# OVER HER DEAD BODY

H.J. GARBETT

Storm
PUBLISHING

Ebook ISBN: 978-1-83700-135-4
Paperback ISBN: 978-1-83700-137-8

Cover design: Lisa Brewster
Cover images: Shutterstock

Published by Storm Publishing.
For further information, visit:
www.stormpublishing.co

ALSO BY H.J. GARBETT

*My Wife, the Serial Killer*

*To Mum and Dad, who encouraged every single page I turned, no matter how far beyond or beneath my years the book in my hands may have been.*

# PART ONE

# ONE

'Ruth,' I quietly murmured to myself. 'This is a really, really stupid idea.'

And the thing is, I've known this was a stupid idea since I first came up with it, months ago. I'd never truly planned to carry it out. And yet, here I was doing it anyway. Besides, was it really the *stupidest* thing a person could do? I wasn't shaving my bikini line with a rusty razor from Nanny's closet after five margaritas; going to the gym commando on cardio day in light grey trackie bottoms; overpacking a rucksack until the zip was barely holding on, with blatant disregard for the bag sizer and my bank account. Even so, I still couldn't think of anything quite as gloriously, catastrophically preposterous as this.

I knew for a fact that a sane, normal person would never even consider passing themselves off as the most notorious serial killer of the past decade while their slightly frostbitten fingers gripped tightly to the rough splintery edges of a box containing a human heart they'd dissected from a dead body a few hours ago. But maybe that's why the TellTale Killer hadn't been caught yet; no one else had been crazy – or stupid enough – to even consider a plan like this.

The biting January wind seemed to career and twirl itself

under my clothes as I lingered rather awkwardly in the shadows opposite Charing Cross Police Station, keeping my eyes fixed on the dull, monotonous atmosphere of the lobby from across the road. It must have been a quiet night for the boys and girls in blue as various officers slowly trundled in and then gently trundled back out. Above me the dim streetlamp flickered. To try and calm my nerves, I counted the seconds between the sporadic bursts of its luminance as if it was lightning: sometimes eleven seconds, sometimes forty-five.

I waited for a few more minutes – or if you prefer, five flashes of streetlamp – making sure no police officers were lingering clandestinely outside the building, ready to tackle the suspicious-looking hoodlum leaving a rustic wooden box on their doorstep.

This was all definitely illegal, I was sure of that, but I had no idea what crimes *exactly* I was committing, nor even how long my sentence would be if I was caught. I figured that, in this case, ignorance was probably bliss. And anyway, my actions were sort of justified. See, this was all in order to catch a *real* criminal, the Tell-Tale Killer, who, two years ago, carried out a string of murders from September to December 2023 and deposited the raggedly cut hearts of his victims in random locations across west London. They had been discovered by binmen, commuters and once a young, innocent child who had been curious to peer inside the plain, coarse wooden box left in their local play park. Safe to say, I imagine she probably didn't bring it to school for show-and-tell day. This was the killer's sick little homicidal trail of breadcrumbs, and yet no one, not the police, not the media, not the true-crime junkies, had been able to follow them, and even come close to catching him. There seemed to be no rhyme or reason to the choice of victims, but the pattern never changed: he'd kill, leave a heart, the press would erupt in madness, and just as the fervour began to fade, some stranger would find another heart somewhere seemingly random in west London. He killed six people in total and then, just like that, at the height of his infamy, he stopped.

Everyone went into the new year skittishly expecting another victim, but nothing came.

See, I had been pondering on the killer's obsession with hearts just earlier this afternoon as I'd meticulously placed my latex-wrapped finger on the top bridge of my knife and gently pushed it down onto the sternal notch of Mrs Lambert's chest to break the skin. The ancient Egyptians, Uncle Phil had told me a few months ago, had believed the heart was the source of everything that made us human: memory, emotion, intelligence. After death, it was given a special preservation status above all the other organs, so that it could be weighed in the afterlife. The heavier the heart, the more sin you had committed and hence the more likely you were to be devoured by the monster Ammit (you know the one: head of a croc-odile, forelegs of a lion, hind of a hippo and hours of entertainment considering the zoological orgy to result in that conception).

I couldn't tell you whether Mrs Lambert would have been supper for an ancient Egyptian beast as I completed my Saturday afternoon high-stakes game of Operation in the Camborne and Sons funeral home morgue and tidied up the scene. I knew basi-cally no details of her personal life. I didn't like to think I was doing this to someone's sweet old gran, so I told myself during the proce-dure that she was the kind of woman who would purposefully wear white to weddings and enjoyed firebombing rescue dog homes. That made me feel a bit better about what I was doing.

I manoeuvred the organ into the temporary container with a pair of tongs, filled halfway to the brim with my home-made chem-ical concoction: formaldehyde to try and preserve some of the tissues, with a splash of glycerol and a nice little pigment-restoring agent to make it look like it hadn't been gradually decomposing inside a dead body for the past two and a half weeks; a little cosmetic touch-up, if you will. You may be wondering why a funeral directors, of all places, would have access to all of these long-named chemicals. It turns out that, for open caskets, there's actually a lot of behind-the-scenes work from people such as myself to make sure that a corpse is 'hot to trot', as Uncle Phil, otherwise known as my boss, would be keen to say. Luckily, Mrs Lambert's corpse, whose heart I had just taken from her coffin, was due to be cremated at some point next week, so no one would notice her body was heading to the afterlife sans heart. On a sadder note, that meant it was very likely I would be the last person on earth to admire the rather radiant skin she had for a sixty year old who had been dead for a few weeks. I would have asked her for details of her skin care routine if she wasn't, you know, dead.

I had drained the heart from its container, removed the disposable medical drape to prevent any possible mess, and eased the organ into the wooden box I'd picked up at the garden centre on my lunch break. To me, it looked just like something the TellTale Killer would use, and I hoped no one would notice the difference. I also made sure Mrs Lambert's coffin lid was tightly closed shut so no one would ever notice I'd disturbed her final resting place. Uncle Phil always insisted the funeral directors would be open on Saturdays to maximise footfall, and I always drew that shift, but today, for once, it worked in my favour.

Hours later, as I watched another police car indicate left and rumble up to the sally port of the station, I tried to purposefully forget my foray into a pathologist's life, and concentrate instead on depositing the box, which I was holding so close to me that its sharp wooden edges were rather painfully jabbing between my ribs. That, and the conversation I'd had this morning with Detective Carlota, the conversation that had led me to Mrs Lambert, and now this moment. I hated the term Detective Carlota had used: 'cold case'. Like a whole investigation could be compared to a mouldy tuna sandwich. I clutched the box tighter. The TellTale Killer's case would *not* be cold for long, not if I could help it.

There were three key elements to the TellTale Killer's work. The heart, a wooden box (luckily for me never the exact same type), and a cryptic handwritten note. I'd written the note on the ridiculously bumpy bus ride to Charing Cross Police Station:

*This unearthly urge has returned to me, unbidden and unholy. I harbour the ravenous hunger to feel the warmth of a life wilt and wither in my hands. In their last tremble, I knew they realised I had claimed them as my own.*

I meticulously penned the word 'Nevermore' at the bottom of the note, trying to keep it as close to the inconsistent, frantic style of the killer as I could. And I was pretty pleased with the results. Turns out, if you obsess over a serial killer's notes, and said serial killer obsesses over the works of Edgar Allan Poe, after a while it's really not that hard to replicate the house style. Naturally, I wrote the entire message in his cipher, of course, pausing every few lines to check I'd got it right. I had already told the police about this breakthrough with the code, but I doubted they'd truly listened. The actual meaning of the words in the note didn't matter anyway, all that mattered was making them believe the TellTale Killer was finally back.

A ladybird landed on the flickering streetlamp above me and I took a deep breath. At last, I was carrying out the macabre plan I had been daydreaming about for months. I had often wondered, even when the investigation was still active, whether this might give the police some extra motivation. But now that they were actively shelving the case, it was clear they *needed* a fresh spur to get the job done.

It's strange, really, how I could feel such resentment toward an inanimate building. The people inside these walls were the ones meant to stop the TellTale Killer. But they hadn't, they'd failed. The killer had taken six lives, vanished without a trace and now, his atrocities had been unceremoniously labelled as 'unsolved' and I imagined the police were moving on to new, easier cases like stolen parcels or missing wheelie bins.

It was unacceptable. That's why I had to do something.

After a few moments, I realised that just loitering under the broken lamppost wasn't 'something'. It wasn't as if I hadn't already committed one crime today. I was now very much, in for a penny. I picked my spot, right at the top of the concrete steps, just outside the station's automatic glass doors. When a lone, practically vintage, police car rumbled up to the station entrance, I fixed my eyes on the officer in the driver's seat as he parked the car, stepped out and began casually walking toward the doors. This was my chance.

From where I stood, I could just about make out the man at the desk's head start to turn from what I presumed was his game of Minesweeper to the weary-looking officer now walking through the automatic glass doors, his back to me. I darted across the quiet road, up the steps, and tossed the wooden box down in front of the entrance. Then, without glancing back, I sprinted away, my heart pounding as I dashed frantically back across the street.

I say sprint, but it turns out, I had been woefully optimistic about how fast I could run. My running could be better described as a sort of limb flailing, wheezy kind of speed-hop.

Nevertheless, I bolted as fast as my legs would carry me back across the road, ignoring the blare of a car horn that I just narrowly managed to dodge by flinging my body forwards. Just my luck: an empty street until the exact second I try and run across it. I tried to seamlessly leap over the kerb in the same movement, but the tip of my shoe caught on an edge, sending me tumbling and crashing onto the pavement, my chin scraping against the cobbled tarmac, my glasses springing off the bridge of my nose.

Shit.

It hurt like a bastard, but I pushed myself up, slapped my glasses back on my face and rapidly dashed into the dimly lit alleyway leading to the high-rise block of flats opposite the station. And I kept going until my legs gave out, which, embarrassingly, only took about forty-five seconds. I slumped down onto one of those dead people memorial benches: 'In memory of Sandra', I could picture the inscription reading, 'she really did despise this shithole.' I tried to get my breath back. Note to self: I really needed to get back into shape. Maybe those other people in their late twenties who trade in all remnants of their personality to become marathon masochists – or marathon dickheads, Greta and I used to call them – were actually onto something.

More important than the state of my own pounding heart, though, was the state of Mrs Lambert's. I had done it. The box was deposited. The police would find it and reopen the case of the Tell-Tale Killer and finally bring him to justice with renewed motivation. All I had to do now, was wait.

I couldn't shake the thought, though. This was a stupid idea, a really, really preposterous level of stupid. But then again, when has pretending to be a serial killer ever exactly been a smart thing to do?

# TWO

I'd often wondered why the killer chose hearts as his signature. Perhaps because it's the one organ we sense the most in our bodies: hammering against our chest when we lock eyes with a soulmate, settling and slowing when we lie beside them in bed, and seeming to split in two when their lover admits they've been sneaking late-night meet-ups with a bloke called Bill they met outside a Slug & Lettuce in Croydon.

I dawdled home, occasionally glancing over my shoulder to make sure a police car wasn't in pursuit of the ridiculously unfit lady who had just left a suspicious-looking package outside Charing Cross Police Station. Ben and Bill's cars were fortuitously absent from the driveway and I thanked all of my lucky stars that they were clearly out of the house as I slid my key into the polished lock of the black fibreglass door. I had no desire to explain where I'd been or what I had done forty-five minutes ago, least of to all to Bill, who must have been the world's most fastidious SS interrogator in a previous life. I slipped inside the house, brushed the dirt and mud from my shoes on the mat, untied the laces and carried the shoes as I ambled down the corridor. Only a few moments later, I begrudgingly put them on again, then exited through the door from the living room that led to outside, crossing the garden to the small annexe, affectionately dubbed 'the shed' by my hosts, that was for the time being what I called home.

The shed was small, larger than your average bedroom, mind you, roughly five metres by three, but it straddled an odd line between a chic modern style and a bizarre take on antiquity, refusing to fully commit to either style. Sleek recessed lighting illuminated the annexe, yet a lone porcelain sink and rusty-edged mirror sat awkwardly in the corner beside a walnut desk that was in desperate need of revarnishing. Ben told me once that he and Bill had bought the place hoping to run the shed as an Airbnb for some extra income, but – for now – I'd rather spoiled their side-hustle plans.

I closed my privacy curtain across the onyx grey bifold doors behind me. Every part of my legs still ached from the forty-five-plus seconds of running I had done this evening, as though someone had gripped each inch of my leg muscle and furiously twisted it back and forth in a vicious Chinese burn. There must be a more politically correct term for that now?

It was a throbbing reminder that I had just left an actual, real human heart on the steps of the police station. My guilty conscience seemed to flare in my aching calves. What on earth had I been thinking? Did I really just do that?

I took my customary daily glance at my crime wall. I wasn't crazy, I didn't truly believe that some clue would magically reveal itself to me, and I would miraculously come that little bit closer to catching the TellTale Killer. But it had become a habit, so today, like all days, no game-changing revelation occurred to me.

I had littered the plain cream wall with photos, Post-it notes, newspaper clippings and anything else that had been connected to the TellTale Killer. It had been far easier to display at my old flat, where I could spread everything out across the entire studio, dividing it sensibly: primary and secondary evidence, rumours and hearsay versus concrete verified facts. But in the shed I had to be at least a somewhat considerate guest and avoid plastering all four walls of my hosts' annexe with my gruesome patchwork wallpaper.

I had learned that lesson when I lost a sizeable chunk of my security deposit thanks to the copious amounts of Blu Tack I'd used in my last flat before I was unceremoniously booted out for multiple late rent payments. That was when I had my, you know, my little breakdown after Greta.

Ever since Greta's death, it felt like I had spent nearly every waking moment trying to hunt down the TellTale Killer. Most of my weekends had been spent locked inside a room studying every known serial killer, trying to figure out how and why they operated and if I could use any tidbit of knowledge to get a little closer to understanding this one. I know what you're thinking, saying I was obsessed was probably a bit of an understatement, but I am nothing if not self-aware. Somewhere along the way it became wired into me, this quiet conviction that I was the one who had to catch the TellTale Killer.

But if there was one thing that I had managed to ascertain above all else through my studies, it was this: serial killers really are a bunch of profoundly egotistical wankers.

See, they don't see their killings as grotesque acts of violence – actually, quite the opposite. They view them as some kind of exquisite deeds worthy of some twisted admiration. And let's be honest, don't we all love a disgusting spectacle? We all slow down to gawk at horrendous car crashes on the motorway, unable to avert our eyes from something so terrible. We all try and peer into the white forensic tents with police tape wrapped around it. We all glare upwards, wondering if the guy threatening to jump off the rooftop is actually going to leap. We know we shouldn't look; we all know it's in bad taste, but we all look anyway, we can't stop ourselves.

Serial killers, intentionally or not, understand our compulsions. They may not all do it in the same way, but the Zodiac Killer, the Son of Sam, the BTK Killer, even Jack the Ripper sent letters to the press and the police, they mocked and goaded the authorities, dared the papers to highlight their crimes and of course, despite the horror, we were all too happy to lap up everything they published. We found the horror of it somewhat exciting.

I glanced once more at the photographs of the six handwritten notes from the TellTale Killer I had pinned to the wall. Each one was left with the extracted heart of his victims; all written, of course, in his trademark cipher. The TellTale Killer had a very obvious obsession of his own, with Edgar Allan Poe. His rather egregious moniker was coined by one of the trashier tabloid media companies – unfortunately, one I used to work for – when they caught on to the MO of extracted hearts left at crime scenes and the only decipherable text on the notes: 'Nevermore'. It was reported that sales of Poe went up by an incredible 700 per cent when the 'TellTale Killer' began to be plastered across the head-lines. Look, serial killers aren't exactly known for being creative pioneers but even by those standards, his whole routine was giving 'plagiarised murder chic'.

For those who've never had the delights of studying Poe for A-level, allow me to be your helpful study guide. He was an Amer-ican writer of Gothic tales of death and dread and very rarely strayed outside that territory. 'The Tell-Tale Heart' is one of his more famous short stories about a man who murders some old codger, hides the body under the floorboards, and then convinces himself he can hear the man's heart thundering beneath his feet. Hence, I assume, where the TellTale Killer got his inspiration for yanking the hearts out of his victims.

Furthermore, our friend Edgar had been quite the fan of cryp-tography back in the day, even penning a snoozefest essay titled 'A Few Words on Secret Writing' which I had now read cover to cover a few dozen times. So, being a card-carrying member of the Poe-diphile fan club, it seemed the killer had continued on Edgar's niche passion with leaving cryptic notes when he deposited his victims' hearts.

Take Henry Morgan, victim number three, nothing left of him other than his heart and a jumbled mess of quill-penned letters:

*V avmkqr siaivxy fvv lreqiee,*
*sotrgomes hyi ueihj at umimii iqhimoyomfz hf xrem qv mglrqim,*
*M cabxiq eih gdopiq jjv Yug wmrvt nlehzgr,*
*fpx eahymak.*
*Is ktiehrv mydnzvh,*
*as eyussdiax aicx,*
*bf vrgfseubx'w jvvxy.*
*Ivzgu pzh dq hf yahzvjfoeh,*
*Glzvv ug es qmqmeq zra rbxigf hyi brzw nq tfvpi ptfz clvfigzve.*

How was anyone supposed to make sense of that? But when you've spent months, immersed in the dreary works of a nine-teenth-century author, becoming something of a reluctant aficionado of the chap, you begin to see the patterns start to slowly emerge. It was almost six months to the day after Greta, around June 2024, when I finally dragged my festering self into the shower, that my brain began to connect the dots.

The word 'Nevermore' scrawled across the killer's notes and also repeated again and again throughout 'The Raven', was quite literally the key. Poe had written about using keywords in Vigenère ciphers, where a certain word or phrase shifts the letters in a message according to the recurring pattern. So, with shampoo still frothing and bubbling in my hair, I threw myself onto a chair and frantically began to utilise the method, scrawling notes on any spare piece of paper I could snatch up, my hands still damp and smearing the ink. Rapidly, the jumble soon began to unravel:

*I waited beneath the heavens,*
*expecting the hands of divine retribution to tear me asunder,*
*I longed and prayed for His fiery justice,*
*but nothing.*
*No thunder rumbled,*
*no judgement fell,*
*no reckoning's wrath.*
*Which led me to understand,*

*There is no divine law except the ones we force upon ourselves.*

I mean, what an utter load of horseshit, right? Who did this guy think he was? Anyone who knows their serial killers will see it for what it is: his own perverse equivalent of winking at himself in the mirror mid-coitus, a calculated, overindulgent flourish meant to show he's flirting with capture while giving the perception to the media that he was completely untouchable.

The rest of the victims' notes were similar once I decoded them using the same method. They were mostly the killer's musings on the murders he had committed and his general thoughts on death as a whole. They very much veered into the whole 'life is meaningless, existence is insignificant, the most notable thing a person can do is die' kind of territory. But despite cracking the code, eighteen months later I was still no closer to tracking him down; no one was, apparently.

I found my gaze drawn to the mass of leathery brown and olive green rhythmically moving in the corner of my room, the only piece of interior decoration I had in the shed that wasn't somehow TellTale Killer related. That was Toast. Goodness me, where do I even start in explaining Toast to you?

See, amidst everything happening with Greta, my part-time helicopter mum read in a magazine that animals are a great way for people to deal with grief-related trauma. Given the choice, I would have loved a dog, but my mum had a family spaniel growing up, called Sam. He was a lovely, docile lapdog for anyone who spared him a glance, but he had the unfortunate habit of barking aggressively at people in wheelchairs. I think all the social embarrassment she had endured over the years with the dog, including him growling at a young child in a wheelchair at Woolworths, was a significant factor in her deciding not to get me any kind of canine.

So, as a natural alternative, she'd gone with a Russian tortoise. And I don't know if you know much about tortoises, but they truly are dumber than a bag of hammers. Toast didn't do much other than roam around the shed and garden, eat, poo and one time, bite a chunk off the tip of my finger, leading to a frenzied trip to A&E. So here I was, stuck living in a yet-to-be repurposed Airbnb with only Toast the flesh-eating trauma tortoise for company, who at the moment had decided to rather energetically hump her hide in her tank.

This was the other thing about my trauma tortoise: she had some kind of neurological tic that meant she liked to hump everything, seemingly not for any carnal desire but just because she really liked the motion. She humped her food dish, her water bowl, her substrate. Last Christmas, I earned 'owner of the year' status with the gift of a partially deflated football that she just loved to go at for hours at a time.

For a creature famed for its slow, deliberate nature, Toast's sudden bursts of thrusty vigour were, frankly, astonishing. I asked the vet about it; apparently, it's not uncommon for Russians, though it is, she admitted, incredibly strange. Sometimes, Toast would make eye contact with me and the sight would haunt every moment of my waking hours. Her bulbous eyes glaring at me, unflinching, while her lower half assaulted a piece of lettuce.

A knock at the door yanked me abruptly out of revulsion towards my first and only pet. Someone *was* home. I silently prayed it was Ben; I really couldn't deal with any of Bill's scrupulous pedantry right now.

'Hello, dear,' Ben (phew) greeted me as he crept through the door of the shed. 'Heard you come in. Thought you might want a cup of tea?'

'Thanks, love,' I replied with a sigh of relief and a subsequent scowl at my use of the term 'love'. No matter how hard I desperately tried, I couldn't seem to stop calling him that. 'Thought you weren't home, though, no cars in the driveway,' I said as he passed me a rather well-brewed cup of Yorkshire tea. He knew how I liked it.

'Bill's is in for an MOT and service, so he took mine to work today and obviously won't be home until late,' Ben said, as he perched himself on the end of my hastily – and poorly – made bed.

Bill had two jobs. One was as some kind of software engineer, and I had no idea what the other one was, except that it seemed to take up most of his nights, even on a Saturday.

'How was your day? You're late, I almost made you decaf,' Ben asked.

'Oh, you know, dull,' I said, 50 per cent truthfully. Other than my rapid descent into criminality, most of the day *had* been a bit of a lethargic slog. After a year or so of working at Camborne and Sons, my uncle's funeral director's business, it was clear this particular career path wasn't for me. But what else was I going to do? It wasn't like going back to being a journalist was viable.

'Goodness me, she's still going at that hide,' Ben said, nodding at Toast. I guffawed, not even bothering to look at what she was doing. 'Hope she bought it dinner first.' Ben recycled that line at least once a week. I didn't find it funny, not even the first time, but I thought it was polite to my host to pretend I did.

'So, how was your day?' I asked.

'It was... a day,' Ben said with a shrug, which was a slightly subdued response for him. 'And you're still feeling okay, Ruth? With everything about the case?' he asked with one part concern and another part pity that he completely failed to hide, I could see his thinly masked concern by the way the corners of his inner eyebrows tilted upwards as he spoke. I hated the fact that I still knew his face so well. Ben was here this morning before work when Detective Carlota had come round to tell me that they were pulling the plug on the investigation.

'Of course I am. Why wouldn't I be?' This time I was 100 per cent lying, speaking like I was flabbergasted that he was even asking the question.

Ben gestured with an incredulous flick of his hand to the crime wall, covered in my notes, clippings and scribbles; I guess he knew my face too. I just hoped he wouldn't clock onto the fact that I very much wasn't all right considering what I had done only an hour or so ago. I watched his eyes glancing and then examining the clutter of notes.

'It's grown, hasn't it, Ruth? Do *not* let Bill see.'

'Bill is still paying his reparations. He can deal with a bit of mess in the shed.'

'You know Bill's not the one to blame for what happened,' Ben said, a little too firmly for my liking. There was a coldness and warning in the clear and even tone he used.

I mean, to some extent, he was right, but it was still easier to blame Bill. Even so, I had the consolation of knowing that for the rest of their lives (because they were devoted to each other and showed no signs of stopping), their coupledom would forever be associated with Bill and Ben the famous Flowerpot Men of 90s' children's TV. No one had ever hidden a sly smile after being introduced to Ruth and Ben, and in that aspect as least, our marriage had excelled.

'Whatever,' I said, flicking my wrist dismissively, trying to brush off the very conversation I started. 'It's not like it matters anymore.'

I know sleeping in my ex-husband and his new boyfriend's shed wasn't the best living situation, but honestly, it was the best I had. Mum had worked for the Foreign Office for most of her career and, about a year ago, landed her dream gig: becoming an ambassador. And do you know where? The Maldives. Yes, she was now the British High Commissioner to the Maldives.

Fun pub quiz fact: embassies in Commonwealth countries are called High Commissions.

'Oh no,' I often teased her, 'another meeting... on the beach. What a nightmare.'

It was sort of frowned upon for children over eighteen to tag along on postings, though, which is why, after I fell behind on the payments for my temporary piece-of-shit flat after the divorce, they lovingly pushed me and Toast into Bill and Ben's rather guilty and certainly reluctant embrace. I had a slight feeling they were trying to rather indelicately push me into adulthood when they didn't get me an advent calendar last year.

But I wasn't too shocked at the turns which had led me here.

Since Greta, my life hadn't really been about brilliant new chapters; it had been one long exercise in selecting the least terrible alternative.

'So, you're fine, right?' Ben asked, reaching out to curl his fingers around the back of my hand. 'Look, just because they've labelled it a cold case doesn't mean he's never getting caught. Forensics is improving all the time; it's only a matter of time before they nab him and he spends the rest of his miserable life rotting in some prison cell.'

I hoped Ben was right. I prayed the heart I'd deposited at the station would wrench the police out of their complacency, make them pull the old files, examine every scrap of evidence, see what they had missed, and finally make an arrest. I was also praying that somehow it wouldn't end up coming back to me.

'Yeah, whatever,' I repeated, knowing full well this was me just deflecting, pretending I was apathetic to the thing that literally never stopped ricochetting around my brain.

'Right,' Ben said, sensing the brick wall I'd just erected between us. My ex-husband was a charismatic and effusive man. I'd always thought of him as the human form of champagne – but his ultimate skill, I believe, was that he could also work out when he wasn't wanted. 'I'll leave you alone, but Bill won't be back until early tomorrow morning, so just let me know if you need anything, okay?'

'Thanks, love,' I said as I took a sip of the tea he'd made for me while I began booting up my VPN to access DarkCell. Damn, there it was again. I really needed to find some way to stop calling him that.

# THREE

I've always had something of an issue with belching when I'm feeling particularly nervous and it's a very real, reasonably common problem, I've googled it. Greta liked to make fun of it a lot. But that was fair as I would always mock her for still sleeping with three different teddy bears each night well into her late twenties. Apparently, stress can make you swallow more air without realising it, and it can even affect how the brain communicates with the gut. So, I was quietly pleased that as I hung up the call, only a short little burp, easily muffled by keeping my lips tightly shut, escaped my throat. I shoved my phone back into my pocket and switched on the vacuum to start hoovering up any of the stray petals left against the hearse window.

'Who was that, Ruth?' Sophie, my cousin-cum-frenemy, asked, peering down the length of the vehicle from the passenger seat as she sprayed another healthy dose of cleaner onto the console and began wiping it vigorously across the cheap faux-leather dashboard. Sophie, too, had been drafted into the family business by dint of not knowing what else to do with herself. None of Uncle Phil's three sons had any interest in dealing with the dead, so his nieces from his two younger brothers – Sophie and me – had stepped, somewhat resignedly, into the gap. She was, by far, the more capable between us and she liked to remind me so as unsubtly and as often as she could. Truth is, she had always been my least favourite cousin, and we had one who put a hamster in the microwave to see if it would work as a hand warmer.

The hamster, miraculously, was fine.

'Oh, it's just the detective who worked on Greta's case,' I replied. 'She says she wants to speak to me at eleven today.'

'Maybe it's good news?' she said in a tone that was a bit too faux perky for my liking. It wasn't as if Detective Carlota was going to tell me they'd managed to resurrect Greta in some Frankenstein's monster-like experiment now, were they? How good could the news really be? My hope, of course, was that she was going to say they were reopening the case. My worry, of course, was that she knew what I had done to poor Mrs Lambert.

But I didn't want to be rude to Sophie, so I just nodded and made some sort of agreeable 'mm-hm' sound and focused instead on ensuring no rogue petals had got stuck into the one of the hearse's many grooves.

There was a definite chance that Detective Carlota – whose phone voice never gave anything away – might be coming to ask me some very particular and specific questions, like where I was on Saturday night, or maybe more directly: why I'd decided to impersonate a serial killer, and why I'd left an extracted human heart outside the police station. When I woke up on Sunday morning three days ago, it felt like the strangest kind of hangover as I slowly came to terms with what I'd done the night before, or more accurately, the potential consequences of what I had done. I'd had similar mornings full of regret in my life, only this time, at least there wasn't a flaccid dry-mouthed stranger in my sheets, asking whether I believed in the lizard people. But now, with Detective Carlota's impending visit, the murky crimes I'd committed on Saturday – the blurry haze of a woman possessed – were slowly hardening into stone-cold memory in my mind.

'Coming through,' I heard the annoyingly chipper voice of Clive call out as he and Eddie rolled a very familiar-looking coffin from the morgue. Oh dear, I knew *exactly* who was in there.

Urgh. Clive and Eddie, the two trainee funeral directors Uncle Phil had hired just before me, both had what I liked to describe as room temperature IQs. They flicked on the brakes, hoisted it up from the gurney by the huckle and slid it into the hearse with far less delicacy than they'd show in an hour's time in front of the family that had gathered for their last goodbyes.

'And how are you doing, Ruth? Did you have a nice evening last night?' Clive asked as he began tightening the car pins around the edges of the coffin. Don't be fooled by his pleasant-seeming words, his tone was dripping with a vile saccharine ooze that we both knew was insincere. The man often liked to crack glib jokes in the break room about my abysmal lack of social life. Clive gave off that deeply unappealing vibe of someone who clearly peaked in high school and was desperately trying to cling onto it at the ripe old age of twenty-eight.

'I did, Clive. How about you?' I replied. I know I came off as a bit mechanical with how I spoke, but I had always struggled with the right tone of voice with almost everyone, and it was especially bad with Clive, who seemed to find everything I said somehow worthy ammunition for mockery. He shot a look at Eddie, and the two of them broke into an overly masculine baritone laughter. I'm sure they'd both had a very wholesome Tuesday evening researching the best mirror-selfie angles. Their brains, as you can probably ascertain, were mostly protein shake with a very light dusting of oxygen.

I tried not to let their remarks faze me, and rifled through my memories for something comforting: the time Eddie, when he thought no one was looking, picked his nose with such zest he gave himself a nosebleed.

Clive swaggered back inside, quickly conducting his body language into something more proper, as Uncle Phil emerged from the office into the loading bay in his full funeral directors' regalia.

His black top hat perched smartly on his head, and a whipcord coat, which his protruding belly now eked and strained against, was wrapped around him.

'How we doing, gang? All set?' he asked, I think trying to instil some spirit into all of his employees who were, to be honest, just there for the pay check.

'Yep, all good,' I was the only one to reply. 'After lunch, I'll make sure everything's buffed, fluffed and casket stuffed.'

Unfortunately, there was a reluctant acceptance of gallows humour in this place.

'Perfect, perfect. Thank you, sweetheart,' Uncle Phil said with his signature warm smile. I noticed him glance discreetly at the car, double-checking for any stray flower petals; we all knew that was his pet peeve. 'And how are you feeling? After, you know...?'

Urgh. You know what really pisses me off? Mum, Dad and Ben, my *ex*-husband, mind you, had a group chat all about me. With Mum and Dad so far away, Ben would give them regular updates on the *Ruth-Report* on my 'well-being' and, clearly, Uncle Phil now had the same level of intel on how I was.

'Oh, the case? It's fine, don't worry about it,' I said with a scoff and an indifferent wave of my hand. Much like Ben, Uncle Phil clearly knew me well enough that he didn't buy my supposed apathy towards the news that the case had been put on ice. He placed a gentle hand on my shoulder.

'It's okay not to be okay,' he remarked softly. 'You do know that, right, Ruth?'

He must have taken the mental health first aid training to heart.

I'm 100 per cent *not* okay, I thought to myself as I stared back at his prolonged eye contact, realising he had one eyelid that drooped further down than the other. But I was doing significantly better than Mrs Lambert, so there was that.

'It's all going to be all right,' he said when I didn't respond to his remark as he took a glance at his watch and then gestured for Sophie to get in as she diligently wiped a small smudge off the bumper, making sure way too obviously that he would spot her assiduousness. Rumour was, Uncle Phil was keen to retire in the next year or so and she was, obviously, the heir apparent.

Good for you, babe, you've just inherited a building chock full of dead people, hope it makes you happy.

'Ooops, you missed a petal,' Uncle Phil said, crouching down as much as he could without his belt buckle snapping, and holding the tiniest petal from the hearse aloft for both Sophie and me to look at. Sophie didn't say anything, her eyes fixed on me as Uncle Phil turned to see who the suspect was.

It was a pretty tense rest of the morning after the hearse bearing Uncle Phil, Sophie and most of Mrs Lambert's remains left, and I found myself anxiously tapping my fingers or rapping my feet as I watched the computer clock creep gradually towards eleven. Surely, I wasn't in trouble. Detective Carlota wouldn't have called ahead if she was going to arrest me, that's not a thing the police did, right? Or was it? I'd never been arrested before. Would this ruin my mum's ambassadorial posting? I hadn't thought about that on Saturday, but then, I hadn't thought about much other than finding a way to stop the police from closing the case.

She arrived at 10.56, as always impeccably punctual. I'd always imagined detectives would wear dark flowing trench coats with loosely knotted ties wrapped around their necks, but Detective Carlota was different. Notably, she had a penchant for the most fabulous jumpers, they were always professional, usually cashmere, with a range of varied necklines. V-neck, roll-neck, cowl, you name it. She was a stunning woman, with sharp, defined cheekbones and long, dark, voluminous hair threaded with small glimpses of grey all while standing at a height that must have been close to, if not, six feet, with a muscular, verging on stocky build that I imagined put most of her colleagues to shame. If I'm honest, I think part of me might have been a little bit in love with Detective Carlota.

It's funny I still called her Detective Carlota. She'd told me, as soon as we began to correspond several times a week about the Tell Tale Killer after Greta, to call her 'Cecilia' or 'Cis', as her friends and colleagues did; but for some reason, perhaps out of awe or respect, I kept calling her Detective Carlota.

But even my awe of her couldn't outweigh my stifling anxiety that she was here to arrest me. In her classic 'no nonsense' manner, she almost immediately gestured for us to head into one of the office meeting rooms, ones we usually reserved for talking to the bereaved about whether they wanted Grandpops chucked in a hole or deep fried in the flames of a thousand suns.

I offered Detective Carlota tea or coffee, but she politely declined both as I sat down, mentally reminding myself not to tap my fingers or feet too much. She was a detective, after all; she'd know instantly something was up if my body made it too obvious.

'So, something's up,' Detective Carlota said, rather matter-of-factly.

Oh dear.

'Wha... Wha... what do you mean?' I stammered, struggling to hurl the words out of my throat. 'Nothing's up,' I reassured her.

'Something is up,' Carlota repeated more assertively, holding my gaze with no intention of breaking it. 'For the last two years, you've texted, emailed, faxed me – who even uses fax? – at least every other day. You sent me every bit of evidence, every time the case was mentioned in *Metro*, every time Jago Jones writes an article, every crazy conspiracy theory, and then, when I tell you it's gone cold, I hear nothing from you for four days. So, something's up.'

I quickly analysed her words in my head. Was this a trick? Some kind of detective mind game?

'I mean, what do you want me to say, Detective Carlota?' I replied with a nervous chortle. I felt she could sense my unease as she reached across the table and, to my relief, gently wrapped her hand around my own.

'Ruth, it's okay,' she whispered, tenderly. 'I'm here for you.'

I felt my heartbeat ease ever so slightly as my shoulders gradually unknotted and relaxed. Okay, maybe I wasn't about to be arrested after all.

'I wish I had an update for you, I really do,' Carlota continued. 'I hope you know how hard I fought to keep this case going, for Greta, but there was honestly nothing I could do. They took it out of my hands before I even had a chance to say my piece. I'm not even allowed to have any exposure to anything else that comes in regarding it.'

I shrugged my shoulders airily as if to say, *Well, what can you do?*

'I'm going to get this guy, I hope you know that, Ruth. Even if it's the last thing I do in my career, I'll catch him and make sure he spends the rest of his miserable existence locked up in a three metre by three metre cell.'

I nodded as if I understood her determination, but my heart rate hadn't settled enough for me to respond in a coherent fashion quite yet. In the back of my mind, I couldn't shake the lingering thought: surely, they'd found the heart by now. There's no way they could have missed it, lying there right outside the station doors. Or maybe Detective Carlota knew and wasn't telling me, or maybe they'd given it to another detective and she had no knowledge of it at all.

I knew Detective Carlota had transferred from another station outside of London about five years or so ago after some sort of scandal. Since I had known her, all I could infer from Detective Carlota was that she had cocked up in some catastrophic way which led to the relocation. Furthermore, from the little she'd let slip, it was obvious her current employers were yet to fully recognise her talents, not helped by the fact she was the lead on the TellTale Killer case two years ago. But I knew how hard she'd tried to catch him, none of this was on her.

I couldn't tell by the way she spoke if she was blaming herself or itching to prove she could still nail the case, most likely a bit of both. What I did know was that she was wrapped up in it far beyond professional duty; her throwaway remarks made it clear her career never really recovered after everyone at the station decided she was the one who'd let the Telltale Killer slip past them. That can't have been easy to bounce back from.

'Are you with me, Ruth, or off daydreaming again?' Detective Carlota asked warmly, snapping me abruptly back to the present.

'I'm sorry, I was... whatever,' I mumbled, still distracted.

'I just really want to make sure you're okay, Ruth,' Carlota said. 'You've been through so much, and I know how important this is to you. I know how much Greta meant to you.'

Most people didn't mention her name. They only referred to Greta obliquely, as if even uttering it would feel like an iron-gloved fist to the gut. But Detective Carlota never had that instinct. I'm not sure why. People were remarkably peculiar about others' grief, maybe because grief was remarkably peculiar.

I felt like most of the people I spoke to considered losing a friend not quite on a par with losing a parent, spouse or a child; that was *real loss*, I could almost hear them thinking as they tried to prevent their face shifting into a sneer. Look, I'm not vying for a shiny gold medal in the Grief Olympics here, but I couldn't recall a time where Greta wasn't practically industrially superglued to my hip. From nursery to university, and even when she pulled strings to get me my first lowly job at the paper, we were always inseparable, always making our life plans to ensure we'd never be too far away from one another.

I know it sounds ridiculous, but I had always imagined my final days (Ben was bound to 'pop his clogs' in one of his usual harebrained mishaps), unfolding with her; the two of us blind drunk and dosed up on pensioner-strength painkillers, swaddled in industrial-grade adult nappies, hopelessly senile, watching the sunset and spitting at any teenagers who dared make a racket in the park while *Cash in the Attic* was on. It never felt like a fantasy, just the natural order of how things would go. And without any kind of warning, she was ripped from my life.

I tried not to get myself too upset, I couldn't let Detective

Carlota see me cry again. I could tell she wasn't here on official police business; she had made this visit specially to make sure I was doing okay. Maybe it was because Detective Carlota came into my life just as Greta left it and so without meaning to, she had become something of my friend, therapist, my confidante, and everything in between over the past two years in some attempt to fill the void. Sometimes I forgot that, for the most part, she was only doing her job.

'But if something changed, if something big happened, you would tell me, right?' I asked, still not certain if Carlota was being ignorant or deceptive regarding the heart. She could be a hard woman to read.

Carlota nodded vigorously, as though surprised I even had to ask the question, and I believed her. Perhaps the police were purposefully keeping her out of the investigation, maybe she was just as much in the dark as I was.

'Look, Ruth, I just really don't want you to do anything reckless. I've found in my career that sometimes, when people lose someone they love, and the case doesn't get resolved in the way they'd like, they have a tendency to...' She paused as she gesticulated, as if that would help her articulate. 'They try and take the law into their own hands, and trust me, it never ends well.'

Uh-oh, too late.

We didn't talk much after that. I asked her how her kitchen redesign was going, as she'd often referred to the domestic chaos it had caused in her home. She told me she had decided on a bespoke kitchen island with a granite top, and I said that was a great idea. She mentioned this Alba person again, who I presume was someone she was seeing but not yet *official* official at this period of time. Then she said she had to get going as the clock struck 11.15, I guess there were other crimes that needed her attention. The Tell-Tale Killer was now just a simple cold case, after all.

That afternoon, I was looped in to funeral duty which was a pain in the arse. I hated doing the actual funerals – not because they were sad or morose, but mostly because they were just so flipping boring and an absolute, utter waste of time. No shade to funeral fans, but what's the point of a 'celebration of life' when the guest star has already peaced out and left the party? Plus, none ever got points for originality. I felt like I had heard 'Amazing Grace' and 'Angels' at least a hundred times by now, and if I had to listen to Frank Sinatra's 'My Way' one more time, I might throw myself into the grave too. No matter the faith, no matter the person, there were always these absolutely ridiculous customs, superstitions, really, that supposedly made people feel better about someone dying, to give them false hope that they may see their loved ones again.

I did keep my opinions to myself, of course. It wouldn't go down well for our Trustpilot reviews if I told a four-year-old that her teddy would be maggot-infested within a week if she placed Blue Bear next to Nana in her coffin.

Nothing lasts forever right? So what's the point?

Today's funeral was being held at St Michael's Crematorium near Chiswick, which Uncle Phil knew I didn't like for obvious reasons. Not that Greta was actually in her plot in the cemetery next door, of course. Her heart had been taken for forensic testing by the police, and then her dad, desperately hoping they'd one day recover her full body, kept it in his freezer after the police returned it to him, or at least, that was the last I heard about it from Chlo, the last friend standing of all the pals I'd thought I had. So, when they held Greta's funeral (why exactly? I have no idea), the coffin they lowered into the ground was entirely, rather hauntingly, void of anything that belonged to her. The headstone they planted at her grave was purely decorative for a patch of land that remained empty.

For the first six months after her death, all anyone tried to do was get me to visit her grave. Every day they told me it would give me closure, whatever the hell that meant. But I never saw the point. Greta wasn't there. And even if she was, what was she meant to do, talk to me? Was a grave supposed to somehow connect me to her in the afterlife like two cups and a piece of string? I mean, I wish she could hear me, then she'd be able to hear every single last apology that I could say. But I knew I'd never get a chance to rectify the mistake I made the night that I lost her.

The best I could do now was to catch the monster who'd killed her. I could still hear his voice lingering in my head, every timbre of his vocal cord, every inflection, every pause of the words I had heard him utter that night.

'You know, you really should be nicer to your friends, Ruth; you never know when it's going to be the last time you'll speak to them.'

Those words never really left my mind; they were always there, like that stubborn tea stain etched on the rim of your favourite mug.

As we stood at the back of the church, listening to Rich the priest speak about the kingdom of heaven and God's children for the millionth time, I felt my phone vibrate violently in my pocket. I quickly reached in to jam the button to silence the call. I didn't need to check the caller ID to know who it was; the same person who called me every day to check up on me. Good old Chlo.

When the funeral was done, I decided to take a slight detour on my way home. Partly because I wanted to pick up ingredients from the Big Tesco to cook dinner for Ben and Bill – despite my position as the cheated party, I couldn't help but always be conscious of overstaying my welcome in the shed – but also because I purposefully wanted to force my route to pass by Charing Cross Police Station on my way to said Big Tesco. I don't know what compelled me to walk past the station and not just go a different route, maybe I wanted to see if the box had gone, or maybe some messed-up part of my brain fancied tempting fate. As I drifted by the main entrance, I could see that the same lamppost was still flickering across the road, yes, even in the daylight, and I kept bracing for a police officer to suddenly clock me as Saturday night's secret postwoman.

I tried to appear as casual as possible as I strolled past the station, but I couldn't stop my neck muscles from pulling my head towards the direction of the entrance. I attempted to smother and suppress the burp rising through me like a geyser. It escaped through my mouth anyway.

'Pardon you,' the precocious voice behind me chirped while the mother of that particularly vocal toddler stared at me as though I'd just committed a horrendous crime against public decency.

*Come on, love, I haven't exactly streaked through Trafalgar Square. Get a grip.*

The nasty part of me wanted to tell the kid, Santa won't be coming next Christmas because he's developed a taste for venison; but I wasn't a complete monster, so I just let them pass.

I glanced at the police station for just a moment before moving on, as if any longer might cause the police to spot me. But, obviously, there was no wooden box sitting outside the entrance. Someone had taken it in. I just hoped it wasn't an urban fox with a new taste for human heart.

My phone buzzed again just as I entered Tesco, but I let the call go to voicemail. Bless her, Chlo was good like that. I'd dodged 90 per cent of her calls over the past two years, and yet she hadn't been perturbed in the slightest. She always made an effort with me, even when most people had given up on old basket case Ruth. She even had the common sense not to be one of the people to force me to visit Greta's grave.

My only gripe with her: voice notes. Do not, ever, send me a voice note. If I wanted to listen to a podcast, I'd pick one that wasn't her losing her chain of thought every ten seconds followed by a two-minute monologue about the state of her ingrowing toenail.

'Well, hello, Ruthie my petal,' I heard Chlo say as I played it back. 'Couldn't get through as per usual but just thought I'd let you know that I spoke to Ava, and she spoke to Oscar, and he said he and his friend, Nico, would be up for dinner with us tomorrow. Please, please, please come. You don't have to sleep with his friend or anything, but it's going to be awkward if it's just me and Oscar at first, okay? Plus, I need to get you out of your ex-husband's house, all right? So just call me or text me back, let me know, okay?'

I wasn't sure about how this Oscar guy that Chlo knew through a mutual friend she had would feel about me crashing his date, but if Chlo wanted me there, I'd be there. It was the least I could do for her. Urgh, I was going to have to be sociable, what a chore.

I grabbed all the ingredients for a lasagne, as well as a nice bottle of wine from Lisbon that I knew Ben and Bill liked. I must admit, I didn't quite enjoy how quickly the attendant ID'd me as over twenty-five at checkout. I mean, I knew I was a few years past that mark, but the fact she didn't even glance at me before waving it off on the screen didn't do wonders for my self-esteem. Maybe my bad-backed, non-marathon-masochist frame gave me away as someone who had lost the gleam of being below the legal drinking age.

As I began to walk out the shop, all I could think about was what serial killers would do when they didn't get the response they wanted. I know, I know, I'm an absolute lunatic, aren't I? Yet the anxiety I felt only five days ago as I delivered them the heart, terrified they might trace my misdeeds back to me, had now turned to a sluggish, disheartening – poor choice of words, I know – disappointment. They had the heart. So why had nothing happened? No breaking news ticker proclaiming the killer's return, no frantic warning from Detective Carlota, absolutely nothing. Had they just laughed it off as a mockery? Had I been too subtle?

After the BTK Killer received less media attention following his initial spree, he began to escalate, even writing a letter to the media, gloating about the murders and how easily he got away with them. I mean, he got his wish: the police did in fact pay him more attention. But I knew if I was going to escalate in my fake killing spree, I had to be careful, because that's also how they caught him.

Just like that, I had another really stupid idea, maybe worse than the one before. When Detective Carlota told me about the case going cold, I'd half sketched a so-called plan B while cobbling together the scraps of an actual plan to get the police to get their arse in gear. I spun on my heel and darted back into the supermarket, making a beeline for the tech section. The thought of the Tell-Tale Killer's voice echoing around the hollows of my skull gave me a jolt of adrenaline – and, admittedly, another healthy dollop of idiocy – enough to push forward with my poorly concocted plan.

I mean, it wasn't like I was actually killing anyone. Honestly, what was the worst that could happen?

## FOUR

I came home ready to start prepping the lasagne right away, hoping it would be a nice surprise for my semi-gracious hosts. I often imagined that there was a dial above people's heads reflecting their opinion of me. I always tried to keep that dial in the green favourable direction with my hosts whenever I could. But as soon as I wandered through the front door of the house, shoes in my hand, I realised I had stumbled into one of their heated arguments. It was the way the air seemed to hang looming and heavy in the entryway. Maybe Ben had found Bill's cigarettes, or maybe Bill had found a red sock amongst the white washing, or it could be the thing I often heard them argue about: me. I had noticed that Ben was far more diplomatic with Bill than he had ever been with me in their 'discussions', as they liked to downplay them as. Previously, I had always been the one trying to calm Ben down and de-escalate things, but now, with Bill being such an unstable, pedantic firecracker, it seemed Ben had taken on a different, more peacemaker role in arguments. Funny how we change in couples, isn't it? I wondered, not for the first time, why Ben could never be that person for me?

I could hear Ben trying to talk Bill down in the kitchen in as measured and calm a tone as he could manage, while Bill continued barking angrily back at him. I knew better than to eavesdrop; the few times I had – and realised that most of the time it was Bill complaining laboriously about my personal hygiene – hadn't exactly been soothing for my delicate and rather sensitive soul. So, I decided to make myself scarce and quickly headed for the shed. I started to creep down the narrow corridor of the house: the kitchen to the left, study to the right. My route to the shed ran straight on, down the hall, through the living room, and out into the garden. If I could make it there unseen, I could hunker down until this all blew over. The lasagne could wait for a day where I didn't feel the house was about to spontaneously combust with the supernova heat of Bill's rage.

'Oh hey, Ruth,' I heard Bill say through gritted teeth and an overly syrupy tone. I hadn't made eye contact, so I just kept walking through the hallway toward the front room.

'Hey,' I replied quietly, hoping I could reach the door to the garden before he caught me.

'Bill, don't,' I heard Ben grumble from the kitchen as Bill walked through the kitchen doorway, following me.

'Hey,' Bill repeated, more audible frustration in his tone now. I pulled my hand away from the door handle and sheepishly turned around to face him; my hands shoved deep into the pockets of my hoodie. I was *this* close to making it out to the shed unscathed.

'Hey, so, the wall in the shed with all of your photos, why, why, Ruth, why has it got *bigger*?' he demanded, his hands moving furiously, gesticulating in every direction possible. 'And why are you using Sellotape to pin up stupid snippets from serial killers when I specifically told you it was newly painted?'

Are you kidding me? What was he doing snooping in the shed? I know it was technically his property but still, is a girl not allowed some privacy?

'You said "no Blu Tack"?' I protested weakly.

'Sellotape is not better,' Bill snapped. 'Actually, I think, it's worse. So much worse. Do you know how much the paint will be chipped?'

I gulped silently, feeling the very depths of my stomach constrict and tighten as I inspected the laces on the shoes in my hand rather than make prolonged eye contact with Bill. I hated arguing, desperately. All I wanted to do was roll over, admit I was wrong and give up. I couldn't bear to be shouted at by anyone, especially Bill. He had a way of making me feel so small, tiny and insignificant. I suppose I should describe Bill to you, so you have some semblance of what he looked like; I imagine the picture in your mind is quite different to reality. He was tall, bull-necked and muscular, the kind of muscular that hid its six-pack beneath a thick layer of fat. When I spoke of a man so fastidious and pedantic, you might picture someone short, an almost more rodent-like reincarnation of Mussolini, but Bill was nothing of the sort. He was a big man; his frame was so broad he made a bottle of Fairy Liquid look almost dainty in his hand.

'I'm sorry, Bill, okay? I'll take it down,' I said meekly.

'Oh, you'll take it down? Great, are you going to repaint the marks too?' Bill snapped, his anger bubbling and frothing. 'Do you even know what shade it is?'

I realised that now was probably not a good time to tell him that he had a poppy seed lodged in his tooth, staring back at me like a third pupil against the white of his molar. It was the one eye on his face that was currently not seething with rage.

'Bill, that's enough,' Ben said sharply from behind him.

'Stop defending her all the time, Ben,' Bill shot back to him venomously. 'I know you used to be married, but for goodness' sake. Do you know what kind of guy lets his partner's ex stay in their house? An idiot, that's who, an idiot. You, you, Ben, you've made me a complete and utter idiot.'

'Well...' I began, finally raising my gaze to meet Bill's, feeling the flood of angry words, that were permanently swirling and festering in my chest, threatening to launch off my tongue. But I clamped my mouth shut before I could say them. I'll admit, it was only the thought of a house-share with a bunch of raucous gradu-ates that stopped me from saying how I really felt about Bill. I never had had the courage to ever be truly honest with how I felt about that. In some ways, I never really felt like I had courage full stop.

'Oh, ho ho,' Bill fake chortled. 'What were you going to say, Ruth? What were you going to say?' he taunted. Ben stepped forward, grabbing Bill's arm, but Bill slapped his hand away brusquely. 'No, no. Tell us, Ruth?' he insisted.

'Nothing,' I murmured, my voice barely above a whisper. I locked eyes with Ben and saw the clenched, tight jaw and the flicker of anguish, maybe even a modicum of guilt in his eyes. Look, I didn't really understand most people or their funny little reactions to things that, to me, seemed irrelevant, but I could just about understand Ben; I could read it in the way his face would always seem to change and twist. I could tell that Bill's outburst wasn't really about me. Don't get me wrong, this kind of outburst wasn't unusual for Bill – the man could get furious over someone putting forks in the knives section of the cutlery drawer – but today, there was more pain and fury in his voice than usual, like there was something else that had upset him judging by the way that Ben was holding back. There had been a whole conversation that I wasn't privy to. I'd thought more than once about telling him to 'have a wank and get over it, flowerpot boy' during one of his many meltdowns, but that seemed like the equivalent of dumping a petrol station's worth of fuel onto a forest fire.

'Right, I'm going to the shed,' I said as assertively as I could, even though my voice still quivered as I spoke. It was more like pulling the ripcord than actually trying to create any kind of firm boundary, but I'd rather play naked Twister with all the residents of a care home than stay in this conversation any longer.

The truth was, ever since I was a little girl, I'd been a bit of a coward. Greta always seemed to have enough courage for the both of us. If I had to have a confrontation, I'd much rather do it from behind a computer screen. I knew that this was something of a personality flaw, but I needed to steel myself. I often wondered if it came to it, would I be able to meet the TellTale Killer face to face to take him down? It's not as if we'd be having a nice chinwag over a cup of tea. But I realised long ago that I'd somehow been born with a complete absence of bravery.

I snapped open the back door and trudged out, hoping Bill wouldn't follow to continue the taunting. From what I could tell, behind me, I think Ben had managed to hold him back.

'We can't keep going on like this,' I heard Bill say, and then, I think I almost heard the sound of him starting to sob, but I was already inside the shed, door shut, the curtains closed, my headphones on and eyes fixed on the crime wall before I could hear any of his whimpers. I glanced at Toast, who, mercifully, wasn't humping anything at present. However, that was only because she had managed to flip herself onto her back, her limbs occasionally twitching in the air. I reached down and set her right again, avoiding any bites to my fingers in the process.

I could understand where Bill was coming from to an extent; if I had just painted a wall, I'd be annoyed too by a few small chips in the paint. But honestly, I was sure he could remember the shade he'd used by memory, something like White Mist or Frosted Clouds, whatever absolute mundane bland vanilla nonsense he'd used. Though, I had to remind myself that Bill's world was much smaller than mine, I guess. He didn't know what it was like to lose someone the way I'd lost Greta; he didn't understand that going through something so tragic, carrying so much guilt, meant you felt like you would never get to move on from your grief.

Maybe, in time, it would all feel a bit easier. Maybe day-to-day life wouldn't feel quite so heavy. But I'd come to terms with the fact that this feeling was never really going to go away, except for one brief moment each morning when I woke up, just before everything came back as this murky, cold deluge flooding every conscious part of me. By now my grief had a life of its own: odd habits, different moods each day, I almost felt like we knew each other on a first-name basis.

I had realised, during Bill's outburst, that my other hand had been firmly gripping my shopping bag. As I rummaged through it, I found the packet of biscuits I had impulse bought and of course the voice recorder I'd gone back into the shop for. I was mildly surprised they still sold them – when your phone has a built-in voice recorder, who needs a separate device for it? Well, maybe serial killers do. I just hoped voice recorders weren't so rare that buying one would set off internal alarm bells at Tesco. Nah, anyway, I'd been a reporter and used one all the time despite being called old fashioned by half the office; surely that counted as a decent alibi if anyone ever asked. 'I'm going freelance' I could say, if anyone decided to pull me up on it.

Damn it, I really should have held onto that old voice recorder I had used for work. Instead, when my journalism career came to its dramatic, cataclysmic halt, I think I remember it correctly that I had ground the recorder's plastic body under my heel as they told me it was time to leave the building.

What I was about to do didn't feel particularly smart, and part of me wondered if I was falling foul of the sunk cost fallacy. Maybe the police would immediately recognise this as the work of a copycat and disregard it with an exasperated scoff. But I knew I had to try; if I could get Detective Carlota back on the case, she might have a better chance of actually solving it. Of course, just because there was no obvious sign the police had reopened the investigation didn't mean they hadn't, but I was still rather sceptical of their proactiveness. Everything told me they'd probably had their fair share of copycats dumping hearts before, and I was just another one in the pile they casually disregarded as some kind of animal heart that some teenagers had sent in as a prank. I needed to stand out, I needed to shine so that it would set me apart from any other copycat.

They needed to think a life was on the line.

After charging the voice recorder for an hour while I read the instructions, I sat in the corner of the shed and did my best impression of pained, torturous whimpering and crying. I kept at it for a solid half an hour, sometimes pinching my arm as hard as I could to try and make it as authentic as possible. Admittedly, my performance was made a touch more difficult when Toast began her daily ritual of humping her rock and I hoped that the recorder wouldn't pick that up in the background.

Occasionally, I whispered a quick 'help me, please help me' in between. Once I was done, I plugged the recorder into my laptop and did what most millennials did, went to find a YouTube tutorial. I was tempted to search for 'hide identity with free audio tools, no crime' but thought that could be a bit suspect if anyone found a way to glance at my laptop hard drive. But I found some lovely geeky-looking fella who instructed me on what to do. So, following the YouTube tutorial closely, I adjusted the pitch until my faint, indistinguishable whimpers sounded even less like me. Why thank you, BitrateBoffin.

Then I cleaned the recorder thoroughly with alcohol solution and placed it in a crisp brown envelope.

The hard part was the letter. No matter how hard I tried, I couldn't think of a good serial-killer-who-gets-a-stiffy-for-Poe line to essentially say, 'Catch me, or I'll kill again.' In 'The Tell-Tale Heart', the narrator taunts the police officers by inviting them to sit in the very room where he has hidden his victim. He brags about his cleverness, all but daring fate by seating them in the very room where the body lies beneath the floorboards. But I was trying to strike a balance between them investigating the killer and not me, the daring copycat. It was quickly becoming something of a tightrope to master.

I had turned myself into such a reluctant Poe fanatic over the past two years that I felt like I could probably go on *Mastermind* with this as my specialist subject, but I needed something more direct to jolt the police out of their complacency. How could this make them think I was the real TellTale Killer who had just abducted a victim? The key, I believed, was the note. If I got that right, made it sound as close to a serial killer as possible, maybe that would bring this investigation roaring back to life. So, rather slovenly crunching on my custard creams, I began to write in his code:

*I feel this warming affliction swell within me,*
*it sears,*
*it breathes.*
*Is this death not another gift I have bestowed upon those who*
*must, in time, kneel on cold wretched bones to kiss her lips*
*regardless.*
*Did you truly not think my shadow would return?*

Hey, I think that was pretty good. I mean, it sounds pretty menacing, right? But I felt like Poe may have given it a solid B if he was alive today. The truly frightening thing about the TellTale Killer, and his little autobiographical musings, was coming to the understanding over the past two years that once you've read his writings enough times, studied them, analysed them, you realised he killed these people most of all because he enjoyed it. There was no mission, no delusion, no psychosis he was experiencing. He knew exactly what he was doing; and all of it came from a place of hedonistic pleasure. The note left with Lewis Khan's heart described how he took satisfaction in the fact Lewis's family would never be able to bury him, and how absurd and childish he found their grief and traditions. In his note, the killer gloated that Lewis's family too would, one day, just be non-sentient dirt that worms and maggots would lie and wriggle around in. 'The dead have no ear for your drum' he had written. It worried me sometimes, that I might feel the same about death and the superfluousness of funerals as a prolific serial killer, but I chose not to think too hard about that.

With gloved hands, I carefully placed the note inside, pulled the tape across, and sealed the envelope firmly. I had considered addressing the package directly to Detective Carlota, but I couldn't be certain the killer knew she was the lead detective on the case two years ago and so, not wanting to make myself suspect number one, I opted to send it to the police station general post box instead. Besides, if what she was telling me was true, Detective Carlota didn't even supervise the case anymore.

This is the thing no one tells you about committing crimes: the sheer, gargantuan amount of anxiety I was feeling.

With a quiet, Custard Cream-y burp, the kind with a bit of a vanilla aftertaste, I opened the Royal Mail app on my phone and randomly picked a post box I would deposit the parcel in at least two miles away. Truth be told, I hadn't used Royal Mail in years, but it turns out they were just traditional enough to make this whole pretending-to-be-a-serial-killer thing work. I couldn't rely on any postal service that involved walking into a shop with cameras; I had no doubt that could be easily traced back to me in no time. But I'd read somewhere that as long as there were enough stamps, the address was correct, and the contents weren't obviously and outwardly dangerous, Royal Mail was obligated to deliver any parcel that slipped through their post boxes. Had to give them credit even if they did lose the Build-A-Bear voucher my great aunt had sent me in the post when I was nine.

I mean, I know I was doing this all for Greta, to make sure her life mattered, but God, I'm glad I didn't believe in an afterlife of any kind. I can't think of how much shame and embarrassment Greta would feel for all of my actions with St Peter as they too ate biscuits on some kind of stratocumulus cloud directly above me.

# FIVE

'Sorry, I think I may have misheard you, Ruth. It sounded like you said you *live* with your ex-husband?'

'That's right; I do,' I replied, deciding in the moment it was best to be as upfront as possible as I took another bite of the burger while trying not to let my glasses fall off the bridge of my nose. No point in trying to hide any details of my complex and not-put-together life. Dating at twenty-nine is a very different beast to when I was twenty-one. Back then, you could say just about anything, and your date would be chill about it. You were a pothead living with your mum and had a collection of vintage Barbies, and occasionally sold pictures of your feet to creepy old men on the internet? Totally fine. But at twenty-nine, you at least had to *pretend* you've got your life together, you have to know what the difference between an ISA and a regular savings account is. Plus, the options become far more limited.

Nico's brows furrowed instantly, and his friendly, interested body language shifted dramatically. He went from casually slouching against the bar table, a smile fixed upon his face, to sitting upright, arms folded, as if someone had lodged one of the bar's spare snooker cues firmly up his rectum. Now I knew I wasn't good at reading people, and social cues were not my forte, but I gathered he didn't like this fact he had just discovered about me. Ah, to be twenty-one again where a previous sexual fling with a flatmate was practically part of the tenancy agreement.

'That's... interesting,' was all Nico managed to say. I had realised some time ago that 'interesting' was one of those words that rarely conveyed the genuine sentiment of what someone meant to say. It was like when someone says, 'I'm sorry you feel that way,' when they are not in the slightest bit sorry for whatever they've done.

I noticed Chlo, whose hand and attention had been in the iron grip of Oscar's all night, glancing over to assess the situation.

'But it's just until you get back on your feet, isn't it, Ruthie?' she interjected, trying to salvage the disastrous situation unfolding before her. 'It's not a permanent thing. Is it?'

I shrugged and took a sip of the extraordinarily weak margarita in front of me, admiring the ambient lighting of the dark and dingy bar, illuminated by the low Kelvin lamps I was sure I'd once spotted in a HomeSense in Milton Keynes.

Look, I'm a big fan of Chlo, but since my divorce, she loved, nay, was obsessed with trying to set me up, always eager to throw me into the arms of some man who she'd tell me I would absolutely love and fall head over heels for. But if I'm being honest, even before Ben, I only ever had a cursory interest in males, like a tourist glancing at museums on the 'things to do' list: nice if you're in the area, but hardly a pressing priority on your trip. But Nico did seem nice and polite, maybe I should make a little bit more of an effort to be pleasant. The first thing I had noticed about him was how architecturally and structurally impressive his nose was; I wanted to compliment him on just how impressive the scale of it was without taking up his whole head but it was quite possible that it could be taken the wrong way so decided to stay shtum.

'Surely that can't be healthy, though, right?' Nico asked, his face turning back to me, clearly realising there were no other women around to hit on in his immediate vicinity, so he'd have to settle for me. 'You have to see your ex-husband in the same house as you?'

'Not healthy mentally, but very healthy economically,' I said nonchalantly, taking another bite of the burger. 'But after a while, you realise it's probably not as bad as living with your mum and dad.' Nico's expression still looked like a slapped arse, but he did manage a humoured snort at that.

'Where do they live?' he asked, with the smugness of someone who was currently assuming my upbringing. 'Surrey?'

'No, she's actually the British High Commissioner to the Maldives.'

Nico let a small chortle escape at that. I imagine he was probably wondering why I had passed up on what sounded like such a good gig.

'I mean, I won't lie; I've heard worse than that on dates,' Nico said as I examined his expression changing, his body drawing ever so slightly closer to me again. 'Once dated a girl who was convinced the moon landings were fake.'

'They are fake,' I said bluntly, taking a sharp inhale and widening my eyes with fury at Nico. I noticed his mouth drop slightly, just long enough for me to crack into a wide grin as I saw his face physically lighten with relief.

'Oh, shit,' he muttered to himself. 'I thought I'd done it again.'

I laughed with him a little. 'No, no, sorry, I couldn't resist. But I do believe pigeons are government drones and Finland doesn't exist, just so you know.'

'I mean, of course, right?' Nico playfully affirmed. I could feel Chlo's eyes briefly glance in our direction and begin to soften, slightly satisfied that the courting situation had been somewhat recovered for the time being.

'So, what do you do, Nico?' I hated small talk but Chlo insisted it was vitally important for first dates, so I had googled some questions beforehand and wrote them as notes on my phone.

'I work for Transport For London.'

'What part?'

'Security and Operations. I basically look at a lot of CCTV footage.'

'Oh, I was hoping you would be able to make the Northern Line less noisy.'

'No such luck, I'm afraid,' he teasingly remarked. I felt like I was doing well, Londoners love a few jokey jabs at the different Tube lines: how gross and old the Bakerloo was, how busy the Central was, it always worked a treat as an icebreaker. 'And what do you do?' he asked, quickly, barely missing a beat.

'You're not going to like this one bit.'

'No? Try me,' Nico goaded, looking far more interested.

'I work at a funeral directors.'

'Oh wow. That's... interesting.'

There it was again. But maybe it was a little more authentic this time. It looked a little genuine, not loaded with an intense glare, a pregnant pause and vigorous nodding, like you're trying to sound interested in your company's new expenses policy. Maybe he was actually curious to know more about my job. I suppose it *was* quite unusual, and surely it was better than saying I was the regional paperclip auditor assistant for Slough or something.

'Isn't it?' I said, finally starting to feel that while Nico was maybe not second-husband material, perhaps he would at the very least make for some interesting conversation tonight. This felt like the social equivalent of eating my vegetables, I wasn't exactly loving it, but it was satisfying to know it was probably good for me. Plus, it gave me a bit of mental distance from obsessing over whether the recorder had been delivered and picked apart by the police already. It was still hogging most of my brain's RAM, but at least there was something else running in the foreground now.

'And tell me, do you have any hobbies or interests, Ruth?' he asked with a soft smile. Funny, had he also read Buzzfeed's '50 first date questions that guarantee a second'?

'Well, if I had to be honest, I guess my main one would probably be serial killers.'

Chlo's eyes snapped back to me, *What in the Lord's name are you doing?* I could hear her telepathically shout into my mind. *Abort, Abort.*

'Right?' Nico said, really extending the vowel as he spoke. 'Like, what are we talking about here? A fan of serial killers and their work, or...?'

'Oh no, no,' I quickly interjected. 'I'm not a serial killer, or even really a *fan* of serial killers. It's just that after my... well, *our–*' I corrected myself for Chlo's inclusion, even though she joined Greta and my friendship group a bit late. '... close friend, Greta...'

I paused, debating whether to mention the fact that she was murdered, until I realised it was actually relevant.

'... was killed by the TellTale Killer, I realised that society has this strange fascination with serial killers, you know?' I said, stumbling over my words as Nico's face grew slightly aghast. 'I mean, don't you think they're interesting? I guess it's the horror of it? How could anyone ever do what they do? How could anyone be that depraved? There's something interesting to dissect there, right?'

Yet again, not the best choice of words, I know.

I could tell I was losing Nico, at least I think I was; I had to reel him back in – not for my sake, of course, but for Chlo's. There's nothing like a double date mood killer than one party looking like they're absolutely repulsed by the other.

'Like, get this, there's a myth that most serial killers have above-average IQs? Ted Bundy had 136, Edmund Kemper had 145, and Jeffrey Dahmer too, but those are just the highly publicised cases, most serial killers actually have below-average intelligence, if you can believe it.'

That was a really interesting fact, I was sure it would win him over.

'How do *you* even know about this?' Nico asked. There was a look on his face I couldn't quite decipher. I was 61% sure it was disgust.

'Ruthie, come on, that's enough now,' Chlo pleaded, but I

wasn't done. Nico had put the silver dime in the jukebox; he had to let me play. I had to prove to him I wasn't *that* crazy.

Nico's eyes were almost squinting, his rather marvellous nose crumpled up and his upper lip had curved up to reveal one of his ever-so-slightly crooked front teeth. He was actually a very pretty man, I realised.

'It also takes on average about seven years to catch a serial killer, don't you think that's quite interesting too?' I asked, hoping that the more facts I threw at him, the more I could win him back.

'Actually, I think it's a bit sick,' Nico responded, yanking up his coat and turning towards the door of the restaurant. 'Look, I've got to go. Sorry. Early start. I'll see you tomorrow, Oscar,' he said as he practically sprinted out of the door to escape me.

I didn't even need to glance at Chlo to know her eyes were filled with complete disappointment. I could imagine Oscar's were too, especially since I'd probably demolished his chances of getting laid tonight.

I really shouldn't have launched into a lecture about serial killers, but it was all I'd been able to think about for the last two years. Every podcast, documentary, and book I'd consumed had been hooked around an obsession with what makes a serial killer tick, although the BBC *Panorama* special on the TellTale Killer had been bitterly disappointing.

'What the hell was that, Ruth?' Chlo demanded as I took another sip of my third – no, fourth – margarita, still feeling quite out of place with such an extravagant glass in the dark and dingy smoking area that also had the aroma of fresh-yet-also-stale piss. How did they manage that concoction, I wondered to myself as Chlo continued her diatribe.

'Why are you getting so mad?' I asked indifferently after she paused for breath for a second. 'I didn't think he'd be so sensitive about it.'

'You know, murder isn't exactly prime first-date conversation material, Ruth.'

'So, what *is* first-date conversation material?' I asked, genuinely curious, I thought Google and Buzzfeed had me covered. Ben and I never really had a first date; we just sort of ended up in each other's beds after seeing each other in a bar every week for a year, and then never left. Dating was not something that I was particularly skilled at. I had my sexual awakening to a Roman foot soldier with a chiselled jawline in a children's book about the crucifixion and no man could ever really compare to that particular specimen ever since. Perhaps Nico's nose and jawline weren't far off, though.

'Oh, I don't know – boring stuff, like dehumidifiers, credit scores, quality bedding, your favourite type of pasta. All the mundane adult shit. But it's universally agreed, Ruth: you don't bring up serial killers.'

'Well, good to know,' I replied, being a bit facetious and also starting to feel a little bit sozzled. 'But Nico could have been a fan for all we knew. We could have geeked out about the Long Island Killer together.'

His loss.

'Oh my God, Ruth,' Chlo said, incensed. She cupped her hands around her mouth, then dragged them down her taut neck as if trying to massage all of the frustration out of her facial muscles. 'Look, I really didn't want to tell you this before, as I thought that maybe then you wouldn't come, but Nico's aunt was also killed... two years ago.'

'Oh,' I stuttered, feeling the embarrassment and shame begin to rush to redden my cheeks.

'Yeah, I, stupidly, thought it might have been a good idea for you to meet Nico and that the topic would come up naturally and, I don't know, you would talk about it or connect or something; it's not like you'll go to a therapist or a counsellor or anything.'

She said that last bit quite dejectedly, as if she was finally giving up on the beaten and broken Toyota Aygo she'd treasured since her sixteenth birthday.

'I'm sorry,' were only the words I could muster, and I truly was, but I knew Chlo had heard way too many apologies from me over the past few years; I knew a part of her was fed up of trying. I couldn't say I blamed her either. Chlo was a good friend, far better than I deserved. She had always looked out for me, and even before I lost Greta, I hadn't treated her as well as I ought to have. People have limits, I realised, and the dial in Chlo's brain on how she felt about me had clearly swung to the red.

'Look, Oscar and I are heading to another bar. You're welcome to join us,' Chlo said with a half-defeated sigh, gesturing in that peculiar way she did with her hands when she didn't know what to do with them.

'No, no, I'm good,' I murmured, not wanting to further sabotage both of their nights. 'I should probably head home anyway; I have work tomorrow.'

'All right. But call a cab. Don't walk or take the Tube – that would be dumb. Wouldn't it, Ruth?' That felt like a parent cautioning her child not to cannonball full of ice cream into the shallow end of the pool. Her tone was a little condescending, especially in the way she called me 'Ruth' and not 'Ruthie', but I knew she meant well, she was just mad.

I nodded while at the same time tilting my head back to drain the last dregs of my margarita. Chlo was still too annoyed to give me one of her big, warm hugs goodbye, so she strolled back into the bar where Oscar was already holding her coat for her. I could feel the scorching heat of his evil glare as well as the ice-cold chill of his balls from several metres away.

'Chlo,' I called after her before she begrudgingly turned her gaze to meet mine. 'I really am sorry. I didn't mean to mess things up, I promise.'

She gestured lightly for Oscar to move on ahead without her, then approached me and reached for my hand, her fingers loosely encircling my palm.

'I love you, Ruthie. I really do. I love you *so* much, but I think it's time for you to move on from this.' She steeled herself before saying her name. 'Do you think Greta would want this kind of life for you?'

I instinctively pulled my hand away, shoving it deep into my pocket. 'This isn't about Greta,' I muttered as defiantly as I could.

Chlo gave me a lukewarm smile; having known her for over fifteen years, I knew this was the kind of smile that said she finally understood just how much of a lost cause I really was.

'Ruthie,' she said softly, 'I loved her too but for you, everything since her death has been about Greta. You need to come back to... to the rest of your life and...'

She thought about stopping herself from continuing, maybe she was trying to work out how to say this in the least painful way.

'You need to stop living in the night she died.'

Ouch.

I knew I should have gone home, but I waited until Oscar and Chlo were out of sight before slipping back to the bar and ordering another margarita. I drank this one even faster than the first four, then decided that one more would be enough to blur my grief and pain into something minuscule, lost in the glazed, hazy blur of a ferociously spinning room, and to dull the sharp, jagged edges of the memories that had been sitting rather snugly in my head for the past two years.

Maybe Chlo was right. I knew other people who had lost friends in tragic circumstances; they all seemed able to quiet the pain and move on with their lives. So why couldn't I? Why was I stuck in this stage of my life, like it would never end? Why was I trying to imitate a serial killer, hoping it would somehow get justice for Greta? Who does that?

I suppose I could chalk my rather heinous acts up to the sheer weight of guilt I felt, but only now was I coming to the awful realisation that maybe I was actually a terrible person. Awful people mutilate dead bodies; awful people think about telling children that Santa wants to eat Rudloph; awful people push away the people closest to them and end up alone. I mean, I had to admit it: I was pretty awful.

The more I'd thought about it over the past two years, the more I realised I'd always felt somewhat disconnected – from everyone, really – and, quite frankly, Greta had been my only true tether to other people besides, occasionally, my husband. It was always Greta coaxing me to parties, dragging me into university societies, or persuading me to see the film I'd been talking about. Sure, there was Chlo, but she was only ever there because of Greta. Now it felt like we were two bits of wholemeal bread trying to make a sandwich without any kind of filling.

I could feel my stomach begin to churn and my head start to feel dizzy as the alcohol got to work, casually shutting down my neural communication pathways like it was flicking switches inside my mind. I wasn't about to embarrass myself by throwing myself at people or dancing wildly at the disco. No, I'd just drink until I felt on the edge of a blackout – but keep just enough facilities to be able to call a cab and make it home.

So, propping myself up at the world's stickiest bar, I scrolled through the various DarkCell forums that I had saved on my phone, as I did every night. My thumb kept sticking against the screen as I saw CerealKillerCornflakes, having just logged on after a few hours offline, spam through his various harangues to me, most of them ending with 'I told you so'.

He was one of my online 'friends'. And by friends, I mean some basement-dwelling, vitamin D-deficient cretin on the other side of the world that I communicated with on DarkCell. (Let it be known, I absolutely include myself in the basement cretin category.)

My motor skills were faltering as I attempted foolishly to navigate across my phone screen. I could see missed call after missed call, but I couldn't focus my eyes for long enough to see who it was from. Instead, I kept reading the photo of the decrypted note that the killer had left with Greta's heart:

*I feel this existence as a cruel jest,*
*a monotonous rhythm so fleeting and void.*
*Yet she might have known more sunlight to ripple on her skin.*
*As I carved the heart from its broken, freed shell,*
*a tremble stirred within me,*
*so strange and unwelcome.*
*Perhaps remorse; which I must deem weakness.*
*Things so divine feel no such thing as remorse.*

Some nights I'd feel so awful, with nowhere to turn, just desperate for some kind of non-judgemental outlet. More often than I'd like to admit, I ended up DMing the Domino's Pizza account on Instagram, unloading my various woes into the empty void, just to have some kind of outlet, my own personal form of prayer. Reading the killer's words again brought back the question I asked myself every single day. I messaged the Domino's account once again, ignoring the tens of unanswered messages I'd already sent them over the past year.

Why did he pick Greta?

# SIX

## TWO YEARS EARLIER

'So, I guess you've got a pretty major problem, then?' Sam asked, scratching at his scruffy, patchy neckbeard as he leaned precariously over the desk divider, directly violating all concepts of personal space.

'I don't have a problem,' I said, exasperated, glancing at Tasha in the hope she'd meet my irritated gaze. She didn't. She was far too busy scolding one of the interns for using the American spelling of cancelled. I turned to face Sam again. 'I spend nearly fifty hours a week with you all already. I don't really want to spend any more time with you; thanks but no thanks.'

Sam was... a lot. He worked in Sales and Advertising, which shared a section of the office floor with editorial, and my word, he did not know when to 'shut up or land the plane', as Tasha liked to put it. Tasha and I were no longer post-room newbies, where we had reluctantly agreed to be paid tuppence just to pay our dues to break into the journalism industry. Our promotions within the second-most-read paper and media conglomerate in the UK meant we now spent most of our time churning out puff pieces or clickbait in the middle of a billionaire takeover, and getting the worst seats in the office, evidently because we were next to Sam. The only upside to the current events in the UK at the moment was that at least we weren't the interns recycling articles about 'five fruits to stop menopause' into 'five fruits to get a stonking, long-lasting erection'. Although at the moment, everyone in the office had spent all day working on the TellTale Killer story in some way.

While I hated the idea of optimism being mistaken for naïveté, I think part of me had been a little doe-eyed about journalism when I had been a fresh-faced graduate myself. I liked the idea of being one of those people who could speak truth to power, hold the elite to account, inform the public, and apply pressure to those accountable when needed. But the days of Watergate had shifted; now, only those on the highest rung of the payroll got to write those particular stories. Most of the time, I got to write stories about seagull crime mafias in Devon.

'Not even for a small glass of pinot grigio?' Sam asked again.

'Sam, why are you so desperate to get Ruth drunk?' Tasha interrupted, swivelling her chair around to parachute into the conversation, her tone cutting. 'Do you not see the ring on her finger?'

'I have a girlfriend,' Sam protested, his annoyingly pinched voice cracking. 'The hot Swedish one I told you about before. Astrid.'

'Yeah, I'll believe that when I see it,' Tasha grunted, unconvinced, before turning back to the intern, who was nodding frantically, hanging on to every syllable Tasha uttered as though her life depended on it.

'Sam, again, no. I'm not coming to drinks tonight,' I said, trying to sound final and absolute in my tone while Sam looked like something resembling a scorned puppy. 'I've already got plans and besides, do you really think it's a great idea for me to stagger home drunk after dark at the moment?'

It was that which, finally, seemed to shut him up. Sulking, Sam shuffled back to his domain. Tasha tapped me on the shoulder, having awkwardly manoeuvred her chair beside me.

'Do you think "Astrid" is just what he calls his right hand?' she whispered, her wide, mischievous grin plastered ungracefully across her face.

I almost felt bad for laughing. Sam's clumsy attempts at womanising the entire office were legendary. The time he walked into a pillar and gave himself a light concussion while ogling Esha on the far side of the room had practically become a core part of office legend.

'Ooh, speaking of arseholes,' Tasha murmured, nodding toward the door. 'Here comes our very own golden boy.'

Sure enough, there he was, the big Double J as we liked to call him, sauntering in at the end of the work day as though he was only late because he had won yet another award last night to cram onto his desk. Statistically, he probably had.

'I still think what he's doing is in bad taste,' Tasha said.

'Journalism for people with brains the size of peas? That's been a thing for a while,' I quipped, both of us watching keenly as Double J slumped down into his chair on the side of the office with the view of the Thames. Lord, I hated him. The Managing Editor, Deborah, often had me quietly rewrite some of his articles for web, so it didn't sound like an unhinged narcissist had complete hegemony over the newspaper printers.

Reminded me of Orwell, you know, the chap who wrote 1984, the book every red-faced boomer pretends they've read. But it was actually his wife, Eileen O'Shaughnessy, who had a huge hand in shaping his work; editing, rewriting, sometimes inserting her own ideas, and he just took all the credit. God, I knew how she felt. Although, let me clarify, Double J is not someone I'd ever consider nuptials with.

Thing is, despite his ego being the size of the *Daily Mail*'s headline font, I mostly hated Double J because he gave Greta an abundance of passive-aggressive notes when he didn't get his way. She would just be working away in IT and then he would make the odyssey to the floor above, approach her desk wordlessly, and then drop a note about how he wanted his article at the top of the home page or for her to remove some disparaging comments about an article he had written. Man had absolutely no humility or manners whatsoever.

My phone buzzed violently on the desk. It was Greta, letting me know she was done for the day and waiting for me downstairs.

'Right, I reckon I'm done. I'm off for a pre-birthday meal with Greta,' I announced, shutting down my computer.

'Oh, enjoy! Pre-birthday?' Tasha asked.

'Yeah, well, Greta's away in Ottawa on some training seminar for my actual birthday so we're doing it today. It's a whole thing. Talk tomorrow?' I said to Tasha whilst yanking my arms through the sleeves of my jacket.

'I'll be here, like most days,' Tasha replied with a fatalistic grunt, shuffling herself on her wheeled chair back to her desk. 'But please text me when you get home, okay? And be safe?'

'I will, I will,' I said, sounding like a child appeasing a nagging mum although I knew I would have said the exact same to her. 'Besides, Greta's staying at mine tonight, so we'll stick together. Plus, I think there's a police officer stationed every seven yards in Fulham at the moment.'

Tasha gave me one of her sceptical, *don't quite believe you* nods as I swiped away Chlo's messages that were incessantly hogging up the majority of my phone screen. I never understood why all her messages were sent in chunks of ten words or less, if ever she discovered voice notes, I was in deep, deep trouble.

I replied to Greta, letting her know I was on my way down. I had to admit, I wasn't exactly in the mood for socialising tonight, and not just because of the notorious serial killer lurking about London streets. It was more the fact that I felt utterly and despairingly useless at work. Like a spare part created solely to make the lads at the top look even more shiny and impressive. When I joined five years ago, Greta had pulled all the strings she could, despite being a very junior member of the team, to get me an interview. I had thought this was my dream job, a huge media empire with a reputable paper at its centre that had a distinguished reputation for investigative journalism. And at first, I was brimming with ideas, frothing at the mouth to finally write the articles I always wanted to, and they humoured me, letting me write my various pieces in my first few months, despite some heavy editing. But as time went on, more and more of my ideas were dismissed. If they couldn't be condensed into 500 words with a catchy headline that would drag someone in from their Facebook feeds, chances were it wouldn't be green-lit for publication. Eventually, I stopped making suggestions altogether; I had decided that I had quite enough of rejection and would just rather begrudgingly write about how boiling tap water was worse than smoking and could turn you into a senile, impotent human kettle; well, that and Megxit always seemed to get our readers in such a tizzy.

I hurried down the stairs to find Greta waiting in the lobby, wearing her now-iconic beautiful, flowing emerald single-breasted boyfriend coat. She gave me a small wave, and we shed our corporate skins to be real humans again as I broke into a half run across the marble flooring to embrace her, wrapping my arms tight around her petite frame as I used all the strength in my core to gently lift her off the ground. It was ridiculous really, we had only seen each other a few hours ago when I went to bother her in IT. No wonder Sam had once started a rumour that we were both closet lesbians.

'Hello, friend,' I whispered, holding her body close to me. 'How is IT?'

'Terrible,' she replied softly. 'How is Editorial?'

'Terrible.'

I loosened my grip slightly to let her drop back onto her feet as I could feel my back muscles start to spasm with pain.

'Well, you look stunning, petal,' she replied, her voice soft and sing-songy. 'Happy, Happy Early-Birthday. How are you? How was the rest of your day?'

'I'm...' I paused, searching for the right words without being too overly morose. 'I'm okay. It's been a bit nauseating with everything going on, but I'm sort of okay... I think.'

'If you were fully all right, frankly I'd be worried. Come on, let's walk while we talk, you know how much I love Sabroso. Mind if we delegate maybe a few minutes for me to talk about something important? I think I'm just being stupid, but I guess it would be nice if you can tell me that straight to my face.'

'Of course,' I replied, already curious what it might be. She had seemed a bit distracted when I went to say hi to her today, like there was maybe something weighing on her mind.

I liked Sabroso. It called itself a café, but it was really a jack-of-all-trades: sandwiches, coffee, brunch, dinner an all-day menu; the sort of London spot that has to be everything to everyone in order to survive the extortionate rent. It felt a little like it was having a permanent identity crisis. I could relate.

She walked a few paces, then Greta suddenly blurted out the c-word in the lobby, followed by the bizarre suffix '-balls' after it. It made me recoil a little, not just at the shift in Greta's tone but the inventiveness of this portmanteau. She really should be in Editorial, she would be great at headlines.

'What is it?'

'I forgot your birthday card, it's at my dad's house when I stayed over last night! I'm such a silly clot.'

She didn't say 'clot'.

We left the office and strolled along the high street, the road adorned with various Christmas lights that felt quite out of place this year. We chatted mostly about the books we'd been reading, and making the most of the hustle and bustle of rush-hour London. Previously claustrophobic, presently it felt strangely safe being amidst the bustling swathes of people now that there was a serial killer at large. I spoke about how I'd been working my way through a high-fantasy romance that was as thick as, seemingly, the male love interest's erect cock, while Greta, a self-professed Obama superfan, was halfway through *A Promised Land*; this was her fourth read since its release three years ago.

'He soothes me,' she would gently say when I asked her why she was reading it yet again, 'he soothes me more than any other man can, Ruth.'

'Yeah, but Obama, Greta. A yank?'

'He won a Nobel Peace Prize, Ruth.'

I harrumphed as my form of a playful contemptuous snort.

I told her that her current obsession with Obama was fine, but if she started creating a shrine to him within her flat, I was going to start preparing to stage an intervention.

We both tried to tune out the constant adverts on billboards or posters hung up about curfews and safety warnings, but as hard as we tried, it was quite difficult to push something like an active serial killer out of your brain. There was a foreboding feel to the air knowing he was still out there. When you hear about serial killers, it's usually in the past tense: the police caught them, or they died or faded into obscurity. But this one was still very, very real. Even in the safety of your own home, there was an ominous, lingering feeling that you were the one that could be next, the name that would dominate every headline and news ticker.

He had killed three men and two women so far, no real connection between them, but no major differences either. The youngest victim had been twenty-five, the oldest fifty. The sheer randomness of it all was what made it so terrifying. There was no way to convince or fool yourself that you were any less of a target.

One more kill and the TellTale Killer would be the most prolific UK serial killer of the twenty-first century. That was a scary thought.

'Are those new glasses, by the way?' Greta asked as we tried to ignore the foreboding feeling in our guts and tried to settle into the cosy, wholesome ambience of Sabroso to have our pre 6 p.m. dinner like we were pensioners who had escaped the care home.

'Oh, these ones, they are indeed,' I replied, trying not to get distracted as I took my new wire-rim soft square glasses off and handed them to Greta for inspection.

'They're lovely,' Greta said, admiring them before placing them back on my side of the table. I could just about function without glasses, but they were handy if I wanted anything beyond twenty feet to not be a blurry mess of shapes.

We distracted ourselves from the TellTale Killer by talking

about our morally dubious decision not to invite Chlo to my pre-birthday meal as she had been a tad annoying of late, then we spoke about Greta's search for a roommate, how her dad and her brother were doing, her current love-life predicaments, and briefly touched on my own. But it's never very interesting to discuss or gossip about your spouse with a single friend, is it? You just seem to end up moaning about how content and stable you are. I never wanted to be the sort of person who moaned that their loving partner had forgotten to put the dishwasher on to someone who was still frantically swiping right on dating apps. I did tell her how I thought it was peculiar that Ben had been weirdly generous about doing the dishes lately and wearing a new type of aftershave, but that was all I really could add to the state of my relationship. If there was one word I could use to describe my relationship with Ben from day one, it was 'stable'. But though conversation with Greta always flowed remarkably easy with the twenty-odd years of vernacular shorthand we had developed between us, I still didn't feel like I could totally relax, even within the confines of a very safe restaurant with plenty of people about. I knew Greta had noticed my nervousness.

'Are you worried?' Greta asked attentively. 'You do seem quite worried about all this.'

'I guess I feel... weird about it,' I admitted. 'I think it's mostly work, just how I can't get away from it *and* how we seem to be covering it.'

'I did see the headline from the other day,' Greta said, with a knowing nod and a shuffle of her butt into the back of her plastic chair. 'I mean, we're making bank at the moment but no one on our floor feels great about the reason.'

'I don't think any staff other than big Double J and Deborah does,' I said with a grunt. 'Even my dad called me to complain about the headline.'

'"*He Will Hunt Again*,"' she intoned, mimicking a deep, dramatic voice with some kind of thunderous bass behind it.

'"*He Will Kill Again*,"' I corrected with a dry almost-laugh.

'And yet we had the highest-ever daily readership on that day. The board apparently cracked champagne. It's kind of revolting, isn't it?'

'Do you know if they're closing in on him or anything? I saw the Home Secretary talking about it yesterday,' Greta asked, as she took a dainty sip of her chai. 'But don't know if the police are saying any different?'

Frankly, any scrap of news I managed to wrangle from my contacts at the Met was about as useful as a jalapeño-flavoured lubricant. No matter how hard I pressed for details, anything that might help me track the killer down, or at least help someone else in doing so, was always frustratingly vague and unhelpful, like they were verbally redacting everything as they said it in real time. All I'd really ascertained was a) every victim had been travelling alone when abducted, b) each attack occurred not too far away from a Tube station when they were last sighted, and finally c) the killer seemed to move and operate in plain sight, which was hard to do in London; somehow he had found a way to just completely blend in.

I think I had been channelling all my nervous and anxious energy into the belief that I could gain some sense of agency by trying to track down the TellTale Killer and play some kind of significant part in his downfall. But no matter what I did, I just didn't seem to be getting anywhere and the feeling of being the next person on his hit list seemed to feel ever more omnipresent. I couldn't stifle the almost suffocating feeling that I would be the next person to die.

'Would you speak at my funeral?' I asked Greta as she took a bite of her club sandwich, her favourite. She rolled her eyes as she munched, her exasperation delightfully exaggerated.

'Ruth, you're doing it again,' she responded, covering her mouth to hide her vigorous chewing.

'Doing what?'

'You've gone off on some very tangential train of thought and assumed I've followed you, but alas, I am not telepathic, petal.'

'Well, you know me well enough that you should be,' I retorted with a smirk.

Greta snickered and took another bite, letting out a big sigh as she chewed heartily, her thoughts mulling over my question to distract her from the bread being a little stale. I took a glance at the window behind me while she continued to eat. I hadn't realised how dark it had got; we ought to have been home by now.

'There's just so much I could say about you, Ruth. Too much to fit into a eulogy. I'd need to write a whole biography, I'd call it *Tea, Biscuits and a Long, Long Life of Bad Decisions*.'

It's like I said before, I really wished that Greta would do a secondment in Editorial, she was truly gifted at headlines.

'You could say whatever you wanted in a eulogy,' I continued. 'I mean, you could say she was an absolute dickhead to me on a vast variety of occasions.'

'Well, can't speak ill of the dead, now can I?' she replied glibly.

'I don't know why people are so sensitive about not talking ill of the dead. I mean, it's not like I'll be able to hear anything you say about me anyway, so what's the matter?'

'Well, what if reincarnation happens?' Greta asked. I loved the way her brain worked. 'If you're suddenly now a lion with a hankering for tourists then I don't want to be eaten if I decide to do a safari in Tanzania.'

Greta and I had talked before about what we'd want to be reincarnated as. We went back and forth for a while, and eventually, she told me I was probably some kind of doe, which made sense: non-confrontational and all-round pretty chill. After a bit, she said she liked the idea of being a ladybird. She told me that she'd found out, while she had holidayed in Amsterdam with her dad a few years ago, in Dutch the name for ladybird means 'the Lord's most beautiful creature', which sounded a little vainglorious. Imagine explaining what your name meant to a Dutch dung beetle, that had to be awkward.

'I feel like I need *something* for you to talk about in my eulogy, though. Like something important; be nice to have some kind of award by the time I died, not something as lofty or glamorous as a Nobel Prize like Obama, but maybe something relatively mild from the Press Awards,' I remarked. 'Just some kind of trophy with my name etched on to show my life wasn't a total waste, that there was some meaning to it. I don't want to spend my life being an uncredited copyeditor for Double J.'

'You'll get there, Ruth, I know you will, it's only a matter of time,' Greta reassured me. She continued speaking but I found myself going into Ruth-mode and beginning to slip into something of a daydream.

I could picture it now, one of those glitzy, fancy award evenings, where my name would echo through the room as the winner. I'd ascend the stage, the applause thundering around me. No one would dare to say it outright, but they'd all know I'd been the favourite to win by a mile. After all, I was the woman who took down the TellTale Killer. What an accolade. How would one even try and attempt to catch the world's most wanted man, though?

'Would you help me catch the killer, Greta?' I asked, abruptly interjecting whatever Greta had been saying, probably something about some bad date she had gone on. I knew my mouth had been robotically repeating, 'right,' for the past few minutes while she had been speaking.

'What?' she said, like she had misheard me at first.

'The TellTale Killer. Would you help me try and catch him?' I asked, almost a little bit giddy at the idea forming of us working together to take him down. Starting to visualise my route to being a proper journalist.

'Did you not hear a single word I just said?' she asked. I couldn't quite work out her tone at first, it sounded a bit angry.

'Oh, I'm sorry, did I zone out again?' I asked, a touch dumbfounded. 'I just think maybe as a duo, we could actually stand a chance.'

It took me a second to analyse her face. I visually scrutinised how her brows wrinkled, and her jaw started to clench. Oh no, I recognised how her face looked when she was angry, she was definitely mad at me. Really mad.

'You're telling me you weren't listening to me just now?' Greta asked, her eyes almost bulging out of their sockets, refusing to blink as she glared at me.

I thought about lying and dredging the recesses of my memory for a phrase, or even a word I could recall, but I must confess I couldn't think of a single thing she'd said to me while I thought about getting some two-kilo golden trophy.

'It's just, I think I've figured out his pattern,' I said, reasoning that if I explained why I was so immersed in my own thoughts, it might justify my space-out. 'All the people who went missing were travelling alone when he abducted them. I think he's targeting people near Tube stations and I wonder if between the two of us – you by the station, me on standby – we could align to the killer's system and then find a way to...'

I trailed off, I could see her eyes only further widening with rage at every word I spoke. I half expected her eyeballs to ping free and skitter across the table between us like two loose marbles.

For a few moments, Greta gently parted her lips to speak before sealing them shut again, leaving me in silence. After what felt like a taste of eternity, she finally found the words she wanted to say.

'So, after ignoring what I just said, you're also saying that you want to use me as bait?'

'Well, no, don't say it like that!' I exclaimed, noticing the ever-deepening crease in her brows. 'Saying, *I want to use you as bait* makes it sound like I'm treating you like you're expendable, which you're not. I just need to find a way to draw him out, and I can't exactly do that by myself.'

What had she been talking about that had got her this upset?

Greta let out a venomous, mocking laugh, more biting than I'd ever heard from her before; there was a callousness that I didn't quite recognise from her. 'Unbelievable, Ruth. Seriously?'

My mind raced. I truly hated seeing Greta upset and I hated

the way her words pierced through the air and directly into my chest. I didn't mean to, but I could feel my eyes begin to moisten and well up at the mere thought that Greta was angry at me. We hadn't argued since we were eleven and I chopped the heads off her Barbies.

'Greta, I'm sorry,' I said, the words spilling out too fast for them to be comprehensible. 'I'm so sorry I wasn't listening and I'm sorry that I asked you to...'

'Oh no,' she shot back, her voice still rippling with rage. 'It's perfectly clear what you think of me, Ruth. Crystal, crystal clear. I can't believe I just told you what I found out today, and you just completely zoned out. You always do this when I try to talk about important things, you just zone out. Clearly I'm not important to you!'

'It's not like that!' I protested, stumbling over my sentences again as an effervescent sort of panic bubbled up inside me. My thoughts scrambled, desperate for a way to fix the situation that had spiralled out of control so rapidly.

'Greta, please, listen to me—' I tried again, but she was already shoving her belongings into her bag. She hastily wrapped the remains of her sandwich in a napkin and crammed it inside, inadvertently knocking my glasses off the table.

'Please, don't leave like this,' I pleaded as she stood abruptly, her chair scraping against the tiled floor, some of the nosy patrons in Sabroso twisting their heads around to take a glance at the commotion unfolding.

'No,' she said firmly, her voice trembling with anger. 'I was telling you something important. I need to get away from you right now, Ruth – I'm just *so* mad at you.'

She had never spoken to me like this before.

I gently tried to grab her arm just to stop her, even for a moment to calm her down, but as quick as a whip, she slapped it away.

'Okay,' I whispered, swallowing hard. 'I get it, I do. Just... can you text me when you get home? Please?' My voice cracked with desperation as I hastily used my sleeve to wipe away the tears now streaming down my face. She was already striding across the café floor. I thought about letting her go for a moment but there was no way I was letting her walk home alone to cool off – not on your nelly, not with the TellTale Killer still at large. I followed her, but the further she got from me, the harder it was to see her clearly without my glasses. I knew I didn't have time to go back and scoop them up if I wanted to catch her. I couldn't bear the thought of losing her, so I stumbled forward, trying to keep my eyes fixed on the distinctive emerald green of her coat. As I precariously pushed open the door and craned my neck in every direction of the busy London street, I couldn't see a glimpse of that signature verdant green. It had been lost, engulfed somewhere in the crowd.

I'd lost her. I'd lost my Greta.

# SEVEN

## PRESENT DAY

I came to rather unexpectedly with a jolt. My poor stomach churned brutally, and my forlorn head throbbed even more so. Unsurprisingly, given last night's margarita consumption, I felt as though I'd been bundled up and shoved into a 1,400 RPM spin cycle. I raised my hands to my head and yanked on a few thick clumps of hair in a vain, stupid attempt to alleviate some of the intense pounding in my forehead to no real effect.

It was only as my blurred, glazed vision began to clear that I realised I wasn't in my bed in the shed, rather I was on the nice plush white sofa in Bill and Ben's living room. Oh dear. I was in very dangerous territory right now. Six margaritas + white sofa = very, very high risk.

The soft clank of a coffee mug hitting the coaster reverberated in my skull, echoing through the centuries to my early caveman ancestors. I let out a small yelp, grabbed the thick velvet cushion my head had been resting on, and slapped it over my face to try and block any further auditory or visual stimuli. Why did I always do this to myself? What was wrong with me?

'You were a real pain in my arsehole last night,' I heard Ben say, muffled through the fabric. 'Far worse than the anal fissure of 2022.'

I remembered the anal fissure. It was a dark time for both of us. We don't suggest taking up yoga anymore.

'I'm sorry,' I muttered through the cushion. I raised it a little bit to reveal my mouth. 'I really am sorry. Did I not make it to the shed?'

'You don't remember how dazzlingly paralytic you were, do you?' Ben replied. 'You know we had to put a bucket down there just in case, right?'

I glanced downwards. Sure enough, there was, in fact, a bright red gardening bucket, neatly placed on a piece of kitchen paper to try and protect Bill's expensive wood floor.

'Was I talking about Greta?' I asked, not really wanting to know the answer to that question, but asking nevertheless.

Ben sighed.

'You were going on and on about the argument you had with her in Hammersmith on the night she...'

'I see.' That was all I could about manage to say as a response. My inebriated episodes always seemed to end with me talking about Greta, like the guy in the pub who has a sip of an IPA and tells you about the girl who broke his heart and the family Labrador who died when he was sixteen. I never even came close to finding out what she was trying to talk to me about that night, as much I tried to revisit it. What had been so important? Would things be completely different now if I had just listened?

I knew the answer to that. If I had paid attention, she wouldn't have stormed out and she wouldn't be dead.

I knew Ben was silently a little cross, but he still pitied me too much to say anything. The real issue was his boyfriend upstairs. I winced at the thought of what Bill might say when *he* came down. He had worked again last night, as he always seemed to do on Thursday nights, at his mysterious second job that no one ever talked about. I tried to imagine once what it was. Maybe he was in fact a stripper; I mean, he had the body for it. Maybe his alter ego was Bendy Bill, down at the Magic Mike experience near Leicester Square.

'Oh, and you might want to drink your coffee,' Ben added. 'Detective Carlota is coming over in fifteen.'

'In fifteen?' I said, lifting my head from the sofa too quickly; the room tilted, and my stomach threatened to empty the last of its contents on their stunning wood flooring. I gently lay back down on the sofa to settle my body like I was carefully handling a fragile nuclear bomb. Why the hell was Detective Carlota coming here? Unless the investigation had progressed because of my misdeeds? Or, worse, she was coming to arrest me? This was the third time she was seeing me in less than a week, surely that didn't bode well.

'Yep!' Ben answered with a forced enthusiasm. 'She kept ringing and ringing your phone at midnight when I was bringing you back, so I picked up and told her to come by at eight.'

From the stairs, I could almost hear the distinctly passive-aggressive rhythm of Bill's footsteps as he descended, followed by the very distinct scent of antiseptic ointment and Tiger Balm. Do strippers use Tiger Balm?

'I tried to let you sleep as long as I could, but I figured you'd need some time to clean yourself up before she gets here,' Ben added in a viciously calm monotone, a trait that had landed us in trouble in the early days of our relationship when I didn't really understand communication was all in the *way* people spoke, less about the actual words they said.

Bill materialised at the bottom of the stairs, glaring at Ben with a look as if to say, *Are you done now?* He placed a hand on Ben's back. That was about the full extent of their physical affection when I was around, and I'll give Bill credit for that. He wasn't one of those hyper-jealous maniacs terrified about Ben and I still having any kind romantic feelings, so felt the need to form a limb prison around their significant other. But I also think he just wasn't a big fan of public displays of affection in general.

Ben reached for the navy padded jacket I'd bought him for Covid Christmas in 2020, the first year we were married. Meanwhile, I ever so carefully tried to shift my body upright, moving at a gentle pace to avoid ruining any more of Bill's pristine house, but this time with the added risk of the walls being painted a new colour called Salt-Rimmed Lime.

'Where are you off to today?' I asked, suddenly aware that I needed to be at work myself in an hour and both of them would have normally left by now.

'Nowhere important,' Bill answered promptly before Ben could respond. Ben gave a weak smile as Bill rather hurriedly ushered him out the door, his hand still firmly glued to Ben's back, almost obsessively rubbing as if he were trying to coax a genie from his spine.

Something was up between the two of them, something I couldn't quite place. Ever since last Saturday, possibly longer, Ben was a shade more subdued and Bill was even more irritable than usual, which I didn't think was even possible.

The thought of Carlota's fast-approaching visit left me experiencing a strange curling and winding in the depths of my gut.

I didn't feel strong enough to trudge the ten or so paces to the shed, so I barely had enough time to down the lukewarm cup of coffee, tie my greasy hair into a ponytail, and splash water on my face before I heard a firm but gentle knock at the front door of the house. It was 7.58. Detective Carlota was punctual as ever.

I opened the door to find her visibly relaxing at the sight of me. Today, she wore a stunning lime-green cowl-neck jumper that suited her olive skin tone and stocky build beautifully, paired with navy slim-leg trousers. As always, phenomenal.

'Thank God,' she said, stepping forward and suddenly yanking me into a close, tight embrace. The warmth, and sheer strength, of her arms wasn't surprising given how muscular her frame was. Then, just as swiftly as she had grabbed me, she stepped back as if to correct herself. 'I'm sorry. I shouldn't have done that. Sorry.' She seemed flustered, a rare sight for the usually impeccably composed woman I had known for the past two years.

'Would... would you like to come in?' I asked, once I had found my voice, still shaking off the surprise of the spontaneous embrace.

She nodded silently, stepping into the entryway, removing her shoes and taking her usual seat when she came to visit at the dining table. I busied myself with the kettle, knowing perfectly well exactly how she liked her tea at this point. With tea, there comes a point where you're locked in for life. If you've always had one sugar and a dash of milk, that's it, that's your tea now, forever. You ever want to maybe experiment and dabble in having it black? No. That's it. No takebacks.

'So,' I began as the water boiled, 'if you don't mind me asking, what prompted that quite dramatic show of relief just now?'

Detective Carlota hesitated as she took a deep inhale through her nasal passageways.

'When you didn't answer your phone last night, I panicked. I couldn't rest until Ben picked up and told me everything was okay.'

I was glad she couldn't see my face as I poured the water into the pot. Why would she assume something had happened to me? There was no way she could have known the heart, or the voice recording, had come direct from me, right?

I tried stretching and contorting my expression into one that looked like a mild surprise before placing the pot of tea in front of her.

'Why?' I asked bluntly. 'Everyone misses calls, I was just out with some friends.'

She drew in another sharp breath and somewhat bashfully folded her arms, placing her palms around each respective rib.

'Ruth,' she paused, 'darling, you know I've told you about as much as I can about this case, maybe far more than I should have at times.'

I nodded, that was true. She'd even skipped the department Christmas party the year before last to calm me down after I'd bombarded her with texts about a news clipping claiming to reveal the Telltale Killer's secret identity was actually ex-deputy prime minister Nick Clegg.

Detective Carlota shifted restlessly in her chair before speaking again, a little uncomfortable as I could see she was still trying to find the words to speak her mind. Looking more like she was about to try and explain to me how when a daddy and a mummy loved each other very much...

'I do need to tell you that the investigation into the TellTale Killer hasn't reopened, nothing has changed there...' She said it as if she was trying to manage my expectations somehow but then her voice dwindled and faded as I poured the tea from the pot into our mugs.

'But there have been some odd developments,' she began, searching for the appropriate phrasing, clearly running through the police guidelines in her mind as she spoke. 'Yesterday, the station received an anonymous recording. It was of a person who was clearly in some sort of pain. I was working late last night and the moment I heard it, I thought it was you and I just felt my whole body freeze. That's why I called you so frantically; I genuinely thought you were in trouble. I'm sorry, but I just needed to come here and tell you the reason I called you two dozen times. It was... stupid of me.'

'No, no, I completely understand. But that's nuts. Who would do something like that?' I muttered under my breath, feigning disbelief as best I could while using my mug to hide as much of my culpable face as possible. My audio manipulation clearly needed some work. I thought I had messed around with the pitch so it was basically unrecognisable, but there must have been something else in my cadence that almost gave me away. Damn you, BitrateBoffin, you've just earned yourself an unsubscribe.

'Honestly?' Carlota took a sip of her tea, like she could relax now she had finally ripped off the plaster. 'In my line of work, nothing surprises me much anymore. But we have methods to work out where it came from.' She paused, placing her mug down with a sigh while I felt my heart stall in my chest. 'Probably just a stupid prank, we've had a few of those lately. But I'm just glad you're okay. When Ben answered your phone and told me everything was all right, I don't think I've ever felt such relief in my life.'

The faintest, tiniest glimmer of moisture in Carlota's eyes as she spoke did make me feel a little bad, honestly. It was, at least, nice to know she cared about me. But I was too busy choking back the froth of frustration that my plan still hadn't fucking worked. I'd given them a heart. I'd given them a recording of someone clearly being held hostage. What more did they want? My mind scrabbled for something else to say, anything that wouldn't accidentally betray just how deeply I was involved to her.

'I guess there really are some pretty sick people out there in the world,' I remarked. You know who I was talking about.

I think this was the first time I'd ever properly lied to Detective Carlota since I had known her, and more than the toxic deluge of margaritas still stirring in my gut, that betrayal made me feel utterly sick.

'Yeah,' Carlota responded, resignedly. 'There've been some odd things happening, some things that I just can't seem to work out.' She stopped herself, clearly realising she'd said way too much, forgetting I was just a limpet clinging onto her friendship, rather than an actual colleague or peer.

She paused for a moment before changing topics.

'Did you at least have a good night, darling?' she asked, rousing herself out of her mini reverie.

I did my best to force a tight smile. 'Truthfully, Detective Carlota, I can't say I did.'

Carlota only stayed for another ten minutes or so as I found out more about her kitchen renovation. She had been debating between halogen, LED and/or CFL lighting for her shelving, while making reference to this mysterious Alba again, who she still didn't refer to explicitly as a girlfriend. After she left, I dawdled over to the shed to change out of my clothes from the night before and grab my funeral director's garb. Toast watched me slack-jawed the whole time, perv.

I took a second to open the one drawer I had in the shed and smooth my hand over the green piece of fabric again, the torn scrap from the coat Greta had worn practically everywhere. I remembered how that coat was the last thing my blurry vision could make out before she vanished into the crowds that night. The next morning they only found that torn piece of fabric, hanging on some wire fencing, about three quarters of a mile from Hammersmith Station.

I walked back into the house and stepped into the power shower Bill had installed a few months ago. As the hot water hit my skin, the drunken slur of my thoughts began to gradually lift, giving way to something that I assumed was probably a kind of sober clarity.

I realised, in that moment, how comforting the idea of an afterlife would be. The thought that all of this might be temporary, just a short, dismal prologue before some promised eternity. But I knew that wasn't the case. The truth was simpler and colder: the case remained unsolved, the TellTale Killer was still out there, and Greta still unavenged.

As I ate a microwavable carbonara ready meal – because yes, you *can* eat dinner for breakfast; not doing so is just what Big Food wants you to think – I realised that I knew it was a really stupid idea to continue in my mission. But the only thing left in my life with any real meaning to me, any real significance, was avenging Greta and making sure she wasn't forgotten. And for that to happen... the faux TellTale Killer would need to strike again.

Just then, I heard a ping. Weird, it was an Instagram notification. I almost never got messages on there, mostly because I so rarely used it. I careered over to check, half expecting it to be something important. Domino's? Domino's? Domino's? Why were they messaging me?

Please, I'm just the intern. We'll give you a free
pizza if you just never message us again.

# PART TWO

# EIGHT

Percy Wilson had been forty-nine at the time of his death a few weeks ago. A nasty, despicable man, he had been universally detested by his neighbours and community for being a deeply racist, sexist, classist and xenophobic piece of work. He had gleefully funnelled his extravagant earnings from the high-interest small loan division of his brutal banking firm into climate change denial organisations and Stalin fan clubs. On some nights, for his own twisted amusement, he'd either place fake reduced stickers on items at his local M&S or watch videos of abandoned puppies and kittens online, laughing deeply until his stomach hurt. Percy had no one he loved and no one who loved him. So, when he died suddenly and alone in his home, the world barely seemed to notice.

Of course, I had no way of knowing if any of that was even remotely true. Similar to Mrs Lambert, I had chosen purposefully to keep any details of his actual life out of my mind. I still felt this knotting and writhing in my gut when I thought about Mrs Lambert and what I did to her, and the idea of doing it again was only tolerable if I imagined a real execrable excuse for a human being.

'You okay, my sweetheart?' Uncle Phil's voice broke through my daydream, jolting me out of my dark fantasy about Percy slipping laxatives into the broth at soup kitchens for his own twisted pleasure.

'Yes, sorry, Uncle Phil,' I murmured, blinking a few times to reorient myself in reality. I turned my attention back to the spreadsheet of the various coffin costs on my desktop, which had become the closest thing I had to a romantic partner lately with all the time I spent staring longingly into its pixels, and all the time I shouted obscenities at it when my Excel formulas didn't work.

Fun fact for you: coffins are marked up absurdly high. Uncle Phil, being an ethical man at heart, had always tried to keep prices fair, but despite his efforts, people always insisted on paying more for a coffin, convinced that an expensive version would somehow maybe ease their grief or maybe be more respectful to the departed. So, to please our customers, we charged at least three to four times the original wholesale price. Uncle Phil had experimented with lowering coffin costs and focusing on service, but oddly enough, people seemed more willing to shell out rather exorbitant amounts for a premium coffin than for any other part of a funeral.

'Where are Sophie and I today, Ruth? Is it St Pancras, for Tom Newson in bay one?' Uncle Phil asked.

'You are indeed,' I replied, not needing to consult the spreadsheet to answer. I always seemed to remember where everyone was going on a given day.

'Brilliant, thank you, sweetheart. I know I can always count on you,' he said warmly while leaning over the desk. It was a slightly cruelly disguised insult from fate, realising I'd become a reliable linchpin in a job I didn't really enjoy and had only intended to do temporarily while I got back on my feet after being sacked from the paper. I have to admit, I had kind of baulked at the idea of working with Uncle Phil when Mum and Dad first brought it up as they were planning their move to the Maldives. At the time, I'd been cocooned in blankets and going by the maxim 'you are what you eat', was 70 per cent raspberry jelly. I think they thought of it as a way for a trusted family member to keep an eye on me while they were sunbathing on the beach with a Mai Tai on taxpayers' money.

'Uncle Phil's funeral directors? Are you joking?' I'd said, spitting projectiles of gelatinous comets across their faces.

Still, as mundane and sluggish as each day was, I confess I had come to appreciate the little – albeit dull – rhythm it gave my life.

'By the way, I meant to say...' Uncle Phil began before checking over his shoulders to make sure no one was overhearing. What was he about to tell me?

He shuffled a little bit forward so most of his torso was hanging over my desk.

'... I've got some very exciting news to tell you.'

'Oh?' I said, not totally sure what emotion to convey in my voice? Excitement? Confusion? Fear? Why couldn't he just tell me now?

'All will become clear soon, Ruth, my dear,' Uncle Phil said with a fluttery wave of his hand and then a small, short cackle before he choked a little on something stuck in his throat. 'Right, think it's time for us to go, Sophie,' he said as my cousin finished talking to Claudia, the office administrator, and gave me one of her fake smiles as she passed me on the way to the hearse. She was probably practising for the day she became my boss and could tell me what to do. I'd quit before that happened, no way was I taking orders from the girl who was still in nappies aged six.

Every time I got a 'good job' or a 'well done' from Uncle Phil, I swear I could feel a twinge in my neck from across the room, like she was itching to drag a knife across it.

Exciting news, though? I wonder what that was all about? Redundancy for Clive and Eddie? Now, that would be very exciting news. I would want a front-row seat to that, popcorn in one hand, slushy in the other.

Once Uncle Phil and Sophie left, I got back to thinking about the next stage of the operation: Hearts and Crafts.

I checked my phone, wondering if Chlo would drop me a message at some point today asking if I got home safe. But she didn't and I can't say I blamed her, honestly. I knew I'd have to reach out first and try to patch things up between us. I wasn't quite sure how to start. Chlo had, admittedly, always been the one to make peace between us if we ever fell out, so I was in uncharted territory. Which, I know, makes me sound awful, but I've had a lot on. How do I start? 'Soz, babes. Hope you still got laid?'

Luckily, as the morning continued, the office only grew quieter and quieter. While early week usually had our busiest days, it had been a stroke of luck that it was a particularly hectic Friday. Then again, it was January, which unfortunately meant it was a very good season for business.

I'd had my eye on Percy Wilson's – or whatever his actual name was – coffin as an involuntary donor for my scheme from the moment I clocked in today. I remembered from the calendar that he was scheduled for cremation tomorrow, and at forty-nine, his heart would probably look young and fresh enough for a police forensics team to believe it belonged to the person the TellTale Killer had presumably captured, recorded their whimperings and then subsequently killed after receiving no response. This part of the plan hadn't been meticulously considered. I'd thought one heart and a voice recording would be enough to get the case reopened but evidently from my conversation with Detective Carlota this morning, more was needed.

The only snag was that Percy wasn't a woman, and his heart needed to play the part of one to match the audio recording I had sent to the police. Ordinarily, this wouldn't be an issue, but women's hearts are, on average, about 50 grams lighter than men's. Still, I was going to take the chance that, in traditional Shake-spearean fashion, his heart could perform a gender-flipped role in my grand production without arousing too much suspicion. While I was no biologist, surely the vast varieties of body types between men and women meant that it would be difficult to distinguish sex from heart alone.

I began formulating my strategy. The Chuckle Brothers, Uncle Phil and Sophie, wouldn't be back until around 12.30 if my rough guess was right. Claudia, the only other person in the office, was the one variable I had to consider. I just needed to find a way to get her on her lunch break early and that would give me a solid thirty minutes to get in, retrieve the heart, and get out.

After my carbonara breakfast this morning, I'd snagged one of Bill's fancy vacuum-sealed meal prep containers, the kind he used to store his more extravagant dishes for his day job as a software engineer. It was airtight and smell-proof, and its thick, onyx-black coating meant no one could peer inside and wonder why my lunch looked suspiciously like a canopic jar.

Once home, I'd transfer the heart into another of the wooden cases I could buy at the garden centre on my way back. How I'd send it and what message it would contain, I'd work out later.

Percy was slated for cremation tomorrow which meant I had a limited window if I wanted to pickpocket his heart. I went into the morgue briefly to go check on his casket and a small card on the gurney confirmed he was prepped, suited, and ready for the service – meaning no one would be opening his coffin again before then. Result.

Trying to appear as casual as possible, I began mentally ticking off my checklist: gloves, surgical scissors, suture thread and needles, face mask, bottles of my chemical concoction to keep the heart fresh, everything I could get my mitts on. I went back and forth between the morgue and my desk as I placed the various items neatly in a carrier bag beneath my computer so I could easily snatch it up and head to the morgue when the coast was clear. I wasn't about to explain why an Ann Summers bag was lurking in the morgue containing dead body equipment, not when Claudia had a habit of wandering in unannounced. Far safer to stash it beneath my desk, where I hoped no person would dare investigate anyway. While I had attempted to be at least a little clandestine, I realised at around 10.30, that I needn't have bothered; Claudia's small, short snores from the other side of the office confirmed she wasn't paying too much attention to what I was doing.

I felt my phone buzz as I sat back down at my desk and snatched it up. It was CerealKillerCornflakes, my virtual true-crime penpal on DarkCell. I preferred these fringe forums to the over-moderated public ones, where any useful information was almost always filtered out by moderator zealots before I could even glance at it. Unfortunately, a good portion of the posts on DarkCell actually fawned over what the TellTale Killer had done, instead of trying to understand or help catch him. But occasionally, someone would post something useful: a police leak, a clandestine case update or bootleg footage would surface.

However, I chose to keep my interactions with most of these people to a bare minimum, maybe except for CerealKillerCornflakes. Most of my conversations with him as my own username: StabithaChristie, consisted of us insulting each other over our various TTK theories, but he never showed the same level of idolatry for the TellTale Killer that the others did, hence why I slightly tolerated him. He still got on my tits, though. The man clearly didn't get out much and I had a feeling his brain would explode if he realised he was actually talking to a woman that wasn't his mum.

He was replying to a message I'd sent him the other day, in which I explained my reasoning over something we often debated: that the TellTale Killer might be quite content to fade into obscurity, never to be heard from again, vis-à-vis the Jack the Ripper.

*Sorry, Stabitha, but your point is, quite frankly, dumb. All curds, no cream*, he began, I could imagine him pushing his glasses up the bridge of his nose as he typed out the message. *The one thing TTK probably hates more than getting caught by the pigs is being forgotten. And last week, my contact in the police said the case is now officially classed as cold.* I mean, that was public knowledge, not exactly ground-breaking investigation skills there, friend.

*I'm telling you, there's no way this guy is just sitting back and retiring. Some serial killers sure, but killers like TTK can't resist the urge. It's not just about getting away with it; it's about seeing how much they can get away with, he wants to live forever in social consciousness. Mark my words: now that the case has gone cold, we'll see him strike again any day now. They always do and then I can tell you, I told you so.*

As much as I hated to admit it, CerealKillerCornflakes was

right. The whole world knew how much this sicko loved the lime-light, no way could he give that up.

I couldn't help but wonder a thought that hadn't really crossed my mind until now: if what I was doing, and what I *continued* to do, actually got out to the press, how would the real-deal TellTale Killer actually respond to my copycatting?

*Okay,* was all I replied to CerealKillerCornflakes's long stream of messages. I knew that would irritate him.

NINE

One of the odder things about working at a funeral directors was Uncle Phil's insistence on still having a Christmas party to keep morale up. Last Christmas, I somehow had booked someone called 'Swedish Elvis', which turned out to be his self-imposed title. However Swedish Elvis, as it turned out, was rather *handsy*. Things took a peculiar turn when he began grinding on Uncle Phil mid-'Love Me Tender'. Not exactly the sort of thing you expect to witness at a funeral directors do...

Sophie had made a point of undermining me during the party, loudly musing, conveniently within earshot of Uncle Phil, that maybe I shouldn't organise the Christmas party next year. It was Machiavellian complaining disguised as a cool casual banter, which I didn't love. I'd planned to get her the make-up bag she'd been hinting at for months for family Christmas, but instead, I got her a padlock from Poundland purely out of spite for her comment.

Why I'm bringing it up is because what I'd learned at that Christmas party, while Uncle Phil was wrestling a gyrating Elvis off one of the show coffins mid-'Burning Love', was that Claudia adored Harry Styles far more than a woman in her fifties reasonably should. It was the kind of obsession that felt... long-term and durable. So, when I mentioned, casually, when Claudia finally stirred, that I'd heard someone had spotted Harry down by the Gail's about half a mile away, she was out the door before I'd finished the sentence, leaving me blessedly completely alone in the office.

I waited for a few moments, just to be certain she wouldn't suddenly reappear – perhaps remembering that Harry was on tour in Rio – and catch me elbows deep in old Percy. After a safe period of time, I snatched the Ann Summers carrier bag from under my desk, shrugged into my thick coat, which I knew I'd need for warmth, and headed for the morgue.

I glanced at the clock as I walked in – 12.02 – and placed my bag of goodies on the side countertop. I had it all worked out: ten minutes for the extraction, ten for clean-up, and another ten to double-check everything – no evidence, no crime. I knew my anxious soul would need the time to make sure there was absolutely no trace of what I'd done.

The weak link in my plan was speed. There was no time to move Percy from his coffin to one of the gurneys, where we usually prepared the bodies for presentation, so this procedure would need to be performed in-coffin.

My eyes did, however, lock onto another pair in the room: Henry. Henry the Hoover. Two great white eyes stamped onto his cheery bright red face, staring at me with a kind of sneering moral authority.

'Please don't judge me for this, Henry,' I pleaded.

He didn't even blink.

I hauled open the heavy oak coffin lid and took a quick glance at Percy, who I was still mentally branding as the epitome of human arseholery to get me through this. But forty-nine really wasn't old, especially when there was still so much life left for him to live. I tried not to let the thought settle too deeply, but I couldn't help wondering: what had Percy been thinking on the day he died? Was he buried in paperwork or arguing with his spouse about where to spend Christmas? What issue had seemed so cataclysmically important at the time, only to be rendered meaningless now that he was gone? Now that they would never argue about Christmas, or anything else, ever again.

I remember turning twenty-five and feeling a quiet grief in realising my youth was officially behind me. But now, four years later, I thought of everyone like Greta who never even made it that far. Not everyone is lucky enough to grow old, I thought to myself, we really shouldn't think of it as such a curse.

It was 12.05 and already I was feeling myself going into Ruth-mode while staring blankly at the extraordinarily bloated chest of the dead husk in front of me, some kind of water damage surely, by the way his body looked. I didn't dare look at his head. I feared he'd have one of those expressions fixed onto his face that would look too innocent or too pure for me to extract a heart from. No, all I needed to do was get in his chest and get his heart out. I didn't need to see any identifying features to remind myself this had been once a living human being.

I threw on the face mask, laid down the medical drape, unbuttoned his suit jacket, loosened his tie, pulled back his shirt, and got to work.

I'm sorry in advance about this.

I worked with precision as I gently carved my entry point with the scalpel around Percy's flesh, and armed with a copious supply of kitchen towel, began to mop and dab any of the dark, clotty fluid that was starting to leak out of him. After making my careful incision, I lifted the skin and snipped away the arteries and the venae cavae connected to the heart. I retched a little at the smell, partly due to the fact I was still dreadfully hungover, and the heart absolutely stank of a vague marine-like taint and a faint coppery tang, but I just about managed to find the fortitude to continue.

The heart that I had extracted looked pallid, waxy, and oddly preserved, its usual shape somehow distorted into something I hadn't ever seen before.

I didn't have much time to inspect it but to me, it looked far more bloated and puffy than a normal heart. But I ignored my misgivings; I was committed to this heart, and I needed to continue with the plan. Using the tongs and ensuring there were no rogue drips, I carefully transferred the heart to Bill's fancy storage container and sealed it as tight as I could.

Quickly, I cleaned up the last bits of blood with kitchen towel and readied the suture needle and thread to prepare to tighten Percy back together. This part wasn't strictly necessary, I realised, it wasn't like anyone was going to see his body again, but somehow it felt wrong to leave him quite so ... open like that.

Uncle Phil knew a lot about burials and death practices, which is a little weird if you think about it; you wouldn't expect someone owning a Subway franchise to know the history of the sandwich. By the time the Christmas party last year had crept into the small hours, Uncle Phil had had about eight too many and collapsed into a sofa. Claudia and Swedish Elvis were slow-dancing to 'Are You Lonesome Tonight?', her hands, with suspicious regularity, straying to his buttocks. It was there on that sofa where Uncle Phil had told me that in the Middle Ages, it was actually quite common for royalty to have their hearts buried separately from their bodies. They were often preserved with mercury, mint and frankincense, owing to the belief that the heart was the receptacle of a person's whole life.

Still, I don't really understand the fascination with the heart. Why not the lungs? Lungs are very important. Or the kidneys? Or the liver? What makes the heart so romantic, so special? I wonder if the other organs ever got jealous of all the attention the heart seemed to get.

I had just began poking and piercing my way with the needle through Percy's skin, admiring how fast I was being with tidying up my handiwork, when a sudden jolt in my leg made me shriek aloud to myself. My stitching went awry as I realised it was my phone that was buzzing and vibrating incessantly against my thigh. Ripping off my gloves, I yanked it from my pocket to look at the caller ID.

Uncle Phil.

Did I pick up? No. But what if it was an emergency? Or worse

– what if he was waiting outside the morgue, about to stroll inside to see me suturing like a madwoman on one of his corpses? My gut made the decision before any logic in my brain could get in the way. I swiped to answer and pressed the phone to my ear.

'Uncle Phil, hi! How are you?'

'Ruth, sweetheart, good to hear you. The funeral's done, all went well. We're just heading back now.'

I glanced at the clock: 12.15. If they'd just left, they wouldn't be back from St Pancras until about 12.32. Perfect. An extra two minutes that would be sorely needed to finish my work here.

'Are you free to talk?' he asked.

'Urgh, yeah, of course,' I replied.

For some reason, I thought this would make me seem less suspicious. Damn, should have told him I was on my period. Nothing ends a conversation with Uncle Phil faster than any kind of menstrual logistics.

I fumbled to put the phone on speaker, resting it on where two lips of the coffin met. I resumed stitching Percy's chest, my hands moving faster and more rapidly now, trying not to be clumsy and make any stupid mistakes.

'Well, first off,' Uncle Phil said, 'I've been reviewing the itinerary. I want you to check on Justin for the service at 10.30 tomorrow. Make sure he's in tip-top condition.'

My hands froze mid thread. I'd been so careful to strip away any hint of the person he may have been; the unlucky man I'd nicknamed Percy was, it turned out, actually called Justin. What if he wasn't the sort to lob rocks at care homes but had spent his life building schools in impoverished countries and I'd just been rooting around his chest like it was a box of bric-à-brac? Annoyingly, now I knew he was called Justin, I wouldn't be able to refer to him as anything but.

'Of course, Uncle Phil,' I said, getting stuck on one of the hardened, crusty bits of Justin's flesh with the needle. 'May I ask why?'

'Sorry, say that again, Ruth, sweetheart? You're a bit echoey, it sounds like you're in the morgue.'

My chest lurched as I tried to steady my voice, I leaned closer to the microphone, not even trying to object to his comment.

'Why?' I asked again.

'Oh, well, Clive has marked him wrong, it's actually an open casket viewing before a cremation. Just want to make sure he looks as good as possible for the family; his sister-in-law is a friend of mine.'

The heart in my own chest tumbled, then sharply plummeted. A brutal lurch of panic took hold – cold, sharp, and paralysing – like a wave of sub-zero frost spreading rapidly from within me. I felt it claw and ravage its way up my throat, choking, freezing me in place.

'Goodness me, I hate London traffic,' Uncle Phil groused. 'You still there, Ruth?'

'Uh-huh,' was about all I could manage to say, my voice barely audible even to me. I couldn't even think about what to say when all I was thinking was how the hell was I going to make this body presentable for an open casket in less than twenty minutes?

Desperate, I switched my phone onto airplane mode, ending the call abruptly. Uncle Phil would think the line dropped, and I wouldn't have to explain any of the sheer terror in my voice if I continued the conversation.

But now what? I couldn't put the heart *back* in his chest – that would be impossible. Worse, I could now see that the central chest cavity was starting to collapse in on itself, the skin sinking in a way that very blatantly screamed, *Error Error: critical organ missing*.

I had to act. Quickly. It was now 12.20. Grabbing the surgical scissors, I rapidly undid my careful stitching. Think. Think. What could I use as a substitute?

As I worked, ripping apart the stitching, my eyes fixed upon a dark, clotty ooze which began to bloom and blossom across Justin's crisp white shirt, as if an old fountain pen had exploded inside him. I cursed – my scissors must've somehow nicked the skin. Whether from dead or living bodies, blood notoriously sets fast, and it was too late to even try and wipe it clean. So, I now had a second problem; I needed something to mop up the blood *and* fill the cavity.

Henry continued to watch from the corner, scathingly.

And then it hit me.

Justin, I don't believe your soul continues to exist after your demise, but if it does, wherever you are now, I am so, so sorry for what I did next. When this is over, I'll bring flowers to your grave every month, but right now, maybe you should look away.

I grabbed a nearby roll and began to stuff handfuls of kitchen towel into the cavity where Justin's heart used to be, like I was stuffing the prized turkey at Christmas.

I used nearly the entire roll, pushing more and more thick wads of kitchen towel into his chest until his shirt seemed to rise to an acceptable, anatomically correct level again. I stepped back and waited for a minute, holding my breath, watching for any small sign of it sinking back down. It seemed like it was stable, and I certainly didn't have time to check things a third or fourth time. This would have to do, he just had to stay like this for a day, that was perfectly possible.

As fast as I could, I set to work re-suturing his skin much faster than Uncle Phil had ever taught me, the faint pierce marks from my first attempt barely visible but just enough to guide me. My hands were trembling so violently I had to force myself to focus. I distracted my mind to try and keep it calm, listing every kind of pasta shape I could name in my head: spaghetti, penne, percy, *damn*, tagliatelle, orecchiette.

My hand that was holding the quivering needle between my thumb and index finger spasmed from the tension and the sudden twitch sent the suture needle tumbling from my grip, rolling off Justin's water-bloated belly before clattering to the floor.

Snatching it up, I instinctively moved it to the sterilising solution, only to pause mid-action, realising this probably wasn't necessary and would only take up more of the very little, precious time I had left. The clock read 12.24. Pacing quickly around the morgue, I gave myself fifteen seconds to clench and unclench my fist, trying to coax some blood flow back into my hand. Meanwhile, the white-hot frost in my chest that I knew to be a cocktail of adrenaline and fear seemed to stretch further, creeping into every corner of my body now, from my head to my toes, numbing my body parts and quivering my skin. You really need a steady hand for this kind of work and the emotions I was currently experiencing were not assisting.

I hunched over Justin again to continue the suturing, telling myself to be slow and steady, all the while going through all the pasta shapes I could still think of: ravioli, agnolotti, conchiglie, Lamborghini – wait no, that was a car.

Before I knew it, the suturing was complete. I wasted no time buttoning up his shirt, just doing the top two buttons and then carefully pulling his suit jacket over the thick black spot that had bled through earlier. Luckily, it seemed any more of the bleeding was happening towards the back of his body; no one was ever going to see that.

I scanned the morgue as I gingerly stepped away from the coffin, my eyes darting from corner to corner of the room. Had I left anything incriminating out? Anything obvious? No security camera had suddenly been installed? Nothing seemed amiss.

Ripping off my gloves, face mask and flinging down the needle I had been using, I bundled them up and tossed them into the bin. Would someone notice a missing scalpel? I didn't have time to dwell on that.

I took a step back and let out a small, shaky sigh of relief. Glancing up at the clock, I froze, hands suspended, the way they do when 'Time!' is called on *Bake Off*. *Cadavre servi cru.*

12.30. On the dot.

I took one last look at Justin in his coffin, inspecting and scrutinising every visible inch of him. In my experience, open caskets didn't encourage long, drawn-out glances. Nobody really wants to linger on the sight of a dead body – especially not of someone they loved. But everything seemed, dare I say it, immaculate. Mission successful.

The morgue door swung open with a jarring creak, and I lurched upwards as Uncle Phil entered. He'd made good time.

'Hello, hello,' he called out in his usual sing-song tone; not even being in a morgue could dim his relentless cheeriness. 'Thanks for checking. How's he looking?' he asked.

'Not bad, I think,' I replied, trying to mask any of the anxiety that was still coursing through my bloodstream by speaking purposefully slowly. I picked up the container I'd left on the counter and held it close to my chest. Wouldn't want Uncle Phil accidentally opening that on a whim, curious to know what my lunch was.

He flashed me one of his signature grins, then glanced over at the cadaver.

'Bad death for poor Justin,' he said. 'Good thing Sophie worked on setting his face. I don't think I'd have done nearly as good a job.'

I nodded; I didn't want to look at Justin's face but I knew it was true. Sophie was exceptionally talented at setting the faces of the dead. Also, my aunt had told me, with some irony, that she was a gifted part-time life-drawing artist. Essentially, if you weren't moving, Sophie could make you look good.

'How was the funeral?' I asked.

'Standard,' Uncle Phil said with a bemused shrug. '"Amazing Grace", "My Way" – the classics.'

'Of course,' I said with a smile, an overexaggerated nod of my head and a hopefully not-too-nervous chuckle.

'Oh yes, Clive and Eddie will handle the wake. But they did say they'll give us a five-star Trustpilot review, so no complaints there,' he added, pulling up the lone creaky-wheeled stool in the morgue and groaning slightly as he perched on it. Uncle Phil was a bit obsessed with Trustpilot, almost had a breakdown when he got a one star review once. 'Right, Ruth, I need to talk to you about something serious, do you have a minute?'

'Sure,' I said, glancing around for another place to sit but he'd taken the only stool, so I shifted awkwardly to lean backwards on one of the counters, trying to make myself look comfortable and not let my eyes wander to Justin's coffin. Was a morgue really the best place to have a chat? Maybe Uncle Phil wasn't bothered by anything dead-related, after so long in the fast-paced, dynamic and exciting world of cadavers.

'I've been doing a lot of thinking over these past few months,' Uncle Phil began. 'About my career, about everything we've accomplished here, and how proud I am of it all. But also, about how much time I have left on God's green earth and how I'd like to use it. And so, Auntie Ingrid and I were talking, and we've decided to finally take out the camper van and travel across Europe, visiting the Menin Gate and Tyne Cot and the like.'

'Okay,' I said, hoping he'd get to the point quicker. Was it a secondment or something? Did he want to me to be his driver on this grand tour? My pulse was still violently racing from the chaos of tearing a heart out of a corpse not twenty minutes earlier. I tried to read his face, searching for any indicator of what he might say next, some hint of sadness or contentment, but I couldn't read him. He wasn't making eye contact, which I normally chalked up to being a bad sign.

'I've really loved having you join the team. And while I know the business is called Camborne and Sons, I always thought of the name as more of an aspiration than a promise. You know my sons, none of them were ever really interested in the family business. But then you came to work with me a year or so ago, and every-thing just seemed to fall into place. I...'

'Uncle Phil,' I interrupted as gently as I could, knowing he had a tendency to ramble on and I had little patience for conversational filler: land the plane. 'What are you trying to say?'

'Well,' he said with a nervous chuckle, 'I guess what I'm asking is... would you like to take over the business?'

'Oh!' I exclaimed, genuinely quite stunned, that was not at all what I thought he was going to say. I instinctively placed the container on the side, worried that the shock was going to make me drop it. 'Oh, Uncle Phil, I don't really know what to say.'

'It's fine,' he said, moving closer to reassure me and lovingly grab the hands that went to reach to my face. 'Absolutely fine. Don't say anything now – just think about it. I've always wanted to keep the business in the family, and I can't think of a better option than you.'

'Thank you, Uncle Phil. But... what about Sophie? I thought she's always wanted to take over? And she's been here for longer than me?'

'Ah, Sophie... I think it's best she remains where she is. I want someone like you, Ruth, someone I can trust.'

Yikes, if only he knew.

'I just want someone in charge of Camborne and Sons who's got real spunk.' Poor choice of word, but I wasn't going to inform him of the modern-day usage. 'By the way, have you seen her life drawings? Absolutely awful, I can't believe we got them as Christmas presents from her,' Phil continued. 'Anyhow, Ruth, sweetheart, just mull it over, that's all I'm asking at this point. No rush, no commitment yet. We can talk more in a few days, all right? Just, please, listen to your heart.'

I couldn't help the way my eyes flicked to the container I was clutching.

# TEN

I probably shouldn't have called her a hag, that was rude. But if you're bag blocking seats on the bus on a busy Friday afternoon, you pretty much do deserve to be called a hag. There had been no seats left on the bottom level, and when this woman who looked like a shrivelled old plum, in a tartan scarf, ignored my polite requests to move her bag, I lost it a little bit. I wasn't about to risk it with a man-spreader on the top deck; I wanted *that* free seat.

But I definitely shouldn't have grumbled under my breath that she was a 'vile old hag'. I decided it was probably worth making my escape before I got booted off the bus by some social justice vigilantes. Besides, the woman looked like she was in her hundreds, she might soon be one of my clients, then who'd have the last laugh?

'Should have given up your seat,' I'd say as I doodled a vulva on her cold cheek like Greta and I used to do. I wouldn't actually do this, by the way, I'm not that awful, but it was a fun thing to think about when I was feeling incandescent with righteous fury.

Walking home, with a single rucksack strap over my shoulder and Bill's bougie container clutched to my chest, did give me plenty of time to think, however. Feet dragging, I mulled over Uncle Phil's offer. It was flattering, I suppose, to be offered to step into the role as the big cheese, and having the supreme power to immediately show Clive and Eddie the door was certainly alluring. Yet this job was never meant to launch my career in funeral directing. Humbling as it was to be given the opportunity, working for Camborne and Sons – or Camborne and Nieces as it should really be called – hadn't sparked anything inside me, and didn't I owe it to Uncle Phil to feel more excitement at the thought of career advancement there? The hard cold truth of it, I suppose, was that I still didn't really know what I wanted. Going back to writing or journalism felt like a dead end. There was no significant other I had to factor into my decisions, and I wasn't shelving any grand passion. After Greta, I'd mostly been treading water because I had no idea where I wanted to swim. I was almost thirty, wasn't I meant to have some kind of direction by now?

Ten minutes into my walk, Mum finally got decent-enough signal on the beach I imagined her sunbathing on to call and ask how I was doing.

'Can't believe it's been over two years since Greta,' she had murmured in the first few minutes of the call as if she had finally galvanised enough courage to address the elephant in the room. Funny how when someone dies, their name can be used as a noun for the day they died too.

I told her I was doing okay. She and Dad sent their love and ran through their travel itinerary: they'd be in Sri Lanka tomorrow and I wished the population of the country well.

Mum and Dad always considered themselves a superior tier of Brit abroad, after all, between them they spoke about eighteen languages. So instead of the classic 'DO. YOU. HAVE. FISH. AND. CHIPS?' they'd bellow at some poor restaurant staff, they'd simply ask for the Yorkshire Tea Gold in Tamil in the tea-growing region of the central highlands.

Bill and Ben's cars were both parked in the driveway which was a semi-positive omen: Bill was home, but at least I had Ben to take some of the brunt of his pedantry for me. Thinking ahead, I carefully opened my rucksack, slipped the container inside and made sure it was completely obscured from sight. If he saw that I'd taken one of his fancy lunchboxes he might combust so violently they'd name the city-sized crater after him.

'Hey,' Bill greeted me from the kitchen, tilting his head slightly past the door frame as I walked into the hallway. The waft of his secret cigarettes hit me like an uppercut to the jaw. As I walked towards him, I noticed he had an ever-so-fresh crescent-shaped scar etched onto his jaw that was far too deep to be from a razor but I didn't have the courage to ask him about that. How I wished it was a secret stripping injury though.

'Hi,' I replied, with as much energy as someone who worked a full-time job as well as moonlighting as a part-time cardiovascular surgeon was able to rally. I brushed my shoes on the doormat with an almost devout precision. Bill watched my every minute move as if inspecting the soles of the boots to ensure not one tiny speck of dirt had made it inside. It took me a little while to fully unlace my shoes so I could yank them off, and made me quietly pray for a Velcro comeback. It wasn't just the tobacco that was nauseating to my nostrils, it was the cloyingly floral red in his hand that hit my nose before I even clocked the glass. The pungent scent made me gag a little; I still felt quite fragile from yesterday. I took off my rucksack and placed it by the door to the garden, praying he wouldn't notice the faint clang of the container in my rucksack shifting against my notepad.

'You haven't seen my lunch container, have you?' Bill asked, certainly sharply and maybe a little – albeit rightfully – accusatori-ally as I joined him in the kitchen to wash out the mug from this morning I had forgotten about.

'No,' I replied on an inhale as I scratched my chin with my index and middle fingers. 'No, I haven't, I'm afraid. When did you last have it?'

His eyes narrowed, lids drooping as his eyebrows clambered up his forehead in a clear expression of disbelief. I know it's one of those really annoying questions, but I thought that was the go-to thing to say when someone said they lost something. Surely that's better than just, 'I don't know.'

'Bother,' he muttered, enunciating the final sounds of the word with an unconvinced and almost growl-like groan. I realised, as his hand missed the side to steady himself, that this clearly wasn't his first glass. Normally Bill was a whisky man so I was surprised he was hitting the vino tonight.

'Do you want a glass of wine?' he asked, luring me into the kitchen when all I wanted was to make my escape to the shed. 'There's enough left in the bottle,' he remarked.

I was surprised by the generosity. I don't think Bill had ever offered me anything. I was too dumbfounded to answer straight away, so he continued speaking.

'Ben's gone to bed, and it's a Shiraz. Don't know how good it'll be in a few days so may as well make the most of it.'

'I'm okay, actually,' I stammered, still startled by his apparent generosity. I worried he might be offended, but at the moment I could barely stomach anything other than water, let alone wine.

'Suit yourself,' he muttered, refilling his glass. He twisted his body to face me and then pouted his lips as if he was trying to detect the location of an ulcer within his mouth. 'Listen, Ruth. Ben and I have both *really* loved having you here, we really have. You've really been such a delightful guest to have around the house...'

Uh-oh.

'But things are really difficult for us right now, and I don't know how much longer we can put you up for, I'm afraid.'

He gave an overexaggerated attempt at a pained wince before loosening his facial muscles to drink a few more significant gulps of wine, staring at me the whole time he did it.

'Oh,' I said quietly. It felt strange hearing this from Bill instead of Ben. I thought when I had outstayed my welcome, Ben would be the one to take me round the back of the barn with the shotgun. Maybe Ben couldn't face telling me and had sent Bill to do his dirty work. I tried to keep my composure despite the drop in my stomach, maybe that was why the two of them had been acting so weird of late. 'That's okay, Bill. Seriously, no worries at all,' I replied, trying desperately not to let my voice quiver.

'I'm so sorry,' Bill said flatly, without even a fake trace of emotion in his voice. 'But it's been well over a year now, and we all knew this was temporary, while you got back on your feet.'

'Yeah, yeah,' I said, my voice unnaturally high as I nodded vigorously, trying to appear agreeable while I stared down at the material of my boots. Inside, I was panicking. Where the hell was I going to go now? What the hell was I meant to do now? I couldn't afford anywhere by myself on my salary. I would have to take over the funeral home, if only for the pay bump it would provide and potential accommodation if I was brave enough to go full-vampire and sleep in a coffin.

A long pause stretched out between us. I kept standing there awkwardly in the kitchen, hands in my pockets, while Bill leaned on the kitchen counter with one hand and held his wine glass with a 'you know, I actually went to a wine tasting experience once' grip in the other.

'It's just... Ben and I, we need our space. We need time to be a couple right now, you know. You understand, right?'

I would have made eye contact, but the shock of being told I had to leave still left me reeling. I wanted to glare at him; to tell him how audacious it was for him of all people to say that to me, maybe even to sock him in the jaw. I hadn't punched anyone in my life but Bill was certainly the person I had wanted to hit the most. But I didn't. I just nodded and repeated, 'Yeah, yeah,' in an unnaturally high tone yet again. There I was, yet again, being a coward.

Slowly, I turned and made my way to the shed, trying to retreat from probably the most awkward encounter I'd ever been in. 'I'm just a bit tired, so I'm going to... head out,' I said meekly.

I could still feel Bill's eyes watching me, like a lion observing a felled antelope. I left through the living room door and carefully trotted along the garden path to reach the shed and once inside, I drew the curtains across the glass doors, dropped my rucksack with a thud, and collapsed onto the bed. Staring up at the ceiling, I let my thoughts churn. What the hell was I going to do now?

I needed some kind of therapy animal, so I walked over to Toast, picked her up, and held her gently, but firmly, against my bosom as I lay back on my bed, stroking her shell. I hadn't tried this before and she didn't seem to enjoy it; her limbs flailed slowly, like she was trying to swim through a pool of treacle. So, I put on an Enya mix on my phone, I knew she liked that and sure enough, it seemed to calm her down almost instantly. I just really hoped that she wouldn't start thrusting the air while I held her close to me, that wasn't what I needed just then.

I lay there for at least ten minutes, lost in a deep spiral of what-ifs, whys and maybes. Wondering what would have happened if Greta had never died. Maybe we could have lived together again, like we had before I married Ben. Her place had been lovely – a tiny but quaint two-bedroom, one-bathroom apartment above a small independent DIY shop in Richmond. She could barely afford it, but I felt like we would have made it work between us; with me contributing to rent, batch cooking and throwing on blankets instead of turning on the central heating. She had been talking about how she wanted to zhuzh it up a bit and I'd have loved to make that a project we could have both worked on together.

Sitting up abruptly, I felt my anger at Bill – and subsequently myself – bubbling to the surface. Why did I just stand there, silent? Why didn't I say something? Why didn't I argue back? I had never even spoken to him about the fact that Bill knew Ben was married when they began their fling. Somehow, I had always felt it would have been way too awkward for *me* to bring up. Firstly, why would it have been awkward *for me*? Secondly, while I knew I wasn't the best house guest in the world, I did keep to myself, gave them plenty of alone time, and paid £250 rent, despite having no hot water in the shed. From another perspective, I was a five-star Airbnb guest, a very reliable source of income for their expensive vino fund.

Vindicated by my rage, I placed Toast – who was now trying

incessantly to bite my finger; she had a taste for human flesh after all – on the bed, snapped on a pair of disposable gloves, yanked Bill's container out of my bag, and carefully twisted the lid open. The stench hit me like some kind of poisonous cloud, and I gagged, retching loudly as the dead-cum-embalming smell overwhelmed the small space. This was so much worse than Mrs Lambert. But after a moment, I steadied myself, steeling my resolve yet again as I continued the procedure.

So, my life was spiralling deeper into disaster by the second. No matter. Maybe there was one part of it I could still control. If I could be the one to find the TellTale Killer, to tear *his* heart from his chest, then maybe – just maybe – all this pain, all this grief, all this guilt burning inside me would mean something. It would have some kind of purpose.

I carefully placed the heart in the wooden box I had grabbed from the garden centre on my way home. I then shifted into what I would call *serial killer mode*. I knew serial killers were antisocial, emotionally detached, and usually saw the world with a healthy dollop of nihilism, and right now, that wasn't a million miles from where my own head was at.

I kept watch on the house through a narrow slit between the thin curtain and the glass, making sure Ben and Bill didn't suddenly decide to make a surprise appearance at my humble abode.

If my plan was to succeed, the police needed to believe – truly believe – that the TellTale Killer had returned in all of his fury and was about to strike again and again. My goal was that they'd realise the case should never have been declared cold and deploy every single shred of resource that I wasn't privy to into finally tracking him down with the important addendum that it wasn't actually me they were trying to locate.

So, if I were a serial killer, craving attention from the police and having my offering of Mrs Lambert's heart and a recording of my next victim ignored, how would I respond? I would retaliate. I would escalate, like a toddler throwing a tantrum because their mother had the audacity to focus on another child for a brief moment. That's how I felt right now, that's how *he* would feel too.

I tapped the pen against my desk in some kind of restless thought, racking my brain for some line that would spur them into action. What would push them over the edge, make them sit up suddenly and realise they were dealing with more than an elaborate hoax?

I let the killer's stream of consciousness play out in my mind. The TellTale Killer craved fame, reputation and most importantly: immortality. The lack of attention would lead his frustration to boil over, driving him to lash out in a way he knew they couldn't ignore. My hand moved faster than my thoughts, scribbling words in code, each stroke flowing with a rather unsettling ease. I didn't even need to glance at the cipher to know what I was writing.

*I shall see a thousand rivers of blood spilled,*
*To raise a mountain of bones*
*beneath these vacant heavens,*
*I will cut,*
*I will carve,*
*I will tear a thousand lives into pieces,*
*in defiance of this rotten, hymnless void.*

Was this a bit much? I feel like it was a bit much. I might have gone a bit too far in some places, but I was no poet and frankly, all I needed was some kind of reaction from the police. Go big or go home, right?

I slipped the coded message into the wooden container holding the heart, then pushed the box into a padded package. I scrawled on the front, in bold letters:

***For the Attention of Detective Cecilia Carlota.***

<h1 style="text-align:center">ELEVEN</h1>

In the dead of the cold January night, I crept out of the shed, carrying Justin's heart in a box tucked within my tote bag. The streets were expectedly busy for 11 p.m. on a Friday, but I moved through London with purpose, keeping my head low and my grip tight around the straps. When I reached the Lidl a few miles in the other direction of where I had deposited heart one, there was only a group of youths loitering outside, smoking cheap joints and lounging back on their BMX bikes. For a moment, I wondered about the possibility of them mugging me before promptly realising that my only possessions were a phone about eight models too old for them to make a profit on, and a human organ. Probably not something they had on their mugging wish list. Luckily, however, they seemed far too stoned to even realise I was there.

It was only when I overheard them debating their preferred type of quinoa that I realised they weren't just stoners. They were the worst kind: middle-class stoners.

Keeping the brim of my cap low to obscure as much of my face as possible, I approached the obnoxiously bright yellow locker. I presented my phone, showing the QR code to the sensor and after a loud shrill beep, one of the metal hatches swung open with a clang. Without hesitation, I tossed the package inside, slammed the door shut, and quickly made my exit into the night. forwarding the successful deposit email from my burner account using a VPN (you can never be too safe) to Detective Carlota as I did so.

And here's the thing: I felt bad. I really, really did feel bad about it. Like, horrendously bad, like I had an even worse churning and rolling in my gut from knowing I had intentionally done something truly ghastly. It wasn't just because I had yanked yet another poor person's heart out of their body, but because I couldn't help wondering how devastated Detective Carlota would feel when she inevitably came to pick up the package. Would she think this was all her fault? Would she somehow blame herself for all of this? Of course, she wasn't at fault, not even slightly. None of this was at all on her shoulders. Yet, Carlota was the only detective I'd spoken to throughout the whole investigation who genuinely seemed to care about the people affected by the killer's death toll, and because of that, she was the only one who, I believed, could actually do something about reopening the case. It all felt terribly manipulative, and part of me wondered if it was too late to turn back, to somehow change the recipient to one of the other random police detectives who had worked on the case. But I knew it was too late. Eventually, the ends would justify the means. I had to keep telling myself that. None of what I was doing was physically hurting anyone living, at least, right? This was all for the greater good.

I tried not to let the previous night's guilt catch up with me as I walked to work early Saturday morning, keeping pace with the small creek murmuring beside the road up to the office. As a comparatively pleasant distraction, I pondered what the TellTale Killer was doing this very instant. What was he up to, what was he thinking? Was he in fact on one of those 'cooling-off periods' like CerealKillerCornflakes seemed to believe? Simply going about his mundane day job, quietly reliving his so-called glory days when no one was looking, blissfully unaware that I was still coming for him? Part of me wondered if maybe the Telltale Killer was already dead. I didn't believe he'd taken his own life in a fit of remorse, of course, but maybe some freak accident or an unexpected bout of illness had abruptly claimed him and he'd popped his clogs with no one knowing who had been behind the most famous man in the UK for the past two years. Deep in my gut, I didn't feel that was true. Some unshakable part of me was certain he was still out there somewhere, just waiting for the opportunity to finally come back.

As I approached the office door of Camborne and Sons, my stomach stirred again, and I took a small, quiet burp to myself and stopped for a moment to gather my thoughts. I knew that approaching thirty meant hangovers could now stretch into days, but I had a feeling this was less from the alcohol and more my body rejecting my moral failings. The fact I hadn't managed a proper number two in several days was also, in its own way, mildly concerning.

I glanced at my phone. I usually ignored notifications, but four missed calls from Uncle Phil stood out. That wasn't good. Perhaps he just wanted an instant answer to the job offer? Or maybe he'd discovered what had happened to Justin and was phoning to interrogate me, before trying the police when I didn't pick up.

Summoning every ounce of Ruth moxie (or spunk as Uncle Phil would call it) I had, I pushed open the door. I barely had a moment to even let my eyes adjust to the overbearing fluorescent lights before Uncle Phil clocked me from across the office floor. He moved towards me faster than I thought his wiry, sexagenarian frame would allow. It's true, Pilates really was working a treat for him.

'Ruth, I need you,' he said, slapping both his hands around my arms, his tone unusually intense. 'Why weren't you answering your phone?'

'Uh... sorry,' I managed to say, my shoulders jolting upwards and feeling a little flabbergasted by the sudden urgency from the permanently chilled, jovial man I knew so well, wondering what on earth had caused such a massive change in his persona.

'Sophie's called in sick, Eddie was late, and I need someone to help on the doors with the 10.30 Open Casket at Rodborough

Hall. But there's a mile's worth of roadworks, so we've got to go. Now.'

'Sure,' I said, though I was so taken back by his frantic energy that I felt like I couldn't really say anything but yes. I was about to ask him what exactly I was meant to be doing but Uncle Phil had already scurried off, vanishing into the cavernous depths of his office like a mole in some hysterical fury.

Uncle Phil always insisted on four people – two on the coffin, two on the doors – and he very rarely deviated from that. I knew this funeral mattered to him, and there was no way he was letting Eddie or Clive near the entrance again, not after one of them tried to chat up a middle-aged widow at a service a few years back.

'Find your smarties!' he called from around the corner. That was his term for smart undertaker clothes. 'And let's get Justin sent off. They've paid us a lot of money for this, so it needs to go amazingly.'

The mention of Justin was enough to give my tummy another long, hard twist. Justin. Also known as the heartless man, who was now 70 per cent kitchen roll, and potentially the most absorbent human being in history.

I snatched up my – don't laugh – smarties, and darted into the loo to change.

I had barely finished tying my Windsor knot when I heard Uncle Phil already rapping sharply on the toilet door.

'Come on, Ruth, we need to go!'

Hurriedly throwing on my waistcoat and buttoning it up, I half sprinted towards the hearse already waiting with the engine rumbling in the loading bay. Uncle Phil had left the passenger door open, presumably for expediency, and was gesturing for me to get in like a commander pushing paratroopers off the plane door in Operation Market Garden. Meanwhile, the dunce brigade, otherwise known as Clive and Eddie, were just finishing up securing old Justin's casket in the back. They looked genuinely panicked, a strange contrast from their usual smug smart-aleck demeanour.

We sped off from the building and practically drifted to join the road opposite, and it was as we careened around the already tight corner, made even tighter by Uncle Phil's frankly erratic driving, that I heard a sharp metal *click*, followed by the unmistakable sound of a thick wooden coffin tumbling onto its side in the back of the hearse. Uncle Phil instinctively slammed the brakes so abruptly that the coffin, now flung open, sent its occupant sliding towards the front of the vehicle with a loud *thud* into the glass separator.

Shit. Was this how they'd catch me?

A hot ripple of terror flared and pulsed beneath my skin, my throat twitching as another belch begin to gather, or at least I hope it was only a belch.

I'd never moved so quickly; I tumbled out of the passenger seat and leaped into the back of the hearse, desperate to at least try and erase any trace of my tampering before Uncle Phil had even managed to unbuckle his seat belt. Clive and Eddie had already stopped their car and were charging over to assist.

Thank the Lord. From my quick assessment, it looked like the body was still intact; together we eased Justin back into the coffin and hauled it upright as a few passers-by stopped to wonder what exactly was happening. As a funeral director, you try not to buy too much into the whole superstitious angle or you would never be able to get anything done, but this felt very much like what some people would call an omen.

Despite Uncle Phil's slightly manic urgency and his frantic incoherent mutterings about the incompetence of Clive and Eddie the whole drive there, we made surprisingly good time getting to practically crumbling Rodborough Hall. It wasn't one of the nicer places we worked at, but we knew it well as a good-value venue: varnished wooden floors, high sash windows, and that little serving hatch connected to the kitchen. It was a community hall, really, a one-size-fits-all venue for any local need; you could still smell the Malbec from the Women's Institute going cray cray on Tuesdays.

Clive and Eddie arrived in the other car not long after and carefully helped haul Justin's coffin onto the gurney before wheeling it into the extraordinarily dull community hall that looked like it hadn't changed since the Queen's coronation. While they did that, I busied myself arranging some of the overly pungent flowers his family had chosen at the entrance of the hall: tuberoses and gardenias, terrible, terrible choices in my opinion. They had blooms so strong they left tears in your eyes before you even saw the person you were here to mourn.

I glanced at the flowers spelling out the word 'DAD', an obvious bestseller in funeral floristry. However, the other arrangement made me pause and recoil for a moment. I squinted at it, double-checking to make sure I hadn't misread or somehow accidentally jumbled the letters when I was preparing them.

'KNOBHEAD.'

I frowned, checked again, and even considered the possibility of some very rare Dutch surname. But no, it was exactly as it appeared. Triple-checking that I wasn't suddenly losing the plot, I caught Uncle Phil's eyeline. He still looked frazzled from this morning's chaos.

'Uncle Phil, is this right?' I asked, gesturing toward the rather explicit arrangement. 'I'm really sure I want to get this right.'

He gave it a glance, then rolled his eyes with a long, drawn-out resigned sigh. 'I'm afraid so...' he replied.

I scoffed, the flowers had been placed so intricately, so carefully, to spell out a word that was meant to evoke some kind of sentimental meaning, yet here it conjured the absurd image of someone with a phallus for a cranium. *Each to their own, I guess.* Could it be a term of endearment, somehow?

As I finally laid out the 'knobhead' flowers in the centre of the hall, I saw Eddie and Clive finishing up with preparing the coffin. Clive began rolling the gurney outside, and I crept over for a quick peek. The fact that no one was screaming or flailing their arms in alarm reassured me that things were, probably, still okay. I peered inside and saw Justin's chest looked fine, no sign of the dark bloodstain on his shirt nor the fact he was currently storing a wholesale supply of kitchen towel in his ribcage. His face retained the serene, neutral expression that Sophie had perfected. No one would even know he was missing a heart, why the heck was I even worrying?

I let out what had to be the quietest burp of relief ever attempted.

'Nasty way to go,' Eddie muttered behind me in a grumble.

The only thing I hadn't properly clocked in the chaos and havoc of what had been the past twenty-four hours, were the sunglasses. Someone had fitted a pair of thick black plastic frames wedged over his slightly puffy, plastically enhanced face, great slabs of make-up painted on in wide brush strokes.

'What's with the shades?' I asked Clive, bracing for a stupid answer from him.

'Oh, the fish in the Thames ate his eyeballs, like reverse caviar.'

Gross. Also, I didn't think he knew what caviar was.

But before I could ask for any more details, Uncle Phil's hissing voice cut through the air.

'People are arriving, Ruth,' he said, loud enough to echo faintly around the hall but still laced with the strained pretence of a hushed, clandestine tone.

With everything set up, Uncle Phil and I took our places by the door, ready to greet the mourners. Being on the welcoming committee with Uncle Phil was always a little bit nerve-wracking. The man was a pro – the David Beckham, if you will, of funerals – and that came with a strange level of particularity about the smallest things.

'Don't say "good morning",' he'd once instructed to me, 'as some people might hear it as "good mourning" or wonder why the morning is even "good". And don't smile too much, but don't look unfriendly either and don't say "how are you?" as chances are you're going to get a stupid answer back. Basically, only speak if you need to.'

There were countless little nuances to keep in mind when dealing with people about to say goodbye to someone they knew and loved. Or thought was a knobhead. For them, it was one of the most upsetting days of their existence. For us, it was just a standard Saturday morning service and we would be thinking about what we were having for lunch. Obviously, I wasn't thinking about lunch, I was still wondering that maybe I'd gone too far in sending the heart directly to Detective Carlota.

I assumed my usual stance, hands clasped tightly behind my back, and mentally rehearsed the standard line:

*'Hello, thank you for coming. Please take all the time you need to pay your respects.'*

It was a phrase I'd heard Uncle Phil use before, and I figured sticking to his example was the safest bet. People in black attire began parking their cars and trickling in, the one commonality was that no one really wanted to be there, no one was power walking to make sure they were the first in line or striding to the community hall with a swift sense of purpose. Everyone was dragging their feet, seeing just how slow their legs could carry them.

Turnouts at funerals varied wildly. Some were tragically quiet, with only a handful of attendees, while others felt more like herding unruly fans at a derby match. I remember one young chap who came to the office one day and explained he'd been diagnosed with a vicious terminal case of prostate cancer. But he had been very clear that he wanted his funeral to be a celebration of his life, rather than a solemn affair. He didn't want anyone to feel sad that he was gone, but rather happy they had known him.

He had grand plans: he'd asked his friends to wear the most offensive outfits they could think of. So when the day finally arrived, the atmosphere was... bizarre, to say the least. I wasn't quite sure what to make of Hitler wrapped up in chains and tight black latex, closely followed by a number of even more offensive costumes that I won't mention. The real kicker was him changing all the hymns to craptacular songs from the early 2000s. If you've never seen two dozen grown men cry while trying to sing 'Unwritten' by Natasha Bedingfield, I can tell you it's quite an unnerving sight.

A young family came walking up the path towards me, all four of the children dressed in suits. The oldest looked around thirteen, and the youngest, a tiny lad no older than five, seemed to be trying to rip off a suit that looked like it was bought at Build-A-Bear. The parents gave me a polite nod as they passed. I hesitated, debating whether to mention the fact it was open casket. Surely, it would be immensely disturbing for a child that young? But I decided against making assumptions. Instead, I offered the usual line and let them join the queue towards the coffin. Judging by the steady pace of arrivals, this was shaping up to be a medium turnout for Justin, nothing at all to be sniffed at. The worst funerals were the quiet ones.

Then came a small group of men, all in their forties, all wearing long coats and flat caps and reeking faintly of booze. There was always one drunk person at a funeral, whether you ended up noticing them or not. However, it was looking like there would be at least eight of those delightful caricatures today. One chap caught my eye as he shoved a very obviously open can of Stella into the pocket of his thick tweed coat. I groaned as I steeled myself for the interaction, Uncle Phil had a very strict policy on this.

'Excuse me, sir,' I said, keeping my tone polite and hoping he'd be obedient. 'I'm afraid there's no drinking allowed inside today.'

'What?' His sunburned face blossoming into an even deeper shade of tomato red. 'What do you mean, no drinking inside?'

'Sir, this is an opportunity for family and friends to pay their respects,' I said, already knowing this was going to be an unpleasant affair and hating the fact I was needing to be confrontational already. 'The venue has made it very clear that no—'

'What a load of bollocks,' he snapped, cutting me off with a spray of beer-coloured spit as he spoke. 'I can't have one drink to cope with the pain of losing my best mate?'

'He was everyone's mate, Rob,' someone quietly muttered from his little pack behind him.

'Sir, I understand this is upsetting,' I said, trying to make my tone even more diplomatic.

'You're not letting me in to pay respects to my best friend? What's next? Going to say I can't even wear my hat, is that it?' he cried.

'Sir, please,' I said, noticing that his tantrum was now starting to block the entrance. Not only was a bottleneck forming, which was very bad for funeral people flow that Uncle Phil placed a lot of importance on, but I could see mourners inside the hall craning their necks to see what exactly the commotion was about. Meanwhile I was willing to bet my entire net worth of fourteen pounds that this chap was the guy who'd decided having 'knobhead' in flowers would be so outrageously funny that everyone would adore his witty and cerebral attempts at mourning.

I had hoped the incident would have been resolved quickly, but I suppose I'd let my naïveté get the better of me. The sight of Uncle Phil stomping towards me, a scowl firmly plastered across his face, made me wonder if he regretted offering me his job yesterday.

'What is going on here?' Uncle Phil asked, his tone making it clear he had no intention of approaching this sensitively.

'We're living in Nazi Britain, that's what's happening,' the bloke shot back, his voice as loud as his wheezy, nasally vocal cords would allow. 'This is nonsense,' he shouted, waving his arms around like an infant mid-tantrum. Some of his less inebriated mates began chiming in, trying to calm him down and reason with us.

'What if he just doesn't drink while he's by the coffin?' one of his slightly more sober chums suggested as a negotiation tactic. 'That'd be fine, yeah?'

'No,' Uncle Phil and I said in unison.

The tension grew and thickened as all of our voices rose to try and speak over each other. I didn't even realise who was shouting at who now when somehow, a young child's voice seemed to pierce right through the chaos.

'Mummy, why is Uncle Justin melting?'

My head snapped around to follow the voice, the words

instantly striking a whole new level of anxiety and fear into me. It was the kind of horror I imagined a rodent may feel just as they saw the wingspan of an eagle block out the sun from above.

From my small elevation of the entryway, I had a clear view of the casket and more specifically, Justin. The young boy I'd noticed earlier now stood frozen in fear, watching a scene that could have been ripped straight from some awful VHS Eighties body horror film. Justin's chest, once still, tight and puffed, was not only sinking but it was starting to collapse in on itself. It was as though an unseen vortex were drawing the wings of his ribcage inward. His suit crumpling and creasing towards the black, gory, bloody centre, as the fabric of his shirt distorted in a way I didn't even realise was possible, like a soufflé five minutes out of the oven.

The commotion of the blokes behind me dissolved into a form of background static. I could only stare at Justin's stoic face, shades still fitted on the nose like he was the Fonz, giving the impression he was just so relaxed and oblivious to the grotesque transformation overtaking the remainder of his body a few inches below.

'Ayy,' I could almost hear him say.

See, I think I may have gone too far.

# PART THREE

# TWELVE

## TWO YEARS AGO

## Greta

*I must tear*
*and shred*
*these feeble creatures to a desire of darker bliss*
*that lurks within these veins.*
*These ruptures I leave for you are my offerings,*
*perverse tokens to you tortured rats bound and imprisoned by your*
*wasteful grief.*
*As flesh and stone alike shall crumble into dust*
*and rot,*
*so too will your vaunting convictions decay.*
*Yet I, remain.*

As I read the passage again and again on my computer screen, it felt more and more like there was something strangely familiar in the writing, something I couldn't quite put my finger on entirely. Why was the message giving me an uncanny feeling of déjà vu?

'Greta?' a voice called out, snapping me out of my concentrated glare of the article about the TellTale Killer's most recent murder on my screen.

'What?' I asked, a little dazed, trying to track where the sound was coming from and who was disturbing me from the swathe of IT tickets that I really ought to be actioning at manager-mandated speed. As the voice echoed through the circuitry of my brain, I registered its familiar tenor instinctively as a 'green' voice, friendly and amiable. By contrast, the deeper, bass-heavy tones of a more dominant speaker, e.g. my boss, would have registered as 'red' in the synaesthesia of my mind. Maybe I had been working in IT for too long.

Ruth came up to my desk and placed a refreshed cup of tea in front of me, made exactly how I liked it. Dash of milk, no sugar, because I'm not a psychopath.

'What up?' she said with a sly, sarcastic grin. 'We still on for my pre-birthday dinner tonight at Sabroso?'

'Of course we are,' I replied. 'Now stop nagging me, I have a lot... of work to do.'

Crikey, I did love Ruth, but she had always had a tendency to be a bit intense. Not in an 'I need to move house and change my number' kind of way, just a 'full-on' kind of vibe. She was such an isolated soul, bless her, latching onto the few things that truly mattered to her: me, her work, and her husband. And sometimes, I worried it was in that particular order. Throughout their whole marriage, I had tried to make sure that Ruth and Ben had their space, but I sometimes felt that she kept dragging me in to be a reluctant third wheel.

I'd mentioned to Chlo a few times that I thought Ruth needed more friends than us, but Chlo never seemed as concerned as I was about Ruth's rather limited social circle.

'What work do you have to do in IT anyway? Wiping people's search history? Telling people to turn it off and on again? I reckon you're just reading Obama for the eighteenth time,' Ruth teased lightly.

'I'm not reading Obama,' I said, exasperated. Technically, I was *listening* to his smooth dulcet tones as he told me of 'A Promised Land', while the hardback lay nestled in my drawer at work, but I didn't have time to get into the nuances of what exactly constituted reading right now. Besides, I won't be shamed for reading Obama, God forbid I like a stable, charismatic politician. The fact he was rather handsome had nothing to do with it.

'Don't *you* have work to do?' I replied. 'I've heard it's busy on your floor.'

'I do,' Ruth admitted, not missing a beat. 'But it's probably just me editing old golden boy's articles again or Sam pestering me to go drinking with him this evening no matter how many times I tell him we've got my pre-birthday meal, hence why I have come to disturb the sanctity of IT.'

I laughed as Ruth started fiddling with the things on my desk, deliberately, because she knew it annoyed me.

'What's the word of the day?' she asked.

'Wabi-sabi,' I replied, just about being able to recall reading it this morning when I flicked it over on the 'word of the day' calendar I kept in my bathroom while brushing my teeth with a toothbrush that was as flat as a dab. What an absolutely horrendous Secret Santa gift. As a journalist, however, Ruth always had an interest in expanding her vocabulary.

'Wasabi?' Ruth frowned, half convinced I'd mispronounced it.

'No, no, *wabi-sabi*. It's Japanese.'

'Meaning?' she asked, now pulling open my drawer and stealing one of the biscuits I kept for when my blood sugar crashed.

'I can't remember exactly,' I admitted, twisting my hands around my head as if that might somehow coax the word's meaning out of my skull. 'But it's the idea of accepting imperfections, accepting that nothing lasts forever, that things are impermanent and incomplete and finding some kind of beauty in that.'

'Weird,' Ruth said, crunching noisily on my biscuit. 'I don't get it.'

Out of the corner of my eye, I saw my superior eyeing Ruth with that look I knew all too well. So, with a widening of my eyes that clearly meant 'take me seriously', I began to shoo Ruth away.

'I'll see you downstairs later, okay?' I said with a laugh. 'Now get out of here.'

I couldn't afford to get in trouble again for chatting with Ruth. People already knew we were glued at the hip and not always, strictly speaking, professional with our interactions. I loved Ruth, she was the kindest person I knew, but she could sometimes get too wrapped up in herself. There was so much I tried to tell her, but it always felt as though she had a habit of drifting into her own daydreams, lost in her own head every time I tried to speak to her about something of significance. Part of me wondered how Ben was with her; I'd noticed him acting strangely of late when I was round, cagier and more introverted, but I hadn't dared bring it up just in case I was imagining things.

I think when it comes down to it, more than anything, I just wanted Ruth to be brave. She lived her life so cautiously, so carefully, she very rarely ever took a risk or stood up for herself. It was hard to be friends with someone who lived life so extraordinarily safely.

As I sorted through the various IT tickets being raised, I glanced over the TellTale Killer's note that the paper had published on the website one more time. That was when it struck me, how I recognised it. As I read, I could almost feel the connections forming in my mind, like pieces of a jigsaw slotting into place. Was it really what I thought it was?

I quietly made a note, pulled Obama out of my draw and slipped it within his thick, well-articulated pages, and trying to avoid the watchful eyes of my superior, began a small little piece of investigative journalism of my own.

# THIRTEEN

## PRESENT DAY

### Ruth

I was coming to the abrupt realisation that I would quite like to visit Australia if I ever got the chance. I had first considered it when I was a postgrad for a little while, blissfully wondering if I could swap the UK's consistently wet, rainy climate for something that felt at least a little bit more exotic. But then I remembered: the trade-off would likely include spiders the size of dinner plates and snakes that would lurk in the pipes of your toilet, and that was a bit of a dealbreaker for me. I didn't want to be subjected to a surprise nibble in the middle of the night while trying to have a wee.

It was probably in poor taste that staring at Justin's collapsing cadaver is what brought the idea of a visit to Oz back to the forefront of mind. But it wasn't my fault that if you squinted hard enough; his sagging, misshapen chest now almost resembled the Sydney Opera House. The jagged contours of his defined ribcage reassembling the iconic white sails of the landmark, their sharp points jutting upwards into the thin flesh. I know that's an utterly revolting thing to think – I'm sure you're scrunching your nose up right now or your facial muscles have shifted into something reassembling disgust – but I was just trying to find some semblance of a silver lining in a situation where I was, quite clearly, well and truly fucked.

Operation: Hearts and Crafts had now hit a small speed bump, an unfolding crisis I would now refer to as 'Chestgate'.

I must have made an absolute hash of extracting the heart. Rigor mortis hadn't exactly made things more stable internally nor had his little joy ride in the back of the hearse, but still, how incompetent could I have been for the man's chest to literally collapse in on itself during his own funeral? Perhaps the fact I was rushing during the extraction and then distracted by Uncle Phil's phone call had meant that I had made some critical mistake while I was rummaging around in there. Maybe I had damaged his ribcage or accidentally shuffled around some organs that led to the implosion of his chest cavity. Whatever had happened, I was really hoping that they wouldn't be able to trace it back to me. It's not like the mass of kitchen towel in him was printed with tiny idents of my name on it or anything.

Uncle Phil was outside the hall, pacing up and down the street with his head in his hands, guzzling every Capri-Sun he could get his hands on. Every so often, he would solemnly mutter, 'I'm finished,' to himself under his breath. Meanwhile, Clive couldn't stop throwing up on the foot of an old oak tree, and Eddie was rubbing his pal's back affectionately. Meanwhile, I sat on one of those dreadful, cheap plastic chairs you'd find in a primary school classroom, which made sense as I heard the hall functioned as a hub for the guides and brownies on a Thursday. I watched the chaos unfolding before my eyes; a small squadron of police officers and forensic scientists were darting in and out of the hall while trying to keep the increasing number of bystanders at bay. I'd been trying to eavesdrop on their whispered theories about what had happened, but I hadn't had much luck picking up on what they were saying. I was feeling strangely calm about everything, which shouldn't have surprised me, from what I'd read there was an odd sense of relief from criminals when they finally realised they were about to be caught, knowing they wouldn't have to deal with the unrelenting anxiety anymore somehow outweighed the idea of life imprisonment.

I saw Uncle Phil stumble wearily into the venue, his face as pale as Justin's flesh.

He clutched yet another Capri-Sun in his hand, the plastic packaging crinkling in his grip as he squeezed the last remnants of orange-flavoured liquid straight down his gullet. He always kept a stash of them in the boot of his car for dire emergencies, bought in bulk as the only real hedonistic pleasure he had for himself. All men have their vices in times of struggle; for some it came with a straw. As he made his way over to me gradually, part of me was worried he might go into cardiac arrest right there and then, but then I remembered the copious amounts of artificial sugars and preservatives he had just consumed would keep his heart beating for the next two hundred years.

'How are you doing, Uncle Phil?' I asked, struggling to hide a smirk at the image of him tossing the empty pouch aside as if it were a four-shot glass of whisky he had just downed.

'I've been better, Ruth. I've been better,' he replied, his frail voice trembling. 'How did this happen? How did we miss this?'

'I don't know,' I said, feigning ignorance for the umpteenth time and silently hoping I was getting better at it.

'We should have checked. I don't know how we could have, but we should have checked,' Uncle Phil intoned as if he was giving himself a firm telling-off, wondering how much his TrustPilot rating would suffer for this.

'Checked what, exactly?' I asked, a little confuddled as to how, unless you were me and had certain insider knowledge, anyone could have foreseen this happening.

'His heart, Ruth! That he still had a heart!' Uncle Phil burst out with a sudden intensity that made me reel, nearly toppling from the tiny chair I was perched on. Until that moment, I hadn't thought him capable of frustration. Worry, yes, but any kind of anger had never really seemed in his nature.

'I'm sorry,' he added almost immediately, his tone softening and mellowing quickly. 'I'm a bit stressed.'

'That's okay,' I said, leaning forward to place a hand on his remarkably hairy arm, hoping it would feel somewhat reassuring to him. 'It is a very stressful situation.'

'This Justin fella... he died in a not-so-nice way,' Uncle Phil muttered, running a hand over his silver stubbled chin and then across both of his cheeks. 'Maybe that's something to do with it. They found his body in the Thames a few weeks ago. Drowned, they think.'

'Oh?' I said, keeping my eyes firmly on the corpse in the centre of the room. Not making eye contact with Uncle Phil, or, for that matter, with the guest of honour we were so rudely discussing.

I watched one of the policemen, donning one of their standard high-vis jackets, interviewing someone wearing a very elegant black dress. My eyes lingered on a face that I could only describe as 'sharp' as she delicately dragged out the last tissue from a crumpled packet, to gently dab her eyes as the policeman continued to mutter something to her. I noticed the mascara that had been impeccably applied was ever so slightly staining the tear trough. I had the conversation at least once a month about people asking me what mascara they would recommend for a funeral, worried that it may run during the service. I could tell by the way the mascara had blotched on her skin that this was one of the ones they had advertised as cry-proof. However, unfortunately, they hadn't ever really made a mascara that could cope with the very real impact of grief.

My conscience ached a little as I watched the woman take another glance at the coffin, her face quivered slightly as her eyes flicked away from it.

One of Uncle Phil's favourite impromptu lectures, usually delivered whenever we were stuck in traffic, was that while most cultures believe the soul departs the body the instant death arrives, nearly all still treat the corpse with dignity. I couldn't quite share that instinct. I really shouldn't care, there was no real meaning to a dead body other than the one society had prescribed onto it. But I'd convinced myself that all of my efforts were something of a victimless crime, that no one was getting hurt. But now I knew this was completely my fault: I had taken the last memory this woman would have of her loved one and warped and twisted it into a grotesque, mangled version of its former self. I wish I could say that realisation stopped me in my tracks, made me pause and reconsider what I was doing, but it didn't. Greta would have told me to stop now, if she'd been here. She'd have told me I'd gone too far, but Greta wasn't here, was she?

From behind the woman, a familiar figure began to appear within my peripheral vision. Dressed in one of her signature spectacular jumpers that seemed to hug her muscles, Detective Carlota was something of a pleasant sight for my sore eyes until I had the unfortunate realisation that this would probably be the woman who might very well be reading me my rights before escorting me to a police car in the not-too-distant future.

'Detective,' Uncle Phil said, running his hand through his floppy, dishevelled hair and stepping forward to greet her. He knew her well from her various visits to see me at the office over the years. She returned his greeting with a warm smile and a shake of his hand before he politely excused himself to fetch yet another Capri-Sun from the hearse glove compartment. If there were a twelve-step programme for Capri-Sun addiction, Uncle Phil would've been the perfect candidate.

As my uncle slipped from her sight, I expected that warmth to linger when Detective Carlota turned to face me. It didn't. I could almost see her expression crystallise, her features sharpening, her eyes narrowing and lips tightening as though I'd just casually mentioned at a fancy dinner party that I liked mayo on my roast dinner.

'Ruth,' she said, pausing as if weighing each of her words carefully. 'So how are you doing?'

Oh, I didn't like her use of 'so'. I could tell from the sibilant hiss of the word that she was beginning to see me through a different lens. If even I'd picked up on it, her change in tone must have been glaring.

'Been better,' I replied, eager to skip any chit-chat. 'Not exactly the kind of thing you want to happen when working at a funeral. Not great for business.'

'No, I can't imagine it is,' she said with a level of fake decorum that I could easily see through. 'I've been chatting to some of the other officers – from a cursory glance, it looks like the man's body has been tampered with in a way that the post-mortem didn't pick up or, more likely, it happened afterwards.'

She inhaled sharply, then slipped her hands deep into her pockets.

'And again, from this cursory glance, his heart is obviously missing. Awfully peculiar, right?' she asked. 'Even more peculiar that you're here.'

I stumbled over my words as I tried to answer her, caught off guard by her interrogatory tone as well as her frosty demeanour. Some awkward guttural gibberish slipped past my lips as I scrambled to reorient my thoughts.

'Detective, we at Camborne and Sons are the largest and most popular funeral directors across three London boroughs. If someone dies, it's very likely their paperwork will come across my desk.'

I thought that was some good reasoning to come up with in the moment and I hoped I sounded unperturbed. Her expression flickered for a moment, an ever so slight recoil at the eloquence and maybe my own frostiness in my response.

'I suppose that's true,' she replied. 'I'll be interested to see what the examination reveals when they compare the body now with the original post-mortem.'

I couldn't quite believe her words, I felt as if she was accusing me, as if she thought I was the one behind it. I mean, I *was* the one behind it but still, I would have appreciated at least a modicum of trust. From her perspective, why would the person obsessed with catching the TellTale Killer be the one involved with this? Were my plans to pretend to be a serial killer really that transparent to a police detective?

'So will I,' I said, keeping my tone as steady as I could. 'I imagine the records will tell us what may have happened. Besides, we have 24-hour CCTV in the office, so it'll be useful to see if anything was tampered with on our end.'

Why on earth did I say that? I was practically inviting an investigation onto myself.

'So you...' she began, her eyes contracting slightly as if she were about to ask the question of my involvement outright. But then she stopped herself, her expression softening into a smile that made me feel deeply disconcerted.

'It was nice to see you, Ruth,' was all she said as she walked backwards for a few steps before rotating and joining her small congregation of police officers to presumably discuss some kind of organisation around the crime scene. I kept my eyes locked on her as she received instructions from whoever was in charge, rather begrudgingly. We both knew she should've been the one giving the orders.

As the conversation between the officers seemed to drag on, she tilted her head barely perceptibly, eyes flicking towards me to pin me with a very particular kind of look. That was the moment I realised just how spectacularly I'd cocked this part of the plan up.

Yet each time the faintest pang of remorse or regret tugged at me, some small urge to turn back, I reminded myself: the killer was still out there, and I remembered what he'd said to me that night on the phone. That was when I muttered to myself, almost as a little tiny vow, *in for a penny, in for a pound.*

# FOURTEEN

I didn't dare take the bus again after the hag incident, so I trudged home, past a lollipop lady for some youth club who looked like she moonlighted as a bailiff, and just to crown the already shitty day, I watched a pigeon swoop down to the pavement for a grotty crust of bread, only to be blindsided by a reversing delivery van. Blink and you'd have missed it. Unfortunately, the pigeon did not.

As I walked home, passing the Saturday night revellers, I decided that loneliness must be our default as humans. We heap on distractions in an attempt to blunt its sharpness: we ring friends on the commute, share flats we could afford to rent alone, and leave the TV or radio on so the silence feels less existential. I mean, come on, there's a reason body pillows exist. And Fleshlights. But two years ago, I learned that even in my small circle, people don't much fancy the company of someone perpetually sad with a life in pieces; apparently, that's a bit of a killjoy. And yet, although I've felt more alone these past two years than ever before, today I realised I felt lonelier still.

I was being kicked out of my ex-husband's house, I had alienated all my friends, Chlo still hadn't called me but that may be because I still hadn't had the guts to send the apology text. My colleagues either tolerated or hated me, even the detective I once saw as something of a confidante now viewed me as the prime suspect in a crime I had actually done. Mum and Dad were still practically off the grid on their grand diplomatic tour and I couldn't even land a one-night stand, let alone a second date because I talked too much about serial killers. The only consistent form of contact I had in my life was some sweaty virgin called CerealKillerCornflakes who liked to say, 'I told you so.'

There was only one car in the driveway, I noticed, when I finally made it back to the house. I whispered a few short 'pleases' under my breath and as I got closer, squinting my eyes to try and make out whose car it was, I felt the smallest flicker of happiness in my chest when I recognised the shape as Ben's. At least I wouldn't have to deal with Bill tonight, I didn't think I had the strength to endure that. He was out again, maybe *he* was having an affair? Now, that would be ironic, but strangely that thought just made me feel quite sad for Ben.

'Hello? Anyone home?' I called out as I opened the front door, but there was no response. I was just about to head out to the shed to retire for the night when I heard the loud groaning creak of floorboards above me, followed by the appearance of Ben, wrapped snugly in his dressing gown. It was only 5.30 p.m., yet somehow, he was already in his cosies. That was weird.

'Hiya, Ruth,' he said, offering a smile that seemed almost to pain him a little.

'Hiya, love,' I replied, not even bothering to correct myself this time. 'How was your day?'

He cocked his head to the side and gave a little wince which transitioned into something of a grimace.

'I've had better days. How was yours?'

I mimicked him, tilting my head and contorting my face into something equally pained. He laughed, then hopped off the bottom step of the stairs and headed into the kitchen to put the kettle on.

'Bill's working late again, so I was thinking of ordering something in that we could discreetly dispose of later without him noticing, something chock-full of preservatives and MSG. What are you in the mood for? I could kill for a tikka masala,' he said, his tone lined with a mischievous tenor.

'Go on then,' I replied, realising I was actually quite hungry. 'You know what, I'd love a bhuna.'

The food arrived only half an hour later. I hate to admit it, but this place was better than the Indian food we used to get when we were married. Ben worked in private equity, which meant he came home late a lot, so takeaways had often been the easiest option for us both.

I was expecting to head out to the shed to eat by myself, but Ben told me to stop being silly and began setting the table. This was unusual, considering that I'd often spot him and Bill from the shed window watching something on the telly while they ate their dinner from their laps. But instead, Ben and I sat at the dining room table and talked about things almost like we were still a normal couple. It was surreal, but a nice temporary distraction from the failure of the operation: Hearts and Crafts. I filled him in on general updates, who was annoying me at work, with a small splash of politics and local affairs for good measure. I didn't mention Justin, but I did tell him about Uncle Phil's offer.

'That's... great?' he said, trying to mask his clear uneasiness.

'You hesitated,' I snapped, pointing an accusatory finger at him. 'That was a trademark Ben pregnant pause, right there.'

'I didn't hesitate, I was just swallowing the rice, that's all.'

'Why did you hesitate, Ben?' I interrogated.

'Look, Ruth, we both know your destiny is not to be the managing director of a funeral home. For some people, yes, that is their calling. But not for you.'

'So, what is my destiny?' I asked Ben, one part jokingly, one part sincerely. 'Please, tell me what my destiny is because I, frankly, don't have the foggiest. Other than being a miserable wet old fart. Sometimes we don't all get our dreams and our callings, sometimes we've got to settle for the least-worst option and maybe that's being the boss of a funeral directors. So, please tell me, O wise one, what my destiny actually is?'

'I can't tell you your own destiny, only you can do that,' Ben said with a glint in his eyes like he was quoting some saccharine Disney film I hadn't seen.

That was an annoying response, I really wanted someone to tell me my destiny at this point.

'Ben, can I ask you a question?' I said after a minute.

'You just did,' he replied. We'd had that exact exchange so often when we were married, and I always fell for it.

'Why did you ask me to move in? I don't think I ever really asked at the time with everything going on. You know, my melt-down and everything.'

Ben groaned in a strangely thoughtful way and dragged out a breath as he bought some time to answer by wiping any orange tikka stains off his chops with the edges of a crisp white napkin.

'I think it was a few reasons. First, I was worried about you. Second... I'll always love you, though it's a different kind of love now I suppose. And third, well, maybe, kind of a bit of guilt.'

It was funny, hearing him say that. I'd often wondered if guilt ever gnawed away at him, if that was why he'd let me stay in the shed. Clearly, it had, and apparently guilt comes with heavily reduced rental accommodation.

'I just wish the humping flesh-eating tortoise hadn't come with you.'

We cleaned up after talking for another hour while reminiscing about memories from our marriage, not in a way that ignored the awkward pretence of now being divorced, but as if they were genuinely happy memories we could look back on without all the grief of me smashing glasses and photo frames as well as the endless hours in lawyers' offices negotiating the various assets that we had collected throughout marriage. Ben had been a little more distant with me over the past week or so, not uncharacteristically so, but enough that I'd felt it. Now, though, I felt closer to him again. It was nice. As he said, it was a different kind of love we had for each other now. Not the sort where I could confess what I'd done to two dead bodies; I loved him enough that I wouldn't put him in that position.

'I'm going to miss you, Ruth. I really am,' Ben said, then his expression faltered and hardened, as if he'd immediately realised that he shouldn't have said that. This was after Bill had slipped in from his mysterious second job, grabbed what sounded like a bag of ice cubes, and gone wordlessly upstairs to bed, leaving us to clear away all evidence of our takeaway crimes before he could notice a thing. Ben didn't say any more but placed an arm around me and pulled me closer to his chest for an embrace. I had forgotten the smell of him, having not been this close to him for a while. It was bizarre to smell his earthy, natural scent again. I think it was the deodorant he liked that he bought from LIDL.

'I'm going to miss you too,' I replied earnestly, the weak part of me – the part I thought I kept under constant suppression – feeling small droplet pangs of deep affection for him again. 'You'll come visit, right? Wherever I go?'

That felt bizarre to say. But despite all the terrible things he'd done to me, I still wanted Ben in my life. Did that make me pathetic? I really hoped it didn't. It wasn't that I thought we'd rekindle our marriage in any way; it was more that, when you've lived through so much with someone, it feels wrong to simply discard them, no matter what they've done to you. I still felt like he belonged in my life in some way and also, I needed at least one friend in my life now that Chlo had disowned me. Even if I did walk in on him six months ago pleasuring himself to something in a homewear catalogue.

'What do you mean?' he asked, visibly confused by what I had said. 'You planning on going somewhere?'

'Well, Bill,' I said, a little confused, 'asked me to move out yesterday. I thought that's what you meant?'

I could feel the goosebumps prickle my skin as I witnessed the fury ignite behind Ben's eyes; I remembered the look well, it was as if you could almost see every single facial and body muscle tighten in sync. I swear, one time I had even seen his rotund ass cheeks clench in unison. What surprised me even more than I could ascertain was the tiny flicker of recognition in Ben's eyes, as though from my words he recalled a conversation with his beloved I was never meant to hear or know about, and it only seemed to enrage him further.

'Would you excuse me, Ruth,' he said as politely as he could, 'I need to talk to Bill.' He became the literal visual manifestation of smiling through gritted teeth as he twisted his body around almost robotically and began to stomp up the stairs.

Confused, and unhappily certain I was the cause of Ben's now booming voice, I decided it was probably best for me to make haste out of there and into the safety of the shed, and see if CerealKiller-Cornflakes was online.

I couldn't help but wonder what the police were up to at that very moment. Did they think the bona fide TellTale Killer was finally back? Or were they desperately trying to pin the body mangling and heart gift baskets on me? I had no idea. I wondered if this was how real serial killers felt, a morbid cocktail of anticipation, dread, and excitement. It almost quieted the memory of that voice, the voice that wouldn't leave me, that echoed through my head whenever I thought back, as I often did, to that night.

# FIFTEEN

## TWO YEARS AGO

'How long?' I demanded, my gaze inadvertently drifting away from him. My eyes landed, rather sadistically, on one of our wedding photos perched on one of the shelves. There we were, twenty-three years old, each flanked by our respective parents, all big, dumb, innocent smiles. I was never going to be able to look at that photo and not feel pure hot-blooded rage again. Greta storming out of the café and into the crowds and now this; this was really turning out to be quite a shitty night in the life of Ruth.

'We...' he began to speak, but faltered, unable to finish his sentence. I forced myself to look at him to see what had interrupted him. But all I saw was his whole body shaking with emotion, his eyes bloodshot red as he tried, and failed, to keep the tears at bay. He placed two fingers on the bridge of his nose and squeezed as if he was trying to pinch the plumbing to the tear duct. 'Nothing has happened. We... I haven't... done anything.'

'Is that supposed to make me feel better?' I snapped, the rage still piping hot in my chest. 'Good for you, Ben. Does that make you feel morally superior? That you managed to control yourself not to...' I couldn't even finish the sentence; I didn't even want to breathe those words, that made me feel sick, into existence.

'No. No, of course not, I'm just trying to say...' he began.

'God, I... I can't even look at you, Ben,' I interrupted, cutting him off before he could string another stupid, whimpering sentence together. Just because I didn't want to speak, didn't mean I wanted to hear his voice.

I averted my eyes from him again, my chest twisting with an unfamiliar, excruciating pain. So, this was what heartbreak felt like I guess, I had never really experienced it before. To me, it was a stinging, relentless tearing that left me feeling equal parts numb, hollow, but also overflowing with anger.

Suddenly, all the strange interactions over the past six months made sense: his vague excuses, the friends he was hanging out with that he couldn't quite name, the signs I had ignored because I trusted him. I imagined that people in the future would tell me it wasn't my fault, that he was completely to blame. But I still felt stupid. Stupid for not confronting him sooner, for brushing it all aside and burying that suspicion deep down in my gut because I didn't want to argue with him.

'So,' I said, summoning the courage to ask the question I dreaded. 'What is this conversation?'

'What do you mean?' he asked, his voice still raspy as he paced slow circuits around our living room.

'You know exactly what I mean,' I said, staring at him as he faced away from me to glance out the window. 'Is this an "I'm leaving you" conversation or a "please, please forgive me, take me back" sort of conversation?'

Despite everything I had just learned, part of me still hoped it was the latter; I prayed and begged it was the latter.

Ben sighed and pivoted his body slowly to face me again, the same moronic expression still fixed onto his stupid face. That was all it took for me to understand what he was failing miserably to say.

All I could think to do now was leave. So, I turned away from him and grabbed my handbag, stuffing anything I could think of into it – clothes, pants, deodorant, phone chargers – good luck messaging your boyfriend without any phone battery, Ben – whatever was within reach of my hand was being furiously tossed and squashed into it. The more crap I crammed in, the more my knock-off designer bag looked moments away from complete structural collapse.

'Ruth, please,' he said, his voice almost strengthening a little now as if he was trying to exude some authority to stop me. 'Please, don't go. I'll go. I should be the one to go.'

'You really think I want to stay in this house now? The house we built our lives together in, after what you've just told me!' I grabbed the framed photo of our wedding I had been looking at earlier, hurled it to the ground and thrusted my socked foot down on it. The glass cracked instantly and I'm sure some of the shattered edges went up and pierced into the sole of my foot, but frankly I was still too angry to care.

'Ruth, stop, you're going to hurt yourself!' Ben exclaimed, walking towards me, faking some kind of concern for me. He didn't care for me, though, he would never have done this if he actually did.

'I'm going to Greta's,' I spat at him, my voice hoarse from all the screaming and shouting I had just done. 'She can talk to you about picking my stuff up.'

'Ruth, come on,' he pleaded, the desperation and exhaustion he was feeling clear from every word he spoke. 'Please don't leave by yourself. Not right now. Go if you want but let me drive you or call a cab or something first. It's not safe with the TellTale Killer!'

'No,' I shouted, grabbing the TV remote and throwing it into my overstuffed bag, along with the hardwood penis ornament we got in Greece that I hated. I didn't really know what I was going to do with that, so I flung it in his direction.

'There is a killer on the loose, Ruth.' Ben vociferating again, gesticulating wildly. 'This isn't safe. Please.'

'I don't care. Just looking at you makes me feel sick,' I shouted, throwing open the front door and slamming it shut behind me with all the force I had. The Christmas wreath, previously perched on the door, went flinging into the bushes from the impact.

Yanking my phone from my pocket, I scrambled to call Greta. I'm sure she was still furious with me from earlier tonight, after what I had asked her at Sabroso. She still hadn't responded to my apology text, but this was now beyond our petty arguments. Extenuating circumstances and all that, surely. She had to put her anger at me aside for this, I know I would for her.

The phone rang and rang, but she didn't answer. My rage only growing, I fired off a quick text as I continued storming down the street, desperate to get as much distance between Ben and I as possible.

> Look, I'm so sorry for tonight, but please, I really need to talk to you.

I could see something in my peripheral vision and glancing over my shoulder, I saw Ben stepping out of the house and beginning to follow me.

'You don't have to speak to me,' he called after me, his voice loud enough to reach me fifty or so feet ahead of him. 'But I can't let you be out here by yourself. Please, just let me drive you somewhere.'

'Fuck off!' I roared back at him as loud as the roughness in my throat would allow.

I called Greta again, hoping my text would put my incessant calling into context. I picked up the pace of my footsteps to try and outwalk my soon-to-be ex-husband as I kept my phone compressed tightly against my cheek, waiting for the moment the aggravating buzzing sound of an outgoing call would finally end. Still nothing.

> Please, please, I need to talk to you. Ben has been cheating on me.

My fingers were fumbling over the touch keys of my phone as my walk became dangerously close to a jog to outrun Ben's much longer legs. But the messages were still only showing as delivered so her phone must not have been out of charge? Maybe she was in the loo, but then everyone brought their phone to the loo with them, what else would they do with their time? But just as I was about to try sending yet another text, the read receipts popped up. She was seeing my messages, she *was reading them.*

My breath faltered as I stared at the screen, waiting for her response, any kind of response from her. But there was nothing, absolutely nothing. Not even the little icon showing she was typing a message. She must just be... staring at them.

'Please, Greta,' I begged under my frantic breath, my finger hovering over the call button again.

I waited until I reached the end of the cul-de-sac before I jabbed my finger into the phone icon again, pushing the phone tight to my ear. I glanced over my shoulder to see Ben was still behind me like he was some kind of covert bodyguard for a billionaire.

'Leave me alone,' I screamed at him as, at last, the ringing finally came to an abrupt stop, and I heard the small pocket of silence after she'd picked up, but instead of her sweet-sounding voice who would apologise for not answering and then tell me everything was going to be all right, all I heard was this long, low, croaky breathing on the other end of the line.

'Greta?' I asked.

Still, all I heard was wheezy, raspy breaths. Was this her idea of some kind of joke?

'Are you kidding me? Seriously? Are you *kidding* me?' I snapped, my voice trembling with hurt and fury. 'After all that, now you pick up? You leave me stranded in the middle of Hammersmith with a killer on the loose, ignore all my calls and texts, and then just – what? Decide to answer? You know, you can be an absolutely terrible, terrible friend sometimes, Greta.'

The moment the words left my mouth, I deeply regretted them. I knew I was just projecting onto her, letting all my anger at Ben spill out onto Greta; she didn't deserve that.

'Hello, Ruth,' said a voice. A deep, baritone *male* voice.

'Who is this?' I asked, frenzied, as my nape prickled with a sudden, bristling chill.

'You know, you really should be nicer to your friends, Ruth; you never know when it's going to be the last time you'll speak to them.'

# SIXTEEN

## PRESENT DAY

A pair of elderly Chinese tourists found Greta's heart the next day on a road in Hammersmith about three quarters of a mile away from the station, presumably near where she'd been taken by the killer. I imagine they must have thought it some quaint British custom when they first saw the box, perhaps expecting a poem, or a little knitted character left by a kind-hearted stranger. They couldn't have known that it was the Telltale Killer at work, or that Britons are rarely so innocently kind; we are, after all, a cruel, cold people, hardened by unruly weather and an absence of flavourful cuisine. I had begged and prayed it wouldn't be her, but the police identified the heart only a few days later as belonging to Greta. I hadn't even realised it was possible to identify someone from a heart, but apparently cardiac muscle yields genomic DNA – whatever the hell that is – that can be profiled against relatives of suspected victims. In this case it was her dad, Aleks, who confirmed that Greta had been the latest – and unknown to us, the last – victim of the TellTale Killer.

Honestly, it was his voice that haunted me most. In my mind, I'd always imagined it would be a growl – the verbal form of the sound of sharp, jagged metal being dragged over rugged coal – but it wasn't. It was ordinary, the kind of voice you'd expect from any run-of-the-mill chap I might encounter every day. And that was what I couldn't forget for most of my waking moments: that voice.

As I tentatively slid the headphones from the top of my head down to around my neck, I realised that I could still hear Bill and Ben arguing relentlessly with each other, even from the detached shed. This wasn't like their usual bickering about Bill's smoking habit, this was much, much worse. It made me wonder if Bill had ascended to a new plane of arseholery by kicking me out without even consulting his boyfriend first. But now, it all made sense. I did think it was odd and unlike Ben not to be there when Bill delivered the news that they were booting me out of their casa and why it all seemed quite so out of the blue. While Ben had been cowardly before, I knew that he wasn't intrinsically a coward. I hated to admit it, but Ben was sort of a good man.

'You can't keep pretending it's going to get better,' I managed to hear but the moment I heard my name from Bill's mouth in what could only politely be described as a rather curt tone, I swiftly slid my noise-cancelling headphones back over my ears to try and block him out, this time playing 'MMMBop' by Hansen at max volume as I slumped down on my chair with a long, beleaguered sigh. Please don't judge my happy place song.

CerealKillerCornflakes and I had gone back and forth a few times on the message board on DarkCell. He was trying to lecture me on serial killer psychology again, probably something he'd picked up from a bunch of YouTube videos. I'd have called it mansplaining if he knew I was a woman, but that thought probably hadn't crossed his mind.

The thing we were discussing – like we often seemed to – was how *he* chose his victims. It was something that I'd thought about myself, as I ripped the hearts out of Mrs Lambert and Justin, wondering if there was some common thread I was inadvertently snipping by picking the two of them.

Thing was, no one could see any link between the victims. They were all different ages, half of them men, half women, different ethnicities, no shared causes. Even after deep investigation, nothing seemed to actually connect them. But I still doubted it was random, although CerealKillerCornflakes insisted it was.

*There is no magical tether connecting them all, that's what makes him impossible to track, it was purely who he could get his hands on at the time.*

*Okay, hun,* I replied.

*Stop saying that, you know I'm right,* he subsequently responded.

*Cool story, bro.*

*I actually hate you.*

*Cry about it*

I often wondered if we were accidentally flirting with each other; I actually couldn't tell anymore.

Eventually, I got bored of CerealKillerCornflakes telling me I was 'wrong' yet again and using his favourite line of 'I told you so', so I called him a little wet goat boy, which I knew would annoy him, and went to lie on my bed while Toast, having taken a break from non-copulatory mounting, stared neutral-faced at her own reflection in the glass of her vivarium. I once read an article about a tortoise that could smell different types of cancer in humans. Mine, however, had the libido of Casanova, the intelligence of a rock and a hankering for human flesh.

I wondered what Detective Carlota and the rest of the investigation team were doing at this moment – how close they were to realising I was behind Justin's internal implosion earlier today. I knew that medical post-mortems were usually quite precise, performed by well-trained medical professionals, and chances were, unless NHS standards had really slipped, they would have probably noticed a missing heart when examining Justin. Regardless, I imagined the attention of the police would now be squarely on Camborne and Sons.

I quickly searched Justin's full name online and found a few local news articles about his death while my playlist moved onto 'Barbie Girl'. I'll spare you the grim details, but the reports confirmed what Uncle Phil had given me sparse details of. Poor Justin had vanished a few months ago, only to be found washed up on some Thames riverbank several weeks later, hence why the heart had looked so decayed when I first nabbed it. The police swiftly ruled it a suicide – or perhaps an accident. With no obvious signs of trauma – no strangulation marks, no stab wounds – the conclusion seemed pretty straightforward from a police perspective. The body appeared mostly intact with decomposition being much slower in the cold winter saltwater of the Thames. But even so, his extended river tour had done quite a number on him, to say the least, softening the diaphragm, macerating the tissue, stripping away what little tension and structure was left. So, when the heart came out, there wasn't any pressure or bulk remaining to hold the ribcage up. It just... gave in.

It seemed likely that Justin's body looking like a crushed toilet roll probably had more to do with the cold water he was exposed to than it did with my own tampering, which meant, if you think about it, maybe my heart-extraction skills weren't actually that bad after all.

In my mind, I tried to imagine the police's thought process; how they would try to connect the dots. It wouldn't take them long to realise that the heart I'd sent to Detective Carlota belonged to Justin's body through the same DNA process they'd used to identify Greta. But would they assume it was the work of the TellTale Killer, a copycat, or someone else entirely? Was there any loose thread they could use to trace it back to me?

The TellTale Killer's usual MO had been to take his victims at night and leave the heart somewhere in public the next morning. But I hoped the police might consider another, maybe ridiculous, possibility: that the TellTale Killer had returned after the killing to retrieve his trophy. I pitched the story to myself. Perhaps the Tell-Tale Killer had chosen Justin as his next victim for whatever reason or particular criteria, managed to drown him in the Thames, but was spotted and had to flee – forced to abandon the body before he could finish what he'd started. But of course, being a completionist, he couldn't let one of his killings go unnoticed. People *had* to know it was him behind the murder and so he went back to fetch his heart at a later date.

But that raised a cascade of other questions, not least: how had the heart been removed between the medical examination and the funeral? Medical professionals would have conducted a post-mortem and signed off on the body. Shortly afterwards, it would have been transported by a private ambulance to us. At that point, perhaps five people in the office would have had access to the morgue where he was stored. Not exactly a wide pool of suspects for someone who might just be the most famous serial killer since Harold Shipman.

I wrapped my mouth around my collar again and bit down, as if the pressure on my jaw might summon some miraculous idea to fall into my lap and solve everything for me. How the hell was I supposed to get out of this one?

I had assumed at least some of the press would have picked up the story by now, but when I checked my Google alerts, there was still nothing, no mention of Justin's missing heart or a possible Tell-Tale Killer return. It was as if the police, fully aware of the chaos the TellTale Killer had stirred up two years ago, were deliberately trying to keep this quiet. You'd think that two hand-delivered hearts and a voice recording would be enough to nudge the police into at least pretending to care about the case again, yet somehow I still had the exasperating feeling that they were labelling this under 'nothing to see here'. There was no way the TellTale Killer was ever going to get his just deserts at this rate, not unless I did another stupid thing. It reminded me of something old Double J at the paper used to say: 'You need to control the narrative.'

I leaped out of my bed, snatched my pen out of my drawer and a fresh sheet of parchment, and I began to write in the killer's code once again. Oh, I just knew CerealKillerCornflakes and the Dark-Cell community were going to go mad over this one.

At first, I just posted it on DarkCell to see how the rest of my basement-dweller friends would react. But within moments I realised the post was getting barely any engagement; even the usual serial-killer aficionados seemed lukewarm at best, disregarding it as some weird necrologist nut head fan fiction.

I figured, it was potentially also worth a punt to send it to my old workplace too, see if they'd pick it up and jolt the police out of their indefinite complacency. The main editorial inbox was bombarded with emails by every Tom, Dick and Sally looking for press, so I went straight to the not-so-secret second inbox the editors actually checked, the ones interns would forward the good stories to; I imagined someone would probably see it. It was the furthest I'd pushed my serial-killer scheme, but I didn't trust the police to be quietly on top of this. Maybe a little press pressure was exactly what was needed.

Although as I pressed send, I couldn't help but remember what Edgar Allan Poe himself had once said:

*I became insane, with long intervals of horrible sanity.*

In other words, I was going completely fucking mad.

That was when I heard a faint, rhythmic thudding in the background. I froze. For a moment, it sounded like a dull heartbeat, the metaphorical hearts I'd stolen, still beating somewhere in the ether, thumping now as a reminder of my gnawing guilt.

And then I realised.

It was just Toast, enthusiastically humping her hide again.

## SEVENTEEN

'Ruth, Ruth, wake up,' I vaguely heard someone shouting loudly, their voice pulling me out of a hazy slumber as my heart was repeatedly punching the inside of my chest. I stirred, disoriented, struggling to separate dream from reality. A tall, slim figure loomed over me, faintly illuminated by the tiny glow of a phone torch. The figure shook me again, more insistently now, but I still couldn't make out who it was through my blurry vision and the tiny glow shining in my eyes. It was almost heavenly.

'Jesus? Is that you?'

'Ruth, be serious, come on and stop being stupid, you need to get up,' the voice replied.

Damn, Jesus was mean.

'What?' I mumbled groggily, my voice still croaky and thick with sleep. 'What's going on? What's happening?' I pushed myself upright, realising I'd fallen asleep at the desk with my noggin cradled in the makeshift cushion of my arms. My vision was still foggy, but as I repeatedly blinked, it began to clear. I recognised Bill standing there, dressed in the most hideous pair of pyjamas I had ever seen, burgundy and white stripes. Urgh. The sight alone was enough to make a woman retch. He looked like some kind of Christmas humbug.

'Ruth, Ben isn't well. I need you to drive us to A&E, now,' he said, his voice moderately stable but certainly urgent.

'What? I can't drive. Why can't you drive?' I said with a groan, not really grasping the stress or hurry in Bill's voice, honestly just wanting to go back to sleep.

'Because I've had nearly a whole bottle of wine,' he replied, matter-of-factly. Gosh, Bill really was knocking them back nowadays. 'The ambulance won't come for hours and also, you're allowed to drive with a licence holder. If anyone asks, we'll just say we forgot the learner plates, no one will bat an eye, I'm sure.'

'At...' I grabbed my phone to check the time, 'two thirty on a Sunday morning?'

'Ruth, please. He needs to go to the hospital.'

I groaned as my senses began to gradually return to me and I waved him off, asking for a moment. He hastily complied, stepping out of the shed into the cold. I tried to pull myself together the best I could, throwing on the first hoodie and pair of leggings I could lay my hands on. I followed Bill out to the car, where Ben was already waiting, strapped in the back seat like a child about to go on a family trip to Butlin's.

'Ben, love, what's happened?' I asked, climbing into the driver's seat, as he sat there, clutching a bag of peas tightly to his forehead.

'I fell,' he replied simply.

'Oh, you sausage,' I said, probably with more nonchalance than Bill appreciated as he belted up in the passenger seat beside me. 'Are you sure about this, Bill?' I asked again, really not feeling confident about being behind the wheel of his car, the anxiousness already surging within me. 'It's been ages since Ben and I have been out in the car, I'm really out of practice.'

'An ambulance would take too long,' he repeated. 'The roads will be quiet. Let's go,' he snapped.

I tried to recall everything Ben had taught me as I carefully edged out of the driveway, peeping and creeping even though the roads were mostly deserted at this hour, even in southeast London.

Tentatively, I pressed the accelerator, only for the car to lurch forward with a jolt.

'Sorry, sorry,' I muttered with a scowl as I fiddled with the gearstick. 'I've always been terrible at finding the bite, haven't I, Ben?'

'You have,' he affirmed sedately from the back seat, while I tried to remember which one was the brake pedal. The one on the left, I think?

As I followed the map on my phone, trying to concentrate on both the directions to the hospital and the myriad of driving mantras swirling around in my head – 'slow and steady', 'only drive to where your eyes can see', 'left is best' – I realised I hadn't given much thought to Ben. It was only as we pulled up at Charing Cross Hospital Accident and Emergency that I started to wonder why we were here. Had he hit his head when he had fallen? A concussion, maybe? How did he even fall in the first place? Why was Bill being so cagey about it?

Bill tenderly helped Ben out of the car while I headed to the car park to find a space. I was frankly amazed I'd managed to get us here in one piece and wasn't about to push my luck by attempting to do something miraculous like parallel park. Instead, I sought out the quietest spot at the very back of the car park, with plenty of room to reverse. Even then, I manoeuvred tentatively, finally parking in a way that I would describe as 'good enough'. The lines are more suggestions anyway.

I stepped into the hospital grounds, the frankly aggressive and bombarding sensory explosion of A&E at this hour hit me: drunks yelling belligerently, a few pre-teens yacking up in kitchen bowls and two policemen restraining some kind of mythical being with the body of some ordinary man and head of a traffic cone.

But I couldn't see Ben or Bill anywhere. How had they been seen so quickly at this time of night?

I considered sitting down to wait before realising the only spare seat was next to a very drunk and also very high Michael Jackson who would occasionally scream 'Shamone' before immediately retching into a bucket filled with sawdust.

As I approached the reception desk, I immediately clocked the receptionist with pursed lips and narrowed eyes. I recognised her as the kind of person who clearly valued brevity in conversation; I had seen many faces like hers before. The guy in front of me mumbled something under his breath to her, which to me sounded a like, *It's been up for more than four hours,* before she curtly told him to take a seat. Then I was next in line.

'Hi, my... friend, best friend...' I paused, feeling just 'friend' was far too casual. '... just came in here with his partner while I was parking. His name is Ben, Ben Murphy. I don't suppose you'd know where he is?'

She drew in a breath before a short snort, as if she was sizing me up, weighing the worth of my words. I realised the purple hoodie I had frantically grabbed in my scramble to get out of the door was one that had 'Trauma Queen' plastered over it, which may not be helping my case. Mind you, I'm sure A&E had seen worse and at least I wasn't wearing Bill's ghastly pyjamas.

'They've taken him to the Constance Wood Ward. Ground floor, to your right.'

'Oh, okay. Thank you,' I said with a polite smile, though she didn't return it.

By the time I reached the ward, I saw Bill standing outside one of the rooms, his arms folded tight and his expression, as per usual, stern, but he was still in those hideous pyjamas which made him look like an imprisoned elf exiled from Santa's Grotto for trying to form a union. I raised a tentative hand in greeting as I approached. His facial muscles didn't shift at all; not that he ever looked over-joyed to see me, but I was hoping he would show at least some sign of relief that I had found him in the labyrinthine corridors of the hospital.

'What happened? How did he fall?' I asked, peering into the room, trying to catch a glimpse of Ben through the glazed window but failing to ascertain the real severity of the situation.

'He just fell,' Bill replied, impassive and detached, his eyes still locked on the small, smudged portal into the hospital room.

'Weird. So, he wasn't feeling ill or nauseous or anything like that?' I asked.

'He just fell, Ruth,' Bill repeated firmly, his eyes bulging a little and his jaw clenching.

'Fine, fine. Forget I asked,' I said, trying to sound unfazed as I turned away from him and dropped into one of the barbarically uncomfortable chairs in the sterically lit hospital corridor. I watched the tense lines on Bill's face begin to gradually thaw as I tried to find some kind of seating position that didn't make me feel like I was about to slip right off and onto the floor that had probably seen litres of blood spilled onto it.

'Thank you for driving us,' Bill said eventually, surprising me with what sounded like an actual attempt at gratitude. 'I'm just... stressed. This whole situation is stressful.'

I gave a thumbs-up as a response. I was far too exhausted to navigate the landmine-infested field that was talking to Bill at the best of times.

'And I shouldn't have asked you to leave,' he continued, not making eye contact with me. 'I wanted to say that to your face too. I really thought I was doing Ben a favour with everything going on with him, but clearly, I wasn't.'

'It's fine,' I replied somewhat aloof but attempting to be poised. I tried not to be completely imperious, he was expressing some kind of regret to me, after all, although falling short of an actual apology. Not sure exactly what he meant, though. Why did he think he was helping Ben by kicking me out and what exactly did he have on?

He turned and slumped his body into the seat next to me. From the way he tried to shift his body, he was finding it as obnoxiously uncomfortable as I did.

'But yeah, thanks for not killing us on the way here,' he said wryly.

'Oh, you're quite welcome. I did think about driving us into the Thames but decided against it this time.'

'You might have done me a favour,' he responded, scoffingly.

Were Bill and I having *a moment?* Even though he was his usual self, dripping with sarcasm and lacing his dry cruelty as banter, it felt like he was being just the tiniest bit softer towards me.

'You know – and I don't really expect you to care,' he said, starting up the conversation again – 'but Ben and I were meant to celebrate our anniversary tonight.'

'No way,' I said, forgetting for a brief moment that to Ben, Bill was my replacement. I knew I shouldn't have expressed any kind of sympathy for his cancelled celebrations, but I still felt a little bit bad. 'You should have said. I mean, what happened?'

'I had to work, or I guess I chose to work, anyway, Ben got really mad. I mean, did you not wonder why I went straight up to bed without a word?'

'I just thought maybe you were feeling tired,' I admitted, trying to spare him the embarrassment of knowing I'd overheard the *East-Enders*-style shouting match from the shed. 'I didn't realise you two were upset with each other. I thought maybe he had just found your cigarettes again. Did you really have to work?'

'No,' Bill muttered, a little softly, almost repentant with the way that he bowed his head as he said it. From what I could tell, Bill's second job wasn't really about the extra money. Between software engineering and private equity, I imagined the two of them were hardly struggling to pay a mortgage, even in London. So why he kept vanishing at odd hours and coming home smelling of weird ointments was still beyond me. I still kept coming back to stripper. I could see people going crazy for Ben.

I couldn't stop myself from asking what I said next. Maybe it was the flutter of camaraderie Bill was showing me, or maybe I was still bitter about him trying to boot me out of the shed.

'How many years?'

'What?'

'How many years were you celebrating?'

He harrumphed. It was stupid of me to ask, and he was wise enough not to answer.

# EIGHTEEN

Back when I was younger, Greta and I once got the stern gaze of our teacher when, sat at the back of the class, we decided to draw enormous vulvas on the textbooks. Penises were so overrated and overexposed within the education curriculum but vulvas, now *that's* not something you see doodled in the back of a school textbook every day. That's got some originality, that's breaking new ground in the art of textbook graffiti.

You'd be surprised how hard it is to draw one from memory, from the clitoris down to the labia majora, making sure you got the shape and curve of things quite right. Our teacher spotted it, of course, but I always remember very clearly that we didn't get in trouble for our art pieces.

We didn't get in trouble mostly because Greta's mum was in hospital at the time. While I'll never be thankful that Greta was only fourteen when her mum died, a part of me *is* thankful that, when I drew the fattest labia I could summon, we were spared the wrath of Mr Trimmer's detention, and it was the first time she'd smiled in months.

After that, Mr Trimmer never looked at me the same way again. Probably because I gave one of the labias a very fetching bow tie.

Bill had remained annoyingly vague about why we were here, saying only, and rather obtusely, that 'Ben just fell'. But I could tell there was something he wasn't telling me. After he lent me his charger for my phone that was as flat as a dab, he had claimed he would try to stay awake, but by the time I stirred at 5.30 a.m. on Sunday morning, he was still out like a light, long heavy snores emanating from his nasal passageways. The first rays of a pinky-red dawn were beginning to filter through the hospital blinds, stretching wide across the linoleum flooring.

I rose to my feet, trotted the ten feet over to the other end of the corridor and stretched my arms as high as I could above my head. Then I noticed, through the glazed window to the hospital room, I could just about make out the figure of Ben sitting upright in bed. He was awake, presumably watching TV with the colours of the screen casting an iridescent gleam across his face. I crept into the room as quietly as I could, wary of catching the attention of a rogue doctor or nurse who might curtly remind me of the hospital's visiting hours.

'Hey, champ,' I said, keeping my tone as light and playful as possible. 'I told you if you kept doing it too much you'd go blind or your palms would get hairy.'

'What's up, sport?' he replied, mirroring my tone of fake ebullience. I could see it clearly on his face. He looked tired, no, actually he looked weary. As if someone had taken some kind of industrial-grade emotional vacuum to suck all of the joy and hope out of his face.

'Is anyone going to tell me what's wrong with you, or am I going to have to play doctor and diagnose you myself?' I asked, half joking, but I was starting to feel the unease in my gut. Something wasn't right and it had been that way for a few days now.

He chuckled softly, though the sound quickly faded, leaving behind a brief, pained wince that I'm sure he hoped I wouldn't notice. I pulled up one of the chairs, its design just as obnoxiously uncomfortable as the ones out in the hallway, and sat down across from him.

'I don't want to lie to you, Ruth,' he said, his voice measured and steady. 'But after I tell you this, I want you to promise me that you won't try to suffer with me through all of this.'

'What are you talking about?' I asked, confused not just by his words, but by the mournful and maudlin way he spoke them, as though each word was causing him a level of anguish that I couldn't hope to understand.

'Look,' he said, meeting my eyes, 'one of the reasons I fell in love with you is because you're kind, Ruth. Which is not something that's particularly ubiquitous nowadays. You're kind to people who don't deserve it, and I don't want you to be kind to me anymore.'

I'd be lying if I said my mind hadn't started piecing things together before I sat down, but I didn't want to believe he was going to say what I thought he was.

'So, what is it?' I asked, trying to stay steady, but my voice was faltering and breaking. I wasn't any kind of medical professional, but I at least wanted to know the name of the thing inside his body trying to kill him.

'Glioblastoma,' he said finally, the word landing with an emotional weight I recognised all too well. He must have seen the vacant expression as I tried to wonder what kind of cancer it exactly was, I think I had heard of it before. 'It's a brain tumour,' he clarified, 'a proper nasty, aggressive one. It grows fast and spreads through the brain tissue like a forest fire.'

'And... what? You can't get chemo?' I asked, desperately.

'They can do surgery, and they can do chemo,' he replied with a rhythm to his words, as if he was repeating what he had been told by professionals numerous times. 'They're asking if I want to start next week.'

Something told me that, though he'd stopped speaking, he hadn't said everything he wanted to, so I stayed quiet.

'I'm scared, Ruth, I'm really scared,' he said with a vulnerability I don't think I had ever seen from him before, even when we were married. 'I don't want to die but I'm just so scared how this thing is going to change me. The doctor said as it grows, it'll affect my mood, my personality, I can get violent, aggressive. And I don't want to change, Ruth. And I don't want anyone's last memories of me to be of someone I wasn't.'

His gaze dropped, fixing a glare on some vacant patch of air.

'So, how long are we talking?' I felt like that was the question I had really been waiting to ask.

'I've got about twelve months if I go through with chemo and surgery,' he said with a sigh. 'The doctor said two years if things go really well.'

I felt like I should have started sobbing then, but it all seemed too cruel to process fully. All I could manage was the simplest, most primal thought pounding around my head.

'But... I don't want you to die,' I whispered, as if this would somehow stop the tumour in its tracks, raise its hands as if to surrender and retreat back to where it came from, as if me saying that had some kind of impact.

'I don't want to die either, Ruth,' he affirmed, his voice breaking as I could see him successfully hold back the tears from spilling. He hadn't often cried during our marriage but there was something about him refusing to weep now, that felt even more devastating. 'But them's the breaks, ain't it?' He forced another artificial smile through the tears, though the brittle bravado wasn't fooling either of us.

I knew he was doing his best to try and suppress everything he was feeling for my benefit: the fear, the regret, the grief, the looming realisation of your own mortality. We all know, deep down, that we're going to die someday. But there's a moment when that abstract, distant notion rapidly hardens into a cold, blunt truth. I saw it at least once a week when I helped someone come in to plan their funeral. I think we assume that death will only come for us once we feel sated by life, as though having your life abruptly and tragically cut short is something that happens to other people, never actually to us. In an instant, you feel the weight of every ordinary day you wished away, every postponed moment or holiday, and realise you never had as much time as you thought.

'But you have to get the chemo, Ben,' I urged. 'I mean, I can't remember the details, but I heard about this guy on the news, he had this inoperable brain tumour or something, and he fought it. He lived another six, seven years. There's still so much life you could still have.'

'Ruth,' he said gently. 'You know, the really cruel thing about glioblastoma is that it always comes back. Always. The five-year survival rate? Five to ten per cent, and the percentage it comes back: ninety.'

'How do you know that?' I asked.

'Do you want to know how much time I've spent on the internet researching this thing?' he replied wryly. 'All my targeted ads on my phone now are about cancer, or wills, or skydiving, weirdly.'

I didn't know what else to say, I didn't even know how to react. He turned his eyes to listlessly watch the television as I just stared intensely down at the hospital bed sheets. After staring at it for so long, I now realised its design was made up of thousands of primary colour caducei interlocking with one another.

'Did you not wonder why I've been at home more?' he asked, with a little jest as if it was all one big prank he had been playing. 'I've been signed off work since the diagnosis.'

'I noticed you've been arguing with Bill a lot more.'

'Yeah, that's something for another day.'

'Oh, Ben, love,' I murmured, sliding my chair closer to his bed and reaching out, wrapping my hand carefully around his and squeezing gently. He turned to me, his eyes still glassy and exhausted, and I lifted his hand to my face, nuzzling my lips against it tenderly.

'I'll always be kind to you, Ben,' I said, 'and you know there's nothing you can do to stop that.'

I didn't know if losing Ben this way was worse than losing Greta. Is it better to know someone's days are numbered so you can make the most of them, or to have no idea, and for their last day to feel just like any other? More and more, I felt death begin to take on a shape, its vague, shadowy ambiguity sharpening. It was starting to feel like this vindictive amorphous being, deliberately taking things from me just to see how much it could make me hurt.

Ben didn't speak any more after that, probably realising that another person knowing about his diagnosis made his impending death feel even more real. The life he'd always enjoyed so much was coming to an abrupt end. After a while, he gently closed his eyes, and I sat there, watching him sleep for a bit longer. Not in a creepy way – at least, I didn't think it was creepy. I was just trying to imagine what he might look like dead, to prepare myself for the crushing weight I would feel when I looked into his open casket. Okay... maybe that *was* a bit creepy.

There were no storm clouds bellowing to echo my mood; instead, the Sunday morning blushed pink and red, a 'shepherd's delight', while the sun rose, devouring the colours as it climbed across the sky.

A lovely, soft-spoken nurse came in. Instead of kicking me out for violating sacred visitor hours, she asked if we wanted any tea and then returned with her own personal mug, since the rest of the visitor crockery was in the dishwasher. I promised I'd take good care of it as I lifted it to my eyeline to see why she favoured this particular piece of crockery. The faded but still visible image on the front was one of the Virgin Mary, hands outstretched and immersed in a cloud just outside what I presumed were the gates of heaven with some Italian writing that had been worn away over time.

I noticed at about ten that the TV was still on with the sound muted, and I casually turned my head to see what the headlines of today were. Probably something dire about the economy, I thought, or some middle-aged clot moaning about the colour of bin bags and some numpty marrying a toaster. As I carefully took a sip of tea, I began to process what some half-handsome newsperson was saying.

Oh. No. I read the ticker.

### The TellTale Killer Returns: Deadly Serial Killer Resurfaces After Two Years. Police Issue Warning.

Oh no. Oh no. Oh no.

I grabbed the remote and rapidly cranked the volume up, in the moment not caring if I woke Ben, as I stared, slack-jawed and stunned, at the screen. Every muscle in my body felt like it was burning, frying from the inside out with a crackling, electric anxiety of a million volts. Sweat coated every inch of my skin within an instant, and my breath caught, jagged in my throat, as I reread the headline on the screen again and again, trying to make sense of it.

And there it was, front and centre, in glorious, horrifying detail: the note I'd written, sent to the paper the night before.

*I will strike again.*

The newscasters were already deep into their analysis, speaking in grave, morose tones about the TellTale Killer's return and what this meant for the UK.

Plastered across the screen, I flicked to the subsequent channels doing their morning updates and it was on, every, single one. Another solemn-looking man, another solemn-looking woman, and then three middle-aged women on a bright red sofa discussing whether the TellTale Killer was 'a narcissist, an unstable genius, or just a really sassy Gemini'.

It was as though I'd been playing Buckaroo without knowing it, stacking one thing after another, oblivious to the inevitable chaos that was about to commence. I'd thought I had control, I thought it would never explode to this degree. But in that moment, I understood just how spectacularly I'd fucked up. The muscles in my hand went limp and the mug slipped from my hand and shattered on the hospital room floor.

I am so, so sorry, Mary.

# NINETEEN

My reflection in the mirror was quite a sorry sight: heavy, darkened eyes sunk into the sockets of a pallid, puffy face, and skin that looked devoid of any kind of life. In a way, I'm glad I looked as terrible as I felt, it would have been strange if a runway model was looking back at me in the mirror after the day I'd had. I spent most of Sunday in the hospital with Ben, doing my best to ignore the continuing headlines from the TV in the room. When I told Bill and Ben I was heading home, they both seemed to assume, judging by the ghastly pallor on my face, that I was still reeling from Ben telling me about his diagnosis. And I certainly still was. But I was also frantically trying to untangle the very messy consequences of my own, frankly idiotic, decisions.

I'd been too reckless the night before, so desperate to shake the police out of their apparent indifference that I'd acted on impulse. Had that somehow worked in my favour? Made me seem more authentic as the TellTale Killer?

But I suppose the combined impact of Chestgate and my note had led the press to pressure the police into releasing a statement, which they did on Sunday evening. The police were likely afraid that if they were wrong – and it was the real TellTale Killer – they'd be in a whole new world of trouble. If it came out they knew about the notes and didn't warn the public, it would come back to bite them in the posterior in the most colossal way. They must have decided it had become a matter of public importance to tell people they had received evidence of what they believed to be the Tell-Tale Killer's return.

DarkCell, naturally, was going wild.

*I told you*, CerealKillerCornflakes had messaged me privately at least half a dozen times. *I told you he'd come back.*

No one likes a know it all, especially when they're technically wrong.

*I don't remember you saying that*, I said to him, purposefully just to wind him up.

*I did!* he messaged back.

*Ah must have missed it, I tend to tune you out when you're being smug.*

Meanwhile, the more macabre side of the website had been trying to predict what kind of victim he would target next.

After lying on my bed in the shed for a while, I pulled open the drawer and reached for the ripped piece of emerald-green cloth from Greta's jacket, gently caressing it in my hand for a moment.

I think some people, at this point, would have paused – wrestled with themselves, asking: *Is this what Greta would have wanted me to do?*

Greta would have told me to come to my senses, to go to the authorities and hand over everything to them. She was sensible like that.

She would have tried to be the voice of reason, as she so often was, the one telling the bartender to ignore my request for a chocolate milk vodka, or that getting a Justin Bieber tattoo at the height of his popularity fifteen-odd years ago was a terrible idea. But I didn't have her to stop me from going astray anymore. I was on my own. No one to save me from my horrible, ridiculous stupidity.

I stayed awake most of Sunday night and watched the clock tick over to 7 a.m. Monday morning. I wasn't entirely sure if I was expected at work or not after Chestgate. But knowing that staying home in the shed would likely result in me curling up into a ball of anxious panic for the rest of the day, I decided it was probably best to get out of the house. On my commute, I tried not to dwell on the fact that my imitation of a serial killer had made the homepage of nearly every website I'd checked. I mean, I had got what I wanted, hadn't I? The police were investigating. But how long – if they hadn't already – until they discovered it was just little old me? And more disturbingly, how was the real TellTale Killer taking this development? What was he thinking? Was he on TikTok, liking all the various conspiracy theories about himself.

I was lost in the swirling black hole of my thoughts as I walked up the street, a hundred or so metres towards the funeral directors at the very end of the road. I was vaguely hoping to find some semblance of mindfulness in the sound of the flowing water from the small creek running to my left until a voice, vaguely familiar, suddenly yanked me back into reality.

'Hi,' she said, just as what I assumed was her hand closed around my arm. I turned towards the source of her voice and found a woman with a smile unnaturally fixed to her face, the sort of smile that influencers use when they're trying to sell you their diarrhoea tea.

'Ruth, hi,' she said again, clearly clocking that I still hadn't recognised her. 'It's Tasha.'

It was Tasha? As in the Tasha I used to work with back at the paper? That Tasha? She looked different somehow. It took me a moment to place it, the dullness in her eyes, the lost lustre in her skin. She looked diminished, though I swallowed that thought back before I could verbalise it. I lingered there, frozen in the lane as the cold morning wrapped around me, before realising I should probably speak.

'Tasha, oh?' I said, startled. 'Wow. How are you?'

'I'm good, thanks. How are you?' she replied, not so subtly angling her body in front of mine in a way that suggested this conversation wasn't going to be brief or succinct in the slightest, an ever-so-subtle conversational trap.

I hadn't seen or heard from her in years. She had been wonderfully supportive when Greta first died, but I suppose fourteen days was her limit on compassion, then she had work to get to.

'I'm well, Ruth, I'm well. Look, while I've got you, I wanted to start by saying I'm sorry. About everything that happened when you left the paper. I've thought about reaching out a few times but... What they did to you was really, really shitty. It wasn't fair, and I just wanted to say I'm sorry.'

'Eh, it happens,' I replied with a dismissive wave. I had no interest in dredging up those particular humiliations again; I'd watched that reel enough times in the private screening room of my head.

'Fancy seeing you here, though,' she continued. 'How have you been? I heard you're working at a funeral directors now, is that right? How's that going?'

I wanted to point out to her that I was about fifty feet away from my workplace when the penny dropped with a very loud clang. How naïve of me to think this might be a genuine, serendipitous run-in with an old friend. Clearly, she was the first harbinger of the press storm that was about to descend upon Camborne and Sons.

From here, I could make out two police cars parked outside the office, both in their signature reflective Battenberg blue and yellow, alongside what I recognised as Detective Carlota's vehicle. Of course. Tasha had been waiting for me, realised that she had an *in* with one of the staff already that she could manipulate. Oh, Tasha, you're so much better than this.

'You want to know about the incident yesterday, don't you?' I asked, cutting straight to it. Journalists hated preamble. Deadlines didn't wait for anyone.

'I mean...' she hesitated, the fake niceties slipping fast, 'if you could give me any details, that would be great. This is the TellTale Killer back again; anything you can tell me, anything at all...'

Tasha had changed since I'd known her. She used to be more laid-back and quite happy with delivering the bare minimum. Now she was clearly ambitious, chasing a scoop. I was sure if old golden boy, Jago Jones, still worked at the paper, she was itching to steal his crown. Probably dreaming of media traffic stats and those glitzy, douchebag awards they handed out at the end of the year along with a trip to Barbados.

I realised that if everything with Greta hadn't happened, I'd probably have been like this too: hungry, restless, my neurones constantly firing, thinking of ways to make my big break. It was strange, in that moment, to feel as though I were looking at a past version of myself.

'Sure, sure,' I said brightly. 'Okay, do you have a pen or something handy?'

In response, she keenly yanked out her phone and held it between us, I couldn't help but notice it had been recording for at least thirty seconds already. Snake.

'Ready when you are?' she said eagerly.

'Okay, get ready, because I'm only going to say this once, so listen carefully,' I said purposefully.

'Absolutely,' she replied, her eye contact unbreaking with mine. Her mouth practically frothing and bubbling at what I was about to say.

And then, without another word, I snatched her phone and hurled it into the creek. I heard it land with a very satisfying plop.

'Piss off,' I murmured as I barged past her as she clambered into the ditch to snatch her phone from the watery depths.

'It's the latest model!' she yelled at me.

'Pens tend to work better,' I said.

# TWENTY

Do you ever see people – whether walking past them on the street or sitting next to them at work – and think, *I wonder what your face looks like when you orgasm?* Perhaps it's just me. But as the stern, stoic police officer – his wedding band glinting faintly – finally wrapped up his questioning, I couldn't help but imagine what he'd look like at the climax of coitus. His expression was so rigid, so unreadable, that I genuinely wondered if, even in moments of joy or grief, it ever actually changed.

When I was finally allowed back onto the floor, I clocked that there were four other police officers milling around the office, talking to the various staff members who were in today, and taking statements, while forensic technicians walked purposefully in and out of the morgue, taking photos with their cameras and grabbing almost everything they could lay their hands on, slipping it into an array of plastic bags. Amidst the flurry of activity, Uncle Phil sat in his office, slumped behind his desk, sipping on yet another of his Capri-Suns as he browsed the sub-reddit for funeral directors (yes, it exists). He was drinking again, not a good sign. I half expected him to leap out of his chair the moment I walked in, telling me the whole business was about to implode, but instead, he barely acknowledged my arrival, clearly all of his nervous energy had been completely exhausted at this point.

I excused myself past another burly police officer taking a statement from the clearly nervous Sophie, to enter Uncle Phil's office.

'So... this is a lot,' I said, gesturing vaguely at the scene of organised chaos unfolding around the funeral directors. It was normally ever so quiet here, that it was bewildering to see more than five people on the floor at once.

'Did you see my texts from yesterday?' he asked, his voice resigned.

I shook my head, I really only scanned a lot of my notifications unless they were from DarkCell.

'Yesterday was... a lot for me,' I replied quietly.

'Oh, yes, of course,' he said quickly. I could see the regret form in his face as he squinted his eyes and shook his head, as if scolding himself for asking the question. 'I forgot how hard this must be for you, Ruth. I hope you're holding up okay. I know it can't be easy knowing he's back.'

'It's not,' I replied with a small affirmation, deciding now wasn't the time or place to explain why my Sunday had been so terrible.

'They're shutting down the whole morgue,' Uncle Phil said, dejectedly, flicking his hand to motion to the various police staff. 'All funerals are delayed until they've investigated every single body. They're going through all the security footage, searching for evidence, want to talk to all of us.'

'What do they even think they're going to find?' I asked, dubiously, also realising I was half asking myself.

'Not a scooby,' Uncle Phil replied with a snort. It was then I realised that I couldn't remember the last time I had seen him look so deflated. 'I know in my heart that none of you would even think about doing something like this. What, do they think that Clive has enough brain cells to be the TellTale Killer, Lord have mercy.'

I cast my mind back to the discussion of security footage earlier and felt another razor-edged spike of worry in my chest when I realised they might well show me packing various items into an

Ann Summers bag before disappearing into the morgue for thirty minutes. But we fortunately only had three cameras in the office, which meant they were limited in what they would be able to capture. There was one by the front door, one by the display coffins which had a restricted view to the morgue, and one at what we called the loading bay where we moved the sorry sods into the hearses. Surely, none of the cameras would have caught me.

I figured I could probably bluff my way through that if they did try and call me up on it. After all, Uncle Phil himself had been the one to ask me to check on Justin's body before joining me for the impromptu job offer surrounded by the interview panel of cold stiffs.

'My offer still stands, by the way, Ruth, about taking over the business,' Uncle Phil said, catching my eye and shifting his lips into a kind smile. 'I'm just sorry you might be inheriting such an absolute mess of a company at this rate.'

'Oh, don't be silly,' I replied with what I hoped would look like a friendly smile to him. 'Thank you, by the way. I am very interested.' Fine, I lied, but I figured I should try and keep my options open. 'I just think that these past few days have been such a...'

I made a strange warbling noise with my mouth, waving my hands around my head in a gesture that was meant to convey my internal lunacy. Uncle Phil gave a robust chuckle, smoothed his hand over his chest as if to ease the indwelling anxiety, and took another dainty sip of his Capri-Sun. I didn't know whether to tell him that drinking his problems away wasn't the answer.

A soft courtesy knock sounded at the open door behind me and I turned to see Detective Carlota looming in the doorway. I was still a little unsettled from my last conversation with her, feeling like she had a moderate-to-high suspicion that I had played a part in the TellTale Killer's return; I mean, she was always incredibly perceptive, she was a detective, after all. Still, regardless of that, I couldn't deny how fabulous she looked today, like always. Tall and muscular, she seemed as though she'd just casually stepped off a runway at Paris Fashion Week. Today, she wore a stylish camel-coloured double-breasted coat over a dark cable-knit blue jumper that perfectly accentuated her striking facial structure.

'Mr Camborne, hi,' she said, smiling at Uncle Phil spuriously. 'I was wondering if I could borrow Ruth for a moment?'

Uncle Phil flicked a hand and bowed his head as if to say, *Of course*, and I followed Detective Carlota into the claustrophobic office kitchen; it could barely fit one of us. She placed a hand gently on my upper arm, as though hoping it might feel reassuring to me, but all I could think about was her telling me they had finally found evidence of my tampering and asking me what kind of prison food I liked.

'How are you holding up, darling?' she asked, her voice gentle and delicate, her words seemingly comforting but with very little warmth under the surface. I'd never seen Detective Carlota like this. She'd always been kind and supportive which made the sudden chill of her professionalism all the more jarring; it felt like watching the family dog bare its teeth after taking a treat from your hand.

'I'm okay, I think,' I replied, trying to keep any telltale guilt from creeping unknowingly onto my face.

'Good, good, good,' she murmured. 'Look, I need your help. The police gave a press conference last night dedicated to catching the TellTale Killer; you may have watched it on TV.'

Admittedly, I had only watched the highlights, there was frankly too much TellTale Killer content to keep up with at the moment. The media circus was very much back in town. 'So, I'm still sceptical this is actually him, the real TellTale Killer,' Detective Carlota continued. 'That being said, due to some recent developments, shall we say, it looks like he may have killed two people already.'

Oh, so they did receive my first package. Rude of them not to reply.

'I thought you were off the case?' I asked Detective Carlota. She cocked her head in response, as if to say, *Well ...*

'I'm not the lead, I'm afraid,' she said. 'But seeing as I was the last time he struck, they've asked me to oversee whatever we can glean from Camborne and Sons.'

Good for her. Less good for me.

'But I've spent all bleeding night searching for what could have happened to Justin's body, tracking every single place it went between inquest and funeral. I'm just determined to get to the bottom of this, Ruth,' Carlota continued. I'd almost forgotten this about her. With the Telltale Killer quiet for two years, I hadn't seen this side of her in a while. But I remembered how it was after Greta, when we still thought the killer might strike again: there was a ruthlessness in her, a kind of callous edge. She would do anything not only to bring him to justice, but to be the one specifically who did it.

She gave me a look I imagine doctors reserve for the moment before they mention a colonoscopy.

'I need your help to try and figure this whole thing out.'

'Oh,' I said, fighting again to keep any flicker of compunction or scruple from betraying me. 'You know me, Detective, I'm always here to help.'

Casually, she noted that I'd been captured on CCTV entering the morgue on Friday – I'll leave you to guess which particular occasion that was – but reassured me I'd since been struck off the list of suspects.

'You see, not only do I know you pretty well at this point, Ruth, but I spoke to a surgeon, and she told me that no amateur could remove an entire heart and cover it up in just thirty minutes,' she added, 'especially not someone who works in admin and finance.' I felt an almost overwhelming urge to point out that it wasn't so difficult, provided you had a bulk supply of kitchen towels to stuff the body, but instead I just decided to make my best concentration face as she spoke.

'I'm actually doing some more work on the bodies now,' I said, figuring that not outright denying anything might make me seem less suspicious. 'It's not just numbers anymore.'

Carlota barely reacted, offering nothing more than a slight, noncommittal, 'hmmph'.

'So, I want you to tell me, Ruth,' she said, tilting her head from side to side as if to make sure we were truly alone in the cramped office kitchen. 'If someone was going to steal a heart from this place, which of your colleagues would it be?'

How the hell was I meant to answer that question and not throw someone – and I include myself here – under the bus with my answer?

'Umm, I'm not sure, really. It's kind of a bizarre question to try and answer,' I replied.

'Not Claudia? Sophie? Eddie? Just give me a name, any name. I trust your instincts here, Ruth.'

I felt my eyes widen as she closed in, annexing what little personal space remained between us; her disregard for boundaries felt as palpable as her presence.

The temptation to throw out a name, any name, just to get her off my back, was almost overwhelming. If I were innocent, I probably would have blurted one out randomly already. But that's the thing: an interview is so much harder when you have to think about what an innocent person would even say in this situation.

'Detective, I wish I could help you, I really do, but that's not something I've even thought about,' I said entreatingly. 'I don't think any of us would do something like this. My only thought is that, somehow, the TellTale Killer came back to take his memento from the victim *after* he'd killed him, I don't even know how, but that's the only theory I can think of right now.'

It was the theory I'd come up with on Saturday night, straight after Chestgate. Serial killers, as we all know, are a big-headed bunch, surely going back to take the heart, even at risk of incrimination, was a plausible story that a police detective could believe?

To say Detective Carlota looked unconvinced was somewhat an understatement. She rolled her eyes and begrudgingly gestured for me to follow her, and together we began a slow, inspecting lap around the funeral home. Her questions were insistent, coming thick and fast as I did my best to answer them as coherently as I could.

'Who has access to the equipment used for embalming? Sutures, scalpels, things like that?' she asked as we stepped into the chilly sterility of the morgue, now practically empty of coffins and equipment.

'Well,' I began, 'it's stored in the locked cupboard here, but the keys are kept in a safe box, though. I think it's just Uncle Phil, Sophie and I who know the combination to access it.'

'You *think*?' she asked cuttingly.

'Know, sorry, I know,' I said, correcting myself.

'Interesting,' she murmured. I'm not sure if that was to herself or not.

Her phone buzzed and she plucked it from her pocket and practically crushed it to her ear to answer it. As she briskly walked out of the morgue, I discreetly pulled my own phone out for a moment. I'd barely had time to check my messages in the havoc since Sunday morning.

My parents had texted me from wherever they were in Colombo, saying the news had even reached them there, and asking me to give them a call whenever I had a chance. But beyond that there wasn't much correspondence from anyone. Still nothing from Chlo, either. I would have thought she might have reached out by now.

What I did notice, though, was a new message on DarkCell, but not from CerealKillerCornflakes. Weird. I opened the email notification on my phone, making sure I could still hear Detective Carlota on her call in the other room, sounding like she was obediently taking a telling-off from someone superior even though I was fairly sure she didn't deserve it. How could I, so contradictorily, root for her career as a detective while simultaneously hoping she'd fail spectacularly at investigating me?

As the link to the website loaded, I saw it was a private reply to the post I had made the night before on DarkCell where I had imitated the TellTale Killer. Naturally, I'd used a different throwaway username for my imitation post, I had to be somewhat sensible in my stupidity.

There were two photos that this user had sent me: the first showed some seemingly random letters that were scribbled on a piece of parchment. I knew better than to verbally decrypt it in the morgue where I could be easily ambushed by an officer of the law so I subsequently darted out of the room, gave a quick wave to Detective Carlota and dashed straight into the loo that was rather peculiarly, yet conveniently, positioned only a few paces down the hallway from the morgue.

I didn't recognise the username at all. It wasn't someone I had spoken to on DarkCell in the two years I had been lurking around in that corner of the dark web. I turned the lock on the toilet door, reopened my phone, and took a proper look at the first image: the letters set out on parchment.

*Gs qmcutp e tvzek yoe mf xci iqoumrwo ark we aumxl r xwkxyi hee ooe lvqnicr okxnmi kiqokrrwn.*

It unnerved me slightly that, like a psychological mechanism wired deep into the hardware my brain, the letters seemed to rearrange themselves until I could easily read what they were really saying.

'To vilify a great man is the readiest way in which a little man can himself attain greatness.'

Now, that was from Poe himself. I remembered the quote clearly from when I had read through his entire collection cover to cover. But it wasn't the message in isolation that frightened me. It was the second photo that was attached.

A naked body lay splayed across scuffed wooden floorboards, its limbs shattered, bent and twisted grotesquely into impossible angles. Where the ribcage should have been, there was only a vast, gaping hollow, the chest cleaved open into a cold, empty void.

I didn't know how to react. My hand shot to my mouth but it

was like a scream had already started somewhere in my chest and there was nothing I could do to stop it.

This was him. It had to be him. The actual TellTale Killer had just messaged me. I had consumed so much serial killer content over the past two years and I'd never seen anything like this before. The TellTale Killer had been lurking on DarkCell all this time, silently watching, soaking up and delightfully savouring every word we'd spoken about him. And now, the voice I'd heard the night that Greta died was back.

I grabbed the hand towel, needing something, anything, to shove into my mouth to stifle the sound rising out of me. It didn't work. What came out instead was a slightly muffled, guttural cry, a pained bellow echoing from the toilet stall.

'God help whoever's in there,' I heard Eddie murmur from outside.

# TWENTY-ONE

'Ruth, we need to go now,' I heard Carlota's voice order from the outside the toilet.

'Coming,' I replied as I still tried to make some sense of this really messed-up version of *You've Got Mail*. It certainly wasn't a dreamy, swoonworthy Nineties Tom Hanks on the other end of this line.

The idea that the TellTale Killer might have been lurking there on the dark web all this time, watching his admirers from a distance – that made a chilling kind of sense to me. He wanted to see people guessing and theorising how he had gotten away with it. I bet he saw this as his personal fan community that he had secretly been a part of, like Tom Cruise turning up to *Mission Impossible*'s opening night in a baseball cap and a fake moustache, nodding along as people whispered about how great he was.

I had attempted to look at the photo of the corpse closely in the short time I had, zooming in as much as I could to try and deduce who it could have been. Of course, I would have known instantly if it was Greta, but it also didn't seem to be any of the three females of the six original victims. This was someone new, he was still killing.

'Ruth. Now,' Detective Carlota barked again from outside the toilet.

'Sorry. It's the burritos! Extra spicy!' I blurted out. What a ridiculous thing to say, it was ten in the morning.

I stuffed my phone back into my trouser pocket as quickly as I could, and tried to arrange my face in the mirror into something I hoped looked innocent. I needed, just for the moment, to clear my mind of what I had just seen if I was going to avoid any more of Detective Carlota's suspicion that I was behind this. I know she'd said I wasn't a suspect, but I couldn't shake the feeling this was just her playing good cop, trying to guilt me into a confession of my recreation of the heart scene in *Temple of Doom*. Did she know I knew? Did she think I knew that she knew? It was all far too complex for my already, frankly, feeble mind.

While I still had access to the DarkCell forum account I'd been using for the past two years, I silently thanked every long-forgotten lucky star that I had thought ahead. By posting with a secondary account before posting the photo to cover my tracks, using a fake email and routing everything through a VPN, at least, I hoped, my identity was protected. I didn't know how skilled the TellTale Killer was when it came to tracking someone down on the internet.

As I unlocked the toilet door, Detective Carlota was standing just inches away. The door swung open and almost hit her square in the face as though she had been trying to peer through the subatomic particles of the door to see exactly what I was doing in there. I don't think she would have even believed me if I told her.

'Ruth, I need to talk to you alone. I've found something.'

Nervously, I followed Carlota a few feet away from the loading bay to the car park outside where small specks of snow were beginning to descend from the blank white sky above us. 'God's dandruff,' I knew Greta would call it.

I watched as officers herded a few reporters away; Tasha was among them. Clearly, others had had the same idea she'd had, craning for a glimpse of whatever might be happening inside the parlour.

'What else did you find?' I asked Detective Carlota, who seemed unbothered by the mild tussle between the journalists and the police.

'Not a lot,' she said evenly. 'Nothing here looks out of the ordinary and, between you and me, forensics haven't seemed to find anything major as of yet.'

I lifted a hand to my mouth and let out a tiny belch. It tasted of mild, temporary relief.

'There's a scalpel unaccounted for,' Carlota said matter-of-factly, outstretching a hand to watch one of the small flakes dance through the air, drop and then melt on the centre of her palm.

'Okay?' I said as I felt my guts start to move south, while I continued to try and feign some level of perplexity and look unfussed by her statement. Inside, I was working very hard not to panic. I had forgotten all about that fucking scalpel. In the rush to clear up before Uncle Phil got back, when I was extracting Justin's heart, I had thrown it out with the soiled kit and it would have gone for incineration the next morning. 'Do you think that means anything?' I asked, *faux naif*.

Detective Carlota grimaced. She didn't meet my eye; she kept watching the snowflakes flutter down from the heavens, as if I was only present as a spare body to bounce her own predetermined thoughts off.

'Your uncle. He seems like a nice man,' she said. I didn't think it was meant as a question, but I hurried to agree.

'Yes, yes, he is. Absolutely,' I responded.

I was maybe a little too keen in my affirmation that Uncle Phil was a buoyant ray of sunshine.

She let out a soft grunt, followed by the deliberate exhale of a mind made up.

'I'm going to bring him in for questioning, Ruth. Something isn't right here: a scalpel is missing from where Justin's body was kept, where only a few people had access. Tell me, frankly, do you think your uncle is simply getting too old and careless – that he innocently misplaced a scalpel and Camborne and Sons has become a crime scene through simple ineptitude? Or do you think he had a hand in it? Do you think he's a part of this whole sick operation? I mean, can you see how bad this looks for him?'

I was stunned. I had no idea how to respond. Every word I could think of might incriminate me or, worse, damn Uncle Phil for something he hadn't done. Did Detective Carlota know exactly what she was doing, pulling my strings like some crazed puppet master? Or was this all in my head? Maybe my view of things was skewed by the guilt and anxiety gnawing constantly at me.

'I don't understand, why would you bring him in for questioning?' I asked, a little dumbfounded, while ignoring the question she had asked. 'Come on, you know he didn't have a part to play in all of this. This is a sweet old man. He is the walking definition of harmless.'

'You'd be surprised by how many people seem harmless,' Carlota said stoically, her tone cool and unruffled. 'Look, I know it seems harsh, and I don't take any pleasure in this, but if the Tell-Tale Killer is back, then the only way to catch him is to apply a bit of pressure on people who I think could be involved, which in my opinion, is everyone who works here.'

It was the way she tilted her head slightly, as if to catch more of me in her peripheral vision, that unsettled me. It felt as though she were studying my reaction, testing how I would respond to what she was saying. Surely, deep down, she knew Uncle Phil couldn't have been involved. By now she knew him; honest, decent, incapable of operation: Hearts and Crafts. All I could do was trust the justice system to recognise it too, clear my dear old uncle, and somehow avoid dragging me into the mess I had created. Maybe that was a bit too much to ask, though.

'I'm just terrified things are going to get worse,' she muttered just as I realised that the silence between us had continued to stretch.

'Worse?' I asked, confused by what exactly she meant by that.

'I don't think it's him behind this, the real killer,' Carlota said, her eyes still fixed on the snowfall. 'I know the press want us to believe it is – or maybe they're just chasing a last-minute payday to kick off the financial quarter. But I really don't think this is the same man I was trying to track down two years ago. There's something different about this.'

'So, what do you think will happen?' I asked, trying to find the actual solid point of what Detective Carlota seemed to be musing about, get her to land the plane so to speak.

'Serial killers don't like copycats, Ruth,' she said, angling her eyeline ever so slightly towards me. 'If they think someone's imitating their work, they get emboldened. They escalate. Twenty million Brits consume the news every day, what are the bets the TellTale Killer is one of them. If you're a serial killer with a precise and enact methodology for every victim, wouldn't you be a bit pissed off if someone was trying to imitate you? How would you even respond?'

I thought about answering that. Thought about telling her all the different cases where serial killers had inspired copycats. But then I hesitated, because explaining just how much I knew would probably only end up proving her point. And because I had remembered the message that the real killer had sent me earlier, it felt like there was an active grenade nestled in my pocket that was rapidly leaking gunpowder.

'Look, I just want you to know, Ruth...' Carlota began, her voice purposeful and steady, '... that if you ever want to talk to me about anything, anything at all, then you know where I am. You know, I'm only a phone call away.'

I watched her carefully and saw her tongue nervously trace the inside of her teeth as she hesitated, searching for the right words to say to me next, but her gaze looked like she was still staring into the vague middle distance rather than facing me direct. Was this a tactic she used with people she suspected of crimes?

'And look, if you are involved in this somehow, Ruth, then you need to know that I'm here to help. I always have been, darling,' she said earnestly. It felt like this was the first time she had actually been sincere for our whole conversation, but there was still an ever-so-slight edge to how she spoke, a cold, sharp warning to me maybe:

*You're in too deep, get out now.*

I can't tell you how close I was, right in that moment, to confessing all of my secrets to Detective Carlota. I could only imagine the sweet release and lightness of not having to keep it all to myself, to finally have someone I could confide in, to tell me how idiotic I was being and what I should do now, and to prevent Uncle Phil from having to go through the stress and anxiety of being questioned. But I knew I couldn't. I knew any chance of the TellTale Killer facing justice died the moment I opened my mouth. So I held back and kept my lips pressed tightly together as if they were a barricade holding my confession at bay, even though it felt like my whole world was spiralling quickly out of control like a Reliant Robin caught in an ice slide.

I knew she knew I was involved somehow, and she knew I knew she knew, which, frankly, was a lot for both of us to get our heads round. The thing was, I also knew that if she ever fully clocked *everything* I'd done, I'd be arrested on the spot. I knew Carlota was a stickler for rules, for procedure, so even if it meant forfeiting her best shot at catching the TellTale Killer, I felt like she wouldn't hesitate.

That being said, I knew – more than anything else in the world – she wanted to catch the TellTale Killer. Maybe almost as much as me. I often wondered whether she wanted to do it because she hungered for the justice of this vile human being, or because she wanted to recapture her glory as a police detective. Probably a bit of both.

'Thank you, Detective Carlota. I appreciate that,' was all I managed to reply.

I could see from her face, still not facing me, that that was not the answer she had been hoping for. A sigh, barely audible, escaped her lips.

'I wouldn't tell Uncle Phil about the questioning yet – best to prevent him worrying longer than he needs to.'

Then, without even saying a goodbye or even a casual 'see you later', Detective Carlota simply tightened her coat around herself and strode off across the car park, then drove away.

In another story, Detective Carlota might shine as the valiant, no-nonsense hero, the Telltale Killer would twirl his serial-killer moustache, and I'd be shoved into the morally smudged supporting slot. I'm not wild about that particular billing, but someone has to give the plot a proper kick up the backside.

The moment Detective Carlota's car disappeared from sight, the realisation hit me with the force of a freight train: the message I'd just received was still waiting for some kind of response.

I swiftly hurried back to the toilet, ready to use the burrito excuse again if anyone asked. I haphazardly locked the door shut and yanked out my phone. My fingers darted across the screen to boot up the chat again.

I knew it was reckless. I knew it was idiotic. But at this point, reckless and stupid decisions seemed to be the only ones I was making. If the TellTale Killer had really reached out to me, incensed that I was stealing his thunder, if he was foolish enough to reveal he was the true mastermind behind the murders, this was my chance, perhaps the only chance, to catch him. This was the kind of opportunity I had dreamed of for the past two years.

I couldn't encrypt my own writings on my computer, I had to do it by hand. I could almost feel my heart pulsating and vibrating in my throat as I found some paper – well, a Camborne and Sons promotional leaflet – and a pen that I had left in the pocket of my work blazer. I quickly began encrypting my response. I wasn't paying attention to the words I was forming, only the letters as the ink scribbled across the background of Uncle Phil's very profes-sional-looking headshot where I'm sure he had photoshopped some more hair onto his scalp.

'Isn't mockery the sincerest form of flattery after all?' I replied to him. 'What's next?'

It only took a few moments. I smoothed my palms over my thighs, waiting for a response, not sure whether to stay perched on the loo or risk creeping back into the office, when I felt my phone buzz with his reply.

'Just you wait.'

# TWENTY-TWO

## TWO YEARS AGO

### Greta

I heard Ruth's desperate voice calling after me as I stormed out of Sabroso, but the fury twisting and festering inside me made it impossible to turn back as I merged with the masses of crowds. The only way to stop myself from erupting was to keep moving, to keep walking further away from her.

How the hell could she have asked me that?

There I was, telling her I thought I might know who the Tell-Tale Killer was, wondering if I was going absolutely positively bonkers, and then she turns around, clearly not listening, and asks if I'd be willing to help her catch him?

She was so infuriating. I loved Ruth, God knows, I loved Ruth, but sometimes she was just *so* irritatingly unaware of what was going on around her.

And being completely honest, sometimes I did wonder: if Ruth and I met now, would we even still be friends? That happens with people, right? You get to a point where you wonder what's keeping you together other than just... consistency? And I don't think I'm a dick for saying that. Ruth was just there, blissfully wrapped up in her own little world. She had her job, she had her husband, and she had me, that was all that mattered to her. She didn't care that my life was an absolute shambles. Sometimes, it felt like all she ever thought about was herself and what directly affected her.

I had drafted an email to the Managing Director of the paper, Deborah, on my personal phone, but I hadn't sent it yet. I still couldn't be 100 per cent sure I was right after all. There was no solid evidence I could point to yet, but as I spent the rest of the day digesting and processing, comparing bits of paper to one another, I *knew*. In my gut, I *knew* who it was. I just had to find some way to prove it.

I scribbled the rest of my notes for the clandestine investigation and tucked them into Obama at page 450, probably a page he bangs on about his blissful marriage to Michelle (nice for some) then slid the book into the second drawer down in my desk at work. The book was thick enough, thanks to Obama's penchant for elaboration, that I knew the note would stay put, rather than slipping out as it might from a worn notebook. As an IT professional, I didn't trust anything digital, not in an office full of journalists whose instincts skew overwhelmingly nosy. I knew, from everyone's search histories and keystrokes, how easy it was to read minds in the paper's panopticon.

I kept storming ahead, moving out of the central hubbub of Hammersmith and into the quieter, more suburban backstreets as I approached the Thames. But after a few paces, I started to feel that something was off. When I glanced behind me, I noticed a delivery van moving slowly, trundling in my direction, never quite stopping. It's one of those things you sometimes think about, right? Am I being followed, or is my imagination just running wild? This time, I really wasn't sure. I did what I'd done so many times before: slipped my hand into my coat pocket and threaded each of my keys between the fingers of my closed fist. *Watch yourself, Greta,* I thought to myself.

To test the theory, I took a sudden left down another road. For a moment, I thought I'd lost the driver, but then, only a few steps down this new street, I heard the distinct, low rumble of the delivery van again. I kept walking, trying not to panic. *Keep calm*, I told myself, *keep calm and think of some way out of this.* That was when I heard the engine rev sharply, and the vehicle suddenly shot past me. I leaped out of the way, stumbling and then falling into a narrow passageway, my green coat catching on a piece of wire and tearing a huge shred of it off. Before I had a moment to get my bearings, the van screeched to a halt ahead, then began reversing towards me with alarming speed, mounting the kerb to block me into a small little alley.

'Hey, dickhead! Watch where you're going!' I shouted as it rolled past me. I shouldn't have said that, antagonising someone I suspected of following me was certainly not the brightest idea, but in that moment, I was positively furious that his uber-aggressive driving had just ripped my favourite coat.

But then the van stopped again. The movements this time were more deliberate, more calculated, as before I could really register it, it shifted aggressively and swiftly to block off the entrance to the alley entirely, scraping the already scratched side of the van in the process with a metallic screech. I looked behind me and realised there was a thick barrier of barbed wire. Without even knowing it, I'd been herded, corralled into the exact spot he wanted me in.

That's when the man stepped out of the van. I recognised him instantly, despite his unusual attire. He wore a high-vis vest, a cap, and a dark uniform. I must have passed a dozen people dressed like that in London every day, couriers, drivers, hidden in plain sight. So, that was how the TellTale Killer worked. How no one seemed to have ever been able to track him.

He'd tracked me, though. He must have known I was onto him. From the moment I'd left the office, he must have found a way to keep watching me, then wait until I was alone to strike.

I froze, just for a second, then turned to run. At the far end of the alley, I glanced again at the barbed wire stretched across the top of a gate. I could get over it if my life depended on it, I knew I could, and if I had to resort to physical violence, I knew I would have enough strength and speed to rip the keys across his face. I knew I could make it out of this, I just had to think fast and be smart.

That was when he called out.

'If you run, I'll just go back and take your friend instead.'

My feet refused to move, even though every cell, every fibre in my body was screaming at me to run as fast as I possibly could.

'She doesn't know anything,' I said, not daring to turn my body around to face him. 'I haven't told her shit.'

'Doesn't matter,' he replied. 'You can save her life if you do what I tell you.'

'What do you want from me?'

'Get in the van.'

# TWENTY-THREE
## PRESENT DAY

### Ruth

A sharp blade of dread slid into my chest as the reporter mentioned, for the fourth time this hour, the TellTale Killer's next victim. I had been trying my hardest to ignore the rather grainy news broadcast on the bulky 2005-era TV in the hospital room, focusing instead on digesting the contents of my book about 1840s cryptography. But whether it was because the book was mind-numbingly dull or because of the TV's subject matter, I found the morose news segment impossible to resist.

It had happened at a nightclub yesterday evening, according to a presenter with an infuriatingly nasal voice. It had been Cheesy Tunes Tuesday when someone had handed a thick wooden box to one of the staff members, claiming they had seen some guy leave it on one of the club tables before slipping quietly out the back door. The staff member, probably imagining it was some kind of class A narcotic pick 'n' mix they'd had the good fortune to inherit, took the box to the back of the staff area, opened it, saw that the contents was not a mound of off-brand ecstasy, and immediately called the police. The Eighties jukebox marathon that had all the middle-aged women screaming ABBA lyrics like it was 1989 until their throats were hoarse came to a screeching and abrupt halt when they realised that the TellTale Killer had struck again.

The police arrived swiftly, but the press weren't far behind. Within minutes, it was all the news was reporting on, and the DarkCell forums were ablaze yet again with speculation of what this could mean for the case and who the dissected heart might belong to. Even some newbies had stumbled onto the site and were suggesting their own theories on who could be behind this.

CerealKillerCornflakes had messaged me again. His tone was the same old brand of mildly superior, possibly flirtatious, but I didn't have the strength to tell him he had the brain of a koala and so I let him perform an offended monologue about how clever and intelligent he was.

Unbeknownst to them all, this was the first public kill of the real, authentic, one-of-a-kind TellTale Killer. He was on the first leg of his comeback tour. Had my actions precipitated this? Had I coaxed him back? I felt sick to my stomach as the thought that someone had died because of what I did. As Detective Carlota had said herself, copycats make serial killers feel emboldened – and now, as if trying to show how the real pro does it, he had taken another life. Another innocent victim who I knew would mean absolutely nothing to him. But I knew; I knew it meant another Greta, another devastating heartbreak for all the people who had known who they were.

And this callous killer had messaged me; he believed that I was like him – a fellow traveller whose mind operated on an entirely different plane of rules, morals and values. And could I say that he was entirely wrong? I didn't seem at all to be like anyone else.

I kept returning to and then pushing away the thought of going to Detective Carlota, the idea of confessing everything about the mess I'd landed myself in, and asking for her help so no one else would get hurt. But after the stunt she was pulling with Uncle Phil, I wasn't sure I could trust her anymore. In fact, I didn't trust any of the police to handle this without botching it up and letting the TellTale Killer slip through their fingers again.

I had to face facts: I hadn't just cocked up, I'd orchestrated a full-scale, award-winning, catastrophic disaster. It was me, me who had lured the TellTale Killer back. I was at that special point where mistakes stop being personal and become historical events.

Which is why I decided to message him again.

I know, I know, you're probably screaming at me right now, asking why on earth I'd do that. But I just knew I had to. It was like having that one guy at uni you didn't even like, but still sent out a few feelers to just to keep him as a backup option for grad ball, making sure he didn't lose interest completely. I kept telling myself I would go to the police eventually, but they were a machete where a scalpel – ironically – was needed, something with a touch of moral flexibility. In time, I told myself yet again, the ends would justify the rather disturbing means I was using. I truly believed, in my heart of hearts, I had the best chance of catching him.

'How did you choose this one?' was the reply I eventually went with. I didn't want to come across as overly saccharine; I figured bluntness with a drop of curiosity might work better.

He still hadn't responded, but I hoped he would. I just needed him to let his guard down, to trust me just enough to let me in.

'For the love of God, Ruth, turn that shit off,' Ben said, yanking me out of yet another deep-swirling, all-absorbing vortex of thoughts. I wasn't sure what he was referring to at first, but then I saw him jabbing a finger towards that old television unit in the corner of the room, the nasal-voiced presenter clearly didn't find his own voice frankly as nettlesome as we did.

'They make it sound like it's not actually real people being killed. All they do, all day long, is talk about this disgusting cretin like it's celebrity gossip,' Ben said cantankerously. 'I bet we're missing some major news as well, Wetherspoons might have started a political party, China could be invading Taiwan, Claudia Winkleman might become prime minister and we'd never know. All they're interested in is a murderer,' he grumbled before spluttering a cough. 'Blockheads,' he managed to say through a series of throaty hacks and expectorates. Maybe he was right about the tumour changing his personality; it was like he had accelerated into a grumpy old codger in only a matter of days.

I glanced around for the remote and watched Ben's face shift from anger to a kind of invigorated determination. He hauled himself upright, gripping the IV stand for balance, and padded carefully across the hospital floor in his bright red compression socks. I'd warned him to take it easy multiple times over the past ninety minutes, but he'd brushed me off every time, saying whatever pre-chemo medication they'd administered had given him a sudden buzz of energy. I wondered if he truly hated the news presenting style or if he was causing such a fuss to protect me in some way from having to hear about the TellTale Killer. While he may not have known how deeply I'd gotten myself mixed up in this, he knew listening to this wouldn't exactly be soothing for my soul.

I had tried to reach out to Chlo with an apology, hoping she'd reply so we could talk about anything – even the price of a Tesco Meal Deal – to try and take my mind off things, but she didn't respond. I told myself she might have missed it, though I suspected a quiet friend break-up, it had been almost a week since our double date.

After a few laps of the hospital room to try and get some feeling back into his legs, Ben shuffled back to his chair and quietly pulled what looked like a small glass bottle out of his blazer pocket.

'Is that whisky?' I asked, astonished.

Ben pressed a finger to his lips as he poured a small measure into his plastic hospital cup and took a sip.

'I read somewhere it helps with chemo, so I make sure I never leave the house without it now. I'm just glad Bill has so much, he'd never notice a missing bottle.'

I scoffed at his brazen nonchalance but couldn't help the scowl that came with realising he wasn't taking his treatment half as seriously as he should.

Not only was I dealing with the grief and trauma of watching someone I loved endure a terminal illness, but I also had Ben with an overly forced cheerfulness informing me that chemo had turned his wee a bright neon colour, 'like blue Lucozade shooting out of my dick' as he so eloquently put it. Which, frankly, was not information I needed in my life.

'Just don't let Bill see, I think he'd hit the roof if he knew you were drinking during chemo,' I said, trying to hold back an exasperated guffaw.

'You know he wants to get married,' Ben said, just as I'd finally willed myself back to focus on the most boring book ever written rather than lecture him on safe alcohol consumption.

'Oh, wow,' I replied, caught a little off kilter by how casually he'd dropped that bombshell onto his ex-wife. 'I mean, congratulations? I guess.'

'I don't want to get married,' he grumbled curtly to me in response.

'Oh,' I said, feeling a bit perplexed again but trying to sound sincere in my response. 'Then... good choice? Well done? Congratulations, again? I mean, I don't know the right response here.'

'It's just...' His gaze drifted to the IV as he fiddled with the drip, stopping when the nurse glanced over and shot him a scornful look as if he'd been caught with his hands down his pants. 'We always said we'd never get married, that I'd done it already, and it wasn't us. And now, out of nowhere, Bill is saying he wants to go out and buy engagement rings. Like, I know he's going just as crazy as I am, but he must know he doesn't need a ring on his finger to get my life insurance payout. He's already pencilled in.'

I wasn't sure whether to laugh or not at that comment, so I just gave his knee a light, comforting pat.

'It's like he's trying to cram a lifetime's worth of relationship into what little time we've got left, Ruth. It's exhausting, frankly. He's been talking about going to an all-inclusive in Cancun, about following AC/DC on tour, asked if I'd like to go bungee jumping. I'm afraid of heights!' he exclaimed. 'The man's gone insane. I don't think I'd do any of those things even if I lived to ninety.'

God, death really does make us all a bit loopy.

'How are you feeling about the whole treatment process? It can't be easy,' I asked him. In that moment, I wasn't thinking about the TellTale Killer or the tangle of emotions I was wrestling with; I was thinking only of the man I'd known for so long, trying to come to terms with the multitude of cancer cells swirling poisonously around his brain. He spoke about it only with a kind of artificial optimism that anyone who knew him well could see was a deflection.

He didn't respond to me at first. He just sat there, still and quiet, mulling things over like he wasn't entirely sure himself.

'I've been thinking about what to have as an epitaph,' Ben said eventually, yet again, skirting the question. 'I quite like, "£100 buried here, yours if you dig deep enough."'

'Oh, stop,' I said, rolling my eyes, not even dignifying that with a forced laugh this time. I wasn't about to point out that there wasn't much sense in spending too much time on finding the right words for his headstone. It wasn't like he'd ever get the joy of reading it himself.

'I've started planning a funeral, though, got some ideas that I'll run by you at some point,' he remarked; interesting conversational pivot. But no, before you ask, unfortunately Camborne and Sons didn't offer mates' rates.

'It's just to make things easier for everyone else, really,' Ben continued. 'Do you have thoughts on burial or cremation? Which one is cheaper?'

'I don't really think it matters in all honesty, Ben,' I said, sounding more morose than I'd intended. But it was how I felt, nothing lasts forever, right? So, what's the point in caring about a leaving do you can't even enjoy. It was like what Greta told me on the day she died, what was the word? Wabi-sabi? A whole concept about accepting that things aren't permanent, everything will at some point, wither and die.

'I think I've realised, strangely, that it's not death that scares me most,' Ben posited.

'What is it, then?' I asked when he didn't follow up immediately to his own trail of thought.

'It's, I guess, things being unfinished. You always think you have time and that everything will work itself out in the end. But like Dad, am I going to have to finally be the one to reach out and patch things up?'

Yeah, so this was a sore topic. Ben's dad wasn't exactly tolerant. If I was trying to excuse him, I would simply say 'he's just of that generation' but I don't really think that is an excuse. He actually liked me quite a lot, which was nice, but Ben cheating on me with a man sort of annihilated their already strained relationship.

'More than anything, I just wish I had more time,' Ben murmured. 'Time to leave my mark, time to do something of note... time not to be forgotten.'

'I don't think you're ever going to be forgotten, Ben,' I reassured him. 'I think I'm going to think about you every day for the rest of my life.'

I let the tiniest smile slip onto my face.

'Hey, that's your mark,' I continued, holding back a laugh. 'You've really messed me up over the years. I mean, look at me, I'm going to continue to be a real grief-stricken old lady from the husband that cheated on her.'

Ben returned the smile, though his a little ashamed, as his gaze wondered around the room.

'I suppose that's grief, though, isn't it? To love someone is to accept the absolute, unequivocal, complete and utter certainty of heartbreak,' he mused. 'That's the price we have to pay.'

'Where did you hear that, in a TED Talk?'

'No, *Woman's Hour* on Radio 4.'

Before I could respond, out of the corner of my eye I spotted Bill through the window next to us, wandering aimlessly through the hospital corridor, looking suitably harried. I raised my hand to try and get his attention, but his head spun away from me simultaneously, and he began traipsing down the corridor in completely the wrong direction.

'Just a second,' I said to Ben, as I could see he was beginning to feel a little pained again. I hopped to my feet, walked out into the coolly lit corridor and called out Bill's name just as he was about to wander obliviously into the gynaecology unit. He turned to the sound of his name and, still looking bedraggled but a little relieved, half jogged back towards me.

'Sorry I'm late. It's just been... a day. How's he doing?' Bill asked, the hospital lighting making the sparkly beads of sweat glow on his forehead.

'He's okay, a bit crabby, so brace yourself,' I said, smacking him on his arm like a Sarina Wiegman to Chloe Kelly going on at eighty-nine minutes. 'How was work?'

'Urgh,' was all Bill responded as I noticed him tenderly touch the blistering red wounds etched onto his knuckles. Stripper? No, I didn't put much credence into that theory anymore. Maybe he was secretly a bouncer at a club?

'Thank you, Ruth. I'll take it from here,' he said.

He stepped into the room with a long exhale where he greeted Ben, whose face visibly lit up at the sight of him, with a tender kiss on the lips.

There was a very active part of me still emotionally processing Ben's diagnosis. I really should have hated him, Greta would have, if she were alive to find out what he'd done to me two years ago. When she discovered her few-months boyfriend was two-timing, she waited till he nodded off, logged in to his beloved Xbox, and fired off enough creative abuse to earn him a lifetime ban from the game he'd sunk a year of playtime into. She could certainly hold a grudge and act on it too.

But with Ben, I couldn't bring myself to hate him. Like Greta, I wanted to find a way to avenge him, to do something to spite death, to stick two fingers up and blow a raspberry at the Grim Reaper.

But what could I do, really?

I probably stared at them too long, forlornly looking at the way Ben's face broke into a warm smile at the sight of Bill. I might have continued staring, going well into creepy territory, if the buzz from my phone hadn't shaken me out of my trance.

Every time my phone vibrated with a notification over the past day or so, I'd panicked – convinced it was *him* messaging again – only to feel a wave of relief when it turned out to be the Duolingo owl, berating me and threatening to stomp my legs if I didn't learn French as I'd promised three years ago. But this time, as I checked the notification, that same sickening, gut-twisting dread returned. It was an email from DarkCell, notifying me that *he* had replied.

I couldn't bear to wait a moment longer. With a sinking feeling, heart hammering, my hands shook as I opened the DarkCell message, dreading what I'd find.

It was another photo. But it wasn't a photo of some letters scrawled in ink on any kind of parchment. It looked like it was written on...

My throat immediately began to tighten like the killer's grip itself was around it. I instinctively swivelled my head, trying to control my stomach convulsions as I scanned the corridor for the nearest toilet. As my belly churned and gurgled with rising pressure, I sprinted as fast as my short, non-marathon trained legs would carry me. I managed to spot the women's loo sign, pushed through the door, flung open the first vacant cubicle I saw and collapsed over the bowl, emptying the contents of my stomach with my phone still firmly gripped in my hand.

'At least you got it in the bowl,' I heard the cleaner in the next cubicle say, flat and weary.

I'll spare you the details, but after my stomach had expelled its last contents, I slumped back against the separator, trying to muster the resilience to look at the photos again. If I had a chance to save someone this time, I didn't want to hesitate. My hand trembled and shivered as I opened the website and forced myself to look at what he had sent.

The photos were grainy and dark, like severely deteriorated and bleached Polaroids that had been lost to time. It took my eyes a moment to decipher the actual subject. His message to me looked like he had hastily carved what resembled numbers into the flesh of a corpse, the same corpse, I imagine, he had just extracted a heart from and deposited at the nightclub last night. Had he killed someone just to get to me, or maybe impress me? I didn't have a clue.

12, 1691, 176, 31, 328, 421, 112

As I wiped my sleeve over my mouth, I realised there was no justifying myself as a victim, this was entirely my fault. I was completely accountable for my actions, and now, of all things, I had a serial killer – one whose voice from two years ago never seemed to leave my mind – messaging me directly. Me. Ruth Watkins, who worked at a funeral directors and owned a horny tortoise called Toast, was being messaged by the chap who everyone in the UK was talking about. And I felt powerless to stop his weird murderous crusade. Deep shit achieved. Deeper shit imminent.

Thing is, I didn't even tell you what he wrote in the box with the heart they found at the nightclub.

*I felt the thrill awaken once more,*
*and knew I would never rest again.*

As I sat over the toilet bowl, wiping the drool and vomit from my mouth, the shock and disgust began to ebb away. Something stronger took their place. I'd wanted the TellTale Killer brought to justice for two years, but now it felt as if someone had dropped fresh rage-fuelled batteries onto my spine like a very dishevelled and depressed Duracell bunny. I could mope around or I could do something. If it was the only thing I did with the rest of my life, I was going to bring this fucker down.

I was going to make him regret ever coming back.

# TWENTY-FOUR

I walked to the Tube station from the hospital thinking about the numbers. I stood on the train still thinking about the numbers, even when I got back home and squatted down on the loo, I couldn't stop thinking about the numbers. Unfortunately, whether it was the nerves or the adrenaline, my digestive system remained on strike. I felt like a tube of toothpaste with the cap superglued on. So while I sat there, I scribbled them out on the notepad resting on my thigh again and again, hoping for some kind of miraculous epiphany where I would see how it all made sense and fit together, but nada.

It wasn't like they referenced any kind of significant date I knew of, and they weren't in the right format to be coordinates. I'd tried working out whether there was some mathematical significance to them, adding, subtracting and dividing them, but still no real meaning came from my thorough analysis. Desperation led me to yank my doorstop Poe collection off the shelf and flick through each page. I had hoped the code might be some obscure connection to his writings or even a hint to page numbers or something like that. But that was a dead end too. Besides, how would the TellTale Killer know which collection of Poe I owned? I wondered if even old Edgar himself would be stumped by this one.

When I got really, *really* desperate, I asked a handful of AI models, but none of them churned up anything useful. As a last-ditch effort, I tossed the notepad in with Toast, hoping – rather absurdly – that she was actually some kind of genius tortoise who'd decrypt it like one of those dogs that 'talk' by pressing buttons. But no. You know what she did to it. I don't even need to tell you what she did.

The killer's behaviour was textbook serial-killer psychology: an insatiable need for control, intellectual superiority and attention in the form of power-play. He couldn't simply instruct me; he had the emotional maturity of a petulant fourteen year old running his first Dungeons & Dragons session. More than anything, I knew he would be savouring the sadistic thrill of secondary victimisation; it was a classic trait of serial killers that I had read about again and again in my research.

I zoomed in and studied the images as much as my phone allowed, but I didn't dare upload them to any third-party software for further enhancement. The amount I zoomed and examined was enough anyway. The more I could see the sickening traces of the TellTale Killer's handiwork, the more I wanted to sob and crawl up in a ball thinking he had done something like this to Greta.

You know when ladybirds feel threatened, they crawl into a ball, play dead and bleed from their knees to ward off predators. I kind of wished I could do that about now.

The only thing I had managed to pick up on from the photo was that the victim was male, probably early twenties and had a poorly drawn orangutan tattoo on his leg, splotchy and rugged, and an attempt at minimalism. I did hope that whoever this was had managed to get some kind of discount on that one when he'd seen the finished result. It was such an awful drawing that any attempt to track down the original artist would be futile; who would admit to producing that visual monstrosity?

I spent the next few hours thinking obsessively about the puzzle the TellTale Killer had sent me. The harder I thought, the stronger my urge grew to tear the shed apart in sheer panic and frustration. I couldn't let someone else die.

After a while, I somehow finally slipped into a deep, fugue-like sleep, my notebook acting as my pillow, when my phone rang and jolted me awake. I blinked at the caller ID: Chlo. Chlo?

I answered, confused and half expecting her to now officially verbalise the end of our friendship there and then, listing my failings and what an awful friend I'd been. After the double-date debacle, I hadn't expected to hear from her again, so the call itself made me feel even more disorientated.

'Hi, Chlo?'

'Hello Ruthie, I'm back,' Chlo replied in her usual upbeat tone, no trace of resentment or underlying anger. 'I'll be there in twenty minutes. So, get ready to go and we can catch up then, okay?'

I was confused. Completely baffled, actually. I had no idea what I was meant to be getting ready for – that was until I checked the calendar on my phone and realised we had booked ourselves in to see Aleks months ago. It was an excruciating sinking feeling I could sense in my stomach at realising this was quite possibly the worst possible timing, maybe only matched by your manager asking you if you were free for a 'quick chat'.

'Okay, great. See you soon,' I chirruped, matching her helium-high pitch. Why on earth hadn't I cancelled this? I didn't have time for social calls, I needed to work out what these numbers meant.

Chlo's breezy 'everything's fine' vibe had scrambled my wits; a sudden bout of flu, food-poisoning from a bucket of mussels, Toast needing a haircut would be a better excuse than agreeing to go and see Aleks on a Thursday morning.

Then again, perhaps agreeing to the plans I made a few months ago wasn't entirely foolish. I'd stared at those numbers so long they'd begun to waltz across my phone and onto the wall, and I hoped a brief diversion might carve out a tiny sliver of clarity.

CerealKillerCornflakes and I had shared some truly questionable content with one another over the last year or so, bonded by our mutual strange mix of obsession and revulsion when it came to serial killers. I knew he wouldn't think I was completely unhinged for messaging him this, and I was grateful for the anonymity we'd maintained over our conversations. I just desperately hoped he'd be able to make some sense of what the TellTale Killer had sent me.

*Did you do this?* was the first thing he sent after I forwarded the images with plenty of warnings and asked if he could try and decode what they meant.

*No*, I replied, adding that the puzzle had come via the forum from an anonymous poster; technically true, if not the whole truth. I suspected CerealKillerCornflakes' skull might detonate if he learned the sender was the genuine TellTale Killer.

He went silent for a few minutes; I pictured him weighing up how he could grass me up to the police. Then his reply pinged back:

*What happens if I work it out?*

*I'll tell you that you're a very good boy.*

*Woof Woof.*

*NOO!* I replied back.

It pained me to admit it, but perhaps through some subtle nuance in our messages, CerealKillerCornflakes had proved more perceptive than I gave him credit for, maybe correctly assuming that StabithaChristie was a woman.

I could feel the knots in my stomach writhing and tightening as I counted down the minutes until Chlo's arrival. My mind had become such a tangled circus of chaos over the past few days that I could no longer separate my mild anxieties from the major, world-ending ones. When I saw her pull up to the house and get out of the car, I noticed right away that something about her looked different. Her skin had a remarkable warm glow, though it took me a moment to figure out why. There were a few spotty patches of bright red on her fair skin, but for the most part she looked like she'd been beautifully sun-kissed. Clocking me from the open front door of the house, she charged across the pavement and wrapped me in her bronzed arms, squeezing all the oxygen out of my body.

'Oh, Ruthie, Ruthie, Ruthie, I'm so sorry! I'm so, so sorry,' she said affectionately and effusively as she held me extraordinarily tight.

'It's fine, Chlo, honestly,' I replied, trying to pry myself free from her iron grip. 'I understand you were mad at me. I'd be mad at me too. I get it.'

'What? Ruth, I'm not mad,' Chlo said, confused, squinting her eyes and shaking her head bemusedly at me. 'I just had no data and didn't want to pay those frankly extortionate overseas roaming charges. Oscar surprised me out of nowhere and asked me to come with him to Florida on a business trip for four days. Did you know it's thirty-four degrees there in January? In January, Ruthie.'

'Wait, what?' I said, trying to undigest what I had swallowed as a cold, hard truth over the past week. 'So, you weren't cross with me? Chlo, I thought you were friend-breaking up with me?'

'No, Ruth. Why would I be cross at you?'

'Well, I just thought I messed everything up with that Nico guy the other night...'

'I mean, I was annoyed, Ruth, don't get me wrong. But I understand. You're an absolute weirdo and I kind of love that about you. There's nothing you could do that would stop me from being your friend.'

God, I really loved Chlo. I take back every bad word I had ever said about her. Maybe, just maybe, I wasn't as completely alone as I felt.

'Okay, right. I want to get it out of the way first, then we don't have to talk about it,' Chlo said as we entered her bright pink Mini Cooper and began to chug down the road. 'The TellTale Killer, it came up on my phone the moment I touched down. How are you feeling?' Chlo asked, rather blunt for her but still with a level of delicacy.

'Terrified,' I replied simply and truthfully. 'But not ready to talk about it just yet.' I feared what I might let slip to her.

Accepting that for now, she shifted the subject to her new beau: Oscar. She told me how his job in finance had scored them a trip to Jacksonville in Florida and recounted every detail of their trip, from their impromptu visit to Disneyworld to Chlo popping her cherry on business-class flights.

'I had three wines, Ruth, three. Like, who even am I?' she said with a mock fluster. 'And I could recline an extra ten degrees more than the peasants in premium economy.'

It seemed that thirty thousand feet up in the air, her class consciousness evaporated; I remember when Chlo had stuffed knickers into her coat pockets to dodge the baggage fee for our Ryanair flight.

'I don't even want to ask this, but... do you think the heart is still in the freezer?' Chlo asked, a little way into our drive. The glance she shot me with the question was one that crackled with unease and apprehension.

'Chlo, he hasn't touched a single thing in Greta's childhood bedroom for two years. What makes you think the heart would be anywhere other than the freezer?'

She flinched, clearly forcing the thought aside so she could keep her eyes on the road. As you'll remember, we never retrieved Greta's body, it was only her heart that the TellTale Killer left behind. Greta's heart had been considered primary forensic evidence at the time, but the investigators had extracted every possible trace – DNA, fibres, residues – before finally releasing it to the family in an act of good faith. Most of the other families had chosen to leave what was left of their loved ones in police custody, clinging to the hope that one day technology might unmask the TellTale Killer. But Aleks had made such a relentless fuss that, in the end, they gave it back to him. I pictured it in its cold resting place, unsettlingly close to the jacket potatoes. I had given up finding the rest of Greta's body a long time ago but I think Aleks lived in the liminal space between keeping Greta nearby and wanting to move on.

It wasn't that Aleks wasn't a nice man. He'd always been a quiet, but generally friendly enough chap ever since we had been kids. Chlo had kept in touch with him over the years, stopping by whenever she could to check in on him, but I felt like I never had the strength or maybe the courage to. Seeing Aleks seemed to physically hurt me in a way I've never quite been able to describe. I had heard of grief physically and emotionally breaking people, forcing them into a shape that was unrecognisable, but I'd never witnessed it firsthand until Aleks.

At first, when Greta died, the man simply shut down. He stopped working, stopped eating; the garden he had once doted on lovingly was abandoned to wither. Even the cherry blossom trees that had bloomed and dazzled every single spring since Greta and I were young had shrivelled and wilted. I can't begin to fathom the agony of losing a child. Whenever I saw him, my own sorrow felt almost inconsequential beside his. Maybe that's why I never wanted to see him, I didn't want my grief to feel like it should be lesser than his.

We pulled up to his house, Chlo did an excellent job of parallel parking on the street which I complimented her on, and I begrudgingly got out of the car. As a somewhat united front, we tentatively approached the door.

'You knock,' Chlo muttered, nudging me with her elbow.

'What? Why me?' I cried.

'Because I drove. So, you have to be the one to knock.'

Groaning, and feeling like we had regressed twenty years, I stepped forward and rapped three firm knocks on the door. A moment later Aleks's frail, but stronger than I remembered, silhouette shuffled into view. I hadn't seen him since the one-year anniversary memorial thirteen months ago, and he seemed marginally improved, slightly less gaunt, a hint more colour in his cheeks. Even so, he remained chalk-pale, especially compared to Chlo's Floridian terracotta glow. Is it polite to say he looked far less ghostly?

'Hello, Chloe. Hello, Ruth,' he greeted us timidly as he fiddled with his glasses, performing what seemed to be the closest thing to a smile he could manage.

Chlo was instantly effusive, stepping forward and wrapping him in one of her suffocating signature hugs until I worried he might simply crack and shatter in her arms. Although, it looked like he almost needed that hug. In fact, I think he probably liked it by the way that his hands hesitated at first, hovering in the air before they went to lay on her back. I would hazard a guess that he didn't get hugged much anymore.

He ushered us into the living room, which had been slightly redecorated since we were last here, and offered us tea or coffee, both already prepared in a pot and cafetière respectively, along with an array of quintessentially British biscuits laid out on a plate. I politely nibbled on a custard cream while glancing angrily at some of the other biscuits that had the gall to be on the plate with such legends, particularly Garibaldis, or 'squashed flies' as Greta used to call them.

I looked across the newly repainted living room wall, and my eyes instantly clocked the photos of Greta and me as children, then later as teenagers with Chlo, when she had joined the school in Year 9, and added to our duo. I remember how Greta and I had practically yanked her away from the popular clique to join our small two-person motley crew. I don't know why, but remembering Greta as a child always seemed to break me the most.

There were new photos on the wall now, ones I hadn't seen before, which I guessed he had added sometime over the past year. I took a moment to stare at a new one of us at the beach, both caught mid-conversation as we daintily dipped our toes into the lapping ocean at Newquay. I wondered what benign nonsense had we been talking about; from my reckoning, we must have only been about twelve.

Maybe that was another reason I dreaded setting foot in Greta's dad's house: it somehow crystallised the grief for me. Most days it hovered over me like a private rain cloud, heavy and unseen by anyone else, yet here it turned into a steam locomotive, thundering straight at me while I lay hogtied to the tracks.

We asked how Aleks had been. He said that all in all, he was okay, mentioning that Greta's brother had just got engaged and moved in across the street with his fiancée, though he murmured he suspected they had only done so somewhat begrudgingly just to keep an eye on him.

'When we heard the TellTale Killer was back, we knew it would bring up some horrible feelings for you. I'm so sorry,' Chlo said, with an impressive amount of grace and decorum mustered.

'It's okay,' Aleks said, offering another frail and feeble smile, one that made it painfully clear he was certainly not okay. 'It was nasty seeing the news talking about it again. You know, I think that was one of the worst parts about losing Greta... the way they wouldn't stop talking about her for days on end, like they suddenly knew every little detail about my Greta, like they were almost trying to find some way to blame her, and then, suddenly, out of nowhere, they just stopped caring about her. It was like she vanished from the world the moment people lost interest in their televisions. Everyone remembers the TellTale Killer but no one can even remember my Greta's name.'

I remembered feeling such rage when I saw what they'd done. They'd used a lovely, natural photo of Greta on the beach to announce her death... and then they'd photoshopped it: carved her a stronger jawline, sharpened her eyes, puffed up her hair. I couldn't even find the words. Why had they done that? If they made her more aesthetically pleasing to the public, then it would make her loss feel like more of a tragedy?

'But I think it could be a good thing that he's back,' I said with a half mumble, half stutter, not totally sure how I was going to articulate the chaotic collection of thoughts in my brain. 'Now he's resurfaced the police might finally throw everything they've got at him, that's what I'm banking on. Maybe this time we'll see him behind bars.'

Aleks gave a faint, indulgent smile and shrugged.

'But none of this will ever bring Greta back.'

After a little while of talking, Chlo took Aleks off to lay some fresh flowers at Greta's empty grave. I was told she had a lovely spot at St Michael's. It was a small cemetery, tacked onto the edge of a beautiful park, perched just on the hill above it. I didn't believe in all that afterlife nonsense as you know, but Chlo had told me she liked the idea that Greta could look out over the park at sunset from there.

I stayed behind, obviously. I didn't have the nerve to go to her pseudo-grave at the best of times, let alone today.

As soon as they left, I found myself mulling over what Aleks had said. He was right, none of what I was doing would bring Greta back. Maybe, in some strange way, that's what I had been hoping for all along; that catching the killer would make my grief and guilt magically disappear or maybe even more deludedly, it would miraculously bring Greta back just as suddenly as she disappeared from my life.

I knew Aleks wouldn't mind if I took a small peek in Greta's room. Gently, I pushed open the door covered with old crayon still etched onto it. It was impeccably tidy, her clothes neatly folded away in drawers, her concert ticket stubs still lined up on one of the shelves.

I'd heard that when parents lose a child, they often don't change their room at all – as if clinging desperately to the delusion that their kid was just out for the moment and would come scooting back through the door, demanding to know what was for dinner any second now. But Greta had moved out of Aleks's place a long time ago, so her room sat in that awkward, transitory state: not quite a guest bedroom, not quite Greta's anymore either – a space caught between being kept for her and quietly moving on without her.

She'd be proud of Chlo for keeping such a close eye on her dad. He still had his son, but he'd lost his wife and then his daughter, no one deserved to be dealt cards that cruel. I doubted Greta would be as proud of me.

I smiled faintly when I saw her rather vast array of stuffed toys, looking like they had been painstakingly kept clean and dustless. I remembered playing with them when we were at primary school, making up long, melodramatic soap opera storylines where Arthur the Pig cheated on Edmund the Orangutan in a scandalous affair with Millicent the Ladybird who was in a poly relationship, of course, with a brick we found in the garden. Most kids could be possessive about their toys, but I remember Greta always had no real problem with sharing them with me. Even as we grew up, she was never possessive of anything, she had always just treated me as one of the family.

I remembered how we'd spoken about reincarnation that night at Sabroso, how she'd mentioned ladybirds; what were they called in Dutch again? 'The Lord's most beautiful creature', or something like that?

I remembered, too, helping Ben with some of the general maintenance of the garden around the shed, when he told me that ladybirds really punch above their weight in the ecosystem. They don't live long comparatively, but they do a lot of good for the environment as a form of natural pest control in a short amount of time.

I looked over the other belongings in Greta's room. I glanced at the globe where we had dreamt about travelling the world together, the posters of One Direction we had fawned over, but nevertheless found myself drawn to her bookcase. And there he was, sitting on the top row: Obama.

I picked up her copy of *A Promised Land* and smirked to myself, remembering all the times I'd teased her about her crazed obsession for the slightly self-indulgent autobiography. I took the hardback from its place on the shelf and smoothed my hand over it. I'd never fully understood the love for Obama, if I'm honest, but for whatever reason, he had always been one of Greta's favourites. Maybe she crushed on him but just couldn't ever admit it to me.

I tucked it under my arm, wondering if I could ask Aleks if I could take it home. It was then that my eyes began to drift to, of all things in Greta's room, the orangutan, and I couldn't help but think of that terrible tattoo from the photos that were still traumatically seared into the hardwire of my brain. There's an old Poe story, 'The Murders in the Rue Morgue' – not one of his best, in my opinion – where the witty detective, C. Auguste Dupin, investigates a grisly double homicide in Paris, only to discover that the murderer – of all things – is an escaped orangutan. A ridiculously stupid plot device for a crime story, but the critics and scholars seemed to lap that up like it was genius. What they were smoking almost two hundred years ago I have no idea. Could you imagine if it turned out the TellTale Killer was actually a baboon? Give me a break.

Then it all began to click: perhaps the 'tattoo' wasn't permanent at all but a slapdash sketch, an ink-marker clue the killer had left, his very own Banksy. It would explain the wonky and horrendous artistry of the drawing. Of course, he wouldn't just fling random numbers my way; there'd be some kind of logic, some twisted clue to make it look like a fair game. The numbers couldn't be page references, the story was too short, but word counts? That might just be it.

I pulled my phone from my pocket and began typing a message to CerealKillerCornflakes.

*It's an alphanumeric cipher, I'm sure of it. Can you cross-reference it with the word placement in The Murders in the Rue Morgue?*

He replied a few moments later: *One step ahead of you. I was literally going through the text now.*

Of course he wasn't. He'd probably been just as stumped as I was, at least until I'd spotted Greta's stuffed toy, but I just know he loved to tell me 'I told you so'.

*I bet you were,* I typed back. He didn't respond, which told me everything. He was far too excited.

A few moments later, his next message came through:

*Word 12: I*
*Word 31: to*
*Word 112: me*

Each number matched its position in Poe's 'The Murders in the Rue Morgue'. Strung together, the decrypted message read:

*I want you to kill for me.*

Look, I know, I know, all of this, this whole ridiculous, shambolic mess, was my fault. I can admit that. But still, somehow, I felt responsible for solving it. For bringing the TellTale Killer to justice, as if exposing a serial murderer was my one sole purpose.

I had spent a good ten minutes sitting on the foot of Aleks's staircase, trying to process the killer's message and figure out what on earth to do next, ignoring the incessant pinging from my phone as CerealKillerCornflakes continued to message me with a subsequent barrage of questions.

So, the TellTale Killer wanted me to kill for him. How the hell was I supposed to do that? But at the same time, I couldn't exactly ghost him, I couldn't let him kill someone else, the ball was very much in my court. While he was waiting on me, maybe no one would need to die.

In his mind, I was probably his eager little acolyte, chomping at the bit to do his bidding. He was trying to enact some control. But in reality, I was there thinking how on earth was I going to fool him into thinking I was a budding serial killer, all the while evading life imprisonment?

Ultimately, I only needed him to *believe* I had killed for him. And if I did that, then I could get close enough to catch him. But how the hell was I even going to manage it? Could I steal another heart from the morgue at Camborne and Sons? No, that was completely impossible now. The bodies were no longer there for one, and even if they were, I'm sure Uncle Phil had fitted at least a dozen more security cameras around the whole vicinity over the past few days. Could I maybe fake a heart of some kind? I knew I wouldn't be able to craft something that would reassemble an actual organ. Pig hearts were supposed to be similar to human ones, could I maybe do something with that? No, even if I pulled that off, if the police got involved, they would realise it wasn't human pretty quickly and I'd lose the TellTale Killer forever. It wouldn't take long to be outed as a fraud.

No. This was my chance to finally get him. I decided I would commit now and figure out the how later. The prize hovered tantalisingly close, just beyond reach, but if I could win his trust, I'd edge one step nearer to bringing him down.

I cudgelled every thought in my brain to try and think of some kind of solution to my problem. Grave robbing? Not likely. Even if I had the stomach for it, any heart I dug up would be halfway to mulch, and cemeteries are far too exposed for a covert midnight dig. Perhaps I could lurk around a hospital morgue, pose as an organ-donation courier and swipe a spare one while the staff were distracted. That sounded even more far-fetched. The whole thing was crazy; spare human hearts are not exactly lying around waiting to be borrowed.

And then, it hit me.

There was, in fact, a spare human heart lying about twenty-five feet away from me. A human heart I could get hold of without the need to actually kill anyone.

And look, I know this is pretty horrendous, on top of a succession of horrendous things I had already done. I'm not trying to excuse myself morally at all. But if I could just do this final act, would it make everything I'd done so far worthwhile? For the past week and a half, I'd been pretending to be a serial killer for the police and the media. Now I just had to pretend to be a serial killer to an actual serial killer. How hard could that be?

And in a weird, strange, hereafter kind of way, I sort of felt that Greta would want me to, she did love to share after all.

# TWENTY-FIVE

Chlo and Aleks returned about an hour later. Aleks's face, pale and distant, showed how completely the visit to Greta's grave had emotionally drained him, and Chlo, ever sensitive to people's emotions, had clearly clocked it. She offered gentle goodbyes on our behalf, saying we would love to visit again soon but we really ought to be going.

I asked whether I could borrow Obama from Greta's bookcase. Aleks looked hesitant at first, then nodded.

'Actually, if it is all right,' he said, his voice determined as if he was pushing through any nerves he had about what he was going to ask, 'I would like to send you a few of Greta's things.'

'A few things?' I echoed his words, pausing mid-step, not totally sure what he meant.

'I have been sorting through her belongings,' he explained, voice tinged with hesitation but also some drive to it, like he had prepared himself to speak. 'I am trying to place everything where it needs to be so I can keep moving forward. Some items I just...'

He disguised his sob as a small *harrumph*.

'Some things I can't bear to throw away, but I know that she would have wanted you to have them.'

I could tell he was repeating the words of a professional who had talked through this with him.

'Of course,' Chlo and I replied in unison.

As we left, I noticed one of the cherry trees in his garden had just begun to show the first fragile blush of blossom.

He wasn't moving on, but maybe as he said, Aleks was moving forward.

We got in the car and started the drive back. Normally, we'd listen to the radio anytime Chlo and I were on a road trip, but she had clearly thought ahead, knowing the current media frenzy would only be talking about one thing, and she had already connected her playlist of atrociously awful pop songs as the background music before she had even picked me up.

'Look, you might not want to talk about this, and that's fine. Totally chill, we can just drop it,' Chlo said after a few minutes of us attempting to decompress to the sounds of some teenage pop star crooning melodically about the obscene amount of vagina he'd been exposed to. 'But... do you ever wonder who the TellTale Killer could be? Like, who is he to the people who actually know him?'

'Oh, all the time,' I responded casually. Chlo hadn't seen my crime wall since I moved to the shed. 'Because he has to be smart, like really smart to get away with what he does.'

'Right?' Chlo agreed effusively as we joined Chertsey Road. 'See, that's what freaks me out the most, it could literally be anyone. This isn't just a common thug bludgeoning people to death. It's scary when they're so smart because you know how well they can blend in.'

'It's also scary when they're not smart too,' I replied.

'That's true,' Chlo remarked resignedly.

'Thing is, a lot of serial killers are absolutely excellent at social camouflage. Harold Shipman, for example, he was trusted as a GP in his community before all of his skeletons came tumbling out of the closet. I don't think the TellTale Killer is any different, I think he's hiding right in plain sight, and he could be anyone. A top prosecution lawyer, an all-star police officer. Hell, he could be Oscar for all we know.'

I know talking about serial killers had become awfully typical and commonplace for me, but I thought Chlo may have a little laugh at that; she didn't, not even a smirk. I suppose, if she was falling head over heels for the guy who took her to Disneyland, she didn't want to think she'd awaken to him with Micky Mouse ears perched upon his head, holding a blade to her throat.

'I just don't think I can understand it...' Chlo said, half thinking aloud with me just happening to be present for her soliloquy. 'What is it that *makes* someone so awful, so horrendous? This total absence of any basic human empathy with no guilt whatsoever. I mean, people like that aren't well. Is it a bad childhood? Is it being hit on the head as a baby or something?'

'It can vary,' I murmured.

'I just think, at that point, you're not even human anymore, are you?' Chlo asked. 'You're something else, just a husk of a human. Breaking any kind of human morality is nothing to you anymore. It's... meh.'

So, two years ago, the idea of carrying Greta's cling-film-wrapped heart in my coat pocket was a thought that would be reserved for the very darkest parts of my psyche, yet here I was, doing exactly that to imitate, ironically, a serial killer. Did the fact I was doing this make me a morally devoid husk, too?

See, I was never afraid I was becoming a serial killer, I had absolutely no compulsion to kill or harm for my own hedonistic pleasure. I just worried that, like them, I didn't really constitute a human anymore. I was just something of an empty, emotionally stunted shell, isolated from the world because there was no one else really like me. What frightened me most was realising that the soul most like mine in all the world was also the one I loathed the most. Maybe we were just two lost husks of human beings.

Changing the conversation, Chlo began telling me about a swamp ride she went on in Florida with Oscar and how every year, there was an annual Mullet Toss where thousands of Floridians would stand at the state line and throw dead fish into Alabama. I didn't find that quite as interesting as she did, just sounded like collective littering.

Chlo dropped me home, along with an invitation to meet Oscar again. I agreed, though she did add a condition: no talking about serial killers. A pretty fair and reasonable ask, I felt.

'You know his friend, Nico?'

'Yeah.'

'He thought you were quite pretty, you know?'

'He did?' I responded suspiciously, I was unconvinced. 'What are you trying to say?'

Chlo's face became one big beaming smile as she lifted her hands aloft. 'All I'm saying is maybe give him a call, that's all. Maybe you didn't scare him off as much as I thought.'

It might be nice to see Nico again, he did have one of the most impressive noses I had ever seen. I'd quite like to marvel at that again, was it weird that I wanted to kiss it?

I mostly laughed her off and told her to text me when she got back safe, just as I always did. Though I knew the TellTale Killer wouldn't be operating tonight.

As I began to dawdle towards the front door, Greta's heart still nestled in my pocket, I felt Chlo's footsteps behind me, then her hand reached around, clasped mine, and pulled me backwards into a tight embrace before I even realised what was happening.

'Hey,' I croaked, meaning to come across as soothing, but I think I sounded something like a deflating broken bagpipe, as Chlo coiled round me like a ball python wrapped around its prey, unknowingly and lovingly wringing every last gasp of air from my lungs.

'I don't want you to ever think I'm cross with you,' Chlo said softly. 'I... I sometimes feel you slipping away from me, Ruthie. Slipping away from people in general. And I worry about you, *so much*.'

I didn't quite know how to respond to what she was saying, but the way she held me, close and unrelenting, told me she wasn't really expecting a reply from me. She just wanted me to know how she was feeling.

'And also...' she continued, not quite done yet. 'I miss Greta too. I miss her every day and I don't want you to think I don't. I don't want you to think I've forgotten her. I know things have been hard for you, but I'm always here.'

'Except when you don't want to pay for the data roaming costs,' I said, with a flicker of jest.

This time she laughed at my joke and nestled her chin into my shoulder.

'Sometimes I worry that you pull away from the world because you think it doesn't want you, Ruthie. But I just want you to know... I think the world needs people like you sometimes. People who see things differently to everyone else.'

Sickos? I wanted to reply. But I stayed quiet. It was nice to be held like this again, to be properly hugged. Not one of those fake pleasantries where your nipples barely graze the other person's, but to *really* feel held in someone's arms, like someone wanted to actually be near you.

Chlo left then, and I made my way to the door. Both cars were on the driveway, which meant Ben and Bill were home, probably exhausted after the chemo session that had stretched into yesterday evening.

I let myself in, brushed the dirt from my shoes and peered into the sitting room, curious about the hush that had settled over the house. At first, I saw only Bill, cradling a mug of tea, then, as I leaned a little farther, the outline of none other than Detective Carlota came into my vision. The jolt of seeing her while I had a human heart in my pocket and the TellTale Killer practically on speed dial, obliterated any chance of me registering what outfit she was wearing. So, I'm afraid I couldn't give a wardrobe report on her attire at this particular juncture. Abject dread poured through my veins.

'Hi, Ruth,' Bill said, his tone mostly indifferent rather than hostile.

Detective Carlota smiled, rose from the sofa, crossed the carpet and wrapped me in a hug before saying a word. This one was nowhere as nice as Chlo's. I flicked my coat back and returned the embrace as lightly as possible, determined not to let the defrosting organ squelch between us.

'Hi, darling. I've just come back from the funeral directors. I spent some time with Phillip and then thought I'd come to talk to you. How are you doing?' she asked – flat, but with a touch more empathy than when I last saw her.

'Great,' I said, feigning a kind of fake hyper-energetic enthusiasm, though I couldn't help but wonder what she had asked Uncle Phil, and how he had reacted. Was she getting closer to finding out I was involved? 'Really, really great,' I repeated. I could see from the way her eyes inspected me this was probably a little too much energy from me. I hadn't quite mastered that yet. I don't think I was a very good criminal.

God, poor Uncle Phil. What had she asked him, how much pressure had she put him under? Why was she here waiting for me? Had something he said incriminated me, or worse, had he incriminated himself and she was here to say he'd been arrested, to tell me as a friend? God, I hated this spiral of overthinking. My heart felt as if it couldn't stand another minute above 180 bpm, yet it kept on hammering against my chest like the drummer for Metallica was locked inside my ribs.

'I think I'm going to head up,' Bill said politely as he pushed himself out of the armchair, collected his mug, offered Detective Carlota a curt – but polite for him – goodbye and trundled his way upstairs.

'How is he?' I called after Bill before he ascended out of view.

'He's okay,' Bill replied, though his flat and dismissive tone confirmed Ben had clearly not had a good day.

Neither Detective Carlota nor I spoke a word for a little while, a deeply uncomfortable silence between us until we heard Bill's footsteps patter on the landing before hearing the bedroom door click shut, as if we were both waiting for him to be out of earshot.

'So, Ruth darling,' she said, awfully calm and measured, as if she was considering each word she spoke. 'I'm going to hazard a guess and say that I think you may have something to tell me?'

She knew? How the hell did she find out I was involved? Uncle Phil, what did he say?

It was too much. In that moment, it was all way too much. The hearts, Greta, the TellTale Killer slinking into my messages; I felt like I was completely and utterly spiralling. Lying had become an exhausting full-time job, and I was realising I simply wasn't cut out for it. How did people do it? How did they lie without being completely emotionally drained to a point where their brain resembled the remains of lumpy mashed potato.

'I did it, all right?' The words exploded out of me, far louder than I'd meant. 'Both hearts – yes, those bloody hearts – the one that turned up Saturday before last and the one I posted to you on the Friday after. They were from me. *Me!* I nicked them from the corpses in the morgue. One was Mrs Lambert – lovely skin, very soft – and the other was that Justin chap who had his eyes eaten by fish. I didn't kill anyone, though. I only wanted to give the investigation a bit of a kick up the arse, get you lot to actually catch the TellTale Killer. Only now – now, the real TellTale Killer is messaging me, he's already killed at least two more people, and I think this is all my fault and I'm absolutely losing it. I haven't slept in days, I'm constantly vibrating from raw terror, and for what it's worth, I haven't had a decent poo in four days because my intestines are clenching my whole body like a fucking fist. Not even bloody Senokot can help me. Do you know how many Senokot I've taken over the past few days? Too many! Way too many! But I need to catch him, Cis, I need to catch him before he hurts anyone else.'

Detective Carlota, usually the picture of composure, stared at me. Her expression slid from mild confusion to severe shock.

'Ruth, no... I was about to ask you about your promotion.'

Fuck.

# PART FOUR

# TWENTY-SIX

'So, is this the moment you arrest me?' I asked after there had been yet another deeply uneasy silence between us, my eyes finding their way to the barely drunk, now cold, cup of tea that Bill had got her surely well over an hour ago. I realised Bill must have been quite fond of Detective Carlota, given he'd let her use his cherished Mr Happy mug to drink from.

'Honestly, Ruth... I haven't decided,' Detective Carlota replied. She still looked a bit faint and dazed after my confession; a little broken, in all honesty. 'I'm still trying to wrap my head around this.'

At least she hadn't said yes, told me to stay put and nipped out to her car to fetch a pair of handcuffs. I considered offering her a fresh cup of tea, but even I, with my limited social skills, could tell it wasn't quite the moment. I don't think it would come across quite how I intended.

'On one hand, what you've done is spectacularly illegal, proper go-to-prison stuff,' Detective Carlota said tersely. 'On the other, if your arrest became public, I dread to think what it might do to the case. And you now have a direct line to the actual TellTale Killer. That's a bigger lead than I ever managed.' She paused after she said that, as though an internal processing error message had just flashed worryingly behind her eyes.

See, I think I knew Detective Carlota better than most. I knew she'd tortured herself every day for failing to catch the TellTale Killer and worse, that she hadn't been allowed near the case – or really any important case – since he'd become inactive two years ago. The police blamed her. She blamed herself. And now I was in touching distance of the killer... What on earth was going through her mind right now?

'So, Justin, at the funeral, the open chest... sinking in on itself... that was...?' she asked tentatively, recovering only slightly from whatever had pained her.

'Look,' I interrupted, hoping to clarify, 'that wasn't intentional. Obviously. He took a bit of a tumble on the way to the service and, well, something inside him went very wrong.' I tapped my own breastbone for emphasis rather than explain in any detail the specifics of the slightly traumatic event. 'And I do want to take this particular opportunity to apologise to you, because I know I sent the heart directly to you and that wasn't cool and I...'

Carlota interrupted me with a groan, long and low, while I still sat there like a child waking Mum at four in the morning to announce I had thrown up on the cat.

'It's fine,' she muttered. 'The moment I opened it, it was snatched off me and I was told it was for the case lead to handle. They let me investigate the funeral directors to throw me a bone, but trust me, I am still very much in the doghouse.'

Goodness me, whoever was helming the TellTale Killer case now clearly couldn't find their own arse with two hands and a map.

'When did you start suspecting me?' I asked, genuinely curious.

'Ruth, are you kidding me?' she asked, flicking her hands up, incensed, and her face rankling with red. 'From the moment a heart appeared at the police station's doorstep. You were so obviously involved.'

'What?' I said, a little bewildered. 'How did you know?'

'Because I care about you, Ruth,' Carlota said, raising her voice and emitting a sound that was like a snort and a sigh simultaneously. 'I tell you the case goes cold, and then – magically – the Tell-Tale Killer returns. Of course, the only person mad enough to do that is the person who once tried to fax me a supposed clue when I didn't answer my emails or my mobile. You really think it could have been *anyone* else?'

It was at that moment that I realised maybe I really wasn't suited for a life of crime. Clearly, I was less good at deception than I had believed.

'How was Uncle Phil?' I asked trepidatiously.

She scoffed.

'He was moaning about your aunt, of all things. I knew he'd had nothing to do with this; I just thought you might take the chance to tell me what I wanted to know. Did you really think I didn't notice how anxious and cagey you were at the morgue on Monday? You think I'm that unobservant?"

'Well, no one else seemed to notice,' I said, genuinely bewildered. I thought I had been such a good actor around her.

She slumped back into the sofa, still looking quite incredulous from what I had told her.

After a moment, she held out her hand, presumably for my phone, and I passed it over obediently; this was the woman who had *currently* decided not to arrest me after all.

However, I had to admit telling her the truth felt unexpectedly liberating. I knew prison was probably not far off the horizon now, and I wondered idly whether Uncle Phil's job offer would still be there after I had served my sentence.

'I never wanted to lie to you, Cis,' I said, hoping my tone portrayed the earnestness I genuinely felt. I thought using her first name may have more of an impact too. 'I promise I only did it because I couldn't stand the thought of Greta being forgotten.'

'I know,' Carlota said with yet another weary sigh, visibly flinching at the photograph of the numbers carved into the cadaver as she flicked through my phone. 'That was exactly what worried me.' She dragged her gaze from the picture, eyes scrunching as she tilted her head upwards as if this was how she attempted to will the disgusting images she saw on a daily basis out of her brain.

She grimaced before talking again. I couldn't tell what was going through her mind at the moment; truth be told, I don't really think she knew.

'Every lead is yanked out of my hands. Every scrap of evidence that turns up is taken away. And now the police are panicking because they know the real TellTale Killer is back, and they haven't the faintest idea where to start. Every time I know I can help, every time I *know* I can make a difference to the case, I'm told to stay back. To stay in my lane. No matter how hard I try to do things by the book, no matter how much I give, I'm told to shut up and sit quietly in the corner. And now there's *you*.'

She exhaled sharply. And, with my limited grasp of human interaction, I knew I probably shouldn't interrupt her even though she wasn't actually talking. She was a woman driven to the very edge, her obsession for rules, guidelines and procedure unspooling thread by fragile thread.

I waited for her to finish whatever internal monologue she was lost in, but she just sat there, back ramrod-straight on Bill and Ben's immaculate white sofa, fingertips pressed into her palms, while I watched the sun begin to slide down the windowpane behind her.

Thing is, I think everyone has their limits, the point where they finally tip and do something completely and utterly reckless. For me, it was the case going cold. For Carlota, I sensed it was years of being shunned and overlooked, of knowing she had the capability to make a difference and being denied the chance. And now, at last, she'd finally snapped.

'I know I can catch the TellTale Killer and the IACP guidelines on alternatives to arrest let me delay charging someone *if* it helps with a wider investigation.'

I googled it later: IACP stands for International Association of Chiefs of Police.

'So, for the moment, that's exactly what I'm going to do. I can't say I won't arrest you at some point, though, Ruth. What you've done is... pretty fucking terrible,' Detective Carlota said cuttingly, but there was more fatigue and exhaustion in her tone now than anger or frustration.

'I can't refute that,' I admitted, heart slightly sinking while I clung to the faint distant hope Detective Carlota might settle for a knowing scowl and a slap on the wrist as punishment. I guess no such luck. 'So, what do we do now, then?'

She set my phone on the table.

'We reply,' she said jabbing her finger in the direction of my phone. 'We keep up the ruse we're a serial killer, we tell him it's done, see what he says next and wait for him to slip up. Those guys at the station are panicking, Ruth, because they don't have any kind of idea who this could be. But now, you or...we, I guess, have a direct line to him. This is huge.'

I was a little stunned at the brazenness of this detective. But I suppose, in some ways, she was just as keen as I was for the Tell-Tale Killer to get what he deserved, we just had very different strategies on how to do it. I unlocked the phone and opened Dark-Cell, ready to reply to the killer and see what he would say next. That was when a stair creaked above us; we both jerked round, half expecting an officer had sneaked inside the house to catch us in the act of messaging the most famous serial killer of the decade. But it was only Ben. He looked more fragile than usual today.

'Hiya, love,' I called. Damn it, there it was again. 'Nipping down for milk?'

'Yeah,' he murmured. He always did this if he couldn't sleep. Out of the corner of my eye, I watched as he shuffled to the fridge, filled a glass to the brim with semi-skimmed, spilled some across the worktop, cursed, then dawdled around looking for where he left the kitchen roll while Carlota and I waited in a kind of a tense wordless limbo. She offered a thin, hold-that-thought, how-long-do-you-think-he's-going-to-be smile as we heard the repetitive sound of the kitchen towel going back and forth on the worktops, squeaking like a very tiny mouse with a case of the hiccups.

'I suppose I'll have to brush my teeth again,' Ben chuckled to himself. 'I hate doing that.'

'How was the rest of the treatment?' I asked, knowing I shouldn't, knowing it would only keep him here longer, but I couldn't help myself. I had this lingering feeling that Ben wasn't convinced by chemo, that he didn't believe all the chemicals coursing through him were worth the extra years they promised.

'It was okay,' he remarked, not assuaging my suspicions, and then ambled back upstairs. ''Night,' he added, door clicking shut behind him.

As soon as we heard that sound, Detective Carlota and I magnetically hunched back together around the phone. I typed the message: *It's done. I have his heart*. I thought I'd flip the gender as one more probably vain attempt to distance myself from my crime. I looked to Detective Carlota to confirm she was happy with it and then jammed my finger onto the 'send' button on the screen.

'*No, Cis, step aside. No, Cis, this one isn't your forte. You let him escape once, let someone with more experience handle it.*' Detective Carlota echoed what I presumed were previous remarks of naysayer colleagues in a kind of weary sing-song while she stared at my phone. 'You know why, don't you, Ruth?' I had a medium-to-strong assumption this was another rhetorical question, so I kept the pin in and stayed silent. 'It's because I fluffed it before, let him vanish, and they're convinced I'll drop the ball again. But no one knows more about this case than me, and maybe, well, you.'

I waited, not wanting to speak in case she had more to say but the reply from the killer arrived almost instantly: *Good. I want you to send it to Jago Jones.*

'Jago Jones? Why on earth him?' Detective Carlota asked, staring at the message.

'You know him too?' I replied.

She gave a grunt and a slight roll of her eyes.

'He's like a rabid dog hunting for stories. I've tried to have him blacklisted by the station, but he still weasels his way in whenever there's a whiff of something that's interesting.' That made a lot of sense; the big Double J was well known only because he had a flagrant disregard for any rule or institution. No wonder Detective Carlota hated him so much. The man would do anything for a good story.

So, the TellTale Killer wanted me to send the heart of the victim I had just killed direct to the press, or more specifically, to the journalist who had broken the story years ago and reaped all of the journalistic awards and prizes possible in the process. Was this the killer's way of warning him? Threatening him? Courting his attention once more? I had no idea what I was being used for. But one thing was certain: Jago certainly wouldn't miss his chance to splash this all across the front page, I was sure it would inflate his ego far more than it would potentially terrify him.

'Right,' Carlota said briskly, nervous but determined. 'Our next problem: finding a heart. He still needs to *think* you're a serial killer; any ideas?'

I kept silent, I had almost forgotten all about it. I reached into my coat pocket to pull out the cellophane-wrapped package. Her expression when I produced the defrosting organ was one of disgust, but I don't think I would particularly say surprise.

'Oh, Ruth.'

# TWENTY-SEVEN

When they made the *Panorama* documentary on the TellTale Killer, Aleks warned Chlo and me not to talk to any of the interviewers. He said he didn't want Greta's story twisted and mangled by some twenty-year-old in an editing suite.

When it finally came out, we all watched it privately – trepidatiously, nervously, bracing for the impact – only to find it was less an exposé on the victims and more a glossy puff piece for the Telltale Killer. Now I couldn't help but wonder if there'd be a part two, and if so, whether this would all circle back to me. What would a viewer think at this point in the story, me finally breaking down to a trusted adult? Would they see it as my undoing? The step too far? Turns out, the daughter of the British Ambassador to the Maldives is actually completely unhinged. I dreaded to think if this would absolutely obliterate Mum's diplomatic career.

Detective Carlota had told me that, as long as she knew I hadn't actually killed someone, it was better not to know whose heart it was; ignorance, she said, gave her the smallest sliver of deniability for whatever else I might eventually confess to. I agreed. Because if she knew it was Greta's heart, even the faintest scrap of sympathy she still had for me would have swiftly evaporated.

Detective Carlota and I stayed on the lounge sofa for the best part of an hour, figuring out our next move, and theorising on the killer's.

'I can't believe he kills at random,' she said. 'There must be some connective tissue between the victims.'

I entertained the thought, just for a moment, that it would be crazy if Detective Carlota was actually CerealKillerCornflakes. Though the fact she had never told me 'I told you so' made me think she didn't have the arrogance of my e-friend.

'I've gone over the victim list again and again, there's nothing that links them to Greta. Their jobs differ; they're scattered across several West London boroughs; but other than that connection, it's as though he chooses them completely randomly,' I insisted.

'I don't buy it,' Carlota murmured. 'Even the two poor souls he's killed now must connect to the others somehow.'

I inched forward a little on my chair, ready to posit my theory. 'Have you thought about how gimmicky it's all been, since the start?'

I saw Detective Carlota staring, frankly astonished at herself that she'd gone this long without noticing I was a complete and utter lunatic.

'Why would a serial killer have their own personal branding right from the get-go?' I explained like I was Uncle Phil telling me about yet another death ritual. 'The hearts, the cryptography, the Poe. Sure, some serial killers have developed a "thing", but that usually came from the press. The TellTale Killer's whole persona seemed ready-made from victim one. Don't you think that's weird, how meretricious it is?'

Detective Carlota gave me a look that said she almost understood what I was saying but also that she didn't think any of it had the slightest shred of merit. Still, I couldn't shake the thought. There was something... tacky about the TellTale Killer, something that was hard to completely articulate, almost as if he was inauthentic as a serial killer despite still ticking all the requirements.

We turned to the conundrum of delivering the heart. In the

end, I persuaded Carlota that I should make the drop: I knew the newspaper office, its routines and its staff.

'But let's think like the Telltale Killer,' she said, beginning to pace determinedly around the lounge. I knew not even Bill would be brave enough to warn her about knocking over any of his well-presented décor. 'He sees you've murdered at least two people and is pretty sure that he's the inspiration behind it. Now if I'm a serial killer, that's exactly the kind of attention I crave. I want to be admired.'

'Agreed,' I replied, realising we'd never meaningfully discussed our shared interest; perhaps she had a good true crime podcast or book recommendation. I wonder if she'd be my next only friend on Goodreads?

'We need to provoke him and force a mistake. Stroke his ego and he'll just preen; but if we wound it, he might lash out. He makes a mistake, we get one step further to catching him. We need *him* to be sloppy,' Detective Carlota reasoned aloud.

'So how do we get him to make a mistake? Get him so angry, he drink-drives and we catch him with a body in his car?' It wasn't a ridiculous idea; believe it or not, it was a couple of cold ones that led to Randy Kraft AKA the Scorecard Killer finally being caught by the police after all.

'Jago Jones will publish whatever we send the moment it lands on his desk,' Carlota explained. 'The killer is probably thinking that this will only embolden the myth he's created, he needs the press and people like Jago to enhance the legend he wants. So, let's mock the killer, make him feel tiny, make him angry.'

We agreed to brainstorm what the message should say while I fetched my pen and paper from the shed.

'What about, "The student has become the master"?' Detective Carlota suggested, both hands motioning as if she was some pretentious art fanatic crooning over a life painting trying to find some meaning in the strokes and squiggles.

You know, she really wasn't good at this part.

'He wouldn't say that,' I dismissed the idea, maybe a little too honestly. I grabbed a piece of paper and started to scribble some ideas, trying to get my brain back into serial killer mode. 'How about something like...'

*You were only a cold whisper*
*in the empty dark*
*that thought itself a mighty thunder.*
*And where your breath*
*stirred a faint shadow,*
*mine commands them.*
*Yet the final verse*
*is mine to write*
*And it shall be*
*terrible in its beauty*

Translation: you ain't shit.

I still didn't love how easy it was for me to write as the Telltale Killer. Maybe it's always easy to write like Poe when you've read too much of him, though, or to think like a nihilistic crazy when, deep down, you feel like you might be one too. But for now, I could be grateful for this very niche skill I possessed.

We both liked the message. We knew it would get under his skin, maybe even make him reckless – though, admittedly, we understood the danger: escalation could mean more victims.

'We just have to catch him first. That's the priority,' Carlota said, trying to bury the concern she clearly felt. 'If we wait, even more people are going to die. This is still our best option.'

I really wanted to believe her, but at this point I honestly wasn't sure.

It's funny how we attach feelings to places. The Maldives will always mean my parents abandoning me for their cushy diplomacy gig. Birmingham makes me nostalgic for my uni days. And Hammersmith? That's just memories of a dead best friend, broken dreams, stale coffee, and a printer that always seemed to hate me specifically.

I had tried to avoid Hammersmith as much as I could over the past couple of years, but going to my old workplace to deliver a *heart* to Jago Jones felt downright surreal. I mean, the guy barely spoke two words to Tasha and me in the whole time I had worked there which weren't either patronising or, failing that, condescending. It was then I started to wonder, is there a word for nostalgia, but for when you actually detest the memories being stirred up? Is that just trauma?

I remembered from my time at the paper that deliveries normally arrived at around 6 a.m., so I figured that was the best time to try and deposit the package, early on Friday morning. I was happy to discover that the broken button at the pedestrian crossing had finally been fixed, and that the one independent bakery at Hammersmith Station was somehow still in business.

Keeping my head down beneath the shadow of my baseball cap, I moved quickly through the streets as I approached the offices, trying to look inconspicuous and avoiding the multiple cameras glaring down from above. Just as the delivery truck rumbled towards the back entrance of the building, I slipped across the road and watched as they backed a huge lorry into the bay also used to ship out the morning papers, a space they obviously used less and less now. Print media is dying, kids, support your bookshops.

It occurred to me that I was now imitating the TellTale Killer's methods more than ever. Presumably this was how he had deposited the hearts: dressed as unassumingly as possible, moving at unsociable hours, leaving them in random corners of London to avoid detection. That was the part I still hadn't cracked: how on earth had he managed it? Everywhere I looked, a camera seemed to be watching me. How had he managed to blend in?

From a distance I spotted the same bloke in the loading bay, the one I used to chat to every morning when I started at the paper as an intern.

My first job had been to sort all the various deliveries from the lorry and ensure they reached their intended destinations on various people's desks. I couldn't remember the delivery chap's name, but he always looked perpetually on the verge of a heart attack, his face permanently bright red and flushed, as if he were constantly struggling for breath and was one rogue beat away from cardiac arrest. I thought he'd be dead by now, honestly; good for him.

Unfortunately for me back then, but fortuitously for me today, speed had never been his forte. I watched him carefully as he left the platform in the bay to grab more parcels from the back of the lorry, which was when I easily slipped into the bay and tossed my package seamlessly onto the huge trolley that would be hauled by the latest tortured intern to the post room. It would be on Jago's desk before anyone picked up my meddling on the CCTV.

I then quickly wound my way through the various back streets and alleyways of Hammersmith, trying to lose the gaze of any rogue cameras I could be picked up on if they tried to trace me on playback. Gradually, I could feel my heart rate begin to slow and my palms got ever so slightly less clammy as I walked along the cobbled lower mall, thankful that yet again no police teams had suddenly jumped out of the bushes to tackle me to the ground the minute I threw my package onto the trolley.

I paused for a moment to take in the rusty teal green of Hammersmith Bridge. I checked once more that I wasn't being followed, nor that anyone else was around my immediate vicinity, then let out an enormous belch you could have used to signal a ship coming into harbour. God, I hated this quirk.

I looked back at the bridge. I hadn't seen this particular view in some time. I'd always liked this part of Hammersmith, overlooking the river, though I could never quite put my finger on why. Perhaps it was because this part of London always felt just that little more serene to me than the rest of the city. You could watch the rowers glide beneath the bridge in the early misty morning, and the dog walkers making their way across the path above.

Luckily, the little side street I was now on held one of the few London cafés without CCTV covering every square inch. I slipped inside and ordered a latte before I went in search of the loo. There, I pulled my spare clothes from my rucksack and quickly changed out of my clandestine roadman-gear and into something a little more Ruth. I know this makes me sound like I'm twenty-nine going on a hundred, but the past seventy-two hours had drained me so completely that I just needed one small moment to sit down. To breathe, properly, instead of frantically pant. At the bottom of the bag lay my copy of Greta's Obama I had taken from Aleks's house. I tucked the book under my arm, collected my latte, and went to try to enjoy the crisp January morning in their outside seating.

I had done what I could. Now, it was the Telltale Killer's move in our deranged game of pass-the-parcel. The café was barely a mile from the spot where Greta and I had had our final argument at Sabroso two years ago. I realised I had spent the days since then avoiding nearly every place that reminded me of Greta. I guess it was some kind of crude form of self-preservation, sparing myself the pain and guilt of remembering what I'd done. I think if I paused to reflect, I might think twice and emotionally implode. The truth of the matter was that, however precarious my situation, I was now closer to catching the Telltale Killer than anyone else had ever been.

As I took another sip of my latte, I opened Obama and leafed through its pages on the scratched and stained coffee table that had clearly seen better days, wondering how many times Greta must have read it, turning each page from cover to cover. I remembered how she'd queued outside Waterstones the day it was released – the only person in line, of course, no one else cared *that* much about an American president. She really was his biggest fan. There had been a few times when I'd tried to dissuade her from her love of Obama, but she always waved it off. She hated politicians as a rule, often saying that maybe Guy Fawkes had a point, but some-how, Obama always escaped the full force of Greta's wrath.

I was just drifting through the pages when, like some sort of conjuring trick, a creased white note slipped from the book and drifted to the cobbled pavement below me. I snatched it up before the wind would have a chance to whisk it out of my reach.

Expecting a lacklustre doodle or a harmless reminder pressed to work as some form of bookmark on her eighty-seventh read-through, I stretched out the paper against the hardback cover of the book to inspect.

It was not a doodle. The paper was enormously dense with fading scribbles in, undoubtedly, Greta's handwriting that hadn't changed since Year 7. A few words remained legible: ironically 'handwriting', a hurried 'headlines', and, more unsettlingly, the names of all five Telltale Killer victims up to that point. Beside each name stood a date, ranging from 2019 to 2023, and what appeared to be a different vehicle registration number beside each one. Wait a second, had Greta been investigating the case? The dates on the piece of paper didn't match the victims' dates of death in the slightest, so they must mean something else. What was their relevance?

For the love of God, why hadn't I listened to Greta that night in Sabroso? What had she been trying to tell me?

At the bottom, scrawled in capitals and circled again and again, were the words:

### *MUST BE THE KILLER.*

God, I always knew Greta was clever; two years gone and she was still reminding me of that fact. She'd solved the case of the TellTale Killer and surely, she was now handing the baton to me to finish the job.

## TWENTY-EIGHT

I rang Detective Carlota straight away, but she was already knee-deep in another case; I guessed lesser criminals weren't too willing to step aside so the Telltale Killer could hog the limelight. Plus, I presumed she would face quite a severe slap on the wrist if it came out she was still working on a case she'd been forbidden to have anything to do with. I forwarded her a photograph of Greta's note, and she sneaked away to a stairwell to begin analysing and dissecting it. But she was just as confused and perplexed as me. The relevance of the dates? The number plates that were scribbled beside them? It didn't seem to connect in any coherent way.

'Run it past me again,' she whispered, clearly avoiding unwelcome ears who may be in her vicinity.

'So, the ink's faded with time a little. I guess Greta's pen must have been dying anyway, but I think she must have known who the Telltale Killer was. The note lists five different number plates, each beside each victim's name, and then a date. The dates seem random, all falling between 2019 and 2023, and I can't find any kind of pattern,' I said, almost breathless with nerves and panic.

*Greta*, I thought to myself, *what are you trying to tell me?*

'Look,' said Detective Carlota hurriedly, clearly she was being pressured by some nearby force to hang up. 'We have a window before Jago unwraps the parcel and the headlines erupt. For now, sit tight, I'll drop by tonight and we can go through it together. Please don't do anything stupid or impulsive, okay? We need to be *really* careful here.'

'Of course,' I lied. Sitting tight wasn't really in my nature – just ask Mrs Lambert and Justin. I had been given an incredible clue here, a few loose strands in this case, and I intended to pull them together tight.

Two people were already dead, and I knew that once the deposited heart made the headlines, the killer would soon be on the rampage for his next victim. He would be angry, furious. It felt as though a clock had already started ticking and I wasn't about to let another person die. I couldn't let there be one more Greta.

'Hello?' Nico said with a modicum of hesitation I could hear in his voice as he picked up the phone. I wasn't 100 per cent sure it was him at first; it had admittedly been just over a week since I had last heard his voice. It was deeper and more baritone than I remembered. All credit to him for picking up. If it were me, I'd have ignored the unknown number and googled it like everyone else does.

'Hi, Nico, it's Ruth. Not sure if you remember me, we met a week or so ago, with Chlo and Oscar.'

'Oh, Ruth,' he said with a delivery and diction I couldn't quite read. Was he happy to hear from me, or regretting even owning a phone that I could contact him on? 'Yeah, I remember.' He paused for a moment before continuing. 'Err, may I ask how you got my number?'

'Ah...' I began, aware it was important not to come across as a stalker or my plan would fall apart quite quickly. Chlo did confirm that this guy had thought I was fit, which I hoped would hold me in good stead. 'I asked Chlo, who I guess got it off Oscar. Look, I know this is a bit of a weird thing to ask, but you said you worked at TFL security, right?'

'Yeah, I do.' I could easily sense the sudden shift to nervousness in his voice. I suppose it was a bit of a rather odd phone call for him, some gal from a bad first date calls you up out of the blue and then starts asking you specifics about your job.

'So, peculiar request: would it be possible for someone like me to look at some security footage from, say, two years ago?'

'Well, I mean, it's possible,' he said, a little dazed. 'I just need to warn you that it needs to go through a lot of processes before we can give it the thumbs-up to be released. I can help you fill in the form to put in a request if you'd like, that's no trouble. Maybe we can meet up for a coffee and I can—'

'So,' I interrupted, I had no time to let him finish the end of his sentence, 'this may sound a bit crazy, but I was wondering if you would be able to help me right now? It's a pretty time-sensitive issue.'

'Now? I mean, now may be a bit hard, Ruth. You would need to travel to our offices for a start,' he replied.

'Oh, well, yeah, that's true. It's just...' I decided now would be an appropriate time. 'I'm actually outside your office right now.'

I was beginning to wonder, on a scale of one to ten, how crazy he thought I was. Eleven? It just felt like it would be harder for him to say no if he knew I was only outside.

'Right,' he said, elongating the vowel before he aspirated the sharp clip of the 't', weighing up the options in his mind I imagine. Did the words 'bunny boiler' bounce around his mind? How bad would he feel if he saw a muscular security man tackle a small woman to the pavement while he watched out of a window above. 'So, what, you just want to look at security footage?'

'Yeah. From two years ago,' I said, clarifying the time frame again.

'Right, okay,' he murmured and then expelled what sounded like a long, slightly weary breath. 'Stay right there, I'll come down and get you.'

Nico came down to the lobby promptly to fetch me, sporting a look of trepidation on his face. I tried my best to summon a big grin and wave so that he wouldn't suspect I was here for any kind of malicious purpose. However, he still regarded me with a rather strained smile and a tense, clenched jaw as I curled my arms around him in a light, friendly hug. It was not a full-on bear hug but rather the kind you give when a handshake would simply feel far too awkward.

God, my memory had not done his nose justice, it was a truly great nose.

He swiftly removed himself from my grip and ushered me to sign in at the front desk, got me a visitor pass, and then gestured for me to take the lift.

It was still lurking in the forefront of my cerebrum that Chlo had told me Nico's aunt had also been a victim of the TellTale Killer, but I was hoping this might work to my advantage. Or it might rather explosively backfire. There was a 50:50 chance I feel.

'You're lucky my boss isn't working today,' he mumbled as the steel lift doors clunked shut behind us.

I glanced at my phone. For the moment, at least, my note hadn't set the media into screeching like seagulls over a cold Cornish chip. Still, I pictured the journalists barely two miles away, cueing up television segments and polishing the bad-taste headlines, poised to publish the instant Jago said 'go'. I wondered if, when they saw the heart, their eyes wouldn't roll with horror but with pound signs, complete with a cheerful cha-ching.

'You're doing something with the TellTale Killer, aren't you?' he asked, as if he was hearing my own internal monologue.

'What, no,' I said beginning to feign disbelief but then I was too tired to protest anymore. 'How did you guess?' I replied within the same breath, a little frustrated that I had come across as so transparent. No wonder Detective Carlota had seen right through me.

'Just a wild stab in the dark: I know you're fascinated by serial killers, the Telltale Killer pops up again, and, purely by chance, you suddenly need footage from two years ago? You'll forgive me if I don't buy that as a coincidence,' he said with this kind of smugness I seemed to get a lot from men.

Nico may have been strangely accommodating to the random girl who had just rocked up at his office, but he sure as shit wasn't dumb.

'I know that you probably think I'm nuttier than a fruitcake, right?' I remarked as I glanced at his eyes. He definitely thought I was crazy, but maybe he was also a little intrigued by my whole shtick. He gave a light huff as a response and placed his hands firmly in his pockets, leaning his back against the walls of the lift as we continued to ascend the floors.

'No, not crazy. But it's just, if the police haven't been able to catch the person responsible for killing my aunt, I don't know see how you can. I've spent so much time trying to work out what happened and always found next to nothing. Curds, but no cream. Don't take it personally if I don't rate your chances.'

Curds but no cream? That was a funny expression. Kind of liked it, though, it was almost familiar.

But no, I didn't take it personally as that meant that Nico was still holding on to some slight assumption that I was at least a tiny bit normal.

He led me through various hallways of TFL, adorned with a weird, fuzzy felt carpet in bright, ostentatious colours. I wondered if any of the employees ever had a bad day at work and then decided to delay the Jubilee line just for the hell of it. I could see that Nico was doing his best not to make eye contact or small talk with his colleagues as he guided me into what looked like a small control room. There were multiple workstations arranged in a semi-circle around a large wall-mounted display, showing what I presumed to be multiple live feeds of the various Underground lines. Comforting to know TFL was run on the same vibe as a mid-tier call centre. There was only one other person there, but he seemed too absorbed in what he was doing on his own computer to notice our entrance.

'So, what are you looking for?' Nico asked as he slumped down in an ergonomic office chair and began working at one of the computers. Pressing a key, his screen suddenly mirrored onto the huge monitor that seemed to take up half the wall in front of us.

Nico didn't offer me a seat, which I'd usually count as a mark against him, but I was so full of adrenaline I wasn't sure I could sit down right now.

I told him the date and time and politely asked him to display all the camera feeds at Ravenscourt Park on the night that Lewis Khan died in October 2024. What had Greta found? The dates seemingly had no connection to the victims' deaths. What was she trying to tell me?

Nico grunted affirmatively and then quickly tapped a few buttons, and within moments, four streams of CCTV footage from different angles of the station's exterior appeared on the screen. He gradually began speeding them up as I did my best to keep track of the various car number plates whizzing judderingly past the camera.

'So, is there a particular type of car you want me to try and find?' Nico asked after a few minutes of scanning the footage to no avail. I had tried my best to stay focused and alert on the various number plates the camera had picked up, but it was immensely difficult with multiple streams of traffic shooting across each screen simultaneously.

'I'm looking for a number plate, final digits MDK, but it's hard to try and track all the cars going past,' I said, glancing down at Greta's note again and making sure I had the right number plate corresponding to the right victim.

*Lewis Khan – KV70 MDK – 11/11/2023*

'Oh, I wish you said that earlier,' Nico said with a smirk as he quickly typed something on his computer. As if by magic, there, at 19.03, the exact number plate fitted on a Mercedes Benz electric delivery van. It was an understatement to say that those were pretty commonplace throughout the UK, even more so in London. Everyone needed their vegetable choppers.

'How on earth did you do that?' I asked, flabbergasted. I just hope the masses of security cameras didn't capture the 2022 incident where I got so hammered that I tried to start a fight with Gandhi's statue in Parliament Square. I thought it had looked at me funny.

'Trust me, it's actually more comforting *not* to know,' Nico remarked.

I tried to peer at the windscreen, make out who it may have reassembled through the pixels, but all I could see was a vague, shadowy figure in a high-vis vest in the driver's seat. There must have been some way to differentiate this van, other than its number plate, from the thousands that went through London alone every single day. 'Can you zoom in?' I asked.

Nico tapped another key on the screen and the grainy footage enlarged a little before us. I walked closer to the big screen to try and spot any defining characteristics. It was tiny but I noticed two small, albeit quite deep scratches on the left-hand side of the vehicle just by the back left wheel.

'Okay, now can you go to Goldhawk Road on the 21 October 2024?' I asked. 'DF69 HMH.'

I knew Maggie Dawes' disappearance had occurred somewhere between 19.00 and 20.00, and I had asked Nico to begin the footage at 18.00. He searched for the number plate and there it was at 18.21. The words could not leave my mouth fast enough as I saw it – the same van again and I could see the two distinctive scratch marks clearly despite carrying a new number plate.

It matched up exactly to Greta's note. The same number plate on the same van on the night Maggie Dawes died.

'Okay, thank you, now can you go to Philbeach Gardens on 16 November?' I requested. 'Final digits, CBV.'

I watched Nico's face ever so slightly twitch and grimace. This was where Bea Powell vanished and the way his face dropped, and how the colour drained, told me that must have been his aunt. He nodded without a word and quickly began to summon the footage. I hesitated before finally committing to placing a hand on his shoulder. It felt right in the moment, okay? He didn't react either way to the gesture anyway, so I kept my hand there with no real movement as he began to boot up the footage.

The highlighted mark of number plate recognition flared up on the monitor. I excitedly jammed my finger onto the screen – a gesture Nico clearly didn't love – and tried my best to rub the smudge of fingerprint off the monitor. There it was again – the van with two scratches, again sporting a new numberplate.

It all began to fall into place. The perfect way for the TellTale Killer to hide in plain sight and yet leave no security footage trailing back to him. The most common vehicle in London, the generic delivery van; you'd melt into the background. No one ever looks twice at a white van, especially not if you have a rotating plethora of number plates. In addition to the fact that I bet it's easier to throw a body in there than in a Mini Cooper.

*Greta, you absolute genius.*

'The same van, different number plates,' I exclaimed. Nico slowed down the footage as we both continued to watch the recording of the van pulling up on a street corner, stopping in a spot by an alleyway just slightly out of frame.

I realised Greta's note only listed five victims because, though she hadn't known it then, she'd been number six. I'd considered asking Nico for the footage from the night she died, but without knowing what number plate the van was using on that particular night, I could lose hours trying to trawl through it.

'Is there anything else in the footage that tells us more?' I asked after I recollected my thoughts. 'Anything at all?'

'I'm afraid not,' Nico said regretfully. I gave a little groan and moved beyond his desk to look more closely at a figure on the giant screen that dominated the room. *Who could you be?*

'So, you don't see who gets out?' I asked, my eyes still fixed onto the figure behind the windshield to try and discern some kind of physical feature to ascertain what the TellTale Killer could vaguely look like.

'Oh, it's just some delivery driver shipping out these parcels. It tells us nothing about Aunt Bea,' Nico remarked indifferently.

'Trust me, I've watched this footage hundreds of times, spent hours on forums, trying to work out what might have happened to her. But it's just another one of these unbranded delivery driver clones. Feel like I've made myself go a bit crazy staring at the same sixty-second loop over and over again.'

God, I knew how that felt. It was strangely nice to hear of another bereaved's obsession with message boards, although I doubted Nico went on ones quite as shady as mine.

I then requested the two other camera footages, and sure enough, the van appeared in each one. The timing didn't always align exactly with the disappearances, but it was always there, defined by the scratches and each time sporting a different number plate, always lining up exactly with Greta's notes.

I had no idea how the dates she'd pencilled beside them fit in. I'd asked Nico to check, but no van with those number plates showed up on any of the dates she'd written down. They must be signalling something else.

Now, I was stuck, though; the DVLA wouldn't give out any private information about number plates. Unless, of course, you were a journalist with very good contacts and luckily, I knew exactly who may be able to help. Unfortunately, it meant going back, the second time in a day, to Hammersmith.

'So, you think this is how the TellTale Killer's been operating? With a van?' Nico asked, swivelling his chair to face me again. He was more than a little interested; this was clearly a man invested in making sure the killer got justice. I did like a guy with a moral centre.

'I do,' I replied. 'It makes more than a little sense, right? The perfect way to take his victims, and the perfect way to then deposit their hearts. Hiding in plain sight every time, swapping out number plates so no one catches on,' I said, half explaining the revelation to myself as much as I was to Nico.

It reminded me of David Middleton, better known as the Cable Guy Killer, who used a company uniform as his way to slip past suspicion to kill his victims. Somehow, a brand makes us feel safe; it seems almost unfathomable that someone delivering our parcels could be capable of killing. But that's the trouble with serial killers – they could be anyone.

'That's very smart. You're very smart,' Nico said complimentarily with an ever so slight tilt of his head.

I almost smiled at that. For a moment, I was distracted, not by the recent discovery, but by the handsome man in front of me, lightly flirting with me. It was quite nice, you know. I realised I enjoyed being flirted with, even if I didn't quite know how to flirt back.

'I...' He paused, massaging his throat like he was working through how to physically say something. 'I was a little triggered the night you brought up serial killers. Only because I also spend so much time thinking about them, especially the TellTale Killer. I just want to find out what happened to Aunt Bea. I take it you're not going to tell the police about this?'

'No,' I responded. 'And I take it you're not going to tell them?'

'No,' he remarked, almost like he was a little insulted by the question. 'I mean, in all honesty, I was hoping I'd get to tell you "I told you so" but hey, you were right. I mean, this is frankly outstanding.'

I started to give a polite guffaw and a flick of my hand as a kind of fake modesty but then stopped abruptly. That turn of phrase was familiar, I had heard it... no, read it, in that exact same tone by another person who had a weird obsession with the TellTale Killer. 'All curds, no cream?' I knew that was a familiar expression too.

My finger shot out like a bullet leaving a gun, pointing directly at Nico sitting in the chair.

'No,' I murmured, eyes narrowing and back hunching. 'CerealKillerCornflakes.'

'StabithaChristie,' he responded, rising to his feet, finger outstretched, matching my accusation.

# TWENTY-NINE

I was already at the police station, waiting patiently for Detective Carlota to become available so I could tell her about my discovery. I figured she'd forgive me coming to her directly when she learned of how groundbreaking my discovery was. When the news broke about the heart I sent Jago, almost instinctively, I switched off notifications for DarkCell. I needed to protect what little was left of my sanity if I was going to make it through this, and to try and stop myself from completely unravelling into a messy human spool. It's not as if the killer would leave any breadcrumbs for me now; he'd be done with that. I know serial killers, their egos are fragile things, poor souls.

Naturally, our old pal Jago Jones had been the first to report on the new heart, and, just as naturally, the media storm that followed was immediate. Every outlet was in a frenzy, clamouring over the latest instalment of the Telltale Killer saga. Urgh, talk about sensationalism.

You could almost feel the city pause; a collective intake of nervous breath, as Londoners stopped in their tracks as their phones pinged with the alert and launched into new conversations about the latest development with whoever was next to them. As I moved through the streets on my way to talk to Carlota, I caught fragments of their voices: a mix of terror and disbelief, yes, but laced through with something else; a thrill, the kind you feel in the queue for the really frightening rollercoaster that someone died on only last week.

For all their fear, people couldn't help but revel in the spectacle. A dark, festering part of them was almost excited by it, even though they knew full well the horror of what was happening before them.

But I didn't have time to dwell on social misgivings. The police would be on their way to the paper soon, racing to retrieve the heart and run their DNA tests, trying to identify who the latest victim might be. I imagined I didn't have long before they discovered it belonged to Greta and fully clocked on to what I was doing.

I barely had time to register the other recent development though: CerealKillerCornflakes, my virtual frenemy, was actually Nico. The look on his face was a cocktail of delight and betrayal as we both clocked what had just happened, an accidental physical meet-up between two digital nutjobs. He'd said he wanted to come and help with my investigation as soon as we realised our true identities, but I shut that down quickly and told him not to go blabbing on DarkCell. There was no way I was dragging him into this, and, truthfully, I still wasn't 100 per cent sure he *wasn't* the TellTale Killer. I still felt that I couldn't really trust anyone at the moment, maybe apart from Detective Carlota.

I arched my back, shifting in the hard blue plastic chair, trying to find even a hint of comfort for my lumbar region. Why was a good chair so hard to come by nowadays? Each movement set off an awful, splintering creak, and above me the harsh fluorescent lights seemed to beat down on me like some kind of divine punishment from above. I knew Detective Carlota would make me feel better about the state of things, that she'd know exactly what to do. Mostly, I was just grateful she now knew about it, and was tangled up in this mess with me.

I gripped Greta's crumpled pages of notes and scribbles, reading them over and over again in every orientation I could.

'What are you trying to tell me, Greta?' I whispered, suspending my disbelief in the afterlife, just for a moment, just long enough to hope she might somehow magically answer from the great beyond. Of course, she didn't. Typical Greta, even dead, still terrible at communication.

Somehow, she'd managed to work out that each victim had been taken using a delivery van with a rotating roster of number plates. How? I had no idea, but she had, and these dates she'd frantically marked onto the paper... these dates had to mean something too. Something tied to each victim. Was this connected to how the killer was picking them, maybe?

I was halfway through debating whether to ask the woman at the front desk if I could bother her for a cup of tea – I was feeling quite parched – when a figure slipped out of the police doors and locked eyes with me.

Detective Carlota spotted me, gave the smallest of waves – arm barely above her waist – and tilted her head in a direction I presumed meant she wanted me to follow. At first, I wasn't sure if it was an invitation or the world's laziest arrest. Of course, I did follow, straight into one of the questioning rooms, or 'interrogation rooms', I supposed, depending on whether you were here by choice or not.

'You've got five minutes,' she said as she shut the door firmly behind her.

I smoothed out the piece of paper with Greta's notes inscribed on the desk in the glorified broom cupboard and slid it across for her to examine, to see if her genius police detective brain could make any more sense of it than I could; see something I wasn't able to.

'Greta knew,' I said, explaining what I'd found in her copy of Obama's book and how her terrible handwriting was more than just random, insignificant doodles, it was a series of clues, hints at what she'd been able to uncover, how the number plates were all tied to the same delivery van. 'She must have figured it out,' I affirmed, 'I think she died because she knew who was behind this.'

It took a moment for Carlota to process. I could practically see the loading bar slowly inching across the width of her forehead, this was huge for her too. She'd been working the case for years and only now had a breakthrough this big, handed to her by a dead girl from two years ago on a scrap of paper... one that, on the other side, held nothing more than a recipe for scones we had published on the website a week before she died.

'And I think there's more,' I said, ignoring all the tinfoil-hat, keep-the-government-away conviction I knew I was pouring into my words. 'She mentions handwriting a few times... and she makes a note about what I think is a double full stop or something. I don't know what that means yet, but it's the key. I'm sure of it.'

Detective Carlota looked puzzled at first, as if I had just ranted at her in frenzied gibberish about the mating habits of sock puppets, but then her expression shifted, excitement slowly dawning as she gently and carefully took the paper from me and began inspecting it herself with the same fervour I had just spoken with, realising just how valuable this piece of scrap was.

'I think we've got something here, Ruth,' she said, practically vibrating with discovery, her voice already halfway to telling me to pop open the Prosecco. 'I think we can work with this, see where it leads. Find out what Greta knew.'

'Right?' I said, a little breathless. It was this weird, macabre kind of thrill, knowing we were finally this close. If only I had read Obama earlier, like Greta wanted me to, I could have saved so much time.

'Has he messaged you again?' Carlota asked, slightly indifferently as she held the note aloft to the light as if Greta was crafty enough to have written in a secret ink.

I let out a reluctant, almost confessional exhale. 'I haven't dared check. I know, I know, it's cowardly of me...'

'No, not at all, Ruth,' Detective Carlota said reassuringly, interrupting me as she placed the note next to her and then held out her hand, stretching across the table. 'Just hand me your phone and we'll be able to take it from here.'

I inadvertently raised an eyebrow. Hand her my phone? I was a millennial, after all, we don't just *hand over* our phones that easily.

'What do you mean?' I asked, my body shifting instinctively, almost angling my limbs away from her. Carlota didn't seem perturbed by my movements, she just kept her hand outstretched, clenching and unclenching her fist as though willing me to hurry up and slap the phone in her palm.

'Ruth, you've done a great job. But this is dangerous territory now, okay?' she said. I could feel her stare burning into my temples as I fixated on a small tuft in the carpet. 'Look, I think it's time you stepped back and let the professionals handle this. So, give me the phone and I promise you, you will get front-row seats to his arrest. But I can't have a civilian involved, it's too dangerous. All you need to do now is sit back and let me finally catch the bastard.'

Maybe I would have believed her, maybe I would have handed over my phone, my notes, everything, if she hadn't said *finally*. There was something about the way she said it, the way her eyes narrowed ever so slightly and the emphasis she placed on enunciating every syllable of the word, that made my pulse thicken, my nerves tighten and my skin tingle with the erratic, electric kind of energy I had felt so much recently. *Finally* didn't sound like she was protecting me at all. It sounded like she just wanted the glory of catching him. That's not at all why I was doing any of this, this was never about glory. This was and had always been about Greta.

'What if I don't?' I murmured. It wasn't bravery forcing me to say that, the words just slipped out with my brain forgetting to filter them, I was genuinely wondering what would happen if I didn't.

Carlota chuckled softly, but there was nothing warm in it, nothing that was meant to feel soothing for me.

'Ruth, you've done some pretty illegal things recently. Are you sure that's a good idea?'

Well, now, that sounded sort of like a threat.

She shuffled closer, perhaps realising how her words came

across, and laid a hand on my arm. For the first time in my life, I instinctively flinched at her touch.

'Hey, hey, darling. I'm here to help you, okay? I don't want you getting any deeper into this. It's dangerous, and I think he's very close to finding out who you are,' Carlota said.

I stared into her eyes, trying to read them, trying to see the truth behind what she was saying. I didn't know if I believed her. Maybe she did just want the killer caught and me protected, but what if that ego of hers was talking, and what if it was that same ego that stopped the TellTale Killer getting caught the first time? What if *I* was still the best person to do this? After all, I'd got further than anyone with this, even her, the so-called professional with all the resources at her disposal.

'Ruth. Please. Let me help you,' she said again.

I think, in that moment, she may have truly believed what she was saying to me. I think she really did want to protect me from the killer. But maybe, just maybe, despite my awful social skills, I actually knew her better than she knew herself. I watched her gently place her hand over Greta's notes, her fingertips applying all the pressure on the tiny surface area as they could. She must have had some idea of what was going through my head.

All I could do was draw in the deepest breath I could manage, watching as her shoulders loosened, her muscles relaxed, as though she thought I was about to relent. Then gripping my phone tight, I hurled myself out of the chair and bolted for the door.

I really needed to start training for that marathon.

# THIRTY

I knew Tasha was just as surprised as I was when I called her, asking if we could meet.

I'll be the first to admit I wasn't thrilled about returning to my old workplace – where I think I had a total of three fond memories over the years I worked there – for the second time in less than twelve hours. I also didn't love the fact that I was now a semi-fugitive to the law but I knew that my old chum Tasha was the only person who could help me right now in getting closer to the Tell-Tale Killer. She always had useful contacts, and I needed them desperately.

I could almost hear the sound of the soft foaming noise of her mouth as she began to froth when I mentioned over the phone that I might have a Tell Tale Killer-related scoop.

'Wherever you are, stay right there, I'm on my way,' she said.

'I'm literally about to get on the Tube, don't worry, I'm coming to you,' I had replied as I hopped down the worn, weathered steps of the station.

I knew she was probably still quite furious that I had tossed her phone into a creek when she ambushed me outside of the office on Monday, but I figured that emotion would probably be superseded by the fact she might soon land a real whopper of a story on her desk. But journalists could forgive a lot for a good story and I'm sure she had some kind of insurance for the phone. Rage fades, but bylines last forever.

The Tube finally arrived back in Hammersmith, and as I made my way to the offices, I couldn't help but find my attention drawn to every single delivery van that passed me on the street. That could have been him, I thought, as one stopped at the red lights before I saw another identical one shoot past me on the other side of the road. He could be picking his victims right now with his van, choosing who would be suffering his wrath next as he tried to get back at the smart aleck who was ribbing him online.

I had to presume at this point that Detective Carlota had told all of her colleagues what I had been up to and put out some kind of notice for my arrest. I mean, maybe she *was* just trying to protect me back at the station; this was the same woman who'd been patient and kind despite my constant badgering about the TellTale Killer for two years.

But at the same time, I couldn't risk it. I was the one who'd heard his voice, the one who always felt like I'd always just missed him, like he had just escaped my grasp by an inch. I was so close. It always had to be me. I was the only one I trusted to get it done. Call me a control freak – actually, don't.

I tried not to let myself get distracted by the paranoia and anxiety coursing through me and power-walked as fast as I could to the offices where Tasha was already waiting outside, finishing off a cigarette. It was impossible not to also notice several police cars beside the building, some clearly forensic units. It wasn't exactly surprising, Jago had just received a human heart. I only hoped Detective Carlota was being truthful about not officially working on the case; it would be rather disastrous if she was also on her way here.

Tasha gave me a quick, light hug, her back arched away from me, before we exchanged brief, perfunctory pleasantries, ignoring the swarm of police cars around us. Then, as I glanced over my shoulder to make sure I wasn't being followed, she led me upstairs to the office bullpen. I can't say I loved having to leak this very valuable information to Tasha, but I knew the woman had a DVLA contact from an investigation we'd worked on together way back when.

It was in the lift that I saw the message come through from Detective Carlota, one that I had been expecting. If I'm being honest, I think I dreaded nearly every message I received on my phone nowadays. All it read was:

Ruth, think this through.

Considering this woman had the power to ensure I never saw a lick of sunlight again, I was ultimately pretty happy that was the extent of the message. I wondered how many other messages she'd workshopped before sending that one. Surely she knew thinking things through was not something I had a penchant for.

Tasha sat me down on the spare wonky chair next to her desk and began typing the number plates from my phone into her computer while I casually surveyed the office. It still smelled the same, must have been the disinfectant that the cleaners used. An astringent, metallically sour kind of smell. While it had clearly been renovated recently, it still seemed to me that not much had changed over the past two years; the same headlines were framed and fitted onto the wall, the same harsh sterile lighting. I still saw the same people on my way towards Tasha's desk; although this time, whenever someone recognised me, they quickly turned their heads away. I couldn't help but look three feet across to where I used to sit. There was someone else there now, hopefully they hadn't inherited my habit for emotional breakdowns.

Tasha's fingers danced over the keyboard while she simultaneously kept glancing at the main TV in the bullpen before lowering her gaze back to the screen. The news had slapped on every possible graphic designed to visually scream urgency, a different coloured ticker, the 'breaking' font in the corner pumped up to an even larger headline size. It was practically impossible to ignore, short of wrenching the television off its brackets and hurling it out the window.

'My contact at DVLA is normally pretty quick – my dad did his prostate exam – so we shouldn't have to wait too long to work out who the number plates belong to,' she stated. 'But I mean...' she laughed, 'where did you even get this, Ruth? How did you find this out?'

'Oh, I'm afraid I can't reveal my sources,' I said with a forced sly grin, one that Tasha failed to recognise as completely fake, as she gave a splutter when she tried to sip her coffee.

'Hey, if this gets us any closer to catching the TellTale Killer, I'll give you some credit, of course,' she said with a sprinkle of obsequiousness. 'Lord knows I need something. Our old mate Double J is back to being golden boy again after today.'

'What do you mean?' I asked with a scoff, feeling like we had both time-travelled back to the daily occurrence of us making fun of the little high-flying journalist that could...

'Did you not see?' she said, folding her arms, leaning back in her chair and making sure my replacement wasn't listening to our conversation too closely. 'The TellTale Killer sent him one of the hearts personally today. He practically jizzed his pants.'

'No way,' I said. I think I was too tired to be in any way convincing but luckily I didn't think Tasha noticed.

'Right? So, he's been dodging calls and interview requests from other outlets all afternoon,' she said, her voice becoming a high-pitched saccharine tone. 'Apparently, they're saying it practically confirms his second Press Gazette Award. Everyone is saying that his reporting on this one is a game-changer for journalism. Urgh, give me a fucking break.'

I'd forgotten how much they all loved that word in this office, *a game-changer*. Apparently, it was one of the first things the billionaire owner had said when he bought the paper six years ago: *Make every article a game-changer*. Which, in practice, basically meant: bring in the clicks for the ad revenue and don't criticise the ultrawealthy too much, okay? I mean, good for Jago, I guess. The killer and I had unwittingly given him a major boost in his dying journalism career after he peaked two years ago. Although, I still couldn't quite work out why the killer had asked me to send it directly to him of all people. Why Jago and not another journalist? What was so special about him? Why did he deserve the career boost? Or was it a menacing threat that Jago had obnoxiously misinterpreted?

'I had written this whole piece on Charlie Young; that was the most recent victim,' Tasha said dejectedly, not realising I had kind of spaced out while she was talking. 'Jago wanted to do a piece on him a while ago, but it never came to pass. It was about his whole life, his family and his charity work, but this will be completely flatlined now, thanks to him,' Tasha said, her voice not even attempting to conceal the red-hot resentment she had for the office's number one reporter. 'But I guess that's journalism, right? Best story wins or something like that?'

That was when her head snapped toward something located a few inches above my right shoulder, and I saw her whole body shift and tense as if to try and do all she could to keep her anger buried deep in her stomach and not spewed at whoever was in my blind spot.

'Something small-dickish this way comes,' she murmured with a scowl as, sure enough, the one and only Jago Jones came waltzing over. It was like he was walking to some kind of bass-heavy rock song that the rest of us couldn't hear. His face looked not only as smug as the cat that got the cream but also as if he had somehow managed to snap the neck of the family dog as well.

'Hiya. Deborah wants to speak to you, Tasha,' he announced, his tone dripping with arrogance as he loomed over her small desk. Tasha pointed at me as if that was all the response she had to his sudden demand. My back was still turned to him, but I could smell his rancid breath seeping over the nape of my neck.

'Go on,' I heard him say in this smug, superior tone I thought I had completely extracted from my mind. It was the kind of voice that, once heard, made you question how forgetting it had ever been possible.

'I can't right now; I'm with a source,' Tasha replied defiantly.

'If you want to ignore her, then be my guest,' he retorted, his pitch rising at the end as if goading her. 'But I wouldn't want to be on her bad side at the moment, you know,' he theatrically scrunched his face with a sharp intake of breath. '... restructuring.'

Tasha groaned begrudgingly with a scowl as she rose to her feet and made her way over to Deborah's private office; I could just about catch her grumblings as she walked away from me.

'This morning, Head of Digital, this afternoon, post girl,' I had just been able to make out her say.

I had assumed Jago Jones would make himself scarce at that point, having successfully irritated Tasha and won some petty game of dominance before moving on to find someone else to sadistically toy with, leaving me to have my third mental breakdown of the day. But his curiosity must have gotten the better of him as, instead of leaving, he swung around the desk, dropped into Tasha's seat, and faced me directly.

The moment he slumped down into a manspread, I saw the flicker of recognition in his eyes. He remembered me but he couldn't quite place where from. I really hoped he didn't assume I was one of his previous conquests.

'You...' he said, his index finger outstretched in my direction. 'You... you used to work here?' You wouldn't be able to tell he was guessing from the confident bravado with which he spoke.

'A while ago, yeah,' I responded, as I hoped and prayed this interaction would be mercifully brief. I couldn't deal with Jago right now. I was just wondering who was going to get me first, Detective Carlota or the TellTale Killer.

'Rachael, was it?' he said with enough false confidence that I almost had to rethink my own name.

'Not quite. Ruth,' I corrected.

'Ruth, I was going to say Ruth,' he said with a self-aggrandising laugh as he slapped the table obnoxiously. 'So, what brings you here, Ruth? You looking for a new job? I mean, I do need a new assistant after mine went home "sick" today. He was the one to unbox the heart, bless him. Blood all over his white chinos. John from accounts heard him throwing up so hard in the bog that he almost baptised himself.'

Gross.

'Just catching up with Tasha,' I responded. I didn't really care for Jago Jones asking me these annoying questions, it was none of his business. What I really wanted to do was perform a strong backhand to his face and be on my way, but now I was going to have to wait until Tasha came out of Deborah's office, and it looked like Jago had absolutely no intention of leaving anytime soon as he began fiddling with the various trinkets on Tasha's desk, rear-ranging them just for the thrill of it.

'Let me guess,' he said drolly. 'You're talking to her about the TellTale Killer? You're not another one of those nutcases who think it's Nick Clegg, are you?'

I raised both my palms upwards as if to non-verbally say, *maybe*. I didn't want to confirm nor deny, but I could see that my discomfort around him was, in a way, somewhat enjoyable to him. He wasn't making it a secret that he was getting off a bit on this.

'I don't want any more of that second-rate journalism here. Let me tell you, the number of people who come in thinking they've magically solved the case of the TellTale Killer, you wouldn't believe it.'

'I'm sure I wouldn't,' I said, still slightly bemused at his presence. What was he hoping to accomplish by talking to me?

'How much do you know about serial killers?' he asked probingly, hoping to get some response from me as his eyes locked onto mine. I jutted out my bottom lip, cocked my head and shrugged my shoulders nonchalantly.

'A little,' I lied. Maybe one of the biggest porkies I've ever told in my life.

'A little?' he said, placing his hand over his mouth and chin, as if to hide a small part of his face from me. 'Some people are really fascinated by them, you know.'

'Well, I'm not the least bit surprised,' I replied, trying to keep my cool and not let Jago Jones see that my mind was working away furiously trying to decipher his game. I gestured with a wave of my hand to the TV behind me. 'When you see how much the press talks about this, is it really a surprise that people get pulled into it?'

'Well, we have a public responsibility to report on it, you know.'

'Sure, but don't you think it gives madmen like *him* something of a platform?' I argued back. You know, I blamed the exhaustion. After so long running on anxiety alone, I didn't have the energy left to be careful with what I said anymore.

All I wanted now was to catch the TellTale Killer. I knew how he was operating – I could almost *feel* him, so close I could practically smell his stench. I just needed this arsehole in front of me to stop talking.

'Come on, there's always going to be serial killers. I mean, look at Jack the Ripper, Ruth. That was the nineteenth century, way before the internet and the true-crime bubble. You really think he was just an egomaniac doing it for the publicity?'

'Have you not read any of the *Pall Mall Gazette* or the *Star*?' I asked, a little bit of patronising slipping into my voice. 'You know, newspapers weren't all that different back then from how they are now, they've always been starving for some sensational story. Of course, they thrived on all the lurid details of his crimes and the public lapped it up in record-breaking fashion, feeding all of their fear and fascination. A notorious serial killer and a hungry press, it's always been the same. They basically feed off each other.'

That seemed to stun him a little. You know, in 1896, when Alfred Harmsworth launched his lively prestigious paper, the *Daily Mail*, his motto was 'Get me a murder a day'. I couldn't help but see the connection again. The Zodiac Killer led to record readership for the *San Fransico Chronicle*; Son of Sam did the same for the *New York Daily News*. It was symbiotic.

'Yeah. Well, I'd better be going,' Jago remarked, clearly I was boring him, probably because I was right. 'Chances are the Tell-Tale Killer has probably gutted another person already.'

In the reflection on the shiny back of Tasha's computer, I caught him glancing at me at least twice as he wandered back over to his corner of the office. It was then I felt the faintest pinch of curiosity.

'He's such an arsehole,' my replacement whispered to herself as she cast an evil side-eye at him. I decided against giving her a high five but only just.

'Hey, I'm Ruth,' I said, pushing my chair over to introduce myself to the woman, someone who looked like she'd also had the passion for journalism drained out of her by working at this paper; her youthful good looks ebbed away by the soul-crushing aura this place emitted. 'Quick question,' I asked. 'Do you still have access to the travel logs? You know, back from when we used to visit sources listed in the database?'

'Yeah,' she replied, as if I was some pensioner asking a teenager if I could borrow her skateboard to do an ollie.

'I was just wondering, would you be able to check something for me? It'll be really quick.'

'Sure. Why?' she asked, instantly suspicious, her guard very much up. I had to change tactics.

'If I told you it might get Jago Jones in trouble... would that be enough?'

That was all it took, clearly. She booted up the reports on her laptop and looked at me like she was positively enthralled at the idea of Jago getting some sorely needed discipline.

I asked her if anyone had visited Bea Powell on the date listed in Greta's note, back on that supposedly mundane Tuesday in May 2024, six months before she died.

'Yeah,' she said, eyebrows raised after she rapidly tapped her keys across the keyboard. 'Would you believe it? The one and only Double J,' she quietly announced with fake zeal; she wasn't very good at hiding the dejection.

I gave her the next name. 'Lewis Khan in November 2023?'

She nodded. 'Jago again, funnily enough.'

'And did he visit a Charlie Young? The latest TellTale victim?'

'Yeah, a few months ago.'

Wait a second...

I heard the very distinctive sound of the email alert from Tasha's computer, a sound I remembered I had heard countless times throughout the day when I'd worked here – and, though I knew it was an awfully terribly nosy thing to do, I couldn't help but lean over the desk to see the preview that had slid across the far bottom left-hand corner of the screen. It was her contact at the DVLA replying to her.

I could just see the first lines of what he had written: *Checked it. All number plates registered to a business address belonging to the legal name of Double J Limited. Say hi to your dad from me.*

As Greta would say: *what an absolute clot.*

However, that was also when my self-preservation finally began to kick in and I knew I needed to get out of this office. I jolted up from my chair without saying goodbye to my replacement and began walking – quickly, but not too quickly – towards the lifts on the far side, keeping my eyes fixed ahead and daring not to glance back to see if Jago Jones was watching.

But despite all the evidence that had just been dropped on me, I couldn't resist testing my hypothesis a little further; I needed absolute certainty of what I thought I had just discovered. I reopened the browser on my phone as I kept my steps fast and purposeful and booted up DarkCell. I typed the first message that I could think of in my mind.

*I know who you are,* I wrote. It was dumb, stupid – I knew it – but it was the only thing that occurred for me to say in that moment, something vague and obscure enough to avoid completely revealing my hand if I was wrong about this, yet potentially sharp enough to strike a modicum of fear into the killer. I hit send and stabbed the lift button simultaneously. As the doors began to close, I could just about hear Jago's phone cheerily chime with an email alert. In that fraction of a second, his eyes snapped to mine, just as the doors clunked shut, severing our connection.

## THIRTY-ONE

Well, what the hell was I meant to do now? I couldn't exactly go to the police. My last encounter with them had involved me sprinting out of the station with my phone clutched in an iron death grip, and an officer of the law at the front desk shouting after me to stop. And what concrete proof did I even have against Jago at this point? His address registered to a list of number plates linked to vans spotted near locations where people had presumably gone missing as victims of the TellTale Killer, logs showing he'd visited each victim between a few months and a few years before they died, and a strong suspicion he was the one messaging me on DarkCell.

Nothing strong enough to take to Detective Carlota even if I wanted to go back. And yet I knew. Right down to the calcium in my brittle bones, I knew it was him. It all made sense. Didn't it?

And Greta had known, too. Greta had found out it was Jago — it was right under her nose, literally. Jago and I worked on the floor just below her. We all knew Jago was a sicko. But why did he do it, what was his *raison de tuer*, if you will? It reminded me I'd read about a chap called Jack Unterweger in my research: an Austrian serial killer who was also an author and journalist. He appeared on television, lectured at universities, and even worked for the national public broadcaster, reporting on murders of sex workers in

Austria and elsewhere in Europe. It turned out he was the one committing those very crimes. There he was, getting a payslip covering atrocities he himself had carried out.

I'd always thought that was madness; surely murderers keep a low profile after a killing. But then there was another man, Vlado Taneski, who did the same, writing freelance pieces about murders he had committed, hoping it would kickstart his budding journalism career. I remember thinking how bonkers and far-fetched that sounded. Only a truly idiotic serial killer, I thought, would report on his own foul deeds. Or maybe someone so deeply egotistical, they wanted everyone to know about their crimes. They wanted, that badly, to be admired for what they did. Yeah... that sounded a lot like Jago Jones.

I hurried towards the Tube. Jago couldn't possibly know where I lived... could he? But an unsettling feeling had lodged within me. He was a journalist, he was really good at finding out information.

I wove through the swathes of tourists and lunged between the closing Tube doors as my phone buzzed in my pocket: an unknown number. I was in no mood for another wretched call about car warranties or mobile phone networks, but I reluctantly picked up anyway, just in case it was Bill or Ben calling from a different phone in case of an emergency.

'Hello?' I said.

'Ruth!' a voice said. The audio seemed to crack and fizzle through the line but I had just enough signal to hear the voice; the tinniness bouncing around my ear delayed my recognition of the caller. 'Just asked for your mobile from Tasha, and I thought I'd give you a ring. It was lovely to see you earlier, I truly appreciated you dropping by.'

My pulse lurched into my throat as I gripped the handset, willing my fingers to hold steady. *Tasha, you absolute imbecile.* I wished that the water from the creek had actually completely wrecked her phone, then maybe she wouldn't have had access to my number. But beyond my anger, I felt a bone-deep fear. It was that voice again, the one that had haunted my thoughts, never leaving me for more than a heartbeat. And now, after two years, we were talking again on the phone.

'My pleasure,' I said, keeping both of our façades intact for the time being. I'd be damned if he could detect any nervousness or anxiety in my voice. 'It's always good to revisit the old stomping ground. I know how frantic things are for you at the moment, though.'

If I'd had any real courage, I would've gone back and killed him on the spot; found a knife, any rusty old thing, and driven it straight into his chest to puncture his heart. Hell, I heard someone died after being hit with a can of baked beans, I could have popped into Tesco on my way there and tried that. But something made me hesitate, made me feel like I was playing chess against someone multiple moves ahead. Besides, if anything went wrong with that plan, I'd just be crazy Ruth who, in an act of envy, tried to kill an award-winning journalist.

He chuckled, letting a mild, fake amusement linger between us.

'You bet. But you're welcome any time, you know that. I'm calling because I valued your...'

He paused, thinking of the exact right word to say to me within the hundreds of thousands that existed in the English language.

'... Your discretion, I guess, back in the day. I trust you haven't mislaid that particular tendency, despite having left us. As you know we're part of a media conglomerate that has standards and, when people can't keep matters to themselves,' he gave a cantankerous *harrumph*, 'well, it seldom ends well for them.'

The fucker was threatening me. He was actually threatening me. Thing was, I was finding him weirdly charming as he was telling me he would kill me if he had to. I guess it made sense right? Monsters weren't monsters twenty-four hours a day?

'Totally see your point, Jago, I do. But some stories aren't meant to stay buried, I feel,' I replied as coolly as I could while I trudged down the carriage and sat down on a spare seat as far away from everyone else as possible. 'Sooner or later, they all deserve a bit of daylight. Don't you think? That *is* journalism.'

To cope, I curled my hand tightly around the handle of the seat, rocking back and forth, hoping the motion might offer some scrap of comfort. All I wanted, in that moment, was for him to be a little morsel afraid of me, for me to feel like I had at least a small chance of bringing him down. For all he knew, I was a killer too.

'I don't disagree. Look, I remember all the work you did proofing my articles back in the day. I know you always looked up to me,' he said smarmily.

'Why?' I asked, the mask in my voice ever so slightly slipping. It was rage, fear or something I couldn't describe that was floating to the surface. 'Why are you doing this?'

He gave a hollow bellow down the phone as if I was a toddler who had asked him to give me back my nose.

'That's a fake laugh,' I murmured, mostly to myself. 'A really bad one. You're not fooling anyone, you know. Tell me, why are you doing this?'

'Ruth, you don't know why you're asking me this,' he hissed as with a slow, clunky jolt, the Tube began to leave the station. 'In some ways, I always felt we were a little bit alike. Even back then, your writing was always sharp, unsentimental, you looked straight at things others refused to see. You cut through everyone else's nonsense. We're both chasing the truth. The only difference is... I never stopped when it turned ugly.'

'Greta,' I blurted out, the name tumbling out before I'd even realised I'd spoken. 'Do you remember Greta?'

He paused again, just for a beat, but it was the kind of pause that felt like he was mentally rifling through a catalogue of his own crimes, as if he was perusing his fucked-up murder rolodex.

'I do. I remember Greta. God, so sad what happened to her, I really do miss her,' he said, his tone almost wistful. 'I think, the amount of notes I wrote her; she became fluent in the Jago Jones calligraphy brand.'

Oh! Well, that made sense. In her notes, the scribbles that were now in Detective Carlota's possession had mentioned 'handwriting'. And Greta had been inundated with those passive, and sometimes outright aggressive messages he used to leave on her desk whenever he wanted her to make edits on the website. I bet she recognised his handwriting from all the notes he had left her.

'Her only mistake was figuring out too much.' I almost heard him give a smirk as he realised he had said more than he intended. 'Look, Ruth, I wasn't going to tell you this, I didn't want to upset you. But I wonder... if the Telltale Killer might've come for you, too. Just imagine, if he saw you both in that café that night, and convinced himself she'd told you everything. I wonder why you were left in peace then? I think she begged. Over and over. Begged him to spare your life, promising the killer you had absolutely no idea. Even when she was dying, I wonder if she pleaded for me to leave you alone.'

There aren't words for how I felt in that moment, so I won't try to even begin to describe them. But I was sure, with heart-obliterating clarity, that he was telling me the truth.

My mind had never once entertained the thought that Greta had been trying to save me on that night. I'd thought, for the longest time, that she'd spent her last moments hating me, wishing I had died instead of her. He didn't mean to do it, but the TellTale Killer had given me a very small mercy.

'So, what's next for you?' I asked casually, hoping he'd answer with something I could use to track him down. Was I worried he might say my name in response? Fairly. But I was determined enough that, if the price of his justice was my life, I was mostly willing to pay it.

'Next?' he responded, almost amused. 'I guess there's always been one person I've wanted to properly interview, that I'd be keen to reach out to... but that would be telling, wouldn't it?'

Yikes, was he talking about me?

I could feel him holding his urges down, biting back the words he so desperately wanted to spill. He thought he'd found someone enthralled by him, obsessed, like some devoted K-pop fan stanning over this idol, and he wanted to tell me everything he was going to do. But, in the end, his instinct for self-preservation just about won out. I just wondered who on God's green earth he was talking about...

'Well, delightful catching up,' he said at last, blithe as ever. 'Must dash.' The line went dead.

I might've found it properly bone-chilling if a dishevelled, 90-per-cent-alcohol bloke on the train hadn't stood up and yelled mostly incoherently to the whole carriage:

'Who wants to see how many Babybels I can fit up my bum?'

And there were indeed takers.

# PART FIVE

# THIRTY-TWO

You know it's weird – real serial killers rarely resemble their fictional counterparts. On page or on screen, they are often given a code, a neat rationale, because we, the audience, find comfort in believing that something specific, something rigid, drives the horror they create. We want a simple reason for them doing what they do. The truth is, unfortunately, a little more prosaic. Most killers are fuelled by narcissism and the thrill of control; above all, they do it because they want to.

I was finally facing that truth. Right from the beginning, the TellTale Killer had been Jago's own invention for the papers. The man craved the limelight, and now both halves of his nature were revelling in it, one collecting journalism prizes and front-page headlines, the other supplying the atrocities he so brilliantly reported on.

I hadn't stopped running since the Tube, terrified I would get home and find either Jago waiting for me with a cup of tea in the kitchen and Ben's heart nestled in his hand, or Detective Carlota, saying I had won an all-expenses paid trip to jail. Either way, I needed to face it. I pelted up the path, grabbed my key and rammed it into the lock before thrusting it open.

'Ruth? Hi?' Bill's voice floated from the landing as I slammed the door shut, wind-tossed, skin moist and face flushed. 'You okay?' I heard him say.

'Fine,' I lied as I inspected the downstairs for any sign of Jago and/or Carlota. I had a feeling that being honest with Bill wouldn't do the investigation any favours. The man was wound pretty tight, even on a good day.

He slowly descended from the top of the stairs, uncharacteristically, and infuriatingly, in the mood for some chit-chat. Exactly what I didn't have time for right now. Could he not have picked any day of the previous few hundred I have lived here for a chinwag?

'So, Ben's taking a nap,' Bill said, reaching the bottom of the stairs and rather awkwardly slapping his hands together. 'And I just wanted to take a moment to say thanks, Ruth. For everything you're doing for Ben and me. We really do appreciate it,' he said, genuinely earnest.

'No problem,' I said, my eyes darting towards the clock on the wall to see what time it was. 'Has anyone called for me? A detective? A journalist?'

'Nope, no one, as far as I'm aware,' Bill replied, really not picking up the urgency in my tone. 'It's funny, though, I've just been working on a bid for overhauling the Met Police's software, actually, maybe you could introduce me to someone?'

I know it probably seemed rude, but I didn't even bother to laugh at that comment.

Bill lingered, exhaling as he shuffled a little closer to me, his heels scuffing the floor like a teenager caught out smoking weed in the greenhouse. 'Look Ruth, I know I can be an arse sometimes,' he said frankly. 'I'm working on it, I've always had a problem with my... feelings and I guess, feeling them. Honestly, a lot of days I'm not particularly fond of myself. So, I'm trying to get better.'

I caught Bill's eye and realised I had been nodding along, over and over, but not taking in a whole lot of what he was saying. My mind was still locked on Jago and his next move. And what about Detective Carlota, was she going to give all of my evidence to the police? Was she planning to arrest me just to keep me safe in a prison cell?

'I don't know how long we've got left with Ben,' Bill went on, the tone of his voice continued to progressively soften and weaken, showing a level of vulnerability I'd never seen from him before, 'but I'd really like for you and I to still be in touch after he's... gone. I know I can get quite angry but I am working on it and I guess, what I'm trying to say is that I don't really want to be on my own and, I think, I'd miss you.'

'Don't talk like that,' I snapped rather curtly as I walked out to the shed to make sure neither Jago nor Carlota were hiding out there, waiting for me. Bill was a bit taken back by that, but I think he assumed it was just the months of resentment finally coming to the surface. I just didn't want to think about Ben right now. Besides, the man still had years left to live, even with his diagnosis. Right now, absurd as it sounded, a deranged journalist was more of a threat to Ben's life than his brain tumour. But despite every passive-aggressive word we had exchanged with one another, there was a new sincerity in Bill's words, an honesty I'd never heard from him before. He was trying to open up to me; I only wished it had come at a different time, when I might have been more receptive, but it was a morsel of comfort, nevertheless. On the off chance I did make it out alive from this, it would be nice to have a friend.

'I understand,' he responded as I opened the shed and checked every inch of it for intruders. It would have been nice if Toast had some security impulses as opposed to carnal ones.

'Look, you mustn't breathe a word of this to him,' Bill continued as he followed me inside, 'but... Ben is not sure he wants treatment anymore. Last night, just before the detective came by, he said he wanted quality, not quantity, with... his life.'

I kept searching frantically around the shed, which made Bill realise he had to spell out exactly what he meant when I didn't react right away.

'I think he wants to stop chemo entirely.'

While most of my focus was firmly locked on Jago, this news

still managed to rattle something loose in me. I stopped dead, that familiar, sinking weight settling into my chest like an unwelcome guest I'd never once invited to stay.

I watched Bill slump against one of the walls of the shed, clearly devastated, his hands falling limp against his lap as his head bowed forward a little. Clearly, he had been needing to talk to someone about this.

'I don't think he wants to keep fighting anymore,' he said quietly. 'He says he wants some grace in his death, whatever the hell that means.'

I suppose I'd half expected it. Ben hated the chemo, dreaded what it was doing to his dignity. I knew he would be worried about becoming a burden – though, of course, both of us would do anything for him. I mean, Bill and I would struggle to make each other a single cup of tea if our life depended on it, but for Ben, the rarest Chinese blend wouldn't be too much trouble. We both loved him, we both knew how important he was.

'You think he'll really stop?' I asked, scanning Bill's face for the reassurance he didn't seem to have. 'He can't do that. That would mean... just a few more months.'

'I do,' he said quietly. 'I think he just wants to enjoy what time's left, without being in a hospital ward. He's tired, Ruth, he's so tired.'

My phone vibrated, forcing me to shove all the complex feelings I was experiencing to the side. Was it Carlota? A message saying get ready for my mugshot? Or Jago? Saying get ready for stabby time. Who was to know at this point.

It was a DarkCell message, and it was not from CerealKiller-Cornflakes.

The note was brief and to the point:

*You're going to die, just like her.*

And then came the photos, of what was left of my Greta, still dressed in her ripped emerald coat, the lone piece of which lay in my cupboard drawer.

I hadn't realised that I hadn't moved for a few minutes until Bill's voice came from close beside me.

'Ruth,' he said, eyes wide with horror as he took in the contents of my phone screen. 'What the actual fuck?'


'So, wait, one more time,' Ben said, his eyes squinting, fingers perched on his temples, 'explain it to me again like I'm an idiot.' I could tell he was trying desperately to digest what I was telling him, but he still couldn't quite wrap his head around it. I can't say I blamed him, though, this was quite a lot to drop on somebody all at once. Bill was still pacing endlessly around the front room, storming from the monstera plant all the way to his vinyl collection before swivelling around and repeating the circuit. Meanwhile, I sat on the lone blue ottoman with my hands placed gently on the corresponding knees, facing both of them. I knew Bill probably hadn't meant to, but the tall black standing lamp illuminating the room had been angled directly at me, almost like it was some sort of interrogation tactic.

'What's there to explain?' Bill rasped, his voice hoarse from the hour of loud voices and curt words, yet still no sign of any kind of communication from Detective Carlota. 'Ruth's gone absolutely bonkers, she's a full-blown nutcase.'

That felt a bit uncalled for, but maybe he wasn't completely wrong. I had gone quite crazy over the last thirteen days.

'Right, Bill, you need to calm down,' Ben said as gently as he could, outstretching his hand to him before pointing to outside the room. 'Go get some red wine or have a smoke or something.'

Bill grumbled something curmudgeonly under his breath as he stomped away to the wine cabinet they kept in the study.

'Oh, Ruth.' Ben sighed wearily in a tone that was reminiscent of our marriage when I would tell him there wasn't enough money in the account when the direct debit went out; his voice blending compassion at the mess I had landed in along with the very clear revulsion of what I had been doing secretly over the past few weeks. 'What have you done?'

'None of you understand,' I muttered sullenly, avoiding eye contact with Ben, I didn't want to see any shame he had for me in his eyes.

'No, trust me, Ruth, I really don't,' Ben replied, exasperated, still looking visibly frazzled, trying to figure out how I'd managed to get away with this undetected right under his nose.

See, after Bill had seen the photos of Greta on my phone and also witnessed the absolute emotional state I was in, I realised three things. One, there was no magical, IQ 5000 lie I could conjure that would explain away why I had pictures of my dead friend on my phone. Two, I was utterly exhausted with lying. And three, I was scared, really, truly scared. At that point, it just made sense to come completely clean to Bill, and Ben too. I mean, at this rate everyone in the UK would know what I had been up to by their Saturday night dinner.

That brief moment of reconciliation Bill and I had shared was instantly shattered and he'd awoken Ben and told him to get ready for the craziest story he'd ever heard.

See, I know why Jago sent it: he wanted to scare me. Sure, maybe he still thought I was a budding serial killer, but he definitely knew that I knew his identity, and he didn't want me blabbing. I also imagine he was still mad at what I had said in the note and wanted to try and terrify me into submission.

And it should have. The photos should have destroyed me, should have absolutely obliterated me, but the more I thought about it, the more I realised I was... almost okay. Seeing Greta like that was horrifying, yes, but he'd unknowingly given me a bleak realisation: my mind had finally accepted that she was dead. Gone. He had completely crushed all hope of seeing Greta alive ever again and I had to be at least a little bit thankful to him for that. Nothing that I could do now would bring Greta back.

'So, that heart of the man that they found at the nightclub, that was... you?' Ben asked, still trying to make sense of this.

'No, that was Charlie Young, *that* wasn't me,' I said. 'I haven't... actually killed anyone, I do want to make that clear.'

Ben made a small grunt as I watched him assume his stern thinking face.

'And my food container going missing,' Bill burst back in, now holding a mightily large glass of wine in one hand and a cigarette in another. 'Were you behind that too?'

I rolled my eyes. Was that really the thing Bill was most interested in right now? You know what, it was probably worth getting everything out in the open at this point.

'Yes, Bill, I did use your food container,' I said on the exhale of a sigh. 'I really don't think you want it back.'

Bill gagged as he desperately tried to hold his gulp of red wine in his mouth without dribbling it on his very expensive flooring. God, that felt good. That's weird of me to say, isn't it?

'And you've been communicating with the killer?' Ben asked, ignoring Bill darting to the sink to retch. 'The actual TellTale Killer?'

'Yeah, it's a guy called Jago Jones, who works at the paper.'

Ben's face flashed with a small glimmer of recognition. He remembered that name back from when I worked there. I had moaned to Ben several times about how much I despised him.

'A journalist?' Ben asked. 'Moonlighting as a serial killer?'

'I guess all serial killers are moonlighting as something,' I responded. 'It's not really a full-time career path.'

'And who else knows?' Ben asked, remaining impressively stoic throughout the proceedings.

'You two, and Detective Carlota,' I explained. 'About me, not about Jago Jones. I guess it would be safe to say that I am currently awaiting arrest from her. She told me to "sit tight", but I ran out of the police station instead. I couldn't let him get away again, Ben. I just have to figure out some way to catch him.'

'Great, so you're on the run from the law too?' Ben said. He seemed to have given up sounding surprised at least. It really had been quite a day.

'Sort of,' I said, tilting my palm back and forth. 'Think of it as a kind of scenic detour from authority in the midst of some bad life choices.'

Ben gave a long groan.

'And so what's your plan, Ruth, to even try and catch him? You're barely five feet tall,' Bill interjected, returning from the loo with his trademark condescension, guzzling the last of his red wine as he finished his sentence.

'Bill, you know what? You're not helping at all,' I replied spitefully before Ben could try and defuse the situation. 'So, you can just leave and have a wank to different types of paint swatches or whatever gets you off.'

He looked frankly appalled that I said that.

'I'm not helping? You're the one who just invited a serial killer into our lives,' Bill exploded. 'He could have found out where we lived and be on his way to kill us all right now.'

'Let's all just calm down, okay?' Ben said again, trying to be the voice of reason between two very tense people but I could tell he found my paint swatches remark a little funny. 'We're not going to come up with a solution if we're all biting each others' heads off.'

'There is only one solution,' Bill chimed in. 'And that's to go to the police, the *proper* police, and tell them everything, right now.' His voice climbed higher and higher in pitch and became more chipmunk as he repeated, 'It's the only option, the only option.'

Ben nuzzled his head into his hand, as if he found Bill and I as infuriating as each other, and I couldn't help but wonder if Ben was now considering what Bill had said. Would he try and make me go to the police? Would he think that was the best option?

'What you did, Ruth, was stupid. Very stupid,' Ben said, cutting through a silence that had grown heavy and overlong after a few moments. This situation definitely ranked higher on the awkward scale than when I had to tell my dad that Ariana

Grande's 'side to side' was about being fucked so hard you couldn't walk.

Ben had told me that there was a thing called 'chemo dreams' where people would have these vivid and disturbing nightmares throughout the whole treatment process, I wondered if he thought he was experiencing one of these currently.

'I know,' I replied simply.

'Just... why? Imitating a serial killer? Did you not think about any of the consequences?'

'Yes,' I said with a scorned mumble, which was true. 'They just didn't seem as important.'

'Just... what even goes on in your brain to even make you consider doing something like that?' Ben asked, his tone laced with a genuine disbelief. Clearly surprised that someone he thought he knew so well could stun him this much.

'Oh, I don't know, maybe the same kind of crazy that leads someone to refuse treatment for a brain tumour,' I replied, hoping that he would feel the same bitterness that I had just received.

Ben's face lit with anger, though not directed at me; he twisted his head to Bill. 'You told her?'

'I needed to tell someone!' Bill responded with a half squeal, his eyes suddenly flashing at me with betrayal. The chain of anger flowed freely between the three of us like a kind of toxic triangle.

'And he used up all your mint tea tree shower gel because he likes the way it stings his balls,' I said. I'd been sitting on that one for three months, ever since I'd overheard him confess it, drunk as a skunk at a dinner party, while Bill was out of the room.

I could tell Ben was just as furious about that as he was about the treatment reveal.

'Psycho,' Bill hissed at me.

'Shut up, flowerpot boy,' I shot back as I watched his eyes blaze with fury. I knew he'd hate that.

'Stop,' Ben groaned, his eyes practically bulging. Oh, he definitely thought he was having some kind of crazy 'chemo dream' now.

'What are you even doing, refusing treatment?' I said, seething, to Ben.

'We're not focusing on me right now,' Ben said, raising his hands to his head. 'Christ almighty,' he muttered to himself. He gritted and ground his teeth as he mulled over what to do next and how to extricate us from the precarious situation I had landed us in. At that moment, I realised I had, in my own strange way, made Detective Carlota, and now Bill and Ben, accomplices to my scheme. And I could hardly imagine that any of them were too happy about that.

'How close do you think you are to being able to bring him in, Ruth?' Ben asked, in a different tone now, like he was done processing and was finally trying to be pragmatic.

My ex-husband had obviously changed a great deal since we'd first met, and even more so since he and Bill had become a couple. Exhibit A: picking up skiing as a hobby, when he'd always hated the cold. Still, I was confident I could still read his face better than anyone else, and I saw something there. It was as if he, too, loathed and abhorred the TellTale Killer almost as much as I did. And while he probably thought I was crazy, it was like he understood where I was coming from.

He repeated the question, realising I had once again got lost in the deluge of thoughts in my mind.

'Ruth, do you think you have enough to bring him in?'

'I think I can do it,' I said. 'I have a plan.'

I had absolutely no plan. Not even the tiniest remnants of a plan. Pretty much since the start of this, I had been winging it.

Ben glanced at Bill, clearly bracing for whatever insane reaction was about to come his way.

'Ruth, if you think you can do it,' Ben said, steady and serious, 'then I'm behind you all the way. You just let us know how we can help.'

Before Bill could even open his mouth to scream in protest, my phone buzzed on the table. I reached for it instinctively, but Ben got there first, probably trying to spare me from another photo of

Greta. It was a phone call, and I tried to make out what the tiny voice was saying as I watched Ben's face drain to a deathly hue, his features becoming even more pallid than they already were.

'Thank you,' he said quietly into the phone. 'I'll let Ruth know.'

Then Ben turned to me, his throat looking like it was pulsating with a set of repeated nervous swallows.

'That was the police. Detective Carlota's gone missing. They said she's been in contact with you and wanted to know if you knew anything about where she may be?'

In that moment, in a strange, dark way, it seemed my problems had solved themselves; Jago wasn't coming to kill me, and Carlota wasn't coming to arrest me. But, of course, that small gift only left room for a far bigger crisis to be dealt with.

## THIRTY-THREE

'Has he messaged?' I asked. A question I'd once posed twenty years ago about the boy on the bus I liked, was now about the serial killer lurking in my phone. Ben shook his head, eyes glued to the phone screen before glancing back up at the crime wall. The three of us had relocated to the shed, hoping that the crime wall I had created over the years would give us some kind of clarity about the situation. It didn't.

'No,' he replied. 'He hasn't. Some guy called CerealKiller-Cornflakes is messaging you, though.'

I groaned, pressing my hands tight to my face before flopping my body back onto my bed. *Go away, Nico, leave your incredible nose out of this.*

'He wants me,' I whispered, in this regard about the TellTale Killer, but it probably also applied to Nico. 'And if he can't get me, he's going to kill Carlota.'

'What if we just leak it to the press right now?' Bill asked, trying for once to be helpful, bless him. 'Tell the whole world who the TellTale Killer really is?'

'Then he'll just kill Carlota for the sake of it,' I half repeated, a little incensed at Bill not thinking his question through. 'I won't let her die, I can't. Even if I have to go to him myself as some kind of sacrificial lamb.'

'And are you considering that?' Ben asked gravely. 'He could just end up killing both of you at this rate. I mean, that's kind of his whole thing, you know, killing.'

'Well, you live, you die, and that's it, isn't it?' I said with my best attempt at a nonchalant shrug. 'This is my fault, anyway. I dragged him back into the spotlight. I could have just left well enough alone and that might have been the end of it. This is pretty much entirely my fault, actually.'

No one in the room – not Bill, Ben, not even Toast – challenged me on that statement, so I guess they knew it was at least partially true. I watched Bill scrutinise the crime wall, taking in every pinned photograph and hastily scrawled note I had made, his upper lip twitching slightly as he registered just how much territory of the wall I'd claimed with my various reams of paper. I could practically hear his teeth grinding at the small factory's worth of Sellotape I'd used. I appreciated he was trying to keep that repressed right now.

I glanced at Toast, hoping for some kind of idea. Her eyes seemed to shoot off in two different directions before she violently sneezed and, at the same time, smacked her head against the glass, probably annihilating her one last remaining brain cell.

'So, Jago Jones actually visited all the victims?' Ben asked as he took a glimpse at one corner of the crime wall. 'Before they died?'

'Yes, some a few months before, others a few years,' I replied despondently. 'I think so, I imagine that's how he picked them. He probably had their obituaries written out before he even yanked their hearts out of their corpses.'

Ben fell silent, then leaned forward to stroke his chest as if coaxing out a thought. I wanted to tell him he was wasting his time: a team of police detectives and an army of online sleuths and I had been poring over this case for two years without so much as a breakthrough. I couldn't see how he was going to make this all fit together.

Ben leaned back, brow furrowed as he picked up the tablet he had brought with him to the shed, as if it would be of any use.

'Suppose there is a narrative,' he posited as he typed something in and began scrolling down the screen. 'He never filed a story based on any of the visits to the victims, did he? Or the connection would have been caught. Maybe he was refused, denied the chance to report on something. Perhaps that's what drove him: his own weird, warped sense of justice.'

I sat up from my bed and straightened my back; maybe Ben had a point, it did make a disturbing kind of sense. Every time Jago had spoken to me, or the TellTale Killer had left a note about his 'story', he'd been talking about enforcing his version of the world, a self-appointed, self-justified crusade. There were very few things that made a journalist more angry than being denied a good story by an unhelpful source.

'I don't know about the others,' Ben murmured as he swigged what was left of Bill's wine. 'But I know Lewis Khan was working at Cobra Electrical and they were right in the midst of this pretty massive scandal. I imagine being told you can't get a story you want is going to be pretty frustrating for a psychopath. Say he made his list for years, all the people who refused to let the truth come to light, and this is how he enacts his version of it, by, you know...'

Ben rather gratuitously mimed a stabbing motion towards Toast, who just looked up at him from her tank as if to say, *Hey, what the fuck, bro?*

As much as it irritated me and hurt my own ego to admit it, I had to concede that Ben was quite likely right. There always had to be some kind of reason for why Jago had picked his victims. Urgh, I was going to have to tell Nico he was right about this too.

It struck me suddenly that maybe Jago hadn't abducted Detective Carlota to get to me at all, but because she too had refused his 'story' and he actually had no idea how closely our lives were actually tangled. I remember that only last night, Carlota had told me she had tried to get Jago blacklisted from the station due to his sneaky journalistic endeavours.

Was this really what I was dealing with: an angry little boy who, when told 'no', decided to kill people? How could someone who'd evaded the best minds in the country have the emotional maturity of a toddler?

I was still the only person, other than maybe Carlota, who'd figured out he was the TellTale Killer. Was there still time? Could I still save her?

Bill exhaled a long, heavy, weary breath that could power an offshore wind farm.

'I'm off to pour another glass of wine,' he announced and dawdled out. Ben and I naturally turned to look at each other as Bill gently clanked the door of the shed shut behind him.

'Can I have my phone back now, please?' I asked Ben. He hesitated, then sighed, like he was admitting I was bound to make a foolish choice with or without the device. We sat in another long silence, our eyes fixed on the crime wall, trying to see if there would be anything there that could save Detective Carlota.

'So, Greta knew,' Ben said quietly, a note of sadness, almost wistful, in his voice. 'She was the one who figured it out first, before anyone else.'

'Yeah, I think so,' was all I could manage to say at this point. My mind was a mess of various complex thoughts and feelings, so it was difficult to manufacture a coherent sentence.

'She was always so smart, so clever. I still miss her a lot, you know.' He hesitated for a moment. 'I mean, I know you know it always bothered me how close you two were, but... I did really like her, Ruth.'

I tried my absolute hardest to muster a smile, something that might try and ease a bit of the guilt he was clearly carrying right now.

'I know you did, love.'

I thought about correcting myself then, but at this point I realised I couldn't remove that word for Ben from my vocabulary, like a juicy Bolognese stain on a crisp white linen shirt. No matter how hard I tried, it was here to stay.

'I suppose it's like what you said, right?' I replied. 'To love someone is to accept the absolute certainty of heartbreak.' I tried to repeat what he'd said to me in the hospital two days ago. Ben smirked, slightly bemused that I'd remembered his bit of Poundland philosophy.

'I think that's only part of it, though, Ruth.' He began, with a look in his eyes I couldn't quite read. 'I think it's true, but also if you cling too closely to the dead, then you just end up becoming a ghost too.'

I knew what he was implying about me; I knew what he'd always thought about how I handled my grief for Greta but that had never once verbalised. But now I was wondering if, by choosing this neat, tidy death by refusing any further treatment, he was trying to stop me mourning two people and becoming even more of a ghost.

'So, you know, I kind of thought Bill was lying when he told me you weren't sure about continuing treatment,' I said. 'It didn't really sound like something you would do.'

'We're talking about this now?' Ben asked with a laugh that was half sincere and half exasperated. 'Is this really the best time? We're meant to be working out how we can catch a serial killer while you're on the run from the police.'

'Well, I highly suspect that I may be either dead or arrested in twenty-four hours, so yeah, I'd say it's a fine time to talk about it,' I responded. 'This may be our only chance.'

Ben scoffed before he replied.

'I just don't want to suffer, Ruth. I want a few good months of making memories with Bill, and then I just want to pop my clogs, and for that just to be the end of it. I don't want to drag it out any longer than I have to. I'm over chemo, I'm over hospitals, I'm over all of it. If I'm going to die, I'm going to die. I want some control in it though. I don't want to slowly grow into a cold dead body, I want you, Bill, my parents, I want you all to have a clean break. No more pain and no more grief needed than necessary.'

I didn't know how to reply to that. Was there such a thing as a clean-break death? I didn't know how to convince him that he was making the wrong choice. Was it even wrong, if it was his choice to make?

'How long would you live without chemo?' I asked quietly, making the cardinal sin of asking a question I didn't really want to know the answer to.

'They reckon about four months, max. For two months I should be all right with the medication, but after that... high risk of hospitalisation and then obviously I'll...' He didn't finish his sentence.

'Right,' I sighed, giving him the courtesy of not letting him speak about his mortality. I watched Toast, who, as ever, was refusing to read the room, straddling her favourite ball. We tried to ignore it.

'Look,' I said, not really knowing what I wanted to say but speaking anyway, 'I don't want you to think I'm not supporting you in... you know, your choice to not do treatment. But from my perspective, there's still so much life left to live, and I'd do anything, anything, to have more time with Greta. God, do you know what I'd do right now if she were alive?'

Obviously, Ben didn't answer.

'I always thought it was corny, so corny, when people said they'd give it all up for one more day. But I would. I absolutely would. And I know it's selfish of me to say, but I want as many days with you as possible, Ben. I don't want you to suffer either, but when I think of how much time we could still have...'

It felt as though Ben and I were both struggling to finish our sentences, as if our thoughts needed more time to connect and construct than our neurons could even manage, leaving us grasping for the words to try and express how we felt. I wished, desperately, that I could gather the thoughts and feelings in my head and shape them into something that made sense to someone. But I never felt I could. I never seemed able to tell Ben how I truly felt.

'I guess this won't be one of your fonder memories to look back on from your deathbed, right?' I asked.

'No, probably not this one,' he said with a thick layer of face-tiousness, staring at Toast doing her thing because that was better than looking at my crime wall. 'I just want to choose how I go. I don't want it to be after months of lying in a hospital bed, slipping in and out of consciousness and family members saying goodbye to the shell of person I was. But at least I have time. At least I can go and patch things up with Dad finally.'

'That's true,' I said. Ben and his dad hadn't spoken in years, so it was nice to hear that he was open to the possibility of finally repairing or mending things. I hoped his dad would be too. Maybe this was a kinder hand from fate than just being hit by a car, maybe now he had the ability to make things right before he died. Was that a better way to die? To know beforehand so you could make amends? I had no idea, frankly.

I couldn't help but think about what had been going through Greta's head in her final moments. What does someone who knows they're about to die think about? Did she hear me on the phone, telling her what a terrible friend she was, when she had possibly just sacrificed her life to save mine? God, I really could be awful sometimes.

'I need to know why you're doing this, Ruth,' he asked, like a senior Sunday-school teacher who'd just caught me taking a leak in the holy water.

'I need Greta to matter,' I said.

'Do you know the great lie about life?' Ben posited after what I presumed was his own moment of small, internal reflection. 'The great lie is that our lives need to mean something, that we need to be the founder of a tech start-up, or invent a cure for Alzheimer's. That we need to make a notable dent in the universe, just to matter, just to have significance. But I don't believe that anymore. I hope you know that bringing the TellTale Killer to justice won't make Greta's life worth any more or less. The fact we're still talking about her, two years later, that we miss her, *that* is proof she meant something.'

'Now, was *that* from a TED Talk?' I said with a light smile creeping across my face.

'That one was,' Ben affirmed, his eyes drifting upwards as if it was to remember which one it was. 'Everything ends, often before we feel it's meant to. But that doesn't mean it matters any less.'

I didn't know if he was referring to our marriage, his own life or Greta's but it reminded me of what she'd said the day she died. Wabi-sabi, her word of the day, the beauty of things being temporary.

As much as I wanted to keep sinking into the deep-and-meaningful conversation with Ben, I knew I'd have to move sooner or later. For now, I was one step ahead of the TellTale Killer, he didn't know I knew about Carlota and if I wanted to stop him from taking another life, I had to do something.

'You said you'd help me, right?' I asked Ben as I tried to figure out exactly how I was going to get through this.

'Always,' he replied, without a moment's hesitation. 'Till death us do part, right?'

I snorted. I thought those vows were redundant when the divorce papers were finalised.

I can't pretend it was bravery that was pushing me right now. In fact, I didn't even know if this was the right thing to do. I just knew that two years ago, Greta had done the same for me. She put her life on the line to save mine. Greta's life had always meant something, but saving Carlota felt like it would let her death mean something too.

Urgh, and anyway, what's the worst that could happen? Getting killed by a serial killer? Eh, no biggie. That was when Bill burst back through the shed door, a notepad clutched in one hand, a pen in the other and a laptop shoved under his armpit. He looked frantic, wild-eyed, jabbing the pen at me as if it were a weapon.

'Right, Ruth, I know I freaked out a bit and I know we've had our differences in the past, but whatever plan you've got right now? Scrap it. I was having a glass of wine and I was thinking and I think whatever you're planning... it's a bad idea and you need to stop it, right now.'

'What?' Ben and I said in unison, both staring at him, beyond baffled. I think even Toast was so astonished by Bill that she stopped doing her usual humping to look at him judgementally.

'I've been thinking,' Bill said breathlessly, barely stopping to let any of his words register. 'About your crime wall, about the Tell-Tale Killer, about Jago and how he's just generally in love with himself. It's like you said: they've all got massive egos and ego makes you do stupid things. Jago *would* probably write the obituary for his victims before they even died. And I think I've got an idea. It's crazy but it might save Detective Carlota. I mean you might die, Ruth, that is the only caveat, but I think it will save her. Because the TellTale Killer still thinks you're a serial killer like him.'

He paused for a fraction of a moment, trying to remember what else he had come in to say.

'By the way, you mentioned you had a friend who still worked at the paper, right?'

Don't know if I would describe Tasha as a friend exactly.

'Yeah,' I said, but I was still processing Bill's sudden willingness to help with all this. 'But why would that matter?'

It was like Bill was purposefully pausing for dramatic effect.

'You know about how they caught the BTK Killer?'

'The floppy disc situation?' I answered; of course I knew how they caught the BTK Killer, I'm just surprised that Bill did. I suppose his job was all about computers and software, maybe that was something they taught you in whatever techy school he went to.

'Okay. So how would you feel about meeting Jago... face to face again?' Ben asked, somewhat trepidatiously, still channelling the wild-eyed energy of a hamster who had been dunked in an espresso. 'Tonight.'

'What?' Ben blurted, his shock plain, but Bill barely registered.

For Ben, meeting a notorious serial killer face to face probably sounded downright mad. Bill and I were clearly more unhinged than he realised.

'It would ideally need to be near Hammersmith, near the office,' he said to me, ignoring his boyfriend.

'I know a place,' I replied quickly.

# THIRTY-FOUR

## TWO YEARS AGO

### Greta

You know, it is funny what your brain thinks about when you're approaching your very last moments. For me, my mind went back to a nativity play from when I was about six in Year 1 of primary school. I remembered I had been given the privilege of playing Shepherd #2 and dressed up in a tea towel that my grandma had got us from Malta as authentic shepherd head garb. I can vividly remember peering through the gap in the curtain to see the audience and feeling a version of that same creeping dread curling and coiling in my stomach.

There was a vague, almost diluted memory that was finding its way into my mind's eye. I remembered Ruth, who played Innkeeper #2, and was incredibly pleased with herself because she got to say 'bog off' to Mary and Joseph in front of an audience of adults, coming up beside me. I caught the fear on her face, and could see she was nervous by the way she was reaching and clenching the fabric of her skirt. She just looked how I felt in all honestly.

'Don't worry,' I remember saying to her. 'You can only be brave when you're afraid.' That seemed to help. That was the day when I felt we had truly become friends, and we'd been inseparable ever since, until, well, right now, I suppose.

Later, she found out I'd lifted it from a handmade kitten poster in Mrs Todd's Year 4 classroom but the fact we kept talking about it twenty-five years later meant that it had still been significant.

I just hoped Ruth would make it out of this. I hoped and prayed that Ruth, Chlo, my dad, my brother, would all be all right, that somehow they'd all be okay in the end. They could be sad for a while, that was fine. Actually, it would have been weird if they weren't, but I really didn't want this to destroy them. Honestly, when you're dying, you don't wish the worst on anyone... except, of course, if relevant, the person killing you. More than anything, you just kind of want everyone you love to be okay, to know that they're going to be just fine without you. More than anything, you just wish you had more time.

But I knew Jago had made one fatal mistake, one he didn't even recognise with the size of his ego. He messed with my Ruth. It might take time – years, maybe – but if anyone was going to get to the bottom of this, it was her. From the words he'd spoken to her on my phone as I began drifting out of consciousness, I knew she wouldn't stop to make him pay for what he did. I knew she'd figure it out some day.

All I needed now was for her to be brave.

# THIRTY-FIVE

## PRESENT DAY

We reached Hammersmith sooner than I'd expected. It was 8.30 p.m., and Sabroso wouldn't close until 10 p.m. if Google was correct. Meeting in a public venue afforded me a very hollow and fragile sense of safety, no guarantee against a knife to the heart, of course, but I suppose there's always a small sliver of protection you feel being a in public setting – it's why you break up with someone in a Starbucks in Birmingham New Street Station as opposed to the hammer section at B&Q. Much as I love London, I doubt it matters where you are: when January is cold, wet and dark, it is unavoidably depressing.

I tried to focus my mind on the present. We had something of a plan; it wasn't the best plan in the world, concocted as it had been by Bill while he was practically buzzing off sketchy red wine and half a dozen cigarettes, but it was a plan nevertheless. Ultimately, it had been decided that I was going to be human bait, ironic considering it was what I had once asked Greta to do. I'd lure Jago out from wherever he was keeping Carlota, hopefully before he killed her. Bill believed it would be the same address the number plates were registered to: a glorified storage unit near Battersea. We were betting that I was the shiny object Jago couldn't resist. He still thought of me as his acolyte, his imitator. If I promised to come alone and unarmed and did it at short notice so it looked a little spontaneous, I knew he'd gobble up the bait. He couldn't risk anyone tarnishing the TellTale Killer 'brand' if my antics came to light, and he'd see this meeting as a chance to snuff me out for good. As Detective Carlota once said to me, serial killers really don't like copycats.

Ben was my backup, parked outside in his car like a terminally ill guardian angel, ready to intervene if things went bad. And Bill... well, he was about to break into my old workplace. I mean, this whole plan had been his idea, I suppose; if he was foolish enough to think it would work, I supposed I was foolish enough to try it. One more stupid decision on the pile hardly mattered now.

Of course, the risk was undeniable. There was every chance I would not make it out of this alive. A woman walks into a café to confront the serial killer she has been antagonising, intending to continue to do so, now to his face. No one in their right mind would exactly bet on a happy ending.

I had one goal: I had to keep him talking for as long as possible.

*Get ready*, I texted Tasha, just after she had told me she had given her entry card to Bill outside the office, I realised this was maybe the last text I would ever send.

*Ready*, Tasha responded instantly.

Outside Sabroso, I pressed my face to the glass, searching for Jago's silhouette but saw no one resembling him amongst the few customers inside, most typing away on their laptops. The restaurant still had its dim lighting and an excess of bizarre decorations crammed into every spare corner and ceiling recess. I spotted the same table where Greta had left me that night and tightened my grip around the small scrap of green fabric in my pocket.

You know, if Sabroso weren't so tangled up with my trauma, I'd probably frequent it quite often. I've always had a soft spot for things that don't fit neatly into a mould. It called itself a café but kept the kitchen going late; old, exposed brick, modern art décor, wine bottles and plants dotting every spare inch. Not the worst place to die, I suppose, at least it wasn't a Costa.

I decided it was best to go in and take a seat, maybe even order a latte. But as I stepped forward, something seized me without warning and yanked me violently backwards.

'Ruth, no. I can't let you do this,' Ben said, out of breath, dragging me forcefully backwards, away from Sabroso.

'Ben, please...' I struggled against him, trying to plant my feet, resisting his pull. He wasn't meant to be here, this wasn't the plan we all agreed on. We knew the risks, we all knew this was the cost of saving Carlota.

'Ruth, I'm sorry, but I can't. I just can't,' he said, his voice tearing and breaking. 'I won't let you die. I can't let you die.'

His grip tightened even more as he hauled me backwards. I fought back as hard as I could, trying to make myself heavier, harder to move, but despite the chemo, he was still stronger than me. A few passers-by cast us bemused glances, weighing whether to intervene, then, realising I was not truly calling for help, moved on. This was London, after all. We clock it, we tut and then we move on.

I found myself on the cold slabs of pavement, my rear impacting the ground as I tried to make myself a dead weight. But still, Ben dragged me along, unyielding, determined, a man utterly convicted in what he was doing.

I ground my teeth as I twisted my forearm desperately, trying to slip free from his grip, when suddenly, a figure brushed past us both.

That was when Ben's grip suddenly slackened, and my arm recoiled, slapping onto the cold, hard pavement.

He staggered, his breath catching in his throat as his hands suddenly snapped to clutch at his side. His body swayed slightly in the wind, before his legs gave way, and he crumpled into a lifeless heap onto one of the chairs outside the café. To the Londoners walking through the brisk and biting January night, he'd look like just some drunkard who'd overdone it again.

'No,' I screamed, primal and raw, as I scrambled to his side. I slapped his face repeatedly, desperate to get him to regain consciousness, but the only response from his body was the hot blood seeping through my fingers as I pressed against his wound.

No, no, no, this was not meant to happen.

'Ben. Ben!' I shouted raggedly. He was losing consciousness. Even before I turned my head, I knew who the figure was. He had been watching, waiting somewhere for me to arrive first.

Jago stood over us, the knife still in his grip, most of it hidden up his sleeve. He looked down at me, his eyes glinting with a lazy, self-satisfied sparkle.

'Let's go inside,' was all he said.

I was about to call for help – there were still people walking past – but then Jago's hand clamped around the collar of my coat and yanked me back towards his chest.

'Say anything and I'll kill you now,' he whispered gently in my ear.

'Please, please, just call an ambulance for him,' I begged, my voice still shaking. Jago's grip tightened, one hand clamped around the nape of my neck, the other pressing the knife's point against my spine. He forcefully guided me forward towards Sabroso's front door.

'No,' Jago said bluntly. 'Hey, maybe he'll get lucky, and someone will spot him. I *told* you to come alone.'

*Please*, I begged any god who was listening, *let someone, a jogger, a driver, a neighbour, anyone, find him and get him to a hospital before he bled out on a street without anyone even noticing.* I couldn't let him die, not like this.

'Apart from your pal, are you alone?' he asked. I could sense his gaze scanning around the surroundings of Sabroso meticulously.

'Yes,' I muttered as a few drops of rain began to patter down outside. 'I didn't know he was following me.'

'And do the police know where you are?'

'No.'

'Good. Because if I see even a single flash of blue lights, well, wouldn't you know it? Ruth Watkins is the Tell Tale Killer,' he said in a ghoulish newsreader-like tone as we hung about in the small waiting area while I kept my eyes fixed on Ben outside. 'She was caught red-handed having just murdered a dedicated police detective before killing herself in one final lethal crescendo.'

'You took a detective?' I asked, trying to sound surprised by the information.

'Eh, she's not a very good one. She never managed to track me.'

Present tense, that was good. I hoped that meant Detective Carlota was still alive.

We were met by the waiter's courteous smile, obviously completely oblivious to what was going on. He told us they wouldn't be serving food and led us to a quiet table tucked away at the back, no doubt internally deeming us a rather curious pair. What must we have looked like? A sobbing, dishevelled woman who looked like she hadn't slept in weeks, and a man in a £1,000 Armani jacket wearing sunglasses in January.

'Oh,' I said, my voice regaining some of its strength again as I reached out to gently touch the waiter on the arm while he led us to our table. 'There's a chap outside who looks like he might be in trouble, just on one of the chairs. Would you mind going to check on him?'

The waiter turned and glanced at Ben outside, still appearing like he was slovenly slumped on the chair of the outdoor seating. I kept internally praying to anyone who was listening that the knife had missed all of the vital organs.

'Oh, it's probably just one of the local...' The waiter was about to say 'crackheads', but caught himself. I think he figured right that I wouldn't have enjoyed the use of that term. 'One of that lot, you know,' he mumbled dismissively as he laid the menus on the table.

'Exactly,' Jago murmured with a dry laugh. 'It's fine, Ruth. Come on, leave it.'

'Oh, Jago, please,' I said with a theatrical groan. I was trying to play the same game he was. I turned back to the waiter. 'Could you check on him, please. I'm quite concerned?'

'Of course,' the waiter replied reluctantly after a small beat. I could tell he really wanted that tip. I watched as he made his way to the outside seating to look at Ben, he gently tried to awaken him and then immediately called over a colleague who instantly had the phone placed to her ear.

Thank God.

Jago scowled at that as we both watched the scene unfold, furious that I had already undermined his authority. I reminded myself that despite Ben having just been stabbed, my own best chance at survival was to keep Jago talking.

'I've thought of two headlines already, you know: "My Ten Minutes with a Monster" or "Eye-to-Eye with Evil". I haven't decided yet,' Jago said, pitching each headline as if its letters were being inscribed into thin air.

'You really think anyone would be stupid enough to believe that story?' I asked, my voice quiet but trying to sound assured. I clenched the fabric of Greta's old coat as tightly as I could in my pocket, really wishing I had brought a knife of my own.

'Oh, I think you're forgetting how good a writer I am,' he said, smirking and chuckling to himself as he traced a crack that stretched across the width of the table with his finger. 'The article's already written, it's sitting on my hard drive now, ready to go. I finished it while I was waiting for you. And you forget the most important thing, Ruth: how stupid people are. I can put out an article in thirty minutes, watch it go viral, and pouf, public opinion bends and twists exactly how I want it. *Owning the narrative*, that's what they call it.'

The waiter returned then and Jago, wearing a sly grin fixed upon his face, requested, 'A pot of tea for the table. No coffee, or I'll never sleep tonight, and not in a good way.' He flashed a smile, slick and greased lavishly with charm, the kind that left your skin feeling faintly sticky. The waiter chuckled obligingly.

'You know, it's funny,' Jago said lightly. 'This is a first for me. I've never met another one of us in the wild before.'

'One of us?' I asked, my gaze drifting to the table where Greta and I had once sat.

Jago scoffed, as if I were being deliberately obtuse. 'You know. One of the enlightened, shall we say?'

I had momentarily forgotten I was still pretending to be a serial killer, forgotten that he didn't know I was a complete fraud in that regard. I felt like an actor playing Hamlet at the Globe who had just forgotten their lines.

'I never would have pegged you for one, you know, Ruth,' he added with this kind of condescending smirk. 'Honestly, I thought you wouldn't hurt a fly. You know, I've had my work plagiarised before, but never quite like this. Why?' Jago asked, I noticed that the usual haughtiness was still there in his voice, but now it was laced with something more savage and primal.

'Oh, don't flatter yourself too much, it's not very classy,' I replied with more arrogance than I intended. Please don't be mistaken, I was still absolutely terrified, but somehow, I was doing a sort of okay job of seeming quite relaxed in front of Jago. After years and years of trying to track him down, finally sitting face to face with Jago was having a strangely calming effect on me. It was almost reassuring, as if my whole body had agreed to keep me steady and sharpen my focus, mindful of how long I'd worked for this. Funny, really, I can't speak to more than five people without my voice shaking, yet opposite a serial killer I was strangely composed.

Jago flinched at the change of tone and then almost smiled at that. He seemed... excited, like he quite enjoyed the surprise of me talking back to him. He lived a life as a serial killer and a celebrity journalist. I bet people very rarely gave him a taste of his own medicine.

I recalled what I had read at some point over the past few years: some victims had survived encounters with serial killers, not by appealing to any of their humanity or empathy, as those, of course, would be futile, but by meeting them as something akin to equals. Some killers would respond positively to that, enjoy the fact that someone was challenging them while they seemingly held all the power.

'It's funny, you know,' he said, lounging back in his chair, placing one arm on the empty table next to him. 'Because there I was, seeing this person flaunting being the TellTale Killer on Dark-Cell and I thought maybe...' he paused as he debated if he was going to finish his sentence, 'maybe there was someone out there like me. Maybe I wasn't quite so alone.'

And then, with all the physical force of an uppercut to the chin, realisation smacked hard into me.

He still actually believed I idolised him. He wasn't lurking on DarkCell to try and see if anyone would unravel the mystery of the TellTale Killer, he was really there because he adored and relished the attention all these weirdos on the internet were giving him. What a freak, scratch that, what an insecure freak.

I rolled my eyes, then glanced up at the long trail of vines draped from Sabroso's rafters. A little ladybird trotted down a leaf and stopped, as if staring at me. I gave a small smile at it, as if it was here to give me one more form of backup.

'So why did *you* do it?' he asked.

I shrugged my shoulders, worried that if I gave him the answer too early, he'd see no further reason to keep me alive.

Jago shuffled himself on his chair, pushing just a hair's width closer to watch my reaction more carefully.

'You know, I was quite proud of the TellTale Killer,' he mused blissfully. 'Had a certain *je ne sais quoi*, you know?'

'What are you talking about?' I asked, incredulous, as one of my eyebrows hopped up my forehead. Negging a serial killer, quite a thing to be doing, but every second he was here gave Bill an extra second to enact his side of the plan.

He scoffed. 'Oh, come *on*. So you didn't think it was a bit too much? Even when you were recreating it? I want to know your thoughts, honestly. Tell me, I can take it.'

I didn't mean to laugh in his face, but I did, I absolutely cackled. I laughed so hard I was pretty sure the people next to us were wondering if I was having some sort of breakdown. It was probably a bit of nerves, but I knew the more scorned he looked, the funnier I found it.

'The TellTale Killer is absolutely tacky,' I managed between breaths. 'It's really, really tacky.'

'Okay, but over one billion people know who I am, so...' he whined, somewhat defensively.

'Right,' I groaned wearily as it was now my opportunity, to gently push myself across the edge of the table, to cross the Rubicon and show him I wasn't afraid of him. 'You want me to feed your little ego, don't you? Tell you how clever and theatrical the TellTale Killer was. That's why you went all in on the Poe, the letters, the hearts, isn't it? Because there had to be a performance to it, a branding. The press wouldn't just go for any old serial killer, would they? There needed to be a *spectacle*, there needed to be *pizazz*. A killer that was built from the ground up just to get as much attention as possible.'

Jago's grin stretched across half his face; someone finally understood him.

'I mean, you get it, you worked in journalism, you saw how many people reacted when you killed those people. There always has to be a *hook*. I spent days workshopping. "The Dickensian Killer" sounded rubbish, but "The TellTale Killer"? I mean, come on, that's good. Shame that Poe was American, but it was important that he had global appeal.'

'It's quite derivative,' I replied flatly.

'Oh, well look who's talking,' he said with a dismissive wave, as if I were merely teasing him. 'I mean, it's Poe, right? And the angels, all pallid and wan. Uprising, unveiling, affirm. That the play is indeed the tragedy.'

I think he was trying to quote Poe but I don't think he realised that he got a bunch of the words wrong. I don't know whether he thought I'd be impressed, or this was just the kind of shit floating around in his mind normally.

'You're kidding me, right?' I said. 'You know that Poe wasn't some kind of serial-killer nihilist, so I have no idea why you thought he'd be a good choice for your whole gimmick.'

'Yes, he was,' Jago replied with unfounded certainty.

'No, he wasn't.'

*You're kidding me...* Jago Jones had modelled his whole shtick on a collection of writings that he didn't even truly understand. This man had evaded the best criminal minds in the country for two years and he didn't even have any literary critical analysis?

'Anyway, we're getting off-topic. I know what you're going to ask me – you're going to try and understand me because you're obsessed with me and I'd love to say I had some traumatic childhood, Mummy didn't love me or I had some horrendous thing happen to me. But the worst thing that happened to me was breaking my arm when I was fourteen.'

I felt my hands ever so slightly beginning to tremble; the adrenaline was finally getting to me, so I shoved them into my pockets as casually as I could, squishing that green bit of fabric again in my hand. A thick droplet of sweat glided from the back of my neck and traced a slow, tantalising path down my spine beneath my top. I glanced around Sabroso, noticing how the café was growing quieter and quieter as the few other patrons began to head home for the night; it was getting late. The overly eager waiter had slipped back inside just as I caught a flash of blue moving towards us. Jago didn't seem to notice; he was too busy talking about himself.

'Because, of course, there have been others,' he went on. 'I've known I wasn't like most people since I was a lad, I imagine you have too, and that some people would assume there was something wrong with us. Look...'

He jerked his head down and then leaned forward, cupping a hand around his mouth in a mock whisper to hide our conversation.

'... there are some parks and sandpits in Cheltenham you probably wouldn't want to go digging around, let's put it that way.'

But then he straightened back up, his voice sincere, confessional. 'I really did try to go straight, you know? I really did. But, my word...'

He fell silent as the waiter, looking suitably harried, returned with our tea.

'... You know how hard it is to make it as a journalist. That's when I realised, I needed something big if I was going to make my name. And people love serial killers. Crazy, right? Nuts. No matter how many pieces I did on war crimes, climate change or one-eyed cats, my editors just didn't care, and I thought after a while, well... why have I been trying to repress my talent? God loves a trier.'

'And let me guess, because some people denied you a good story in the past, one that you think would have given you a big break, you decided to off them?' I remarked as I tried to wipe away some sweat from my neck that I hoped he wouldn't notice.

Jago cocked his head as if he was a little impressed. I had figured that out as he lifted the pot and poured tea into the two mismatched cups, perfectly in keeping with the quaint, quirky charm of the establishment.

'They denied the truth to the world, I think there's no greater sin than that. They denied me a story, so I made them one. Their deaths right wrongs.'

'Keep telling yourself that, Jago, but we both know you did it for the likes,' I remarked, unimpressed. 'You did it because you enjoyed it and gave yourself a motive to make yourself feel better. Those people died for press coverage.'

'Specifically, my press coverage – that's important,' Jago replied, placing his index finger to his chest in a way I think I'd seen a toddler do when claiming ownership of a train set as he took a sip of his tea. I simply watched the steam dance and drift off the surface of mine, I fear my hand would quiver uncontrollably if I tried to pick it up. 'I mean, come on, hearts in boxes, it doesn't get more gruesome than that. Urgh, I mean, you know what I can't stand? The smell. The smell of...'

'That sickly, sweet rotting smell?' I responded, while he still hunted for the right description. I'd known that scent all too well for the past year or so. He extended a finger towards me, as if I'd just scored a point.

'And look, I'd love to say I was wrong, but with every person that ended up dead, the more views, the more reads we got. People loved that shit. Do you know how much ad revenue we made, Ruth? It basically paid for the new office in New York.'

'And yet, no one remembers the victims?' I said quietly. 'No one can remember their names. Can *you* even remember?'

'Oh, let me guess, you're a killer with values? Well, la-dee-dah,' Jago said, his voice dripping with disgusting mockery before blowing a frustrated rasp forcefully through his lips. 'I saw your messages. You were killing because you wanted to be like me. Because you *knew* you were like me. So don't even try. I mean, Ruth, this is what you need to understand. I killed people and I wrote the stories. But it was still every single tabloid, every news channel. *Good Morning Britain* even had a whole segment on it every single morning with a risk factor depending on what borough you were in. People were entertained by it. People enjoyed it. And you're really going to deny me that? If people didn't lap up the first one as much as they did, I would never have killed any more than that.'

I fought to keep the wrath and ferocity I was feeling from showing on my face. My gut was searing with a supernova kind of rage. For a brief moment, I wondered if I could take the knife from his pocket and kill him right then and there, but I knew he'd see me coming a mile away. There was no way I'd survive the ordeal.

'You know we spoke, right?' I said, my voice more fragile than I wanted it to sound. 'Do you remember that night? The night you killed Greta.'

Jago's eyes narrowed, a painfully slow, very deliberate squint, as though rifling yet again through a thick rolodex of memories he didn't care enough to keep at the forefront of his mind. He tilted his head, almost recalling, but didn't answer.

I saw the barista start cleaning her various tools, which was not a good sign.

'Sorry, guys,' the waiter said as he came over to the table. 'Don't want to rush you, but we're closing a bit earlier tonight because of the TellTale Killer and the police guidelines. We're sending people home in pairs. Sorry.'

Shit.

The panic was coiling tight in my throat. I needed to keep Jago talking to me, I needed time, needed... something. Anything.

'You don't remember at all, do you?' I asked him, recapturing my previous train of thought.

Jago just laughed callously.

'I'm sorry, Ruth, I can't say I do. I don't know about you, but it's all very murky when I kill someone. Do you not feel like that? You don't get that rush of emotion, that hit of adrenaline? That feeling is just...' He faltered, and even as a journalist he knew he didn't have a good enough command of the English language to articulate it. 'What, you don't get that?'

'Oh, I really do, gives me a massive lady boner,' I replied, hoping he wouldn't start to see the cracks in my lie. 'If the feeling was so amazing then why did you even stop two years ago?' I asked.

'Because,' Jago said, elongating the vowels, as he savoured another sip of tea on his tongue. 'Because when old Greta found out about my endeavours, I couldn't keep going until I knew for certain that no one else knew. So, I had to tone down the whole TellTale shtick.'

I narrowed my eyes, not quite understanding what he was implying.

'Look,' he said, 'after your whole, frankly hilarious, meltdown when Greta died, I couldn't risk anything. I had this feeling she might have left you a note or something you hadn't found yet, that's why you were let go, actually.'

It took everything I had to stay composed, to keep from visibly showing that his words had just gutted me. *He* was the reason they'd fired me, not my breakdown?

'But it was you, Ruth, you, tempting me back into the limelight,' he continued, not realising any change of expression on my face. 'I mean, sure, I've picked off the odd person here and there these past two years, I sent you the photos, but it felt too indie, too underground. I'd forgotten how much I loved the front page. That's what I want to keep doing.'

While he was talking, I turned my head subtlety and saw Ben being loaded into the back of the ambulance by a frantic team of paramedics, and let out as small a belch of relief as I could. You know, it's funny, whatever self-hatred I had for what I'd done over the past week or so was ebbing away as I looked at the excuse of a human being before me. I hadn't realised evil could be this arrogant, this self-absorbed, this basic. His code was all based on him being an annoying, snivelly little brat that craved attention.

'See, with Greta, there was nothing special about her. Not like you, Ruth, you're like me because I...'

'You're wrong,' I interjected before he could even finish his sentence. 'Greta *was* special and I'm *nothing* like you.'

My Greta was not a nothing.

If only Jago knew how my grief for her tore me apart every single day. How I'd give anything to spend just one more afternoon with her, talking about Obama and the erotic smut books we had read, and to remind her just how special she truly was. But no, I didn't think Jago would ever understand that.

I glanced at the clock in the far corner of Sabroso. The café was essentially empty now, just Jago and me, and the two staff members tidying up so they could get home, before the Telltale Killer struck again.

Jago tried to smother his smile for the staff, but I caught the slight curl of it. Right, he'd wait for lock-up and then he would strike. I was still on my own, no Ben to protect me now, and no sign of Bill. Had he done it yet? I really needed my *backup* backup.

'But I suppose I have to give you some credit. At the end of the day, I've found the real TellTale Killer now,' Jago said, his intonation suggesting we were coming to the end of our conversation as he swigged the last of his tea. 'I'll write a corker of a book about you, Ruth, don't you worry, and look, I've been thinking about setting up a charity, so I'll make sure some of that money goes towards... something you like. Horses, do you like horses? Or I don't know, diabetes?'

I should have known he was still planning to kill me. But I'd gotten this far, and I had one last ace up my sleeve though I wasn't sure it would guarantee my survival. Actually, I knew it wouldn't, but what a way to go for old Ruth. What a way to finally have the last laugh.

'Right, that makes sense,' I said, somewhat resigned to my death. 'Although... last request and all that. Would you mind glancing at your phone for a moment?'

'What? Why?' Jago scrunched up his nose, almost appalled I had asked him that, like a dad who really didn't want to be involved with the local school fair magician.

'Please, just humour me, Jago. I just want to see the news one last time before I...' I jerked my head to one side and made my best attempt at a death rattle. 'Just do this for me. Please.'

That seemed to intrigue him, wondering why I had such a bizarre request. Honestly, this part of my plan had not been discussed between the three of us, but I wasn't going to die, with him thinking that he'd won. Greta wouldn't have gone easily and neither would I. I just had to hope that, while I'd been talking to Jago, Bill had been doing what he was supposed to and that nothing had gone dramatically wrong in the process.

'Owning the narrative, right?' I said, watching him as he stared at his phone, his mind rapidly working to piece together what was happening before him.

Though my view of the video was upside down, I could see a news reporter sat at her desk, clearly just handed fresh information. I wouldn't exactly call it serendipitous timing, given it was about to lead to my demise.

Do you want to know how they caught the BTK Killer?

He sent a floppy disk to the media, convinced he'd wiped all identifying data. The investigators recovered the disk's metadata, traced it to a computer at his church, and even found his name embedded in the file properties. They had him arrested almost instantly.

And now ask yourself this: do you think someone with as big an ego as Jago Jones, who had evaded the police for two years and then just confessed that he had written most of his articles in advance, would store them on his work computer?

As I mentioned earlier, the thing about serial killers is their absolute, ridiculously sized ego. The longer they hunt, the more untouchable they truly believe they are, not noticing the more and more breadcrumbs they scatter with every single victim they think they claim.

Ego and stupidity often keep very close company.

'... which is, of course, developing rapidly. For anyone just joining us, we can now report that an article has just been released by Tasha Duncan, citing several verified sources,' the reporter announced, pausing for a quick breath. 'We can confirm that Jago Jones, the award-winning journalist, has been identified as the man behind the TellTale Killer. We are told that a substantial body of digital data linking him to the murders has been handed over to the authorities. Police are responding immediately, and anyone with information on Mr Jones is urged to come forward straight away, as we continue to...'

So, it seemed Flowerpot Boy had done his job; it had worked. I'd kept Jago away from the unit where he was keeping Carlota, drawn him out, and in that window of time, Bill slipped into the office across the road using Tasha's ID, pulled what he needed from Jago's computer using his software engineering prowess, and, together with Nico's TFL hits, sent the lot to Tasha, whom I'd primed beforehand. It was all there in tech babble I barely grasped when Bill was explaining it to me: terms like DOCX metadata and EXIF, whatever the hell that meant. If everything else had gone to plan, the police were already on their way to the storage unit and hopefully here too.

'Oh, you think I came here just to massage your ego? To tell you how amazing you are?' I asked Jago, his face still dumbstruck as he tried to process what was happening. I took a big swig of tea. 'No, I came here to see *that* look on your face. You know, I spent the last two years thinking about you – thinking about how I could bring you down – and I never realised how utterly disappointing you'd turn out to be,' I said, feeling a surge of catharsis in the words I was speaking. It was everything I had ever wanted to say to him.

It was then that I saw it as he turned to face me, the monster Jago never truly believed himself to be, finally beginning to surface.

For a heartbeat, life or death hardly mattered. I, Ruth Watkins, had outmanoeuvred the TellTale Killer and was watching him receive, at last, a small, tiny sliver of his due; I was watching his downfall in real time.

'See, Jago, I wonder if you could have got away with it. If you could have made it out the other side scot-free, and kept operating until you died at age ninety choking on a scone, but you made one critical mistake.'

He didn't ask what it was, so I told him anyway.

'You should have never touched my Greta.'

It would have been more impactful if I hadn't belched just as I said Greta, but I felt like I still got my point across in the moment.

What I failed to realise, though, was that with his identity exposed, he had nothing left to lose anymore.

Whoops.

And that was when he pulled the knife from his sleeve, scrambled across the table, and drove for my heart. I threw up my arms in a desperate shield as my chair toppled beneath me as his weight crashed into mine. My fingers in my pocket still clenched tight around the scrap of Greta's green dress.

Two things consumed my mind.

Firstly, I really hoped the police were on their way to rescue Detective Carlota.

Secondly, what animal would I be reincarnated as.

God, I really hoped it wasn't a tortoise.

# THIRTY-SIX

I'd never really imagined what it would feel like, experiencing the funeral directors from this particular perspective. Being there in the lobby, feeling slightly hemmed in by the display coffins, it felt oddly surreal.

I took one last look at the trinkets and traditions Uncle Phil kept on the shelves bordering the visitors' desk in the lobby, a carefully chosen mix of death accessories and regalia, designed to appeal to the widest range of people who came into the office. I suppose we all cling to our rituals around death, little distractions from the sobering thought that death is the end because we want their lives to have had meaning, to have had importance.

'Hiya, Ruth,' Uncle Phil said, the natural glow of his optimism having returned to his face. I forgot how warm and inviting his whole presence was. He trotted up to me and wrapped his arms around me as delicately as he could. There was no trace of Capri-Sun on his breath this time which I took to mean he was doing pretty well, all things considered. I was so thankful he had kicked the habit; Capri-Sun addiction can ruin lives, kids.

'How are you doing? How's everything?' he asked, gesturing to my still broken body.

'Okay, I think,' I said with a short sigh, instinctively smoothing my hands over my ribs as I pulled the plastic Sainsbury's bag from my side. I handed over my funeral directors' clothes – my *smarties*. 'As requested,' I said.

He gave a small, knowing smile.

'Oh, I really should have called, Ruth. They won't need these, you know.'

'What do you mean?' I asked, feeling my face frown ever so slightly.

'They'll bring their own uniforms in apparently, these hideous purple things.'

'Urgh,' I groaned. 'I should've known.'

'Don't worry,' he said lightly. 'I'll pop it in the charity van. They'll find some use for it, I'm sure.'

I was glad things between Uncle Phil and me were... well, not perfect, but certainly better. I doubted they'd ever be great again, but since the sale to the mega funeral-director conglomerate had gone through, there was a fragile but significantly more cordial understanding between us. He'd said it wasn't ideal, but after everything came out, including the news that I'd been, shall we say, *fiddling with bodies* in my spare time, Camborne and Sons' reputation was never going to recover. Of course I felt bad; I'd be an arsehole not to. Still, the fact Uncle Phil was retiring anyway eased my conscience. Sophie, meanwhile, was still glaring the sharpest of daggers at me as she hauled boxes from one room of the office to another. She hadn't spoken to me since it all came out, still clinging to the belief that she'd been destined for the managing director role that I'd callously stolen from her. Oh well.

'So, what day are you officially closing up?' I asked Uncle Phil, as he couldn't help himself from neatening up some of the pens on the visitors' desk.

'July eighteenth,' he said with a few short nods, eyes roaming the room as if trying to memorise every last detail before he left. 'And then we'll be out of here and off to France to spend my pension on wine and cheese.'

The door creaked open behind me, and I turned to see Detective Carlota. She was still recovering from her injuries but, even on sick leave, she looked immaculate, the sharpness on her face had faded a little, her muscular frame had shrunk a bit, but her fit was still excellent – cream blazer and trousers, a white top underneath. It was effortlessly cool.

'You ready?' she asked me bluntly, not even a hello.

'Yeah,' I replied, then turned back to Uncle Phil. 'I guess I'll see you at your retirement do?'

Uncle Phil smiled, though I saw his whole face ever so slightly tighten at the sight of Carlota.

'Are you here to question me again?' he asked, trying to be funny but not doing a great job at hiding some of the fear that she actually was.

'You should be so lucky,' Detective Carlota responded with a wry smile. Oh, she wasn't completely gone.

I turned to face her as she left the funeral directors as quickly as she'd come in, barely holding the door for me as I followed behind her.

'How's the spine?' I asked her as we pulled out the chairs in the small little coffee place a few shops down the street from the funeral directors.

'It's healing,' she said brusquely. Her tone was curt, austere even, but I sensed she hadn't meant to sound gruff or abrasive with how she spoke. 'How're the ribs?' she asked back.

'Healing,' I repeated.

A silence settled between us. It was... undeniably awkward, I can't pretend it wasn't, but I mean of course it was – this was the first time we'd seen each other in almost six months.

I'd been interviewed about that January night multiple times at this point, but I still struggled to remember it with vivid detail. I remembered Jago lunging at me, the knife gripped tight in his hand, and then I remembered he missed. Well, *sort of* missed, he still managed to dig and drive the blade through my ribs, slipping it between the intercostal space, a lucky angle that missed my heart, lungs, and any major blood vessels.

A split second later, he had yanked the knife back out and went to bury the blade in my chest again, but something stopped him.

More specifically, *someone* stopped him.

Even more specifically than that, my ex-husband's boyfriend had stopped him by punching him direct in the jaw.

Bill had infiltrated the paper offices that night, sent the data to Tasha to break the story, and arrived just in time to find no sign of Ben and me in the café about to be made into a human kebab. I'd often wondered where Bill disappeared to on all those mysterious late nights, why he had always been so aloof about it and came home smelling like Tiger Balm and taking copious amounts of ice cubes out of the freezer. Turns out his secret life was something I could never have predicted:

Cage fighting.

And not just dabbling, either. Ninth-best in the country, man was really good. Turns out that was his way of attempting to manage his anger. I wondered how many of his fights had been fuelled by my use of Blu Tack on the shed walls, punching his opponent's face, pretending it was the small scab that had been etched onto the wall. Ben had massively disapproved of Bill's pastime, seeing it as quite barbaric, hence why the subject had been somewhat frosty between the two of them.

I felt supremely glad that he'd found this particular release, as I watched him drive Jago into the floor again and again before he could stab me a second time, his fist hammering down as Jago's skull repeatedly thudded against the wooden boards.

There were times, admittedly, I wished I'd never told Bill to stop, especially when he started smashing dirty crockery across Jago's face. The doctors said they didn't know when exactly Jago would wake from the medically induced coma, but he'd probably just about pull through. The lawyers, however, unanimously agreed that Bill was lucky to have been considered to have used reasonable force in the circumstances. Everyone knew it wasn't true, but he was doing it to the TellTale Killer so no one seemed to care much about how much exact force was exerted on the man who had killed at least eight innocent people.

At the time, everything had felt so intense, as if I was experiencing things in a heightened sense of reality. But now, it was more like all of that evening's events had happened to someone else, or more like a weird fever dream I had experienced after too much blue cheese before bedtime.

'And how many hours have you got left?' Carlota asked. I could still feel the tension radiating from her, the Siberian winter of coldness that she continued to carry towards me.

'Nine hundred and ninety,' I replied with a slight guffaw. 'But you know what? I'll take it. I'd rather be picking up litter and doing gardening than, you know, being in prison.'

'They'd eat you alive in prison,' Detective Carlota said, glancing out the window while taking a small, gentle sip of her coffee. I could tell she was still angry with me by her tone, even if she didn't realise it herself.

'Yeah, maybe,' I admitted, realising that my humour hadn't been warmly received.

She drew a deep breath, resting her hands carefully across her torso. I could tell she was still in a lot of physical pain.

'Look,' she said, 'I'm not going to say I'm sorry... but I *am* going to say thank you. I've thought about it a lot, and I know that what you did saved my life. So... thank you.'

'Ah, it's nothing,' I said with a casual, relaxed smile. She didn't return it. I, personally, held no resentment towards her. I'd heard she'd sent a remarkably persuasive letter to the judge during the trial, one that heavily influenced me getting community service rather than any prison time. She didn't owe me that, but she did it anyway, so there were no hard feelings on my part.

She'd changed since Jago had taken her, that much was obvious. And I wondered what the real issue was. Was she still furious that I'd taken away her chance of catching the TellTale Killer herself, refusing her chance to redeem herself in the eyes of her superiors? Or was being kidnapped by a serial killer simply something you never really could recover from? I didn't know. What I *did* know was that, despite everything, she'd still been sidelined by the station. She told me the current case she was working on was a trail of graffiti on posh people's houses.

Still, I felt a flicker of hope when she mentioned her kitchen remodel was finally finished and that Alba was coming over that evening. Alba, she said, had been a huge help in her recovery so it was good to know she wasn't going through it alone. I sort of felt Carlota needed someone, she wasn't one of those people who could be by themselves.

Funny she mentioned that, I was actually heading to Nico's tonight. Dinner in, a movie on Netflix, and, well… you know what that implies: chill. I was just grateful it was at his place. There was no way I was getting laid in the shed with Toast watching excitedly from the corner, her eyes bulging as she watched us potentially fornicate.

It was only a brief meeting; she'd mentioned when we arranged it that she had just fifteen minutes to spare. So as punctual as ever, Detective Carlota rose to her feet and offered a hand when the clock struck 10.15. I knew better than to attempt a hug, she wouldn't have returned it, so I simply nodded and gave her hand a very formal shake.

'You're a really good detective, Cis,' I said as she grabbed her blazer from the back of her chair. 'I know it's only a matter of time before they see that.'

'Yeah,' Detective Carlota replied quietly, in that way that told me she either didn't believe it, didn't think it meant much coming from me, or had simply given up on the dream altogether.

I watched her leave the café, cross the street and head towards the zebra crossing, lifting a small wave at the stopping cars. It was strange, really. For two years, ever since Greta, I'd felt like Detective Carlota had been looking out for me. And yet, six months on, I suddenly felt like a parent watching their child walk into school for the first time, wondering if they'd be okay.

# EPILOGUE

Tasha rang me again, asking if I'd be interested in a job at the paper. Yet again, I politely declined. I think she still felt she owed much of her success – maybe most of it on the TellTale Killer story – to me, and this was her way of paying it back. But I told her that after I threw her phone into the creek, we were now even. She laughed and told me to call if I ever wanted something, so I thanked her and hung up.

Almost immediately, I dodged yet another call from Chlo. I'd speak to her later, after I'd finished burning the remnants of my crime wall in the garden while I tried to deter Toast from getting too close to mounting the red-hot steel drum. I was incinerating the various things in it while she enjoyed the June sunshine glistening on her shell. Today felt like the right time to do it, to finish with everything.

By the time I got back from meeting Carlota, I'd heard the rather unfortunate news that Jago had finally woken up from his coma but that was just from Nico texting me. The news didn't even make the very edges of the BBC homepage. There was nothing left of him or the TellTale Killer now, his myth had firmly been extinguished that night. People had moved on from him in the era of twenty-four-hour news and would rarely think about him again.

'You ready to go?' Bill asked, as I made sure the flames were out.


I noticed that the last of the bright pink cherry blossoms had just about bloomed across the graveyard as I held the bouquet of flowers close to my chest. You know, I understood the appeal of flowers at weddings, or even as a romantic gesture for a loved one on Valentine's Day or an anniversary. But I had never quite grasped why we so often brought them for the dead. It wasn't as if they could admire the blooms, or breathe in their aroma, or even sneeze uncontrollably from hay fever at the mere suggestion of them. Who really were they for?

No, but then, of course, I remembered. My years working at a funeral directors had taught me that funerals and graves and the like were never really for the dead at all. They had always been for the living. That's what I had missed, we do this all so we can keep a part of them with us. It's never really been for them.

I'd told Aleks a few months ago that I was going to do this, and he'd asked if I wanted him to come with me. I'd said no, politely. I wanted to, I needed to do this alone, but it had still taken me a while to galvanise the courage.

Aleks had come to visit me in hospital while I was still recovering, after he'd realised that the heart in his freezer was missing, and all of the implications of that. At first, I think, just like when Chlo and Mum and Dad found out, he didn't quite know how to process it.

I could tell he wasn't exactly pleased with what I'd done, but he told me he understood. And, more than that, he said he was glad. Glad that, while nothing would ever bring Greta back, the TellTale Killer would never hurt anyone again.

He eventually sent me the things he had told Chlo and I that Greta would have wanted us to have. As I had carefully unwrapped the cardboard packaging and peeled away the layers of bubble wrap, the memories came through one at a time and then suddenly all at once, to the point where I couldn't believe I had forgotten so many fond moments between us. I couldn't help but chuckle at the sight of her beloved stuffed toys and all the various soap opera stories they had been unwilling participants of. Then I saw it, an envelope.

It had my name on the front. It was for my birthday; the one she had forgotten to give me on the night she died. I hesitated at first, the seal was still completely intact. But before I could even have a chance to second-guess myself, I tore the paper open and yanked the card out. On the front, Borat grinned, declaring, 'Your Birthday. Very Nice.'

'So cringe,' I muttered to myself, hoping she wouldn't see me smile.

Inside, in her unmistakable messy cursive handwriting, she had written:

*Hello you, Clot.*

She didn't say 'clot'.

*you are pains in my arsehole...*

(I believe that was meant to be in the Borat voice)

*...but you are the best anal fissure I could ever want. Have a lovely birthday, Petal.*

It would have been nice if she had said something along the lines of always loving me or always being my best friend, but if this was the last-ever thing I'd hear from Greta then at least she was being true to form.

Finally, I had found my way to her grave. I had always known where it was, but I had never quite made it that far up the hill at St Michael's before. I turned to check on Ben. He was fine, leaning against the car I still hadn't managed to crash during our driving lessons, with Bill standing a little further up by the church at the bottom of the hill.

I knew chemo had been tough for Ben over the past few months, but the doctors had said he was making great progress. It turns out that almost losing your life really makes you appreciate having it. At least for now, he had decided, he would keep trying to see how much more he could get. He had told us that, as he'd slumped there on the cold steel chair in Hammersmith, he thought about what I had said to him about Greta, how I'd do anything for one more day with her. So that's what he said to Bill and me: 'I'll give you a few more days. As many as I possibly can. Maybe a clean-break death is overrated.'

Bill, meanwhile, had told me to stop paying him rent and to put that money towards moving out, which I can't say I disagreed with.

I let out a long exhale as I walked the last few steps to Greta's grave, the only sounds around me the distant hum of cars on the road below, the faint rustling of birds in the trees above and the few children in the park opposite kicking a ball. As I smoothed my hand over the cool granite stone, my fingers traced the words engraved for her.

I had always liked that Aleks had made sure it read:

GRETA: DAUGHTER, SISTER, FRIEND.

You didn't always see that word a lot on headstones – friend – but he had always said how important Chlo and I were to Greta and he wanted to make sure we knew that.

Standing there suddenly felt awfully formal, so I slowly lowered myself onto the grass. A small smile tugged at my lips, as if she could somehow see me, a connection point between now and the mythical hereafter that I was almost certain didn't exist... almost certain.

'I miss you,' I whispered aloud. 'I really do miss you, Greta. I don't think I understood, until right now, just how much I missed you. How much space you've left in my life. But I just want you to know that...'

I choked on the words, words I had been thinking in my head for so long but had never quite found the courage or even the ability to say aloud.

'I don't want you to think that I'm ever going to forget you. And I just hope that if you can hear me...' I let out a small, teary laugh, 'wherever you are, you know just how much you were loved, and will always be loved. By me, by Chlo, by your family.'

I had always thought this grief was something quite terrible, something I wasn't meant to hold on to as much as I did, but I didn't think like that anymore. Maybe grief wasn't all that bad. Maybe this heartbreak would never really mend but maybe that was okay, it was always meant to be with me.

I scoffed softly, wiping the tears from my cheek, laughing at myself a little. I could practically see her rolling her eyes at me, fake vomiting in mock disgust, calling me cheesy and corny before giving me a playful slap on the arm and telling me how much she loved Obama.

'The thing is, I don't want to forget you... everything, this grief just keeps you alive for me for a bit longer and I just want you to know how much I'll always love you,' I said, adjusting the flowers for her to make sure they looked nice before rising to my feet.

Down the hill, I could just about see the figures of Ben and Bill waving at me again as they saw me look in their direction. I was meant to drive them both home; good luck to them. But I had asked them to come just to make sure I didn't back out on the way.

Something felt different inside me since that night where I met Jago at Sabroso, as if things were just a little bit lighter, a little bit easier. I think I knew now that the pain wouldn't ever really go away, and somehow, I was feeling pretty okay with that. Greta lived a life full of moments that mattered so much, because they ended.

Nothing lasts forever, right? *And that's the point.* Wabi-sabi, just like Greta had told me on the day that she died.

*Be brave*, that's what Greta had once told me. What she had always told me, right from the beginning, when she had given me those words of encouragement on the stage of the school play. Be brave.

'Right,' I muttered to myself, letting the teeniest, tiniest, smallest amount of hope creep in as I watched a ladybird drift down onto the flowers I'd brought for Greta, slowly making its way across them.

'What next?'

# A LETTER FROM THE AUTHOR

To the reader who has finished *Over Her Dead Body*, an enormous, gargantuan thank you from me. I truly hope you enjoyed the book and found yourself drawn into Ruth's chaotic world of Hearts and Crafts. Believe it or not, this entire story was crafted with *you* in mind, and I hope it made you feel everything I hoped for. I hope there were laughs and I hope there were tears!

If you'd like to stay updated on my new releases and bonus content, you can join other readers by signing up for my newsletter.

www.stormpublishing.co/hj-garbett

If you enjoyed this book and have a few moments to spare, leaving a review would mean the world to me. Even a short review can make a huge difference in helping new readers discover *Over Her Dead Body*. So, if you loved it (or even if you didn't – but hopefully you did, if you made it this far!), please consider sharing your thoughts and telling your friends.

Thank you again for choosing to read *Over Her Dead Body*. I hope you'll stay in touch – I have so many more stories to share with you!

H.J. Garbett

www.hjgarbett.co.uk

# ACKNOWLEDGMENTS

I'm writing these acknowledgements while missing a social event I really should have been at. In 2025, 'Sorry, I don't think I can make it,' and 'Sorry, I'm only replying now,' have been said more times than I can count. As a writer with a full-time job, a partner, and all the joys of adult life, I feel a huge amount of empathy for those who juggle the same, especially those with caring or childcare on top; I have no idea how *they* do it.

*Over Her Dead Body* was made with genuine care, joy, and love throughout every single page of the process. I have absolutely loved writing this book but each draft left me feeling maybe a teeny bit exhausted: delighted by the process and obsessed with the reader's enjoyment of the book, but feeling a little like I was tumbling out of a charred vehicle to hand over the manuscript and give a thumbs-up to the camera before limping off-screen. I am truly indebted to the people who stuck with me this year.

If you're in a rush, in a nutshell: thank you for reading, truly. Your support means the world. This book was written for your enjoyment above all. And this short version of the thanks goes to everyone who bore with me this year, for every message I didn't reply to, every event I missed, and every adult responsibility I delegated.

The longer version is as follows.

Firstly, *Over Her Dead Body* was written before, during, and after the release of my first book, *My Wife, The Serial Killer*. I want to thank those who spent their own money, read it, and recommended it on. To list a few, Tom D, Alex W, Will B, Callum N, Chloe B, Claudia K, Sophie F, Kate G, Elliot R, Lisa G, Gila L,

James K, Fiona F, Georgia V, Maddie G, Kate G, Lewis B, Emily S, Emily T, Emily R, Clara S, plus my Gran, Hannah, Auntie Julie, and Auntie Jayne, thank you for sitting down with my book and messaging me about it. I'm sure I've missed some names; a few of you only told me months later you had bought it on release date. These are simply the ones I found while trawling my messages to make sure as many people as possible were acknowledged. From pre-ordering all three formats to pressing it into colleagues' or customers' hands, your support means so much. Thank you.

To my beta readers, this was very much a first for me. We'd never met in person; I put out a call on Instagram, and you valiantly answered. You gave your precious time and your honest and kind feedback, and you helped shape this book into its strongest form. I'm deeply grateful. Huge thank you to Lucía Uribe, Melissa Tostevin, Carla Magriñà, Brooke, Tamsin Collins and Meghan.

To my family: Mum and Dad, steadfast as ever, who nourished my love of reading from day one and never wavered on my wish to be an author, from my mum taking me, aged twelve, to a 'How to get published' seminar at Plymouth Guildhall and my dad, always giving me faith on phone calls after another rejection email from an agent to keep going. To my sister, for always catching the medical inaccuracies even if I chose to ignore them 'for the plot', and with much love to Denise, may she one day read this when she's much, much older. To Becas, *a minha segunda mãe*, an extraordinarily accommodating host while a fair portion of the book was written at her home and one of the first readers of the manuscript. And to my girlfriend, *meu amor*: thank you for your extraordinary patience, with a man who can be grumpy with writer's block, who had to neglect social plans and domestic errands to sit at a desk, and who was, at times, a bit hysterical when I hit a plot hole. I'm endlessly grateful to you all.

To the two people without whom there would be no book: my agent, Kate Rizzo, who has gone above and beyond with her support, along with the whole Greene & Heaton team, and who has genuinely been the most delightful agent an author could ask for; and my editor, Emily Gowers, the most thorough and fantastic pair of hands throughout this process, who powered through colds and deadlines alike to deliver kind, thoughtful and incisive critiques, together with the brilliant Storm team. I'm endlessly thankful to you both.

Finally, for Matthew. Matt was a dear friend who died way too young at the age of sixteen. I've spent more than a decade navigating the grief of losing him, and, pretentious as it may sound, much of this book is me trying to make sense of his loss and the hole it left in my life that has never really healed. Through Ruth to Greta, I finally said the things I'd been carrying for a long time.